W9-BYO-194

the center of the world

the center of the world

andreas steinhöfel

Translated from the German by Alisa Jaffa

Delacorte Press

Published by
Delacorte Press
an imprint of
Random House Children's Books
a division of Random House, Inc.
New York

Translation copyright © 2005 by Alisa Jaffa
Originally published in German under the title *Die Mitte Der Welt* copyright © 1998 by Carlsen Verlag GmbH, Hamburg. All rights reserved.
Jacket photograph copyright © 2005 by Thomas Schmitt/Getty Images

Chapter 2, "Dumbo on the Tower," was first published by *Rush Hour* in the Spring 2005 issue #3 ("Face").

The publication of this work was supported by a grant from the Goethe-Institut.

All rights reserved. No part of this book may be reproduced or transmitted in any form or by any means, electronic or mechanical, including photocopying, recording, or by any information storage and retrieval system, without the written permission of the publisher, except where permitted by law.

The trademark Delacorte Press is registered in the U.S. Patent and Trademark Office and in other countries.

Visit us on the Web! www.randomhouse.com/teens
Educators and librarians, for a variety of teaching tools, visit us at
www.randomhouse.com/teachers

Library of Congress Cataloging-in-Publication Data
Steinhöfel, Andreas.
[Mitte der Welt. German]
The center of the world / by Andreas Steinhöfel ;
translated from the German by Alisa Jaffa.
p. cm.
Summary: As he works through his often difficult relationships with his single mother, distant twin sister, his first boyfriend, and an odd assortment of friends, a teenage boy learns about the wounds and healing brought by love.
ISBN 0-385-72943-X (trade)
ISBN 0-385-90266-2 (lib. bdg.)
[1. Coming of age—Fiction. 2. Homosexuality—Fiction. 3. Family life—Germany—Fiction. 4. Interpersonal relations—Fiction. 5. Germany—Fiction.] I. Jaffa, Alisa. II. Title.
PZ7.S82635Mi 2005
[Fic]—dc21 2001052987
The text of this book is set in 12-point Garamond #3.

Book design by Trish Parcell Watts

Printed in the United States of America

May 2005

10 9 8 7 6 5 4 3 2 1

BVG

contents

the
center
of the
world

prologue

glass

It was a cold, wet April morning as Glass boarded the huge ocean liner, bound for Europe from Boston Harbor. With the handle of a battered imitation leather suitcase in her left hand, her right hand gripped the handrail of the swaying gangway. The pier was swarming with people, and water surged against the quayside. A stinging, nauseous stench hung in the air, a mixture of burnt tar and rotten fish. Glass tilted her head back and, narrowing her eyes, gazed up at the banks of fat clouds stacked up over the coast of Massachusetts. A fine drizzle spattered the light coat flapping about her incredibly thin legs. She was seventeen years old, and nine months pregnant.

Goodbyes rang out, white handkerchiefs fluttered in the wind, and engines sprang into action. In the middle of the seething mass of people gathered on the pier to wave goodbye to relatives and friends stood a child. Laughing, he raised a hand and pointed up at the gray sky. Seagulls were fluttering in the sea breeze, like confetti on a Fourth of July parade. Moved by this innocent gesture, Glass almost regretted her decision to leave America. But suddenly the steamer picked up speed. With a mournful blast on the horn, it cast off and left the harbor. The bow cut deep into the water. Glass turned away from the mainland. She never looked back.

During the days that followed, the other passengers watched the girl standing at the bow of the pounding ship, gazing fixedly at the ocean, her grotesquely swollen belly pressed against the railing. Defiantly Glass ignored their curious stares and whispers. No one dared to speak to her.

A week after she had left America for good, Glass tasted the salt of seaweed on her tongue. At noon on the eighth day she stepped ashore into the Old World. For hours afterward Glass continued to feel a rocking motion under her feet. She had tried telegraphing Stella several times from on board ship to say she was on her way to Visible, where she wished to stay for an indefinite period. Her older sister, whom she had not seen since she was a small child, and whose most recent letter had arrived only four weeks before, had not cabled a reply. Couldn't be helped. Glass hadn't put thousands of sea miles behind her only to turn back again in her highly pregnant state for nothing.

It took the remainder of the day and half the night to

complete the rest of the journey south by train—the trains became progressively shorter, slower, and more uncomfortable. Nothing about the landscape flashing past outside reminded Glass in the least of America. In America the sky was vast, the horizon endless, at times framed by seemingly unconquerable snow-covered mountain ranges, and the rivers were sluggish and boundless. But here the countryside seemed to shrink progressively as they left the coast. As far as the eye could see, the snow-powdered forests, the frost-stiffened hills and mountains, and the villages and towns in between had the miniature scale of a toy landscape—even the broadest rivers seemed tame. After she had changed trains for the last time, Glass sat alone in the overheated compartment, her hands clasped around her belly, wearily staring out of the window into the ink-black night, wondering whether she had done the right thing. At last she fell into a restless sleep. In a dream she saw an unremarkable brown bird being pursued by a mighty eagle with golden wings. Far below was the ocean, and a zigzagging line of huntsmen were firing this way and that across the stormy black skies until the exhausted little bird gave up the struggle and, folding its wings against its body, allowed itself to fall. It hit the sea like a stone and sank into the raging blue-gray waves.

Glass awoke with a fright as the train jerked to a halt. She felt a sudden cramp in her lower abdomen and for the first time seriously feared the contractions might be about to begin. Peering nervously out of the window, she saw a small station building enveloped in a pool of dim yellow light, and a worn, barely legible sign. She had arrived.

On the platform she was hit by the biting cold. The few people leaving the train fluttered through the darkness like pigeons startled out of their sleep. There was no sign of Stella. Speaking in harsh consonants with much gesticulation, the aged, suspicious stationmaster informed Glass there were no taxis. According to Stella's letters, Visible was in easy walking distance, a mere quarter of an hour from the town, by the edge of the wood on the far side of a narrow river. Unnerved by the old man, whose eyes wandered over her belly like inquisitive hands, and cursing the bitter cold, Glass trudged off in the direction indicated by the stationmaster in response to her repeated mention of Stella's name.

Hardly had she crossed the bridge linking the edge of the town with the adjoining dense wood when her abdomen contracted in jerks like an accordion. Cramps charged through her body in waves, followed by dull vague nausea. There seemed no sense in blindly running back. Glass forced herself to take deep breaths and keep going, calmly placing one foot in front of the other. Soon after the bridge the asphalt path petered out into a forest trail. The ground was frozen hard below a thin covering of crisp snow. If she started running now, if she was to slip, to fall . . .

A quiet crackling noise sounded through the undergrowth. For one terror-stricken moment Glass thought she saw long thin shadows darting toward her, straining dogs, maybe wolves, driven together by hunger and cold. She stood rooted to the spot holding up her suitcase, which suddenly seemed much too small to use in self-defense, and listened, half expecting a threatening snarling sound in the wood.

Nothing.

The next contraction took its time, and Glass marched on, suddenly full of anger at herself. She knew nothing about this country she had so impulsively chosen to come to, nothing, not even whether there were in fact wolves here. And then the rows of trees parted, and her anger faded as the outline of Visible suddenly rose ahead of her in the night sky. Taken by surprise, Glass breathed in through clenched teeth. She had never imagined the house was so big, so really . . . castlelike. She could distinguish the outlines of battlements, gables, and small chimneys, countless barred windows, and a covered veranda. Dim orange light shone through two tall ground-floor windows.

Glass was about to press onward in relief when her knees gave way without warning. She simply sank to the ground as if a rug had been pulled from under her feet. She fell forward. Instinctively she raised her arms; her suitcase slipped from her hand, and before she reached the ground, her hands closed around the trunk of a sapling birch in front of her. Warm fluid ran down her thighs, instantly turning to ice, and froze to her stockings. The palms of her hands were stinging from grazes caused as she fell. Panting, she pulled herself up. The next contraction hit her like an ax blow.

Glass clutched at the tree trunk, threw back her head, and screamed. She was vaguely aware of someone running out of the house, a young woman with long hair that in the darkness seemed a dull red, unlike any color Stella's hair had ever been. When Glass screamed again, it was not because of the tiny little girl emerging almost effortlessly between her legs to face the world, but because of the agitated words of the young woman—for Stella was dead, she was dead, dead. . . . What was more, there was absolutely no chance of calling a midwife for help, as the phone bill had not been paid for ages, and the line had been disconnected. So the young woman rushed back to the house, came back with blankets, and wrapped the little girl in them, while Glass propped herself up against the tree, pushing and panting and screaming, until the first ray of sunlight touched the horizon and finally the boy also emerged from her body, far more reluctantly than his twin sister.

That is how Dianne and I came to be born: two wet little creatures, we dropped onto the crisp snow and were then picked up by Tereza, who from that moment on was to be our friend and companion, counselor and second mother. It was Tereza too who was later to present me with Paleiko, the moody black china doll.

It's a very strange thing, Phil. There are times when he'll speak to you and answer your questions.

Why has he got such a funny name?

That's a secret.

But that was many years later, on a warm summer's day,

when none of us was thinking of snow and ice. Glass, who should know better, still insists to this day that that far-off morning was a magical instant, at the moment of Dianne's and my birth, when night became day and winter became spring. Be that as it may, three days after Dianne and I saw the light of day, a warm desert wind really did begin to blow. It melted the last of the snow, transformed Visible's garden into a sea of multicolored crocuses and swaying white snowdrops, and lasted for an entire week.

part one

attics and cellars

chapter 1

martin's towel

I never even saw most of the men Glass had affairs with. They used to come to Visible late at night, when Dianne and I were fast asleep. Then doors would slam and unknown voices would penetrate our dreams. In the morning we used to find telltale signs of their existence: a warm mug of hastily gulped coffee abandoned on the kitchen table; a toothbrush wrapper in the bathroom, crumpled carelessly and dropped on the floor. Sometimes it was no more than a sleepy aroma hanging in the air like a strange shadow.

Once it was the telephones. Dianne and I had spent the weekend with Tereza, and when we got home, there were the phones in our bedrooms, connected to newly laid cables, and the plaster still damp on the walls. Glass had pulled an electrician.

"Now each of us has our own phone," she stated smugly, with Dianne on her left arm and me on her right. "Isn't that fantastic? Don't you think it's terribly American?"

I'm sprawled on my bed when the telephone rings. The July heat has wiped me out—even at night it crawls through the rooms and passages like a tired animal, looking for a place to bed down. I know who it is—I've been waiting for this call for the past three weeks. Kat (her name is Katja, but apart from her parents and some of the teachers, no one calls her by her full name) is back from holiday.

"I'm back again, Phil," she shrieks down the line.

"Sounds like it. How was it?"

"A nightmare, and stop grinning, I can tell you are! I'm suffering from parental abuse, and that island was the absolute pits, you can't imagine. I want to see you."

I look at my watch. "In half an hour on the castle hill?"

"I'd have died if you'd said no."

"Join the club. I've been bored out of my mind the last three weeks."

"Listen, I need a bit, longer—about an hour? I've got to unpack."

"No problem."

"Can't wait to see you. . . . Phil?"

"Mm?"

"I missed you."

"Didn't miss you."

"Thought so. Asshole!"

I put down the phone and stay lying on my back, blinking at the blinding white ceiling for the next quarter of an hour. The scent of cypress comes wafting in waves on the summer breeze through the open windows. I roll over and get out of the sweaty bed, grab boxer shorts and T-shirt, and pad along the creaking floorboards in the passage to the shower.

I hate the bathroom on this floor of the house. The door frame is so warped, you have to lean against the door with all your weight to get it open. Inside, you're met with broken black and white tiles, cracks in the ceiling, and flaking plaster. The antiquated plumbing takes three minutes before the water finally comes through. In the winter, the rusty boiler connected to it comes to life only after you've given it several hefty kicks. I turn on the tap, hear the familiar wheezing of the system, and once again regret that Glass never got involved with a plumber.

"For the sake of the plumbing?" she asked in astonishment when I once suggested how practical such a relationship could be. "What d'you take me for, darling—a hooker?"

Visible's architect must have been just as crazy as my aunt Stella, who discovered the house, already then in an advanced state of disrepair, a quarter of a century ago while on a trip to Europe. She fell in love with its southern charm, quite uncharacteristic of this part of the world, and promptly bought it. *For peanuts, my little chick,* she proudly wrote to Glass in America. *I've even got some money left over for the essential repairs!*

Stella was financially independent. Hers had been the classic career path of the American high school beauty, not thinking about the future until it was almost over and done with—early marriage, early divorce, overdue but relatively generous alimony payments. The money wasn't enough for Stella to live in great style, but it allowed for a life more or less free of financial worries. It was enough to buy Visible.

Surrounded by an extensive plot of land, Stella wrote, the house stood on a hill overlooking the edge of a tiny town on the other side of the river. The two-story façade with its colonnaded porch, the tiny bay windows and the tall casement windows, the innumerable gables and the battlemented roof were visible for all to see from a distance of miles. Seeking to give it an appropriately American name, she quite logically called the entire estate—the house, with its outhouses and garden sheds at the rear, as well as the huge garden bordering the wood, where life-sized statues of discolored sandstone stood about like lost souls—by the name Visible. It soon became evident that the money left over from the purchase was barely enough to cover the merest fraction of the renovation costs. The masonry was crumbling, the roof leaked in several places, and the garden was a jungle.

In its dilapidated state, Visible seems to be waiting and dreaming of better times, wrote Stella in one of her increasingly rare letters to Boston. *And the residents of the town seem to be waiting too. They don't like this house. The tall windows scare them. And d'you know why, little one? Because you only have to see these windows from afar to know and feel they call for a broader view of the world.*

I grew up with photos of Stella, countless snaps that Glass had dug out from her sister's papers a few months after her death and put up all around the house. They are everywhere: in the dark entrance hall, up the staircase, in almost every room. In their cheap frames they hang there like kitschy religious images, propped up on wobbly chests of drawers and tables, crowding on windowsills and window seats.

My favorite portrait of Stella shows her angular suntanned face. She had large, clear eyes and a lot of laugh lines. It's the only photo where my aunt looks soft and vulnerable. All the other pictures show a mixture of childish defiance and stormy provocation. These make Stella look like glowing steel tempered in fire.

Three days before Glass arrived at Visible, my aunt Stella's broad view on the world proved her undoing. She was cleaning the windows on the second floor when she fell to the drive below, where the postman found her next day. With her head resting on one arm and her legs slightly drawn up, she looked as if she was asleep. She had broken her neck. Later Glass found the cable she herself had wired from on board ship, and the draft of a reply her older, only sister had been unable to send. *Baby, looking forward to you and your offspring. Love, Stella.*

Stella's death affected Glass deeply. She had idolized her sister, even after she had left America. Their mother had died young of the Big C, as Glass put it, and their father had shown more interest in alcohol than in the fate of his daughters. The fact that both of them disappeared to Europe was met with drunken indifference. No one knew what had become of him. Once when I asked Glass about my grandfather, her curt reply was that the continent of America had swallowed him, and she hoped it would not spew him up again. After her initial mourning over Stella, she adopted a pragmatic attitude toward her death. One of her favorite sayings was "As one door closes, another opens." Death had taken Stella from her but given her Tereza instead: not such a bad exchange.

The municipal authorities appointed a local lawyer to go through the dead American woman's papers to establish whether there were any relatives overseas. Too busy to go himself, the man sent a trainee assistant to Visible, a young woman with long red hair, who, once she had got over her quite understandable initial fright, set about helping the two new additions to the family enter the world with impressive efficiency. (Tereza was a city girl but had turned her back on her hometown years earlier to go and study law somewhere in the northern mountain region.)

On the bitterly cold night preceding Dianne's and my birth, Tereza had brought her own sleeping bag and bedded down at Visible, intending to stay until she had completed her search. Here she found what she was looking for, as Stella had indeed left a will. In it she appointed Glass as sole heir to Visible and her entire estate. Things were not straightforward, there were legal complications—Glass was underage, she was an American, and she did not have a residence permit. The fact that she spoke only English didn't make matters any easier.

Tereza took Glass under her wing and pleaded her case with the lawyer. The man was fond of Tereza and took a liking to Glass, and he had friends who in turn had friends in high places. Blind eyes were turned and rules bent, regulations were carefully bypassed and favorable documents drafted. In the end Glass was allowed to stay, but that was only the beginning. Stella had left very little liquid cash, but this was money Glass desperately needed. There was no question of putting Visible up for sale. The house was more than just her legacy from Stella; it was a roof over her head and a haven for her tiny new family. Once again, it was Tereza who saved the day. Through friends at the university she found Glass a job that consisted of dealing with a mound of English correspondence and summarizing articles from international specialist journals.

A year before Tereza completed her studies, her father, a widower for many years, died. He was quite well known as a professor emeritus of botany, the only academic the town had ever produced. Overnight Tereza became wealthy but homeless. She disliked living alone in her father's home, and so she regularly spent the college vacations at Visible. She looked after Dianne and me while Glass first attended language courses and then trained at night school as a secretary.

By this time Dianne and I were four years old and trusting as young puppies. We had instantly taken Tereza to our hearts. In return she ruined our milk teeth with popcorn that she prepared for us every evening before putting us to bed. We would chew the sweet sticky stuff from cracked brightly colored dishes as Tereza read us fairy tales. She would usually nod off over the book, and then we would cover her with a woolen blanket and stick bits of corn up her nose.

Our love for her was blended with respect—after all, like the witches in the fairy tales, Tereza did have red hair. She could reduce us to tiny panic-stricken bundles when she threatened to turn us into frogs.

With her exams behind her, Tereza went to work in a lawyer's office. Two years on she had gained enough experience to set up her own practice in the second largest town in the region, and naturally she needed a secretary. The timing was perfect. Dianne and I were just about to start grade school, so Glass could work half days. Later, when we had learned how to look after ourselves, she took on the job full-time. Then she would get into her car (the old Ford that had belonged to Tereza's father) in the mornings, and come back home in the evening, and always bring us some small present—poison-green lollipops, a little picture book, a record that was quickly played to death.

When Dianne and I got home from school, we used to heat up the meals prepared for us the day before. We didn't need to be supervised or urged to do our schoolwork. Almost all our free time was spent out of doors, in the jungle of a garden and in the woods bordering the estate or by the river nearby. Glass took pride in our independence. As she pointed out more than once, our existence depended on her working, so Dianne and I didn't dare confide in her and tell her how frightened we were of Visible, left all alone in that big house. All those rooms tucked away in nooks and crannies, many of them never used, the immeasurably long and winding corridors, the high walls that gave off endless echoes at the faintest footstep—all this was scary. Visible was spooky, a gloomy, empty shell, and we were never more terrified than when Glass suggested we play hide-and-seek there. Dianne and I shared a bedroom on the ground floor; later on, when we had come to appreciate the privacy offered by the calm and peace of the upper floors, each of us moved into a room of our own up there. I took over a room with an unbroken view stretching beyond the river up to the town on the slopes of the castle hill, whose summit was crowned by an unimpressive early medieval fortress. It was in this room that I came to realize how different my personality must be from Stella's, for the view through the tall windows into the world beyond was never broad enough for me.

The cold shower has woken me up. I pull on my shorts and T-shirt and walk along the labyrinthine passage to the curving staircase that leads down to the entrance hall. There is no sight or sound of Dianne or Glass. Maybe they have succumbed to the oppressive summer air and taken a siesta.

As soon as I step outside, the heat hits me. I grab my bicycle, propped up against the wall, and let myself freewheel down the bumpy unpaved driveway.

The garden resembles a field of waving corn. On either side of the drive, grass several feet high fights with the colorful meadow flowers for a place in the sun. Rampaging ivy clings to the bark of the old fruit trees and poplars, clambering up along the branches and across the gutters to the house, and tumbles down in cascades from there.

During her first five or six years at Visible, Glass attempted to tame this wilderness and conquer the jungle by planting some sort of garden. Her battle dress consisted of a green kitchen overall and pink rubber gloves and boots. Her armory was an array of garden implements enough to transform the entire Nevada desert into fertile soil. Dianne and I, equipped with miniature rakes, spades, and plastic buckets, clustered around her legs when our mother moved into battle, and always stayed near her. But all the weeding, raking, and hoeing was to no avail; the heroic battle against the persistent army of weeds was doomed to failure.

"As if nature's ganged up against me," Glass complained as she sat at the kitchen table in the evenings, exhausted, her hands covered in blisters despite the rubber gloves. "These damned plants—they refuse to grow where I want them to, and spread like wildfire just where I want to get rid of them."

So Glass engaged a gardener by the hour. Martin was not much older than her—a young man with black hair and brilliant green eyes. God only knows where he came from, and that's exactly where he disappeared to. Right from the start, Dianne made no bones about the fact that she couldn't stand him, and avoided him accordingly, but I was enthralled by Martin. When he used to come into the cool kitchen after work on hot summer days, Glass would hand him iced lemonade, and I would bury my face in his sweat-soaked vest. I loved his scent; he smelled of grass and the wide blue sky. As he spoke to Glass he would run his hands down my neck. His fingers had a soft and pleasant touch, in spite of the hard gardening. Later he would tell me stories as he showered, laughing at the end of each sentence; his skin glistened with beads of water, and I would sit on the lid of the toilet, my head propped in my hands, and look at his strong arms, his broad suntanned shoulders, and the place where his slender legs joined. Secretly, I used to take the towel he dried himself with to bed with me and use it as a blanket. That Glass took him into her bed filled me with previously unknown pangs of jealousy, keeping me awake for nights on end.

If Dianne took all this in, I wasn't aware of it. It was only many years later that I gradually realized that at the time not a single detail had escaped her and that my twin sister had spent sleepless nights just as I had done, if for a completely different reason—Dianne hated Glass's having affairs.

chapter 2

dumbo on the tower

Kat and I are sitting side by side on the castle wall. Our legs dangle over the edge of the parapet, and a warm current of air drifts upward. Below us lies the town, spread out like a brightly colored map, fringed by wooded hills and enclosed by the triple bend of the shimmering blue ribbon of the river. In the three weeks Kat was away, I was often drawn to this spot. I find it reassuring to see the world in miniature.

"No violin lesson today?"

"Not the first day home. But I still had to practice." Kat gives me a sidelong glance. "Believe it or not, I really missed playing."

"Couldn't you have taken the thing with you?"

Kat shakes her head, as if reflecting in total bewilderment. "You know, I once saw something on television about Malta—the bridge between Africa and Europe. Crusaders and all that stuff. And windmills. They showed the windmills on television. Oh, and those godawful little crocheted mats they make everywhere all the time. . . ."

"And the guys, the Maltese, what were they like?"

She gives me a shove, almost enough to catapult me into space. Free fall from fifty feet above the ground, and soft landing in a bed of tall stinging nettles.

"Hey!"

"Serves you right. Christ, here I am, pouring out my soul, and all you can think of is the guys!"

"Go on."

She grins, revealing a wide gap between her front teeth that has defied years of wearing a retainer at night. "They were hideous, with big, fat asses—satisfied? Apart from which, Daddy was watching me like a hawk, even if I had felt like it. . . ."

"You wouldn't have let anyone stop you. Not even your father."

"Oh, come on, you know what I mean." She gives me another shove.

"Careful, right? Anyone would think you're good at choosing friends."

"He drove Mama totally nuts as usual, he really did. Culture overkill and all that. You're lucky you don't have a father. . . ."

Kat's eyes are fixed on an indefinite spot somewhere beyond the horizon. She knows she can't expect me to answer. When it comes to father, any father, I'm at a loss—I'm not up to handling the subject. I don't even like to think about it. If I do, then I get the kind of feeling that fills me at the thought of falling off this wall. The difference being that if I fell, I'd know what was waiting for me down below.

As if she guessed what I was thinking, Kat says, "Why d'you never say anything about your Number Three?"

"Because there's nothing to say," I snap back. Up to now, whenever she's asked me about my father, I've always given her a monosyllabic answer. And if it's left to me, I won't change.

"Oh, come on . . . anything."

"Glass has never spoken about him."

"Really?"

"She's . . ." As I search for the right words I look out at the red rooftops of the town glowing in the sunlight. Above them the air is shimmering, held in rippling suspension by the heat haze. "She's drawn a line under all that. The life she had in America is something she's never talked about with Dianne and me. OK, I do know a little about my grandparents, but it's boring stuff about boring people."

Sometime in the first half of the last century our ancestors left Europe for America, unhappy with the political and economic situation in their home country. They crossed the Atlantic in rotten hulks, weathering storms and cold, hunger and sickness, and very soon their descendants spread like dandelion seeds blown by the wind right across the continent, which they called God's Own Land, Home of the Brave, Land of the Free. And brave they certainly were, as well as free, but they never really put down roots. A few ended up in the large up-and-coming cities. But the majority by far, fired by the pioneering spirit and the desire for freedom and undeterred by obstacles, made the arduous trek for the frontier, the mythical borderlands in the West, beyond which—so they believed—the end of the rainbow awaited them.

"And my father . . . ," I go on. "It's not as if I've never tried asking about him. But Glass simply clams up."

"Does it bug you?"

"In a way, yes," I admit reluctantly. The fact that Number Three had walked out on her is the only reason I know that drove my mother across the Big Pond. "It's so . . . incomplete."

I think back to the list I found by chance a few years ago in among Glass's papers, a list of all the men she'd had, neatly numbered with names and dates when I assumed Glass had slept with them. In one place there was just a number. It was easy to work back from the date when Dianne and I were born to the date written next to Number Three.

I've no idea whether that list still exists today. At the time it consisted of about fifty entries. Whether that was few or many, I was in no position to judge. Spread over about ten years, fifty affairs really didn't seem to amount to that much, but it could well have something to do with the fact that very few of the men—in the event that Glass brought them home at all—ever turned up more than once at Visible. As far as I can remember, their faces merge into one another like gray phantom sketches, vague and interchangeable. They played no part in my life, and so even when they did have names, at the end of the day they meant no more to me than they did to Glass—just names on a piece of paper. Of course there are exceptions—Martin with the green eyes and smelling of garden soil is one of them, and later on there was Kyle, the woodcarver with the beautiful hands—but towering above all the exceptions is the nameless man who appeared on the list as Number Three.

"Would you like to have one? A father?" Kat has picked some moss out of the cracks in the wall and is rolling it between her fingers into a small green ball. "I mean, do you somehow miss him?"

"What d'you mean, miss him?" I snap at her. "I've never even known him."

Kat knows very well that she's dabbling in dangerous waters. She can be a real bitch.

She knows how to touch a raw nerve, trampling where no

psychiatrist would dare to tread. Black holes. Get too near them, and before you know it they swallow you up.

But what I consider black holes Kat calls "blank spots on the map of your psyche." She patiently fills in these spots whenever the occasion arises and is blissfully unaware of overstepping boundaries in doing so.

Like now, for instance.

"At any rate, you do know he lives in America," she keeps on, burrowing away.

"America's a big place," I snap. "And that he's alive is pure conjecture. And now do me a favor and shut it."

"OK. Truce."

She throws the wad of moss away with a deft flick of her fingers, and it goes sailing down through the warm air, landing at the foot of the wall among the clumps of stinging nettles. I get a placatory close-up of the gap-toothed smile. "Ice cream?"

The summer before I started school, Glass decided something had to be done about my ears.

"They're too big," she explained. "And they stand out. You look like Dumbo."

We were sitting on a quilt by the riverbank, sheltered from the afternoon sun by tall clumps of impatiens, far away from the town and its inhabitants. My mother reached into a cool bag filled with drinks and sticky peanut butter sandwiches, took out a bottle of Coke, and put it to her lips. Once she'd put it down, there was no escape.

The fact that she didn't like my ears filled me with alarm. I looked across at Dianne, who was standing up to her knees in the sluggish water, hunting for snails on the underside of flat stones. No one would have taken us for twins, if only because—as it suddenly struck me—Dianne had utterly unremarkable ears.

"Who's Dumbo?" I asked cautiously.

"An elephant." Glass placed the Coke bottle back in the cool bag. "His ears trailed along the ground, so when he was running he kept tripping over them. They were just too big."

Dianne waded out of the river and, nimbly jumping over a few stones, clambered through the waist-high grass. The next moment, without a word, she pushed a stone with an unusually pretty pink snail stuck to it under Glass's nose.

"Oh, God, take it away!" shrieked Glass in disgust. "I can't stand those slimy creatures."

Glass lay back and closed her eyes and consequently did not see Dianne marching back to the river to look for more slimy specimens, meanwhile sticking the snail experimentally into her left ear. Into her normal-sized left ear that did not stick out, as I noticed enviously.

I remained sitting on the blanket, overcome by the most dreadful premonitions. I waited for Glass to return to the subject—to explain what you did with overlarge, sticking-out ears so that they didn't trail along the ground—but she'd fallen asleep, and as she didn't mention it again on the way home, I somewhat hesitantly considered the matter settled.

The early evening was taken up with an unsuccessful attempt at extracting the unfortunate water snail from Dianne's ear. Using the entire contents of three kitchen drawers, Glass set to work burrowing away inside Dianne's auditory canal, with the not altogether surprising but painful result that at some stage the foreign body was pushed up against the eardrum. Finally she muttered something about the Eustachian tube. I didn't know what impressed me more—the fact that my mother could utter such a complicated word or that without batting an eyelid, she closed her lips around Dianne's nose and blew into it so hard that I fully expected the snail to shoot out of the ear across the kitchen with the speed of machine-gun fire. When even that didn't help, cursing, Glass bundled us into the car and drove to the local hospital, where a patient young emergency-room doctor rinsed out Dianne's ear several times and with the aid of fine tweezers removed the offending article.

"My name's Clemens," he said to Dianne. "And yours?"

Dianne didn't reply.

The doctor laughed. I looked on as his strangely pink hands fiddled with the tweezers. His nails were cut very short.

The snail was of course dead, but its dirty pink shell had miraculously survived the intervention completely intact. As we were sitting in the car, Dianne let the shell roll across her open palm. "May I keep it?" she asked.

"You know what you can do with it. . . . Oh, sod it, for all I care, keep it," Glass replied.

There was a grinding noise and the car lurched as Glass shifted into the wrong gear. I knew she was furious, unspeakably furious, because on account of a snail no bigger than a pea, she had been compelled to seek help from some unknown person, even if it had been a very nice unknown person. Many years later I found Clemens on the list. Beside his name was the number twenty-four.

By the time we had eaten that evening and gone to bed it was already dark. Glass came into our room and stood by my bed; the light was out, and Dianne was already asleep. She had placed the shell under her pillow, and next morning we would find that it had shattered into a hundred fragments.

As Glass bent over me, it felt as if I was all alone with her voice.

"About your ears . . ."

It was all Dianne's fault! If only she'd left that stupid snail alone, Glass wouldn't be going on and on about my ears.

"You do realize," said the voice, "that they'll do the same to you as they did to Dumbo."

"Who will?"

"Those out there."

I saw the silhouette of a hand pass across the dark blue

square of night framed by the open window. The movement encompassed everything and everyone—the town, its inhabitants across the river, the rest of the world, the universe—and its all-inclusiveness frightened me.

"What did they do to Dumbo?"

Tense expectation had caused me to whisper, and now I got the feeling that the voice was hesitating before answering. Silence wrapped itself round my pounding heart like a rough and shrunken coat.

"They put him in a circus on top of a sixty-foot tower," the voice answered at last. The darkness turned even darker. "They made him jump into a pool of semolina. And everyone laughed!"

At first I was scared stiff of Marthe, the senior nurse. Whenever I saw her charging along the hospital corridor, her head bowed, ready for battle, I pictured her spearheading a march into battle many years ago, ending with the victorious capture of Station 303. It was only later that I realized that under the armor plating of her crisply starched blouse there beat a heart as soft as butter.

"ENT," she snorted in answer to the first question I put her, when I noticed a crucifix attached to her fine silver chain, "means Earnoseandthroat."

Regardless of their age, she addressed her patients as "kiddy," and those, like me, who were there to have their ears treated belonged to the inner circle of the "jug ears." She resolutely refused to pronounce my name properly and called me Pill.

Pill, my little jug ears.

For all the respect she commanded, I instinctively felt that in the cold hospital world with its strange smells, she provided a haven of security. To anchor in this haven all I needed to do, like all the other little jug ears, was to use my enormous ears like sails, especially when Senior Nurse Marthe knew she wasn't being watched by the other staff. Then she would give free rein to her maternal instincts and speak softly and gently, and if you were in luck, you would be pressed to her ample bosom and stroked behind your either still projecting or already manhandled ears.

The name of the doctor who was to see to it that no one would laugh at me on account of these ears was Dr. Eisbert. Dr. Eisbert had a deep voice that inspired confidence. He had deep furrows running down from his nostrils to the corners of his mouth that I considered with some distrust. Furrows like these, I later decided, were the result of lying. Dr. Eisbert explained to me what would happen during the operation. A tiny slit would be made behind each of my ears in order to remove a mass of cartilage.

"You're not going to cut my ears off, are you?"

"No, just a tiny incision," he assured me in his growling voice. "After that we'll sew everything up, and you will have a neat little turban. You'll look like an Asian prince."

"Will it hurt?"

Dr. Eisbert shook his head. Satisfied, I sank back into my pillows. An Asian prince enjoyed royal immunity. None of those out there would ever think of making him jump into a pool of semolina from a great height.

But deep down, I was still uneasy. Earnoseandthroat was a ward not in our little local hospital but in a specialist clinic. Visible was more than two hours' drive away, and so visits from Glass and Dianne or Tereza were accordingly rare. Above all, Glass, who regarded hospitals as breeding grounds for exotic bacteria and generally gruesome deathly places best given a wide berth, clearly couldn't be counted on. She bore the main responsibility for my pathetic state, and for all I cared she could go jump in a lake. And I wasn't too bothered whether or not Dianne came, because I was still convinced that her stupid experiment with the water snail was the cause of my misfortune. It would have served her right if the snail had stayed forever and ever in her stupid head and rolled around with a loud clattering sound every time she moved. Tereza was the only one I wanted to come and comfort me, but she had her hands full with her new lawyer's chambers. I felt abandoned and all alone. Intimidated by the harsh fluorescent-lit hospital corridors, which I feared would swallow me up if I went out in them, I hardly dared leave my room. I spent most of the time patiently filling in endless drawing books with colored pencils.

The evening before the operation I heard terrifying screams and the menacing voice of Senior Nurse Marthe coming from the room next door. It wasn't hard to guess that she was struggling with one of the jug ears.

"Leave off!" yelled a child's voice. "Leave off!"

"Will you—"

"No!"

This was followed by a metallic crash and the sound of breaking china. I jumped out of bed and opened the door. A little white-clad person rushed past me down the corridor. Loosened bandages were streaming down from her forehead, with two angry green eyes flashing below. Senior Nurse Marthe stormed in pursuit, brandishing a syringe menacingly in her right hand.

"Stop running—Pill, shut the door and into bed, into bed!—Stop running, you . . ."

The wild chase shot past me again, this time in the opposite direction. The distance between the little jug ears shrieking in panic and her pursuer was visibly shrinking. Both disappeared from view, and then a last piercing scream from the fugitive announced that the syringe had won the uneven battle.

Not a happy prospect.

Hours later, when the ward had long since settled down for the night, the cautious pattering of bare feet woke me from my uneasy slumber. Jug ears with the green eyes, encased in a knee-length nightgown, head wrapped in bandages that glowed in the dark in a ghostly way, scurried through the open door. It came to a halt by my bed and picked its nose.

"My daddy owns a school," it said.

I couldn't really match that. I didn't know my father, didn't even know his name.

All I knew was that he lived in America. *America* was the magic word I used to say out loud to myself like a prayer, over and over.

The girl, who seemed determined to talk to me, wouldn't let herself be put off by my lack of an answer. "Are you having your ears operated on as well?"

This was less shaky ground. I nodded. "My mother said I would look like Dumbo, the elephant. He had to jump down into a pool of semolina. Everyone laughed at him."

"But later on he could fly with his huge ears, and he was famous and a star."

"Who?"

"Dumbo. Can I get into your bed?"

I folded back the blanket and shifted to one side. The girl who knew Dumbo and whose father owned a school crawled across and snuggled up to me. Her bandage pressed against my face; it smelled of ointment and disinfectant. It had slipped up slightly above the left ear. The place was dark with encrusted blood.

"Does it hurt?" I asked in sympathy.

"Like buggery."

Glass, who was not averse to using strong language herself, had punished me for using this particular word by not allowing me peanut butter sandwiches for two whole weeks. Suddenly I was filled with rage. My own mother had lied to me. Well, OK, that might not be exactly the right word, but she had omitted to tell me a part of the truth. As far as I was concerned, lying and leaving bits out came to the same thing. I would never be able to fly like Dumbo. I would never be famous like Dumbo. That Dr. Eisbert with his deep voice had lied was clear as daylight. I hated him. The Asian prince would wear a bloodstained turban. The operation would hurt.

"Like buggery," I repeated, shuddering. I touched the girl's shoulder. "What's your name?"

"Katja. And yours?"

"Phil."

"I can have ice cream here every day if I ask for it. Cherry's my favorite."

"Mine's vanilla. May I try on your nightgown?"

We got out of bed and undressed. I felt uncomfortable naked, unlike Katja. When I handed her my pajamas, she shook her head.

"Don't need them."

"But my mom says the place is full of bacteria."

"Rubbish."

I was shorter than she was, and her nightgown came down to my shins. It was soft and light; as I let it slide over my head and shoulders, it felt like cool water on my body.

Back in bed, Katja nestled up against me, naked apart from that terrible bandage round her head, and consequently defenseless against all the bacteria in the world. I put an arm around her to protect her. She fell asleep immediately, while I let my fingertips slowly glide over the unfamiliar smooth fabric of the flowered nightgown. "America," I whispered with my eyes shut.

The world had become a dangerous place. At its center there were doctors cold-bloodedly sharpening their scalpels on small children. Nurses armed with syringes chased defenseless jug ears down the neon green labyrinthine bowels of gigantic hospitals. Mothers could not be relied on to help. They betrayed confidence and their own children. In the future I would have to be very careful.

The future is never further away than the next moment. As I heard a deep, worried grunting and opened my eyes, Senior Nurse Marthe stood by my bed like an avenging angel. "Always on the run! You little big ears are all the same." I saw the stiffly starched blouse being smoothed down. "The Lord God doesn't like seeing boys and girls sharing the same bed."

The Lord God, I thought, probably didn't have to be afraid of an operation to remove cartilage from behind His ears, and when all was said and done, He was the one responsible for my landing in the Earnoseandthroat with two misshapen jug ears in the first place.

And it didn't surprise me in the least that He didn't approve of the nightgown. Senior Nurse Marthe had already pulled back the blanket and gently lifted Katja out of my bed when her gaze fell upon me and she stopped short.

"What are you wearing that for, Pill?"

"I'm frightened."

"You needn't be afraid. No one's going to hurt you."

"Yes, they are. Katja said so."

"Take off that nightgown. The Lord God—"

"No!"

The Lord God could go and take a running jump. Stubbornly I pulled the blanket up under my chin, bracing myself for the inevitable thunderstorm.

It didn't come. Maybe it was the night and the silence, or it may have been the warm skin of the little jug ears lying in her arms, that softened Senior Nurse Marthe. Shaking her head, with a last disapproving backward glance, she left the room.

Katja's naked body almost disappeared in the strong arms, but in spite of her delicate back, the head lolling to one side, and the pitiful bloodstained bandage, she didn't look fragile. I began wondering if I would stop being afraid of the hospital if I got hold of enough cherry ice cream. Staring into the darkness, I stroked the nightgown.

"America, America, America . . ."

In the dull heat of the afternoon the marketplace, with its war memorial barely visible under the coating of pigeon droppings and little wedding cake houses, is deserted. There is not a breath of air; nothing stirs. Anyone in his right mind is either in the swimming pool or at home indoors.

Kat and I sit down at a table in the far corner of the

garishly painted ice cream parlor and order gigantic servings of vanilla and cherry. For a while we watch the little kids come in from time to time, slapping their carefully counted coins down on the counter and then disappearing with their ice creams, which begin to melt the minute they clutch them in their tiny sweaty hands.

"By the way, Daddy told me the other day that we're getting a new one," says Kat, interrupting the agreeable silence. The summer holidays end on Monday, and we're starting to talk about school again.

"New . . . does he come from here?"

Kat nods.

"Stayed down?"

"Ran away from boarding school."

She scoops a sticky maraschino cherry out of her sundae before adding furtively, "A boys-only school."

"And?"

"And? Why d'you suppose that lot expels anyone? Maybe the guy felt up one of the other boys." The maraschino cherry bursts open between pearly white teeth. "Doesn't the idea make your lonely heart beat faster?"

"And yours?"

"Well, in case you're referring to Thomas . . ."

Thomas is in the year above us. Last winter he and Kat were an item for a few weeks—just long enough, as she informed me, to lose her virginity and as a result discover with certainty what she didn't want out of life. Including, among other things, Thomas. Kat parades like a hard-won trophy the fact that he is still moping over her. Although she repeatedly assured Thomas at the time that I was simply her best friend, we both know that he is hugely jealous of me.

"And if I do happen to be referring to him?"

"Oh, forget it." Kat grins. "Or show me a guy who's not just good-looking but also has an IQ above 130 and occasionally thinks of something besides football, cars, and melon-sized tits."

"He's sitting right beside you."

"You don't count, darling." She's imitating Glass. She even adopts the same typical gesture, tossing her long blond hair back over her shoulders. "And if you did count, that would mean trouble at home."

That's the sort of trouble Kat would welcome with open arms. Years ago, in Earnoseandthroat, we found out that we came from the same little town. Following this discovery we swore an oath of eternal friendship, and ever since then our relationship has been a perpetual bugbear for Kat's parents. I was the son of that woman—Glass and her notorious way of life were already then the talk of the town—and so Kat was forbidden to be friends with me. Her father is the principal of the high school in the town; he managed to see to it that from the very start in first grade we were put in separate classes. As we moved up in school he intervened in person to prevent his one and only daughter from associating with me. I have often wondered if he really was so stupid not to realize that the more he tried to keep us apart, the more inseparable Kat and I became.

Even back then, for heaven alone knows what reason, Kat took it into her head to want me for a friend, and she's never let go. As she's grown older, over the years she's fought her parents tooth and nail. Obstinately she's disregarded all their bans and prohibitions with that sublime composure and readiness to fight them that so endear her to me. She is totally without prejudice. As if at birth a fairy whispered in her ear that the world was a place without secrets, she is open to everything—you can astonish Kat, but you can never really surprise her. In essence she is still the barefoot little jug ears who gave her nightgown to a frightened little boy. That even then her motives were not entirely altruistic is another story but a blameless one. After all, who wants to live without friends?

I'm more reticent than Kat, less prepared to be wide open. There are things that I keep to myself, not so much out of distrust—there is no one I trust more than Kat—but because there are things that I haven't fully worked out for myself. Like my attitude toward Number Three.

"Another ice cream?" she says, interrupting my train of thought. "Phil?"

"What? Oh, I don't know. . . ."

"Vanilla ice cream is good for the soul."

"Says who?"

"I do."

"I feel ill."

"Force yourself. I'm paying."

She grins and signals to be served. In the course of the afternoon we manage to put away four sundaes. Kat relates details from her disastrous holiday. We laugh a lot.

We speculate about the coming school year and future loves that may be around the corner.

It's one of those hot, sky-blue days that taste of vanilla ice cream and summer and future, when your heart beats faster for no apparent reason, and when you're prepared to swear any oath that friendships never end.

chapter 3

the broader view

When I get back to Visible and close the front door behind me, I hear the distant murmur of voices coming from the kitchen, followed by nervous laughter. Forget the milk I was going to take. Glass is obviously with a client.

"The UFO."

I jump to one side and very nearly lose my balance. Right next to me a gaunt figure has emerged from nowhere and is eyeing me coolly.

"Dianne! You nearly scared me to death!"

She doesn't react as if my sudden demise would bother her too much. As I see it, she's always trying hard to avoid reacting to anything. Her straight black hair is scraped back carelessly from her face. She is pale, and as ever, regardless of the summer heat, she wears an outsized black turtleneck sweater far too big for her and a floor-length dun-colored skirt.

"Why are you eavesdropping again?" I whisper. "You know Glass doesn't like it."

Dianne shrugs. I've often wondered what she gets out of listening in sneakily to the stories these women clients tell. There was a time when we used to do so together purely out of childish curiosity. I soon gave up, first because I lacked a deeper understanding of what these conversations between Glass and her women clients were all about, and then because all that sobbing and crying, the tantrums and the yells of vengeance, gradually began to sound the same. But maybe Dianne just keeps on listening as a way of keeping in touch with the world through other people's emotions.

"Don't get caught," I advise her.

She gives a dismissive wave of her hand without looking at me.

"I'm not stupid, Phil."

Glass feels bound to observe a sort of confidentiality. She doesn't say much about her clients, whom she advises mostly on weekends or in the evenings, after she gets home from her job in Tereza's office. She does not ask for payment for listening to these women, but most of them leave money in gratitude, small or large amounts that Glass puts firmly aside for unforeseen expenses—for a rainy day—occasionally reminding Dianne and me of the fact. This explains Rosella, the enormous pink china piggy bank that sits proudly at the center of the kitchen table, with a smile of eternal happiness etched under its fat snout. Glass bought Rosella at a flea market for next to nothing because its left ear was missing.

"How long's the UFO been here?" I whisper.

"Half an hour." Dianne still doesn't look at me. "She wants a divorce."

"She won't do it." I take off my trainers and place them on the bottom stair. "She's been talking about it forever and keeps putting it off."

"She'd have been better off if she had done it. Her husband is a filthy pig. He's screwing another woman, and the UFO is stupid enough to wash the sheets afterward."

"Whatever turns you on. By the way, I've just been into town. Met up with Kat."

Dianne turns round and silent as smoke glides toward the kitchen to hear better. I really don't know why I keep on trying to get her interested in my doings. In the unlikely event that she isn't totally indifferent to Glass and me, my sister certainly doesn't give any sign of it. Dianne has always been withdrawn, but over the last few years her existence is like an insect trapped in amber. We talk to each other less and less. There was a time when we used to explore the countryside together, wander through the woods, follow the course of the river until our feet were sore. Now when Dianne leaves the house, she's alone; she stays away for hours on end, and if I ask her where she goes on her solitary walks, she doesn't answer. Our conversations fizzle out after we exchange small talk.

I go upstairs, pursued by the UFO's laughter.

The UFO's name is Irene. Two years ago, when her husband had already been cheating on her for a good while and loneliness and despair were gnawing away at her like moths, she announced that on a mild summer's night she had taken photos of unidentified flying objects. The grainy, slightly smudged black-and-white photos allegedly supporting her claim did indeed show a few mysterious white blobs against a dark background. They caused considerable excitement in the town, for after the photos had gone through the hands of all the neighbors and acquaintances, Irene—by now drunk with success—allowed herself to be talked into passing them on to the local press. They were published in the weekend issue of the regional newspaper under the banner headline "UFOs Overhead?" A week later a reader's letter from Dr. Hoffmann, the town's one and only gynecologist, maintained that these images were ultrasound scans of a female uterus. While chatting to the regulars in the local bar, after a few pints he indicated that in actual fact these were images of Irene's uterus; God alone knew how the copies of the scans had come into her possession, and she must have had copies made. It really isn't for me to say that Dr. Hoffmann has deep furrows running down either side of his nostrils, recalling my long-standing suspicion of Dr. Eisbert, executioner of countless jug ears, and so this was a confirmation of such furrows being the sure sign of someone's being a liar.

When Glass heard about the whole affair, she was equally incensed by the indiscretion of the gynecologist as by the term *female uterus*. In a letter to the gynecologist (which was never answered) she wrote that he deserved to get a kick in the masculine balls for gross biological ignorance and to have his license to practice removed. There was someone else who felt the need to take even more drastic action, for a few days later a message in poison-green spray paint adorned Hoffmann's office premises, urging in unmistakable terms that the damned woman-hater should have his willy chopped off. This in turn led to a policeman's turning up early one evening at Visible, a slightly spotty young man in uniform whose extreme nervousness revealed itself in his flushed face and constant fidgeting with his tight shirt collar, but above all by excessive secretion of saliva. This flow of saliva compelled him to pause frequently while speaking, because he kept having to swallow.

"This communication comes from you, right?" he said, even as he stood outside the front door, brandishing the letter Glass had sent to Dr. Hoffmann.

"You bet your sweet little ass it does," replied Glass, prompting the officer's first bout of hiccups.

She led the man into the kitchen and asked whether he had come on an official inquiry, and when he answered in the negative, she insisted on Dianne's and my being present. Then she set about making tea, and there followed half an hour of conversation that was highly instructive for me, with Glass doing most of the talking, mainly dealing with male sexual organs, their general functions, and their potential maltreatment by insulted women.

At some point the young officer, who had meanwhile introduced himself as Mr. Acer, undid the top button of his shirt.

"I'm now asking you perfectly frankly," he finally asked, "whether the graffiti on the wall of the doctor's house was your handiwork."

"And I'm asking you perfectly frankly," retorted Glass, her words unleashing his final attack of hiccups, "whether I look like the sort of woman to waste raw materials in a public place."

Dianne, like me, had listened to the conversation without batting an eyelid. We must have seemed quite spooky to the policeman, as we sat next to each other at the table without moving a muscle, breathing almost soundlessly, and all in all conveying the impression of waxworks intent on murder. In front of us on the table stood Rosella. With her friendly snout, missing left ear, and big eyes, she was the only neutral object to enter the bewildered officer's field of vision in the course of the questioning. But he stared at this harmless piggy bank as if he expected even the pink piece of china to sprout fangs at any moment.

When Acer finally left Visible, he was like someone on the run; he staggered and stumbled down the drive and disappeared into the rust-red sunset like some lone drunken sheriff in an old western movie. He had left his tea untouched. I never told Dianne that weeks later, while hunting for a patch to mend my bicycle tire, I came across a can of poison-green spray paint in the woodshed behind the house—but I was mighty proud of her.

As far as Irene was concerned, by some crazy male logic elevating her on the spot from victim to culprit, she was disgraced, and this is how she came to be a case for Glass. Sooner or later every unfortunate woman from the town or its immediate surroundings who couldn't afford an expensive psychiatrist or cheap lover became a case for Glass.

"It's a kind of life insurance, darling," Glass once explained to me. "So long as they're afraid I might spill the beans about their petty secrets, I have that lot over there eating out of my hand."

She refers to the residents of the town as "that lot over there" because they live on the other side of the river. For me they are the Little People—a term from my nursery days, when I used to think of people who frightened me as tiny, lifeless dolls.

We've never been on good terms with the Little People. Anyone who doesn't come from an old, established family is regarded with suspicion by the townspeople, and this can persist for generations. But right from the start Glass had to face up to more than mere suspicion. Once she started bringing men back with her to Visible every now and again, and because she made no secret of the rapid turnover in her love life, she was met with open hostility. She received offensive letters and obscene phone calls. Once after she had driven into town to do some shopping, she found the paint of her car scratched. She'd only been in the shop for ten minutes; when she came out again, she found the word *whohre* scratched in large unmistakable letters on the driver's door. Glass stuck a piece of cardboard below the scratch marks on which she wrote in thick black letters: Whore *is spelled with only one* h. She drove for a whole hour with it down every street in the town, her right foot pressing hard on the gas pedal, honking loudly, with murder in her eyes. Later, as things came full circle and Glass began selling the nuggets of wisdom learned in the main from her lovers to her women clients, battered by fate or the violence of their husbands, she was granted a grudging kind of teeth-grinding tolerance. There were fewer letters and phone calls, and finally they stopped altogether. But then, as now, it would never have occurred to anyone to include her in the great ballyhoo of the annual town festival, let alone offer her the chairmanship of the local rose growers' association.

For a long time Dianne and I were spared any animosity. That lot over there regarded us as pitiful little creatures who'd had the misfortune to be dumped into this world by a mother who was far too young and totally irresponsible. But we didn't belong to their world—not because we deliberately didn't want to but because we felt that we were different. I couldn't really even have said in what way, whether from inborn arrogance, acquired aversion, deeply buried insecurity, or a combination of all of these. The fact remained that we felt as if there was a glass wall separating us from that lot over there, young and old alike, and that we would have subjected them to the meticulous study of scientists researching the life of ants had we only had the necessary patience to do so. As things stood, we couldn't have cared less about them.

The reverse was not true. Our peers were afraid of Dianne and me, and like all groundless fear, this too proved fertile soil for superstition. During recess at school, our classmates would whisper to each other that one glance from me could turn anyone to stone, a single word from Dianne made the person concerned turn scarlet, or a fleeting touch from our hands would render them speechless. But the kids never went so far as to attack us physically—apart from one single occasion, the Battle of the Big Eye, when Dianne saw to it that they lost the desire for any further battles once and for all—though they mocked us with swear words that were every bit as painful as blows. In the end we clammed up like oysters that keep their pearls safe from robbers.

"Children are wax in the hands of the world," said Tereza when I told her about it. "Open books with empty pages, waiting to be written on by us grown-ups. For the rest of your life you'll never get rid of what's on the first pages."

I knew she was right, for I could see how books were written. There were some classmates who were brought to school every morning by their mothers and fetched again at lunchtime. These were the mothers who sized us up and then fantasized about us in whispers to their children, after which the children would look at us pityingly or disconcertedly when we turned up at school in the morning with our shabby schoolbags, sometimes soaked to the skin without umbrellas or galoshes, or then without a warm coat or gloves, frozen to the bone in the icy winter weather. In the eyes of these mothers and their children, Glass was obviously a bad mother whose indifference caused Dianne and me to suffer dreadfully. It didn't seem to occur to anyone that Glass allowed us the space on which we both insisted loudly, sometimes amid tearful protests. If we didn't wear coats or gloves, it was because we had taken it into our heads to defy the winter. That snow and cold emerged victorious in this unequal battle was of secondary importance. Anyway, we warmed up in the evenings when, wrapped in blankets, we would sit with Glass on the threadbare sofa snuggled up to one another, our feet hidden in thick woolen socks, with the tall bare room lit by flickering candles and the open fire. There Glass drummed into us: *Be strong and defend yourselves. Anyone who hurts you, hurt them back twice over or keep out of their way, but never let anyone tell you how you ought to live. I love you as you are.*

She gave us the feeling that we were unique, and the idea that I should envy other children for their protective, whispering mothers never even entered my head. What I did envy them for hugely was their fathers. It wasn't that I didn't feel sufficiently protected by Glass, even if it did take Dianne and me quite a few years before we learned to face down that lot over there in the same stubborn thick-skinned way our mother did. No, what I wanted was a kind of second authority, an outward-looking, tangible image of the willpower and tenacity that Glass possessed. Glass may have been steering the ship of our lives, but she simply wasn't able, at least so I thought, to cope with the sails at the same time. Since there was no prospect far and wide of a father prepared to take on this task, and Glass was not making any moves to make one of her lovers responsible, I was looking for a substitute. I found him in Gable.

Gable is the only relation Glass is prepared to talk about and the only one I have ever clapped eyes on. He stems from a distant branch of the family, from which he ran away as a youngster—a rebellious black sheep for whom, like Stella, the view of the world could never be broad enough. At the age of sixteen he signed up on the first available ship in the nearest port and unknowingly established the tradition, later followed by Glass, of seeking rescue from emerging problems by escaping across the open seas.

"He's a mariner, darling."

"Is that something like a pirate?"

"Pirate, merchant seaman, smuggler, fisherman, freebooter . . . he's a bit of everything."

So—a mariner. Gable's appearance gives no hint that he has spent the best part of his life at sea. It's useless to search the features of his broad coarse face for the traces that such an existence is supposed to leave behind: tanned weather-beaten skin, dark brows, deeply scored furrows. His stocky body is like a muscular athlete's in top condition but lacks the sluggishness that sometimes comes with it, and despite heavy labor his powerful hands bear no signs of calluses. The only striking peculiarity is a scar disfiguring his upper arm, the sight of which filled me with horror as a child. The scar is large and deep and creeps along below the skin like a pink, rampant web. In the past it often seemed to me that it had a life of its own, for when Gable used to come and see us, its shape seemed to have changed from one visit to the next, like an ameba stretching out its pseudopods in different directions, growing fractionally in the process.

It's nothing unusual for Gable to pitch up at Visible two or three times a year, often as not without warning. He's almost exactly ten years older than Glass, which makes me think that he sees her as a kind of little sister who needs to have an eye kept on her from time to time. This makes Glass wild. Gable's regular offers of money are turned down with equal regularity. I know from Glass that Gable was married for a short while and lived with his wife somewhere out on the West Coast of America. At some stage both the marriage and the home were abandoned. The name of the wife is Alexa, and she left Gable at around the time that Dianne and I were born at the other end of the world. Alexa couldn't put up with Gable's restlessness—the ocean had a magnetic attraction for him, like the moon for howling dogs—and worse still, in emotional terms he was like a block of ice. Maybe things would have been different for the two of them if Alexa had accompanied her husband on his voyages.

Whenever Gable visits he brings us presents. When I was little I would get enormously excited by these little tokens, and later on they would thrill me to bits, all because they came from the sea. Gable used to give virtually unpronounceable names of different coastlines or islands to each of these presents—names that rolled across my tongue like softly shimmering pearls when I repeated them. *Tongatapu*—a black, mysteriously shiny fan-shaped coral. *Semisopochnoi*—dried sea horses with hard little brown bodies. *Kiritimati*—a piece of driftwood encrusted with age-old shells. Once it was a crab's giant pincers, vivid red, as if sprinkled with drops of fire.

Dianne categorically refused to accept these precious gifts. Even early on I never saw her get closer to him than about ten feet—it was as if he was surrounded by an invisible barrier of electric energy, and she didn't want to step across its boundaries. On the other hand, what Dianne did have in common with Gable was a strange kind of reserve—they could both suddenly cut out of a conversation and withdraw into themselves, which I found terribly irritating—but then, of course, it was just this reserve that prevented my sister and Gable from baiting each other. As soon as Gable left us, Dianne would come to life again, and on more than one occasion we then fought over the treasures he had left us, in which she had pretended to have no interest whatsoever until his departure but which she now coveted.

Each time he visited us, Gable never tired of declaring that this was the last time he would come ashore, as he felt ill at ease and couldn't cope on land. As a child, I envied him for being a grown-up. His home was the seas and the oceans. He found his bearings from the stars and the way the waves rippled under the wind that blows only in a certain part of the world, from foreign smells and the changing colors of the water—brilliant blue and turquoise that promise land ahead, a gleam like greenish black ink where underwater ravines plunge to impenetrable depths.

"Won't you take me with you?" I would regularly beg him.

"One day. If Glass allows it."

Glass had brought Dianne and me up to be bilingual, but I didn't need to speak to Gable in English. He could speak more languages than there were seas in the world, and his voice was also as deep as an ocean.

At night I used to take Paleiko to bed with me. No sooner had Tereza given me the black china doll than her promise came true—he spoke to me. Admittedly Tereza hadn't warned me that Paleiko could talk incessantly, that he had an opinion about everything and would bombard me with well-meant advice that was often as unintelligible as the answers he gave to questions I asked him.

"When will Glass let me go with Gable?" I whispered.

Embedded in Paleiko's forehead was a pink stone, a small piece of crystal. I imagined I saw it light up when the cold china mannikin answered: *When you're ready, my little friend. When you're ready.*

I seized on Gable as the father I'd always wanted, who not only would take me in his arms to comfort and protect me but also led a dazzlingly exotic life, with whom one could survive adventures of the kind that made my wildest dreams pale in comparison. I was crazy about the tales Gable told. When he described his voyages at sea, it made the ocean come alive for me. I could feel the pitching of the ship under my feet and the sun burning my skin, or be shaken by violent storms that tore the sky to shreds like a fine silk cloth. Every time Gable left I would be miserable and restless for days; I'd stroke the corals he left behind, lick the salt off the little dried sea horses, and lose myself in daydreams in which I accompanied Gable on his voyages. And whenever I asked Glass when she was finally going to let me go with him, she would listen to her inner self for a moment before answering, "Not yet."

chapter 4

the battle of the big eye

In summer the kitchen at Visible is transformed into an aquarium. The ivy presses against the windows outside, so the light coming in passes through a kind of green filter, making you involuntarily take a deep breath as you enter the room.

Glass is standing at the stove, where she is frantically shaking a frying pan. The air smells of burnt bacon and scrambled eggs. I can see only her back and her blond hair, pinned up carelessly.

"What are you up to?"

"What does it look like? First day back at school after vacation. I'm trying to be a good mother."

"Seventeen years too late."

"Thanks a million, darling." She turns round to me. "Is

Dianne coming down for breakfast as well? Will she want scrambled eggs too, or something—cornflakes?"

"She's never eaten scrambled eggs." I sit down at the massive ancient wooden table that takes up the center of the kitchen. "Or cornflakes either. I've no idea what she eats, probably nothing at all."

"That's all because of TV." She scrapes the contents of the pan onto a plate. "Those American programs are crawling with skeletal women who all weigh less than eighty pounds, and over half that is in their silicone tits! I sometimes think the whole of California is one big anorexia commercial."

"Glass, it's you who watches those programs, not Dianne."

"Then she should, as a warning." The plate is shoved under my nose. "I mean, she is painfully thin, don't you think?"

"How can you tell in the kind of gear she wears?"

Glass sits down opposite me. She herself doesn't have breakfast till she gets to the office; at home she just drinks vast amounts of tea. "I'll be home a bit late tonight," she announces over the edge of her cup.

"Mm . . ." I poke around in the scrambled egg in search of a strip of unburnt bacon. "Who is it?"

"Couldn't it be that I'm simply doing overtime?"

"Come on, where did you meet him?"

She grins. "At the office. He's one of Tereza's briefs, a dishy-looking fraud case."

She blows carefully into her tea. Sometimes I forget she's my mother, she's so young.

"Fraud? Is he the guilty party or the victim?"

"Now, have I ever hooked up with a criminal?"

"A couple of them looked like criminals." I strike lucky and spear a piece of bacon with my fork. "What does Tereza have to say about it?"

Tereza is far more than just her boss. She is absolutely everything for Glass—understanding mother confessor and friend, safe haven among the breakers when life gets too stormy.

"She says the guy is a bad character because he doesn't do his shoelaces up properly—or something of the sort. Apparently that's an unmistakable sign." Glass turns up her nose indignantly. "She's probably just jealous."

"Of the guy?" The scrambled egg is so salty, I push it to the side of the plate. "You're crazy."

"Old love never dies, darling."

"Neither does vanity, it seems. You've been out of the picture for a long time. Tereza has Pascal." Tereza and her girlfriend have been cohabiting for over four years.

"You're probably right." Glass looks thoughtfully out of one of the green-lit windows. "You know, you should have seen her when she helped me out when I was in the shit. At least once a week she'd be standing at the door, always looking . . . somehow all over the place. Her red hair was so wild, you know. And then those gray eyes, so provocative. I was really impressed by her. At first she always used to come with a mound of papers. Then she started coming more and more often, just for a visit, in between times. By then, of course, she was already head over heels in love with me."

All that was long ago. I know my mother never had a relationship with Tereza—Tereza's name isn't on the list. There's no woman on the list.

Glass looks at her watch, gulps down the rest of the tea, and stands up. "I've got to be off."

"Have fun tonight."

"Sure thing." She smoothes down her skirt, runs her hand through her hair, and sails out of the kitchen. "But not too much, for starters."

"Sounds serious."

"I'm going to be thirty-five, darling," she calls from the corridor. "Makes a woman start thinking."

I wait until I hear the front door close and the car start; then I tip the rest of the breakfast into the garbage and go upstairs to pack my bag.

As I pass by the bathroom, the door is open a crack, and I look in—discreetly. Although God knows Glass can hardly be accused of having brought us up to be in any way prudish, Dianne doesn't like being seen naked.

Motionless, her arms hanging down limply, my sister is standing under the shower with eyes closed, her straight black hair sticking to her neck. Glass was right—Dianne is painfully thin. I am shocked at her emaciated form, normally cleverly concealed under outsized shirts and sweaters. At the same time, I find her beautiful. Her protruding hip bones catch the falling water like a bowl and let it pour down between her legs. Her breasts are tiny and brilliant white, almost imperceptible apart from the minute nipples. Above her left collarbone, starting at the neck and ending at the shoulder, is a finger-length red scar.

"D'you still ever think of it?" Dianne has opened her eyes and caught sight of me through the water curtain. "About the battle and the Hulk?"

"Sometimes, yes." My voice sounds cracked. I feel caught out. I'm ashamed of standing here sneakily watching my sister.

"Beat it, Phil." She raises a hand and lays it protectively over the flaming red scar, as if that was the only nakedness she had to hide. "Go on, piss off!"

The Battle of the Big Eye took place on a glorious bright summer's day, not far from the spot by the river where three years earlier Glass had decided that something had to be done about my protruding ears.

Dianne and I had been out for three hours, exchanging the depressing atmosphere of Visible for the open country and the broad sky. Glass must have been home a long time, but she wouldn't miss us until it started to get dark. The corn in the fields stood tall and yellow; the sweet scent of freshly mown hay mingled with the slightly musty smell of drying algae rising from the nearby river.

"At Big Eye," said Dianne, "there are trout."

"So? Everyone knows that."

Big Eye lay about a mile downstream from Visible. The

name sounded imposing, but we applied it to nothing more than the outlet pipe of an underground stream, diverted long ago, that actually looked more like a gaping mouth than an eye. "We could catch one."

"What with? With that?" I pointed to the bow of polished wood and the arrow that went with it, the only one she had—a smooth branch sharpened to a point but without a barb.

"I can shoot with it," she said huffily. "I've practiced."

The bow was a present from a man by the name of Kyle, whom Glass had brought along in the early summer. His angular face, dominated by deep blue eyes, had made an unforgettable impression on me, because Kyle had paid us more attention than just ruffling our hair in an impersonal way, which was the usual kind of notice that most of our mother's lovers took of us. What's more, he was an Englishman; Glass had muttered something about his being a member of the British Allied forces who had deserted from the army. We thought this terribly romantic.

Kyle arrived with an olive-green rucksack and stayed at Visible for almost four weeks. Long enough for Dianne and me to get used to him; too long for Glass, who finally slammed on the emergency brake. She wasn't interested in a long-term relationship.

One evening Glass hadn't yet got back from work, and we were sitting on the veranda, Kyle in a sun-bleached wicker chair, with Dianne and me at his feet. The cool air was filled with the chirping of the first shy crickets. Kyle had broken off a branch of an ash tree from behind the house and was sliding the blade of an army knife along the bark. He had strikingly fine hands with long, powerful fingers.

"Ash," said Kyle, "is a wood that lasts. Something this house, and you and your mother, are in desperate need of." A heap of fine fresh green shavings began to pile up around his feet. "Stability? D'you know what that means? Something that lasts."

I scarcely paid attention to his words. I was watching the bark shavings fly downward and the slender fingers guiding the knife like a delicate surgical instrument.

"Something that lasts," repeated Dianne in a serious voice.

Kyle nodded and carried on working without a word. Finally he carefully rubbed the bare branch dry with a piece of cloth, then cut notches all the way round the top and bottom ends and attached a leathery cord that he dug out from the inexhaustible contents of his rucksack. "Who wants it? Phil?"

I shook my head.

"Dianne?"

She nodded and accepted the bow reverently. Her large eyes were shining in admiration both for the weapon and for the man who had made it. "Tomorrow," he promised, "I'll carve you an arrow to go with it."

To Dianne's huge disappointment he didn't get to fulfill his promise. That night we heard Glass and Kyle having a flaming row. Doors were flung open and slammed shut furiously. By the next morning the wood-carver with the beautiful hands and his green rucksack had disappeared. However, Kyle had left a farewell present—his army knife—and in the days that followed, Dianne was hardly to be seen. She had set out on the quest for an arrow worthy of her bow, and eventually struck lucky.

"Where have you been practicing?" I now asked her.

With a wide sweep of her arm she said, "In the woods."

We kept close to the riverbank, where the ground was soft and as densely overgrown as a jungle. The sultry air swarmed with all kinds of insects. Just one year ago, it suddenly went through my mind, Dianne had only to stretch out her hand for beetles and ladybirds to come and settle on it. She'd held an almost uncanny attraction for all manner of creatures, until Glass put a stop to it one night that I don't like to think back to. She wasn't able to curb her love of plants, however.

Dianne used her bow to push aside the tangled undergrowth and strike a path to let us through. "Meadowsweet, valerian, comfrey." She listed the names of all the pungent-smelling plants that Tereza had taught us on extended walks. "Touch-me-not, butterbur—*Petasites hybrides*—but only the leaves."

We battled our way through the brush for a quarter of an hour. Then, on the riverbank opposite, with its gaping black hole we saw the Big Eye staring at us fifteen feet away. Rising as tall as a man was the pipe at the center of a mound sparsely covered with vegetation. The mound was artificial, its sole purpose being to hold the pipe, from which melted snow and ice would shoot out in springtime like lava from a volcano. Now in the summer the stream had shrunk to no more than a rivulet that dribbled harmlessly into the river.

"We've got to get across."

We left our shoes and socks behind on the bank and waded through the clear water up to our calves toward the Big Eye. From time to time single minnows shot out from under flat stones on the riverbed. The nearer we got to the crater-shaped funnel formed by the water falling down from the pipe, the deeper the water got. Soon it reached up to over our knees and lapped at the hem of Dianne's thin white summer dress.

Her hand shot up. "Stop!"

Cautiously I stepped beside her to the edge of the funnel. "There's one. A whopper!"

As if weightless, the dark fish was floating halfway up the gravelly hollow. Idly it flipped its tail fin. From time to time it turned over on its side, its scales catching the sunlight in a silver-pink gleam.

"A rainbow trout!"

Dianne just nodded, not taking her eyes off the fish for a second. Intently she stretched out the bow, the arrow on the bowstring.

"Will you get it?"

"Bang in the middle. Don't move."

She had as little knowledge of physics as I did; she didn't know that water bends light. The arrow zoomed silently from the cord, missing its target by several inches. It left a trace of tiny bubbles under the surface of the water that bobbed about wildly as the fish shot away in a last flash of pearly pink.

"Shit," hissed Dianne.

"I thought you'd practiced."

Some way away from us, the arrow bobbed up again. It spun round on the surface of the water for a moment before the current seized it and slowly bore it away. "I've only got the one. I'll get it back."

Farther upriver, the water became shallower, and at that point there was a wide ford, with flat stones placed at intervals, where at one time horse-drawn wagons had clattered across. Immediately behind the ford the river bent sharply to the left, and alders and clumps of tall reeds hid it from view.

I followed Dianne as far as the ford, over which the arrow had by now happily sped on its way. Beyond the ford the water became deeper once more and the riverbed far more stony. I stayed standing where I was, laughing as she splashed through the river, her dress bunched up and the bow in one hand, making up the distance, when a shrill voice rang out across the water:

"There they are, that filthy cunt's brats."

I ducked and turned around, terrified. Standing on the ridge above the Big Eye was a group of children. There could have been six or seven of them; it was hard to make out, as they had the sun behind them and their outlines blurred into one another. But unmistakable was the one who was leading them on. It was the Hulk. He stood slightly to one side, his fat hands on his hips, and he was spraying aggression like sparks from a blazing firecracker.

Everyone knew the Hulk. At school he made himself unpleasantly conspicuous, not just because of his high voice, which was in sharp contrast to his bulk and strength, but because essentially he was a brutal thug, feared by all those to whom he denied the favor of being included among his friends. Neither Dianne nor I was a friend of his. Up to now we had imagined that we weren't his enemies either.

"Dianne?" I whispered. She must have seen the children, heard the Hulk. But she wasn't there anymore; she had disappeared beyond the bend in the river.

Done a runner, I thought. My legs seemed paralyzed, my feet frozen solid in the suddenly icy water. The phalanx of children fanned out, and now I could count them. Including the Hulk, there were seven of them. I knew some of them by sight.

"The girl's done a runner."

"We'll still get her."

They let the Hulk take the lead. He was leader of the pack, he had the right to attack the prey; the others would have to content themselves with pathetic pickings. Nimbly the Hulk slid down the sandy hillock. Then he slowed down and, crossing the ford at an almost leisurely pace, advanced toward me. He was a whole head taller than me, and when he finally stood in front of me, I had to look up at him.

"Your mother's a filthy cunt. You know that, don't you?"

When he spoke quietly, his voice sounded less shrill. I noticed a tiny corner missing from one of his incisors. His nose was spotted with freckles.

"Say it: 'My mother is a filthy cunt.' "

I shook my head. He was going to beat me up no matter what happened, and he wasn't likely to fight fair. I was about to get a thrashing worse than I had ever imagined in my worst nightmares. The Hulk was going to kill me, and I wasn't going to defend myself for fear that I might hurt him—an insane idea. But all these terrors couldn't dispel the thought that my sister had dropped me in it and run away.

"Go on, what are you waiting for?" He gave my shoulder an impatient shove. "Say it: 'My mother . . .' "

The other kids, two girls and four boys, had gathered on the bank. Little People, grinning judges, waiting for the sentence to be carried out. Suddenly I was seized by blind rage.

"OK." I took a deep breath and stared the Hulk straight in the face. "Your mother is a filthy cunt."

Whatever that might be.

A snarl of outrage rushed out from behind the chipped tooth. With unexpected speed an arm shot around my neck and clamped against it. A fist sank into my stomach, once, twice. The pain and ensuing nausea were not as bad as the panicky feeling of being unable to breathe. I gasped for air. The Hulk forced me to my knees and as he did he twisted my head round. The world turned upside down—right above me was the glittering water of the river, below me the flickering light in between the blurred dark green of the trees.

Between the trees stood Dianne.

She had appeared on the opposite bank of the river, fifteen feet away from where we were. A breeze stirred the leaves in the trees. Dianne stood perfectly motionless, her head slightly raised, facing the wind, as if studying the weather. She had found her arrow. She drew the bowstring taut, the tip of the arrow pointed at the Hulk.

"Let go of my brother—now!"

I couldn't see the Hulk's face, but I could feel his reply. The stranglehold was tightened even further. I wriggled feebly, a purple mist flickering across my eyes. I wished Dianne would hurry up. I wished she would kill the Hulk.

"And why should I let him go?" he screeched.

"Because if you don't, I'll shoot."

"And what if you hit your brother?"

Dianne probably took him, as well as me, by surprise. Maybe she didn't feel inclined to let herself in for a ping-pong of threatening questions and provocative answers, or maybe she believed that a single warning should be enough to make it plain she was in earnest.

Something whirred. I heard a frightened groan and felt the headlock loosen from my neck. Air shot whistling into my burning lungs; I staggered to one side, and as the mist cleared from my eyes, my gaze fell on the Hulk. Red drops were dripping from his fingers into the water. He was staring in disbelief at the arrow embedded in the arm now hanging limply, as if he was waiting for a puppeteer to attach a string and set it back in motion.

Suddenly Dianne was standing beside me, pressing a stone into my hand. It was wet. "Here," she said quietly.

Taking this as the signal to attack, the other kids came at us, screaming. The stone immediately put the first attacker out of action. I saw his astonished face as I struck him on the temple with it, and then the world turned into a whirlwind of screeching and scratching, hitting, boxing, and kicking. I was no longer afraid; on the contrary, I wanted to hurt the kids, and so I lashed out blindly, seized by a feeling of intoxicating, pounding dizziness. Whenever I met with resistance, I let out a triumphant shriek. Dianne did the same; she hissed like a wildcat and struck out left and right with her bow. It was only when my fists had been pounding the empty air several times that I realized our attackers had retreated. After taking a deep breath, I saw why.

One of the boys, a fellow with razor-cut red hair and green eyes and almost no eyelashes, was suddenly brandishing an open penknife in his hand. I couldn't believe he really meant to use it, as his entire body language—particularly his expression of alarm at himself, suggesting hesitation and retreat—seemed to deny it. But something inside him had already got him going. Like a machine set into gear and impossible to switch off, he took two swift, tripping steps in Dianne's direction.

"No!" I yelled.

The knife flashed. Right beside the strap of Dianne's dress the glittering blade, about two and a half inches long, dug into her shoulder up to the hilt. There was a short, ugly sound, like a fork digging into an undercooked potato.

"Shit!" I heard someone gasp. The boy with the razor cut stepped back. He raised both hands helplessly.

Dianne's eyes narrowed. An upright furrow appeared on her forehead, as if she was seeking the answer to a particularly difficult question. Her right hand was still holding the bow, the left feeling her shoulder in astonishment. Her fingers closed around the handle of the knife sunk into it.

"Dianne," I whispered, for I could see that she was grasping at the wrong angle, but my warning came too late. Her flesh burst open like a fallen pomegranate, spewing out its bright red seeds.

Dianne opened her hand and let the knife drop into the river. "It doesn't hurt, Phil," she said.

"She's . . ."

"Ohhh . . ."

"Beat it!"

The unexpected wounding of the Hulk had drawn the kids to him like a powerful magnet; Dianne's bleeding wound had the opposite effect of repelling them. Loud screams rang out, water splashed, and sand and dust flew through the air. Then the kids grabbed the reluctant Hulk, dragging him after them by his good arm back over the ridge. In a matter of seconds the uproar was over, the ghosts seen off.

Dianne looked up at the hill, at the top of which the dazzling sun had swallowed up our attackers. "I need a new arrow," she said. "He took mine away. It belongs to me."

"You're bleeding, Dianne! We've got to get home."

"D'you know what, Phil?"

"Dianne, we—"

"Next time I'll take my knife with me."

She spoke softly. She was extremely pale. Her dress looked as if strawberry juice had been poured all down the front. By the time we reached Visible, she could barely walk. I held her up and got myself covered with her blood as I did so. I kept whispering meaningless stuff, meant more for me than her. Dianne stumbled toward the veranda, and on the bottom step she sagged and remained sitting there.

As we got near, I had already started yelling for Glass. When she came storming out of the house, she took in the situation at a glance.

I flapped my arms helplessly. "We were—"

"Tell me later. Dianne, get up, into the car at once, quick, quick—Phil, Phil, come here." She pulled my T-shirt up over my head. "Press that against the wound and don't let go until we get to the doctor's."

Glass did her very best to stay calm, but I could sense her suppressed panic; it spread to me like a severe, infectious illness. The car shot through the woods and across the bridge into the town. Although the T-shirt remained dry under my hand, I didn't dare to lift it. *Just because she wanted to help me,* I thought, and hoped that it wouldn't occur to Dianne, who was looking straight ahead impassively, to think of closing her eyes, because then she might die . . . no, then for sure she would die! Tears were dropping on my naked chest and trickling down my stomach, collecting in my navel.

As it turned out, the loss of blood was far less than it seemed. The wound was only really deep at the point where the knife had got stuck; the blade had entered at an angle and merely severed muscular tissue.

"Could have been far worse, missy," said the doctor. "A vertical stab downward and the left lung would have been damaged."

Dianne's face had at last regained color, but now it was me who was pale—I could feel I was pale, watching together with Glass as the doctor's steady hand sewed the edges of the wound back together. I could feel every stab of the outsized shiny chrome needle as it entered Dianne's anesthetized skin, just as if it was going into me.

Dianne had her shoulder strapped up, Glass exchanged a few words with the doctor, and then we drove back to Visible. She sat us down in the room with the chimney, in front of the cold, empty fireplace. Dianne curled herself up in Glass's lap and closed her eyes; I snuggled up to her side. Glass stroked our hair.

"What happened?" she asked.

I told her. She listened quietly, without interrupting me with any reproaches, as I'd actually been expecting. Now and again she just made little sounds of acknowledgment. They sounded like the soft suppressed moans that sometimes came from her bedroom when she had a man with her.

"OK," she said when I had come to the end. "You were absolutely right to defend yourselves. We're not obliged to excuse ourselves to anyone. Anyone at all. Understood?"

I hadn't understood at all, but I nodded seriously. There was no reply from Dianne; she may have fallen asleep, or she may have simply been too exhausted. I studied her face, her black hair, damp with sweat, plastered to her forehead. Then I remembered a question that had been going through my mind for hours. "Glass," I said, "what's a filthy cunt?"

The events of that day were the starting point, paradoxically, for the lasting love-hate between Glass and the Ones Over There. Late that evening, when Dianne and I had just put on our pajamas, there was a loud knocking at the front door. Glass opened it, and we hid behind her. Outside stood a short wiry woman with untidy hair that hung in wisps over her forehead. Her face was gaunt. She wore a cheap summer dress. "Your daughter wounded my son," she shouted at Glass angrily. The shrill voice, inherited by the Hulk, trembled. "I'll report you for this. Someone should have done so long ago, you . . ."

"Filthy cunt?" asked Glass quietly. "Was it you who taught your son that word? My son was asking me just now what it meant. Would you like to tell him?"

Without waiting for an answer she motioned Dianne in

front of her and pulled her pajama top over her head. Her fingers deftly removed the bandage from her shoulder. The stitched wound looked ghastly, the pale yellow hall light turning it into a black-encrusted hollow.

"My daughter was wounded too. She could have lost her left lung. Or bled to death, the jugular vein, d'you understand?"

Carefully she replaced the bandage and pushed Dianne aside. She wasn't speaking anymore; she was singing, her words bobbing like little boats tossed about on troubled waters, carrying us all along with them.

"D'you know what I think? I believe the problem isn't either your son or my daughter or some unpleasant swear word. And it isn't that you and other people consider your children better than mine either. No, I believe the real problem is that you are deeply unhappy. So unhappy that you feel the need to run other people down and slander them, and you use disgusting words to do so, which your equally unhappy little son then hears, as a result of which my children suffer, and on no account will I put up with that!"

The Hulk's mother looked down at the floor in silence. I couldn't understand why she had come only now, hours after the incident at the Big Eye. Perhaps she was a coward. Perhaps it had taken her time to muster the courage to come and confront Glass. And now she'd had the wind taken out of her sails.

"I have a suggestion." In an instant Glass had become calm

personified. I had never seen her like this before; it was uncanny. Behind her back I felt for Dianne's hand. "I'm going to make us a pot of tea, and we'll sit down in the kitchen and talk."

"That's not what I came for," said the woman, who, drawn by the siren's song, had already stepped into the entrance hall.

"And you"—Glass turned to Dianne and me—"go and brush your teeth and into bed. Lights out! I'll come and look in on your later."

The last I saw of the Hulk's mother was her narrow back. Just two months later the Hulk stopped coming to school; the woman and her entire family, including her husband, upped and left town. The fact that not long after, the little knife stabber with no eyelashes also disappeared seemed like magic to me; for a long time I believed that Glass had only to strike up her singsong voice to turn the world upside down or change its course around the sun.

"What d'you think they're talking about now?" asked Dianne, closing the door to our room behind her. "About us?"

"I don't know."

She placed a hand on the light switch and pointed to her bed, where her crumpled pajamas lay. "D'you want to wear my pajamas?"

"No."

"D'you want to sleep in my bed?"

I shook my head.

"Why not?"

I shrugged. I didn't know.

"As you like. I'll turn the light out, then."

I ran across to my bed in the dark and crawled under the blanket. Although I was dog-tired, I couldn't sleep—I was too excited. It had been a glorious day for Dianne and me. We had fought and bathed in blood. We had battled like heroes and triumphed over enemies who outnumbered us. Across the river, over the sleepy rooftops of the town, I knew the first silver threads were already falling into children's dreams that would then weave themselves into the legend of the Battle at the Big Eye. From now on we would be left in peace. We were unassailable. An enormous weight lifted from my chest as the realization spread through me that I would never need to be afraid again.

"You were fantastic," I whispered to Dianne across the room. "You really got the Hulk. That was great!"

"I missed. Just like I did that stupid trout."

Something in her voice made the darkness swirl around me. Suddenly I found myself wishing that Dianne wouldn't say any more, when black bubbles came whizzing through the air and popped.

"You know, Phil—I was aiming at his heart."

I'm packing my bag when I hear the front door shut. Dianne goes to school without me. As a rule, she walks, whereas I go by bike. But today I get the feeling that she quite deliberately wants to keep away from me—and that the door shuts with an unusually loud slam, and that even her footsteps sound unusually loud on the gravel as they recede down the drive. Normally Dianne drifts through the world like a wisp of fog, invisible and as good as weightless, as if reluctant to leave any imprint wherever she happens to tread. Perhaps she's still mad at me for watching her under the shower.

At school the most we're likely to see each other is during recess. There's only one class that we take together. Back in elementary school we started off in the same class, but the witch's offspring in a double dose was just too much for our little classmates, and inattention and panic attacks were the outcome. Finally a few of the teachers approached Glass with the request that Dianne and I be put in separate classes, pointing out politely but fairly unambiguously that this would be best for her own children as well. That's the way it's stayed up to the present, and meanwhile it suits the two of us.

I move to the window just in time to see Dianne's brown-clad figure disappear between a couple of trees. These are the same trees where, years ago, the day after Kyle left us and Dianne returned from her hunt for an arrow, I found deep angry gashes on some of the branches, with the bark hacked away. At the time I had collected soft moss from the garden and stuffed it haphazardly into the biggest of the gaping holes, as if to bandage them like wounds.

chapter 5

red shoe lost in a hole

The fine scar lines behind my ears act like meteorological sensors. A slight prickling reliably predicts any imminent change in the weather. As I padlock my bicycle in the shelter beside the main school building, I look up at the sky. It is deceptively blue and cloudless. Just a hint of sultriness assures me that my scars are right and that there will be rain or even a mighty thunderstorm this afternoon or maybe not till evening.

The school is an architectural leftover from the turn of the century, a massive, four-story building, its solidity unimposing yet reassuring. As a child, I imagined its grayish brown walls were rooted hundreds of feet deep in the earth. A few years ago a modern extension was carelessly slapped onto the rear of the building, a flat, elongated construction consisting of a mass of concrete and steel and even more glass. Thanks to this unadorned appendage, erected under the direction of Kat's father, there are in effect three schoolyards—one in front of the old main building, popular on account of its many shady chestnut trees and the undisputed territory of the older pupils, as well as two more yards to the left and right of the extension, shared by the lower school.

Kat is waiting for me outside the main entrance. She's not hard to pick out from all the other pupils crowding the yard and flocking into the building, not because she is particularly tall or because her hair is pinned up the way that Glass wears it—for Kat idolizes Glass and imitates her whenever she can—but because the stream of pupils parts in front of her, just as the Red Sea must have parted for Moses. Nothing to do with being considerate, but on account of Kat's status. Like me, she is not particularly popular or unpopular. She might perhaps be more popular if she didn't have the headmaster for a father. That's what puts most people off a bit, even though I've never really understood why. Perhaps they think Kat has something like a hotline to God. What I find less surprising is that her directness and her habit of telling people straight out what she thinks of them hardly earn her brownie points.

"Is it me you're waiting for, or are you putting on a show for Thomas?"

She pulls a face, as if she's just bitten into a lemon. "He's already gone in. Walked past me looking destroyed. And I've already seen Dianne."

"She left before me."

"She had some girlfriend in tow."

"Dianne?" I put my schoolbag down. "She hasn't got any friends."

"Are you sure?"

"No."

Kat grins. "Maybe she's starting an anorexics club. The woman goes about in the same kind of hideous gear as your sister. And she's just as scrawny."

"What's her name?"

"No idea. She's not in our year." She's tapping her feet nervously and looks over my shoulder as if she's afraid of missing someone.

I turn round but can't see anyone. "Now are you going to tell me who you're waiting for?"

"Man, have you forgotten? The guy from the boarding school."

"Is that why you're so edgy?"

"I can feel it, Phil." She takes my hand and plants it on her left breast and holds it in place. "Just there. This guy is going to make my life change course!"

"What have you got in there? A compass?"

"My heart's in there, you idiot! My tiny heart that's longing for love."

"Oh, yeah?" Two girls pass us and start giggling stupidly. I pull my hand away.

"The other day you were singing quite a different tune. The other day the most you wanted was a guy who—"

"The other day, the other day . . . That's a million years ago, Phil! He who thinks changes his mind."

"Says who?"

"Says Nietzsche."

"Who's Nietzsche? Is he good-looking?"

A shock of blond hair appears beside us, pushes past me, and the next moment has disappeared in the crowd.

Kat cranes her neck and looks for him. "Hey, wasn't that Wolf?"

"Yes, it was Wolf. What is it? Can we go in now?" I bend down to pick up my bag.

"That guy gives me the creeps. He looks like a serial killer."

"Leave him alone, Kat, OK?"

"Oh, excuse me!" She gives me a mocking smile. "I'd forgotten that you once had a thing with him."

"I did not! We were just friends, and that's long ago. He probably doesn't even remember who I am."

"You yourself said he was a nutcase."

"Yes, he's a sad sack, and now for heaven's sake focus on your little heart, and leave me alone!"

"My, my! We are touchy today." She nudges a little boy from a lower grade who's just caught up with her. "He is touchy today, don't you think?"

The boy shrinks back in terror, like a snail withdrawing its horns, and rushes off.

"Come on, now." I've had enough of Kat's squabbling. "You can look for the new guy during recess."

"Don't even need to." She ambles along beside me, and even the sound of the school bell doesn't make her speed up. "We're taking the same class. I've been having a bit of a rummage through Daddy's files."

"Which class?"

"Handel. Didn't you get a timetable?"

"Didn't look at it."

Handel is the math teacher. The fact that he bears the same name as one of the greatest Baroque composers prompts him every now and again to spout about the relationship between music and mathematics and then go on about how a deeper understanding of these two abstract disciplines is linked to their both being processed in the left side of the brain.

"The faculty of abstraction, ladies and gentlemen, is the basis of all reason, consequently of enlightenment. Reason, logic—anyone who does not cultivate this quality is as much at the mercy of his emotions as Neanderthal man was to the forces of nature. Deep down he will be unable to shake off the superstition that thunder and lightning are signs of divine wrath. He will, ladies and gentlemen, forever cower!"

I am lousy at math, and unlike Kat I'm not particularly musical, and the explanations that Handel loves getting tied up in are frequently so abstract that after the fourth or fifth sentence I can hardly keep up, as a result of which I am bound to conclude that the left side of my brain must be atrophied—even if I do find myself distinctly at odds with the idea of cowering. Maybe Glass could give him remedial instruction and explain that the left side of American brains functions differently.

"I've been thinking," announces Kat as we cross the main building and reach the modern annex. Ahead of us pupils are fanning out toward different classrooms. "What would happen—just suppose—if one of these days you really did fall in love with a guy?"

"What d'you mean?"

"Well, would you keep it a secret, or what? After all, no one here knows that you're gay."

"Why don't you try shouting a bit louder, so everyone will know?"

"Oh, come on, tell me."

"I wouldn't keep anything secret. Just saying it sounds totally stupid."

"You know perfectly well what I mean."

Don't I just—and how! It's one of the blank areas on the map of my soul. Furious, I feel cornered and stop dead.

"Kat, I don't live on another planet, OK? I know perfectly well that this one-horse dump would be up in arms if I turned up with a boyfriend—which I would, if I had one. I also know that some sort of guardians of public morality would slip white hoods over their heads and come riding up on cattle to

Visible at night and nail a dead cat to our door. And you should know that I wouldn't give a shit!"

I walk on, faster than before. Kat trots along beside me. "No need to get so wound up! It was just a question."

A question she quite deliberately aimed right below the belt—the answer has to be theoretical. Turning up with a boyfriend is an experiment that's still waiting to happen. It'll be no picnic, that's for sure—Tereza once assured me of that, and she should know—but it's not something I'm scared of. The wary aura that's enveloped and protected Dianne and me for years, ever since the Battle of the Big Eye, has never quite faded away. And I'm not helpless, I can defend myself. But aside from that, would I be able to live with being labeled? Well, I've had that all my life.

"You know, in this case being open takes two, Phil." Kat won't let go. "What would you do if you had a boyfriend who wasn't keen on being got at and who . . . I mean, well, would prefer to keep a relationship quiet?"

"Relationship? That sounds like getting married."

"And you sound like your mother."

"Glass would never let a word like *marry* past her lips. She considers it obscene."

"Matter of opinion, don't you think?" says Kat. "These people here consider it obscene that there are other things she puts in her mouth instead."

"The people here"—and I point to pupils arriving late and rushing past on either side of us—"are old enough to have their own opinions. What do they need to go dragging around their parents' prejudices for?"

"Because it's easier than thinking for themselves."

"Does that also come from Nietzsche?"

"No, from me."

We've reached the classroom. Kat with her great flair for dramatic entrances lets me go first so that she can then let the door slam violently behind her, with the result that twenty pairs of eyes send us startled looks, and the same number of mouths, which up to that moment had been prattling away cheerfully, now drop wide open.

"Oh, yeah, Madam Headmistress!" a mocking voice calls from somewhere.

"And the top of the morning to you too, toe rag," Kat calls out across the classroom, switching the laughter in her favor. As conversations start up again we look for a table with two empty chairs. We've just sat down when the door swings open and Handel enters the room.

There's no denying that Handel also bears one of the distinctive hallmarks of the Baroque—namely, a certain amplitude and rotundity. He carries his protruding belly—witness to his love of the choice pleasures of the table—before him, obliging him to walk with small, almost mincing steps. The resulting impression of physical lethargy is hugely misleading—it is in direct contrast to his brilliant mental agility.

Handel is not alone. He is followed by the newcomer, walking far enough behind him to demonstrate that he has not attached himself to the teacher's shirttails from any lack of confidence. He stops when he gets to the blackboard, and I can see him only in profile. Handel purses his lips and gestures to the class to quiet down. If the degree of his popularity can be judged by the uproar greeting his arrival in the classroom, he is hugely popular. When the noise has died down, he nods to the new arrival, who now turns to the class.

"Nicholas," he briefly introduces himself, without adding his surname. Barely half those present take any notice. I take a look at his face, and as my stomach shoots down to my knees at the speed of an elevator out of control, I think: *At last—now I know who you are.*

When we were thirteen I gave Dianne a silver pendant for Christmas that I had come across while poking around in the cellar at Visible among rotten wooden boxes and moldering cardboard cartons. In return I received a snow globe that Dianne maintained she had also found, without mentioning where. Maybe both of us scored such a hit with our presents because neither of us had given much thought to whether or not they would please the other.

As far as the pendant—a sickle-shaped half-moon—was concerned, Dianne acted as if it had always belonged to her and had just gone missing for a while. The silver was a bit tarnished, so she took it to a jeweler, who cleaned it till it shone and talked my sister into buying a matching chain. A few small spots that the jeweler had been unable to remove stayed on the moon, but this didn't diminish Dianne's surprisingly overt delight with the present.

For my part, I had scarcely unwrapped the snow globe when something strangely magical happened that cast a spell over me for days. Wherever I found myself standing or sitting I never tired of looking at the silvery white cloud that rose when I shook the globe. As soon as the shimmering snowstorm settled, a small dark house became visible, with orange-red flames shooting out from its tiny doors and windows. And what happened was that a few of the falling snowflakes would always settle on the darting tongues of flame. This was the contrast that fascinated me. How could something keep burning when snow was falling on it? What sort of flames were these that weren't put out by cold or ice? When I asked Paleiko about it, he replied in such a soft whisper that I couldn't understand him.

A few days after the Christmas festivities Glass took me into town. Small clouds emerged each time we breathed out as we trudged across the freshly fallen snow through the silent wood. It was already getting dark when we reached the middle of the bridge leading across the stream.

"Iced over," said Glass. She placed her hands on the railing. From the corner of my eyes I could see she was sizing me up.

I looked down at the rippled blue-gray ice reflecting the light from the streetlamps.

Broken reeds and bundles of lifeless grass coated with hoarfrost lined the banks.

"What are you thinking about?" asked Glass.

"Nothing."

"You can't think about nothing."

"Yes, you can."

I was thinking that the frozen stream was like a runway. Two or three years before I might perhaps still have thought that an airplane might cut through the dark clouds of the winter sky and come in to land, propellers whirring. Out would step my father, who would whisk me off to America. Other children spent Christmas with their fathers.

Glass sniffed noisily. Her hands tightened round the railing. "I'm pregnant, Phil, three months," she said. "I want to have the baby. That's not going to please your sister."

My skin tingled in the cold air. I knew that I was supposed to be glad. Instead what I felt was the sort of sympathy you have for a fledgling that has fallen out of the nest. All I could think was that just like Dianne and me, the baby would have no father.

I remembered Martin's green eyes, the smell of dark garden soil that had clung to him. I wished he was the father, or Kyle, whose beautiful hands had carved Dianne's bow. But both men had disappeared years before.

"Dianne is bound to notice," I said to Glass. "As soon as you get a big belly."

"I've no intention of keeping it secret from her." She sounded almost furious. "But she doesn't have to know right away, OK?"

I nodded, knowing full well that by agreeing I was making myself her accomplice, and returned to staring down at the ice. If you looked hard enough, you could make out flattened air bubbles slowly drifting below. Then I looked up expectantly at the sky, but the dense cloud cover did not part.

By the time we reached the marketplace it had started to snow again. The snow was falling so thickly that it muffled every sound, even softening the noise of cars gliding along through the streets as if in a time warp. Car headlights cast an eerie yellow light. From their position on the tall pedestal of the war memorial, two soldiers looked down on Glass and me with cold lifeless eyes. Most of the shop windows still had their Christmas displays, looking out of place. The holiday crush was over; by now people's thoughts had turned to New Year's.

I stuck close to Glass. She wandered aimlessly from shop to shop, her cheeks flushed bright red and eyes glittering, apparently oblivious to the sidelong disapproving glances thrown at her by some of the passersby. I was embarrassed that everybody knew her and that the Little People disliked her, and irritated that she clearly couldn't care less. We were approaching the church at the northern end of the marketplace leading up to the castle hill when one of Glass's clients crossed the road and recognized my mother. Instantly the woman drew her head down so that it disappeared inside her large coat collar, like a tortoise withdrawing into its shell. Nervously I slid my left hand into my coat pocket and felt for the smooth cool glass of the snow globe, which I'd been dragging around with me for days, and looked in another direction.

That's how I caught sight of the boy.

Just a few feet away from Glass and me, he was standing at the top of the three steps leading up to the church door. As soon as he realized I was looking at him, a hint of a smile crossed his face. He was taller than me, and possibly a little older. Black hair tumbling across a white forehead. Eyes as dark as Dianne's, and incredibly red lips.

Glass had followed my gaze. With a sudden movement she raised her arm, beckoning the boy. There was no way he could not have noticed her, for she was standing right next to me. But he didn't respond to her wave. He remained in front of the church door, still and motionless as a waxwork. He had stopped smiling, but his eyes shone brightly, burning holes in my coat.

"Glass, stop that!"

My voice sounded strange to me. Glass laughed and waved once more. I reached for her outstretched arm, missed it, slipped on the icy pavement, and fell full length on the street. I could taste blood—I had bitten my lower lip—and, cursing, wished Glass to hell. By the time I managed to get to my feet again, my face bright red with shame, the boy had disappeared.

"What was that for?" I barked at Glass. I was furious and confused. The incident was so embarrassing that I could have killed her. "Why did you wave at him?"

Instead of answering, Glass pointed at a man and a woman plowing through the driving snow like leaves drifting in the wind. The man had a misshapen body and dragged his left leg as he walked. The woman's face, half concealed by a fur cap, seemed to consist of parts that didn't fit together, as if assembled by a drunken puppet master. Her mouth was barely visible, a hole no bigger than a dime, her breathing a faint whisper.

"Just look at those poor wretches," said Glass softly. And in a louder voice, "This town is a bloody sewer."

I had no idea what she meant by this, but her condescending tone of voice scared me. She placed her hands on my shoulders, bent down to me, and nodded in the direction of the man and woman disappearing behind a wall of snow, just like the burning house in the glass globe when I would shake it.

"These people," said Glass with a movement encompassing the entire marketplace, "have been sticking together for hundreds of years, and regard this as perfectly normal. But these same people will hate you when sooner or later you fall in love with a boy."

I was still furious with her. But I knew she was telling the truth. Visible was a magical place and Glass was an unusual mother, and the two together created laws that did not apply out here among the Little People. Up to then I had thought that Glass had taken me with her in order to tell me on the quiet that she was pregnant.

But there would have been plenty of other opportunities to do so. Now I was wondering whether the point and purpose of our walk was to demonstrate her contempt for Those Out There. As I recalled the expression on her face when she had spoken about the Little People, I shuddered.

On the way home neither of us said a word. Not until we got home did I muster up all my courage and speak to Glass.

"Why did you wave to that boy?"

She slipped off her boots, shook her long hair, and pulled it back at the neck as she reflected. "Because I could see that you fancied him," she answered at last. "There is such a thing as love at first sight, you know. That can make you forget the cold and the winter."

"Have you ever fallen in love at first sight?"

She straightened her shoulders. "A long time ago. Come on, I'll make us a hot chocolate, darling."

Carelessly throwing her boots into a corner of the closet, Glass disappeared down the unlit hallway. She could find her way in the dark like a cat. As I took off my coat, I wondered whether she had been referring to my father.

Then all other thoughts disappeared. My hands were scrabbling about deep in my coat pockets in the hunt for the snow globe, but all they came up with were a couple of snotty paper tissues. A second attempt proved equally unsuccessful. The snow globe had disappeared. I panicked. It must have rolled out of my pocket when I fell. The TV was blaring from Dianne's room. She wouldn't care if I'd lost her Christmas present, but I did. I shut my eyes to recall the image of the snow globe and waited for the piercing feeling of loss. Instead what drifted before my eyes, clear as a photo, was the face of the boy with the gleaming eyes, and my heart skipped a beat.

I kept my shoes and coat on and ran back to the marketplace. All worries about the Little People were forgotten. I searched everywhere, but the snow globe was nowhere to be seen or found.

I've never forgotten that—you love in order to forget the cold and chase the winter away.

It's midnight before the storm breaks. It started building up in the morning and after that hung uncertain and leaden over the town. I put out the light in my room and stand at the window, listening to the rain come drumming down, washing away the dust from the trees and the sultriness from the air. Visible itself seems to be taking deep breaths of the cool air; it's as if a sigh of relief is passing through the house. I start as the floorboards creak just in front of the door to my room. Outside ghostly flashes light up the sky; an unreal light illuminates each tree and gives each roof ridge on the other side of the stream new, sharp contours.

Out there somewhere is where Nicholas lives. This morning, before he took a seat in the back row of the class to sit with outstretched legs and gaze out the window with evident disinterest until the math class was over, he had given me a passing glance. Which was enough to set my heart racing. I'm certain Nicholas didn't recognize me. Both of us have changed since that winter four years ago. His shoulders are broader, his facial features are sharper, and his black hair is longer than it was then. Only his eyes are exactly as I remember them—bright, unfathomable, and disturbingly dark.

I toyed briefly with the idea of telling Kat that I knew the new boy, that I'd seen him once years ago, and about the deep impression this encounter had made on me. So deep that over the years I kept thinking back to it at every opportunity, appropriate or not. The crushing verdict handed down by Kat during one of the recesses made me decide to play safe and keep quiet for the time being.

"He's a phony."

"A what?"

"A phony. Plays the Lone Ranger—hard on the outside, sensitive on the inside. He's actually weak on the outside and boring inside. Believe me, I know these types—Thomas is just the same. You can cross him off."

"It couldn't be that you're annoyed at being wrong? Because your little compass needle was pointing in the wrong direction?"

"That's life."

She sounded almost furious. I said nothing and felt like a traitor because I didn't share Kat's dislike for the newcomer and didn't want to. I didn't tell her that I found Nicholas attractive, that I found his silent manner appealing rather than repulsive. Kat may cross him off, but I'm keeping my options open. I want to get to know him. I have to. The longer I stare out into the receding thunderstorm, the more determined I become. It stems from the feeling that the newcomer owes me something. It's as if back then in the winter cold he—no, we made a pact with each other that I sealed with my bitten lip and my blood, a pact that has still to be fulfilled.

The crunch of gravel breaks into my thoughts, making me look down just in time to see Dianne's slender figure lit up by sheet lightning as she disappears into the woods. I resist the temptation to call out her name. She obviously thinks she hasn't been spotted, and just as obviously wants to be alone. The creaking of the floorboards earlier outside my door may have been Dianne peering through my keyhole to make sure that I'd gone to bed. I'm surprised, but greater than my surprise is my relief. The insect is leaving its amber trap. Dianne is going to meet someone; I can't believe that she's leaving Visible at this time of night and in this weather just to be alone.

Although it's years since Dianne and I have drifted apart, suddenly I'm overcome by something like jealousy. At one time we used to be inseparable; hand in hand we discovered the world together. We innocently played at doctor, after which we would call each other nothing but "Pipi" and "Pillerman" for weeks on end and laugh ourselves silly, and later on we fought a battle together. Then somewhere along the line, for no apparent reason, my sister stopped talking. She disappeared from sight like an illusion. Whoever she's going to meet now knows more about her than I do.

I don't move away from the window until the thunderstorm has passed. The heavens open, tearing the clouds apart and revealing the moon hidden until now. Full and shining brightly, it hangs above the stream and the town. Paleiko sits quietly on his shelf. I get undressed under his bright gaze and lie down on my bed. I listen to the regular patter of the rain and the distant rumble of thunder. Visible envelops me like a shell. And suddenly I feel like the little boy I once was, a microscopic dot in a gigantic pod. I'm alone. Glass isn't back yet from meeting her fraud case. Dianne has gone off; she doesn't need me. I place my hands across my chest and focus on the rising and falling of my diaphragm, the rhythm of my breathing. In, out, in, out . . .

And then the pod dissolves, leaving nothing but a vacuum, a boundless nothing. I'm overwhelmed by a loneliness that the presence of Glass or Dianne or Kat would not be able to disperse. Even America doesn't comfort me—it hasn't for years, and couldn't. It's as if my mouth is sealed and refuses to utter the magic word.

My hands glide down my belly as if of their own accord, stay there briefly, warm skin on hot skin, and then slowly feel their way farther down, where they find their own practiced rhythm, faster than my breathing, faster than my pulse. I'm counting on this to banish my loneliness, but it just increases it all the more.

"D'you know how to do it, little feller?" Annie Glosser asked me.

"Do what?"

"Get a good feeling. How you can get yourself a good feeling."

A good feeling was being an eight-year-old little feller sitting beside this fat woman on the rim of the fountain in the marketplace under a cloudless summer sky, licking the ice cream she had just generously treated me to. And as I did so, a good feeling was watching the pigeons at our feet, fighting over the fallen wafer crumbs as they dropped. To my intense satisfaction I had Annie Glosser all to myself. The very first time she had shown up at Visible, Dianne had refused to so much as look at this fat woman. Right from the start she kept Annie at the same safe distance she had previously reserved for Gable. I couldn't think of any reason why she rejected her, for Annie was the most harmless creature in all the world. Maybe Dianne simply had the feeling that she shouldn't get in the way of fat people and had to make room for them, even when they were already sitting down.

Annie Glosser lived in a small house painted pale green that, like Visible, stood near the stream and some way outside the town, even though it was on the same side as the Little

People. That was enough to make me think of Annie as far more like Glass, Dianne, and me than like the town dwellers, for Annie, as she had said to me on more than one occasion, and not just being critical of herself because it was me, was a bit crazy. She had come to Visible because some compassionate soul, probably mistakenly thinking she had some problem with men, had assured her that Glass could solve all such issues. But Annie did not have a problem with men. She simply couldn't add. She couldn't make out advertisements in the daily paper for special offers from supermarkets and liquor stores far and wide, particularly special offers on cherry brandy, and as a result she was always afraid of being taken for a ride when doing a big shop. The simplest addition presented Annie with as much of a headache as anyone else would have with the details of the theory of relativity. Glass explained to her that given the extent of her disability allowance, it didn't make a scrap of difference which kind she chose; she could even have covered each bottle with gold leaf if she felt like it. Glass sent Annie back home. "You should stick to this Annie," she advised me. "Go and visit her. You can learn a lot from crazy people."

Glass couldn't have dreamed how right she turned out to be.

Exactly what Annie's disability consisted of I never found out. Perhaps she was nothing more than one of those somewhat rare but highly typical products of this sewer, as Glass came to call it in later years. She was harmless, sniggered at, and, as I imagined with sympathy, must have been a favorite target for cruel ridicule as a child.

"Annie's terribly lonely sometimes," she confessed to me on one of my visits. " 'S'why she's bought herself these little red shoes."

Annie's mentally challenged agility was only seemingly matched by the apparent sluggishness of her physical bulk. In actual fact Annie was surprisingly nimble. In her red shoes she sashayed through the town in an erotically aggressive kind of way, with an occasional saucy lift of her skirt revealing her hefty thighs and chunky ankles for all to see. What made Annie so fat I never did find out. As I never saw her eating ice cream or anything else myself, at some stage I did get the idea that all she consumed was in liquid form, possibly her beloved cherry brandy.

"What sort of good feeling?" I now asked Annie, and scattered the last of my wafer crumbs to the pecking beaks.

"Just come and see Annie, then ya'll see," she offered. She was swinging her legs, frowning with her lower lip stuck out, and looking at her red patent leather shoes gleaming in the sunlight. Maybe she was asking herself why it was that in spite of this lure no man was coming to speak to her. "You come by, 'n she'll have something to show yer, will Annie. And yer'll get another ice cream as a reward."

The very next day I was standing at her door, the first of many visits. The house was surrounded by a small garden luxuriant with greenery and flowers. Annie was the only woman

I knew who talked to her plants. I would sometimes see her from afar, a watering can in her hand, standing on the rose-enveloped path that led through part of the garden. She swung the can to and fro and chattered away to the greenery as if she'd invited guests to a tea party.

By way of greeting, Annie placed her fat arm around my shoulders. Since everything about her was fat and fleshy, I didn't even notice the flabby mass on my back. Far more striking was the protruding lower lip, which always looked as if it was ready to take the next sip of cherry liqueur, or alternatively as if its owner was offended. The other striking thing about Annie was her huge, sleepy eyes. The previous spring, just before the only cinema in the town had closed down, Glass had taken Dianne and me to see *Bambi,* in which to my relief there was no one with ears that were either too big or too small. But there was a skunk called Flower who was always tired, and it was Flower's face that I rediscovered in Annie's good-natured fat face.

I was surprised how tidy her home was. At Visible I was used to dusty rooms with pieces of old furniture and boxes and cases standing about higgledy-piggledy. Here everything was spotlessly clean and in its own place. Annie too. She dragged me into the living room toward a comfortable sofa with a deep hollow in it. With a great snort she flopped down into it. After downing three glasses of cherry liqueur in rapid succession she slurped with her tongue and tapped her forehead with her finger.

"There's a roaring sound in there. It's white. Can yer hear it, little feller?"

I knelt down on the sofa, pressed my right ear against her left ear, and listened for a while. I really did hear a distant noise, but I would have been lying if I'd called it white, and whether it was in fact the roaring, I didn't know either. All the same I nodded. There was an ice cream at stake.

"Sometimes 's'there and sometimes 'tisn't," Annie observed. "When 'tis, then Annie gets spots in front of her eyes. Rushes and rushes, like peeing—eh?"

"Yes."

She nodded, stared into space for a moment with her sleepy eyes, and then heaved herself off the sofa. "Now I'm gonna show yer something, little feller."

She went to a tall chest and, smiling secretively as she drew a little key out of her overall pocket, opened one of the doors. Seconds later she had whisked a television onto the table—not a real television set, but a miniature one made of a garish orange fabric, about the size of a cigarette box, with a tiny peephole and a switch on the side. At Annie's instruction I looked through the peephole and pressed the switch. The little machine showed twelve pictures one after the other, teeny transparencies. Essentially they were all the same—naked women with impressive upper halves and legs spread so wide as to give an unimpeded view into the furthest anatomical depths. I didn't know what to make of this.

"'S'porno, tha' is," whispered Annie, close to me, and

cherry blossoms seemed to waft through the room on a cloud of bitter-smelling alcohol. "Filthy stuff."

"Sporno," I repeated reverently.

"Now pull your pants down."

I placed the television on the table and obediently dropped my pants.

"Now you got to play with yourself, little feller," said Annie in a matter-of-fact tone. "Till the cock crows."

For the sake of the promised ice cream, I followed her command, but without achieving any remarkable results. There is probably nothing in the world more boring for an eight-year-old than an erection that fails to materialize in front of an orange-colored television showing pornographic images. But that didn't stop Annie from showing me with her surprisingly soft and evidently practiced fingers how I should move my hand for the cock to crow.

"Well, don't it feel good."

"Sure, sure." I was getting impatient. The whole business was about as interesting to me as a hole in the air or a photo of a blank piece of paper. "Do I get my ice cream now?"

Annie nodded and belched several liquor clouds into the air in rapid succession. I pulled up my trousers, and the television disappeared back into its hiding place in the tall chest. Annie squeezed her fat feet into the red shoes, and then hand in hand we walked into town.

"Ever pinched chocolate, little feller?" asked Annie on the way.

"No."

"Spat in a church font?"

I shook my head.

"Annie has," she said. Her booming breathless laughter must have been heard all the way to Visible.

Annie seemed satisfied to have taught me something for life, for I was never again offered the television to see the filthy stuff. That was all right by me, for it left more time for extensive visits to the ice cream parlor, which I would regularly recount to Dianne to make her jealous, but without success.

The reason I would vividly remember that day forever and ever and the nonerotic experience on the sofa was because the moment I had sat next to Annie, I instinctively knew that we were both doing something forbidden. Making the cock crow, stealing a bar of chocolate, and desecrating a church by spitting into the font were all one and the same. They were forbidden, and breaking that ban, yes, that was a good feeling, though not in the way Annie meant.

Toward the end of the summer Annie Glosser had an accident as she waddled through the town laden with two shopping bags. The usual white rushing sound must have been going strong in her head; I can think of no other reason why her eyes were blind to the gaping hole in the road, made by workmen, next to a crossing just a few yards ahead of her. Eyewitnesses reported that Annie had been teetering along purposefully toward the site of the disaster, her massive body had split the red and white striped security strip enclosing the construction area, and for a fraction of a second she had hung in midair, as if held by some invisible hand. Then heavy Annie and her equally heavy shopping bags flew downward. When Annie was rescued—a time-consuming exercise, as it was a mystery how Annie had managed to fit into the hole she fell into—her summer dress was soaked red through and through. There was general panic until her two shopping bags were extracted and exposed to the light of day. These were found to contain sharp fragments of at least six shattered bottles of cherry liqueur, whose contents had spilled out all over Annie, but apart from this the bags contained no other form of food, which didn't surprise me in the slightest. When Annie was admitted to the hospital, she was found to have lost one shoe. It must have been left behind in the hole, and was probably set in concrete at a later stage.

Annie had broken her collarbone as the result of her fall. I never saw her again. The same city fathers who after Stella's death eight years before had come forward in the apparent absence of any available relatives once again busied themselves out of similar motives and had Annie Glosser, spinster, admitted to a sanatorium without further ado. At least that was the official version. The schoolkids, as usual better informed through secret sources than the adults, got to the heart of it.

"She's in the loony bin, is Annie. They do things there."

"What sort of things?"

"They pump them full of electricity."

"And injections."

"And freeze them in ice, to stop them moving."

"She's in a padded cell."

"Why?"

"So that in a fit she doesn't bash her head in. She's really dangerous."

"And wears nappies."

That last bit of information was what shook me the most. I was terribly sorry that Annie had broken bones. She must have been in pain, and probably been terrified down there in the hole, covered in sticky liqueur. But the notion of Annie wrapped in nappies broke my heart. Altogether I was certain that everything being done to Annie in the lunatic asylum would definitely not give her a good feeling, and the suspicion overtook me that for Annie the days of cherry liqueur as well as the porno-pic orange plastic TV were well and truly over. I was so moved by Annie Glosser's fate that for a long time had anyone asked me what I would like to be when I grew up, I would have said a psychiatrist. But nobody asked me.

For several weeks I went prowling round Annie's brightly painted house, secretly expecting a window or a door to swing open in friendly welcome. Dianne and I won the Battle of the Big Eye, and I would have loved to tell Annie about it. But the summer passed, and weeds took over the neglected garden, suffocating the splendid displays in the flower beds, and when the autumn winds began rattling in vain at the colored shutters I gave up all hope. But I didn't forget Annie or how to make the cock crow.

Years later, when I had successfully satisfied myself for the first time, exactly as I'd been shown, I bought an ice cream wafer next day in honor of Annie Glosser. I took it and sat down on the rim of the fountain in the market square, crumbled the wafer, and fed it to the cooing pigeons.

chapter 6

or you'll wake them

The rampant deadly thorn hedges had retreated. Once again the flies were buzzing and crawling along the sooty walls, and the cook had dealt the kitchen boy a resounding box on the ears. There was no longer anything to prevent a wedding. I was more than content. I was thoroughly happy.

"But why did the prince kiss Sleeping Beauty?" Dianne wanted to know.

"Because he was in love."

"How could he be in love with Sleeping Beauty when he didn't even know her?"

"Because that's how things just happen sometimes." Tereza closed the book of fairy stories and let herself sink back against the burgundy upholstery of the armchair, promptly making part of its stuffing shoot out with an indignant creak. As she leaned back the light of the candles on our bedside table made her eyes seem no more than two gleaming silver-gray specks.

Dianne pulled at one of her earlobes thoughtfully, her lower lip pouting, visibly dissatisfied with Tereza's answer. I couldn't understand her disbelief. She was being utterly unromantic. For the prince to love Sleeping Beauty was a law of nature, and you simply didn't question laws of nature. What bothered me was a problem of a much more practical nature.

"Where do they live now, the prince and Sleeping Beauty?"

"What d'you mean?"

"You said they lived happily ever after."

"Oh, I see. . . ." Now it was Tereza's turn to pluck at her earlobe. "Well, I expect they live in a beautiful castle."

"Like the one on the castle hill in the town?"

"No, that's far too small and crummy. Real princes and princesses have to have at least . . . well, let's say about a hundred rooms."

A daring thought began forming in my head. "Tereza, are there a hundred rooms in Visible?"

"Definitely," came the answer from the burgundy armchair. "At the very least."

My head was spinning. "Then maybe Sleeping Beauty and the prince have been living here all the time, and we just haven't seen them yet."

Dianne gave a skeptical snort.

"Could be," said Tereza. And then, after a lengthy pause that drove me nearly wild, she added: "Now that I come to think about it, I'm really quite certain that you're right."

I threw back the blanket, jumped out of bed, and ran across the cold parquet floor in my bare feet. Very cautiously I opened the bedroom door and peeked down the corridor expectantly. To the left and right the corridor disappeared in the impenetrable dark. Not a sign of Sleeping Beauty, the handsome prince, or the royal household awakened after one hundred years' sleep. I slammed the door in disappointment and stormed back to bed.

"Really?" I whispered. "Here in the house?"

Tereza nodded earnestly and bent down over us. Her gaze slowly moved up toward the ceiling and then back down again just as slowly. She spoke so softly that I wasn't sure whether I was actually hearing the words or just reading her lips. "If you ask me, Sleeping Beauty and her prince do live up there in the attic. They live there, in love forever. But there's one thing they don't have. D'you know what it is?"

Dianne and I shook our heads. As I hung on Tereza's words in suspense, waiting for her to say more, it suddenly came to me that we would never be able to visit Sleeping Beauty and the prince. Up to now, Dianne and I had never been into the attic. At night there were terrifying sounds rampaging about up there—dormice, martens, or squirrels, Glass maintained, or possibly even rats. But Dianne and I weren't stupid. We knew perfectly well that those noises were made by nightmarish creatures, the most monstrous of monsters, who ever since the beginning of time had been just waiting for two little idiots like us to go up into the attic so that they could use their stumpy yellow teeth to bite our stupid heads off.

"Come on, tell us!" I thumped Tereza on the knee with my fist. "Tell us, what is it they don't have?"

"Sleeping Beauty and the prince don't have . . . popcorn!" yelled Tereza, and in an instant Dianne and I had pushed her aside, shrieking our way ahead of her to the kitchen, which was soon filled with the smell of melted butter and the snapping little pops of bursting corn.

Going up into the bewitched attic was simply not an issue. But as I couldn't stop thinking about the story of Sleeping Beauty, the next day I pressed Dianne into playing a game where we acted it out. We ransacked Glass's wardrobe and used everything that fell into our hands—brightly colored semitransparent lengths of fabric that our mother used for tying up her hair, short skirts, nylon stockings in every conceivable color, belts with all manner of decorations—to dress ourselves up in fantastic costumes. We ran out into the garden, returning with armfuls of wild scented roses that we spread all over the bedroom. We took makeup, lipstick, and powder and painted our faces.

But in spite of all these preparations *Sleeping Beauty* never did get to have its premiere, and that was all because of Dianne. I used all my powers of persuasion to talk her round, but she stubbornly shook her waxen powdered face, which I had taken such care to make up, and kept her scarlet lips firmly pressed together. She simply could not bring herself to climb onto our mother's bed, where I lay, and wake me with a kiss.

That evening, incensed and close to tears, I complained about this to Tereza, and she put her arms round me. She let me bury my face in her red hair, which smelled comfortingly of oranges and almonds. "Don't let it upset you, Phil," she whispered. "I know just how you feel. You know, I always wanted to be the prince. But no one ever let me."

"Why not?"

"That's a damn good question, my little one." Tereza loosened her embrace and took my face in her hands. She kissed me on the forehead, then ruffled my hair with one hand and asked, "Has anyone ever told you how sweet your sticking-out ears make you look?"

Nicholas is so good at sports that the school is toying with the idea of providing him with a personal trainer. His specialty is long-distance running. Soon everyone is calling him the Runner.

He has a sports class early on Thursday afternoons, immediately after my track and field athletics lesson. For the next three weeks, instead of going straight home after my class at the sports ground at the edge of the town, I wait there for a further hour. I shower, change, and go and sit in the shade on one of the spectator benches with an open book on my knees and pretend to be reading.

The country is in the grip of summer. The days are blindingly brilliant, sharpening every contour, so that a single blade of grass looks like a green spear and the sky like crystal-clear water, so that only the force of gravity stops you from plunging into it.

Staring straight ahead into space, the Runner covers lap after lap on the rust-red track, apparently with the greatest of ease. It's fun to watch him. Normally his shoulders are imperceptibly hunched forward, as if constantly on the alert to defend himself if need be. But as he runs, every sign of tension falls away. He appears to float; his strides don't raise the minutest grains of sand, giving the impression that his feet don't actually make contact with the ground.

Just as the Runner doesn't seem to be aware of my presence on the sports ground, he likewise doesn't seem to notice me surreptitiously looking at him in school. Math is the only subject where we're in the same class.

In order to attract Nicholas's attention, I decide to listen to Handel as he drifts from mathematics to philosophy and mental acrobatics. I activate the left half of my brain and do my best to keep up my end in the discussions that arise from time to time, which Handel registers with one knowing eyebrow quizzically raised but which totally escapes the notice of the Runner.

It doesn't take long for me to feel like a complete idiot.

Before Kat has a chance to run a critical examination of my suddenly awakened interest in discourses about emotion and reason, it has come to an end. After three weeks of observation sessions at the sports field, I put a stop to those as well. I get the feeling that in that time I have become personally acquainted with every single leg muscle belonging to the Runner. He proves to be just as reticent, if not as monosyllabic as I originally judged him to be. Contrary to my expectations, he doesn't prove to be a loner, though. Nicholas never needs to be the one to start a conversation; it's the others who approach him of their own accord. When questioned, he gives short but interested replies, accompanied by a noncommittal smile, so there is never the uncomfortable feeling that he may have felt in any way bothered. It's only when he goes off to run that he sets himself apart. Then he avoids any kind of conversation and stands alone at the edge of the track, nervously limbering up, as he waits for the starting signal. From that moment on, each of his movements is as predictable as those of a mechanical windup doll. Running absorbs him utterly. Not until he passes the finish line and with lips firmly pressed together casts a brief glance—never satisfied—at the stopwatch does he change back to his usual self. Then he joins the other pupils and shortly after leaves the sports field, laughing and jostling shoulders with the rest of them.

Good athletes are always popular. Admirers buzz around Nicholas like bees around a honey pot.

"Types like that arouse primordial instincts" is Kat's comment as she sees me watching him. "The pack, you know."

"What d'you mean by 'the pack'?"

"It relies on the fastest and strongest member of the pack to survive. That's why women are also attracted to guys like that." She grins. "They can scent good genetic material."

"If it's only that, then why didn't you stay with Thomas?"

"Oh, don't be so stupid!" she snaps angrily. "What I just said was true of the Stone Age. Meanwhile, there's far more to it than that. Or do you still see mankind running around in packs?"

"Well, to be honest . . ."

"A culture develops only when reason enters the stage. Mind over muscle, diplomacy in place of brute force." She nods, agreeing with herself.

"You sound like Handel."

Kat shakes her head. "No, in this case like my father in one of his liberal onsets. And he's right."

The reasons for the Runner's popularity are more or less all the same to me. Fact is, he has friends. The jaunty ease of Nicholas's manner with others, making them flock around him and bond with him, has a corrosive effect on me in a very short time. Love takes longer. It is slow in coming, like a creeping sickness, and takes hold around my heart like the ivy that almost suffocates Visible in the summertime.

Wolf was the only boy with whom—for a short while years ago—I entered into a kind of friendship. He had the most expressionless eyes I had ever seen, and was really and truly mad. His soul was broken and cold as liquid nitrogen.

The Battle of the Big Eye had won Dianne and me respect; after that we were never bothered again. But at the same time it effectively barred the way to our making friends—Dianne's arrow had sunk deep into the flesh of the Little People, and it was as if it discharged a black poison at regular intervals to remind everyone that we were dangerous and to be avoided at all costs. If at night we figured in the dreams of other children—as I firmly believed we did—it was not as heroes, but as fearsome nightmarish creatures. In the daytime the young dreamers nervously avoided us, and the passing of time did nothing to change this.

I persuaded myself that I didn't need the friendship of other children or miss it. Neither was true. Kat was the first to resist the restrictions her parents tried to impose on her. I didn't get to know her properly until later. And Dianne was often not enough for me. Sometimes I would catch myself silently comparing her with a boy of my age, with whom I could wander through the fields, to whom I might confide my secrets as we each grazed our knees.

It was the whispering that went on as we entered the next year that drew my attention to Wolf, a pale boy who always seemed as if he wasn't quite all there, small for his age, who kept his distance from the other children and seemed to be the same kind of loner I was. "He lives alone with his father" went the brief comments in the playground during recess. "His mother killed herself."

In class he sat alone at a table, just as I sat alone. I watched him. He appeared strangely immobile and feeble. He often seemed to be looking straight through the other pupils at some invisible horizon miles away. Finally, with a pounding heart, I spoke to him and asked whether he would like to sit next to me. Wolf examined me through hooded distrustful eyes.

"Why?" he wanted to know.

"My father is dead," I said.

For weeks on end I was afraid that Wolf might discover the lie and I would once again be just as alone as before. But he never asked me about my supposedly dead father; it was enough to have me as a friend. It was not in his nature to ask about things, and he didn't talk much at all, which suited me fine. At the same time he refused to answer certain questions. When I wanted to know where he had got the key for the old school cellar, which he presented me with one day in his quiet level fashion, he just shook his head without saying a word. He had dry, flaxen blond hair that I would have liked to touch.

We went down to the cellar many times, always in the afternoon, when we could be sure that the school was deserted. The entrance was behind the main school building, a low wooden door with iron hinges speckled with rust, and—judging by the overgrown vegetation in front of it—it probably hadn't been opened for ages. There was a light switch behind the door, but it didn't work. Not until you had gone down by way of a rickety staircase and groped about fifteen feet through total darkness and astonishing cold was there another switch on one of the walls. When you turned it on, you found yourself in a strange alien world.

Rotten wooden walls were all that divided up the cellar into rooms. Naked bulbs shone on countless piles of discarded books, battered atlases, and faded wall maps long since overtaken by history. Down here time had come to an unexpected standstill. Everything breathed decay; even the air tasted old, dusty, and gray.

"There aren't even any spiders down here," Wolf once observed.

I struggled with myself for a long time before stealing two of the ancient wall charts. One of them was an opened-out geodetic view of the globe, and the other showed North America. Wolf helped me to roll up the maps. I let my finger trace the East Coast of the United States. Boston was one of the many fat red dots. I took both the maps with me to Visible. No one was going to miss them.

It was only on our second visit that Wolf and I discovered the display cabinets standing in the far corner of the cellar. Staring out at us through the glass doors were the sad, false eyes of stuffed animals, their fur mangy with bald patches, their plumage dull and faded. There were fragile little skeletons, many different colored birds' eggs, and broken bees' honeycombs, thin as parchment. But what most fascinated us was a row of tall glass cylinders filled with a pale yellow fluid, sealed to make them airtight. They contained fish and rats, frogs and birds, whose bodies and heads had been opened up to reveal chestnut-sized knotty brains, strange organs, and intertwined innards, all faded to a uniform gray.

With this discovery, Wolf lost interest in all the other objects stored in the cellar.

He was invariably drawn to these display cabinets, where his fingers would leave greasy marks as he followed the tracery of collapsed blood vessels and branching networks of fine nerves. On one occasion I laughed out loud, I don't remember why. Wolf started as if I had slapped him. He waved his arms, his face turning bright red. "You must keep quiet," he hissed, "or you'll wake them up. They're sleeping."

That night I dreamed of animals staring at me from dead, milk-white button eyes. They wriggled and twisted their open bodies, trying desperately to gasp for air in this yellow broth that preserved them for eternity. I woke up screaming and saw the pale face of Dianne bending over me. "That's what comes from leaving me on my own all the time," she whispered.

She got back into her bed, turned on her side, and pointedly turned her back to me. I felt miserable, because in the past weeks I had indeed neglected her, but my bad conscience was outweighed by the desire, the longing, the need for Wolf's friendship.

He invited me to his house, where he showed me a picture of his mother, a black-and-white photo of a beautiful young woman with long blond hair almost down to her hips. She had killed herself when Wolf was five years old—had lain down on her bed and with the same scissors first cut off her long hair and then opened the arteries running from her elbow to her wrist. Wolf had sat beside her motionless, his lap covered with blond locks, and watched as his mother's life ebbed away into a stained sheet.

There were times, sometimes lasting mere seconds, when I fancied Wolf was reliving that day; his normally hooded eyes clouded over completely, and he was utterly unapproachable. I only noticed these moments because I sat next to him; our teacher took them for inattention. Once I asked him whether he missed his dead mother as much as I missed my dead father—the purpose of the question merely stemming from the desire to refresh my lie from time to time.

"She isn't dead," answered Wolf, placing a hand on my shoulder as if speaking to an uncomprehending child. "She's only gone to sleep. When she wakes up again, I'm going to give her back her hair."

Now I understood why Wolf was so fascinated by the dead creatures in the display cases. I also realized that he was completely mad, and on more than one occasion Paleiko whispered to me, urging me to keep away from this blond boy whose rare smiles were more fleeting than the beating of a hummingbird's wing. But Wolf was my only friend. Just knowing he existed filled me with a hitherto unknown feeling of happiness that I didn't want to give up for anything in the world. He never let me know what I meant to him. Maybe he just needed someone to accompany him from time to time on his excursions into darkness.

Wolf's father was a pale-skinned, taciturn man who, since the death of his wife, hid himself away from the world, and consequently I rarely got to see him. He never seemed to laugh, and I never saw him touch Wolf affectionately. If he was aware—which I doubt—that his son had linked up with the most insignificant pariah in town, it made no odds to him. He owned an air gun, and Wolf and I would often take this weapon out, collecting old tin cans and other garbage on the way, set these lifeless targets up on ledges or tree stumps, and shoot at them. Every time Wolf aimed he would whisper, "Bang!" It was a harmless but forbidden form of amusement, its main attraction being the thrill of expecting to be caught out at it.

Our strange friendship came to an end when we discovered a bird's nest on one of our expeditions. The nest had been built in a forked branch much too close to the floor of the wood. Five young blackbirds were sitting in it, and the parent bird was nowhere to be seen. The nestlings were crouching down, and it was only when I gently touched the edge of the nest with my finger that they stretched out their necks and opened their hungry beaks. "Oh, look, Wolf, how cute!" I said.

"Bang!" came the monotone whisper, and with a flash from the muzzle that Wolf aimed at the first defenseless down-covered back, the tiny body burst open with a spurt of blood and torn flesh.

I stood as if frozen to the spot as Wolf reloaded and shot, reloaded and shot; to this day I don't know why I didn't hurl myself at him to stop him. Finally he let the gun drop. Then he sat down on the ground and began to cry. "Poor little birds," he wailed, "poor little birds."

And something happened to his forehead: it became furrowed, but it didn't look as if Wolf had anything whatsoever to do with this. No, it appeared much more as if his forehead was being moved, as if an invisible, bitter wind was sweeping across the face and was creating deep waves between the hairline and the eyebrows.

The sight of this utterly horrified me. I left Wolf under the tree and ran and stumbled back to Visible, overcome with the fiercest shame. There I locked myself into the bathroom and cried for hours on end, not for the five extinguished lives of the birds but for the extinguished life of my one and only friend, Wolf.

Later on, exhausted, I went to the bedroom that Dianne and I shared and took Paleiko from his appointed place on the shelf. "Why ever did he do that?" I whispered.

Because he is very, very unhappy, Paleiko replied. *His misery has made him sick. Sick at heart and sick in his head.*

Can't he go to a doctor?

Maybe, but a doctor can help him only if Wolf wants to be helped.

And why doesn't he?

Because his grief won't allow him to.

That same day I decided to leave the room that Dianne and I shared and have one to myself. I took my bed apart, in order to reassemble it in my new abode, but then changed my mind and just took the mattress with me. I took the various parts of the bed up to the attic, which I entered for the first time, my heart pounding. Spiderwebs hung between the dusty wooden beams, from which gray wasps' nests dangled like small balloons that crackled at the slightest touch and crumbled into dust. I found ancient pieces of broken furniture, stacks of yellowed journals and boxes, and cartons filled with useless junk. I didn't find either Sleeping Beauty or her prince. If they had ever existed up there, they'd probably been spirited away by Wolf to his dark domain.

We are standing under the leafy canopy of an ancient chestnut tree in the schoolyard. Kat is sipping milk from a plastic cup. Sunlight seeps through the matte green foliage and falls on her blond hair. August is slowly coming to an end, and the days are getting noticeably shorter. Summer is fading and losing its vigor.

"He collects stuff," I say.

"What?"

"The Runner. He collects some kind of stuff."

I point at Nicholas, who is standing aside from the general break-time tumult with a couple of boys from our year, undoubtedly members of his ever-expanding fan club. Last weekend he came in first in the long-distance event at the regional trials.

"I've noticed it several times," I continue. "Once on the way to the sports ground, then here in the schoolyard. The other day he even fished something out of the wastepaper basket in the classroom."

"What was it?"

"Don't know. I was always too far away."

"You're mad, you know."

"Am not."

As if he heard what we were saying, and to prove Kat wrong, Nicholas drops to his knees without moving away from his circle of admirers. He looks as if he's just going to tie a shoelace. His right hand reaches for something on the ground beside him; as he stands up again, his hand disappears in his trouser pocket. The entire operation is so casual, without any attempt at concealment, that I'm hardly surprised that neither Kat nor anyone else has noticed. It's like that famous story by Edgar Allan Poe where a number of people are hunting desperately for an important letter, turning a room upside down several times over, only to find in the end that the document has been stuck in a picture frame on the wall all along, for everyone to see.

"Well?"

"Could be chestnuts," she says, unmoved. "He ought to leave those to the younger kids."

I point upward, to one of the trees. "They don't start coming down for another week at the earliest."

Kat shrugs indifferently. "D'you want me to drop my milk cup at his feet? Maybe he'll pick that up too. Save me going to the trash can."

"That's definitely not what he's after."

It's not litter he's collecting. There's all kinds of stuff lying around in the schoolyard. Things that have been carelessly dropped or lost. You just have to take the trouble to look properly—a button here, there a comb with broken teeth, a pencil stub, a book of matches, a small lapel pin, maybe a dime. I'm certain that nothing escapes Nicholas's eye. But he's choosy, and it's a mystery what criteria he applies for either ignoring one of these objects or picking it up and pocketing it.

"What d'you think he does with these things?"

"Why don't you ask him if you're so interested? Or don't you dare?" The bell goes for the end of recess, mingling with the sound of Kat crushing her plastic cup.

"What's up? Aren't you coming?"

I follow her in silence. Without knowing it, she has hit my major problem of the moment right on the nail: I've stopped trying to make the Runner notice me. All the same, my thoughts incessantly and obstinately appear to center on the tip of a compass needle that unfailingly stays pointed at Nicholas with stubborn persistence. He has been spooking my dreams for quite a while now. In the daytime, I lose myself in fantasies in which his arms enclose me, or his long legs, which work like well-oiled pistons on the track, rub against mine. I kiss his slender hands, which remind me almost painfully of those of Kyle, the wood-carver. At night I suddenly wake up, convinced that he has just now been standing by my bed, bending over me; blinking in the darkness, I search for his face with its sculptured lines and the glowing eyes. I don't dare to speak to him. For fear of a rebuff, I prolong my wait.

During the next lesson, Handel puts a further damper on my unfulfilled desires. "Now take a close look, ladies and gentlemen, and tell me what you see," he challenges us as once again he imposes one of his notorious intellectual digressions on the math class.

He minces to one side. Sticky tape attaches a poster to the board—a glossy double-spread photo of a naked woman, characterless, plastic, and yet arousing, of the kind to be found in any men's magazine. Chairs scrape noisily and the class resounds with enthusiastic whistles.

"Why don't I see any naked men?" objects Kat beside me, loud enough for Handel to hear. He gives the merest suggestion of a slightly ironic bow in her direction, which is met with a gracious nod from Kat. I'm aware that for years he has been monitoring Kat's progress in violin playing from a distance with approval.

"Where did you get that pinup?" someone calls out from a back row.

"Never mind." The answer comes with a snort of displeasure. Handel spreads his plump fingers and with a dramatic gesture raises both arms as if to bless the class. "What do you see?"

Nicholas's verdict is to disregard the poster and study his fingernails instead. Handel lowers his fat hands in order to stick three more posters on the board in rapid succession. A reproduction of an Expressionist painting, hard-edged surfaces and colors, seemingly born of feverish ravings. An advertisement for an insurance company—a family with a child in front of their home, and a lively dog romping in a luxurious garden. Finally a grainy enlargement of a photograph of a coastal scene—cliffs like the fangs of a long-extinct creature, the sea one seething blue mass.

"You must learn to abstract," says Handel. He has stepped beside the board, his hands folded, his index fingers nervously tapping each other. "Look behind things, distrust the superficial. Do not let yourselves be deceived, and do not deceive yourselves. What do you see?"

What I see is Nicholas slowly closing his dark eyes and nodding.

I often look at the two wall charts I took five years ago from the old school cellar, North America and the world. At the time, after the frightening incident with Wolf that prompted my move to the first floor of Visible, I immediately hung the maps on a wall in my new room. I dug out all the postcards that Gable had ever sent us and began to hunt for all the exotic places they referred to on the map of the world, marking them with red-topped pins. I stuck green pins into countries and towns, oceans, and islands that I wanted to visit sometime, either because of their beautifully mysterious-sounding names or simply because they had famous buildings or wonders of nature to admire. Each green pin was a visual affirmation for me of my intention one day to turn my back on the town and on Visible.

On the opposite wall, sitting in his special place up on a shelf, is Paleiko, staring straight across the room at these maps. His big-eyed white gaze from the black of his Moor's face is full of disbelief and distrust. The crystal embedded in his forehead sparkles like a small star. Paleiko hasn't opened his mouth for years—and never will again, of that I am sure. And yet I sometimes believe I can see his lips move in a dark whisper.

You'll never do it, Phil.

Yes, I will, you lousy spoilsport.

I'll believe it when I see it.

You can't see anything. You're blind; your eyes are just white blobs of color on black porcelain. What's to stop me from disappearing from here?

Every single additional day that you spend here. You're getting used to the world of the Little People. Your footprints are sinking deeper with every step you take here. Your horizon shrinks each time you look out of the window.

You can't judge. I'm stronger than you think, Paleiko.

You're weaker than you think.

Sorry, old friend, I don't see it that way.

Really? Then you're the one who's blind, Phil.

I don't like Paleiko's distrustful gaze, nor do I trust his admonishing criticisms. The simplest thing would be to turn the doll around to stop it seeing the two maps and, best of all, me. But I don't do so, because I believe that Tereza gave Paleiko to me for a good reason. Those who don't learn to watch out for themselves need a guardian to watch over them.

chapter 7

on board the *nautilus*

The library at Visible is huge, flooded with light at all times of year, thanks to wide double French doors. Wooden strips divide the glass up into a lattice, but the paint on the dividing strips has long since flaked off. Grimy glass panes that haven't been cleaned for an eternity split the daylight passing through into radiant oblique shafts—Glass calls this phenomenon "God's fingers" because they resemble the fanned-out sunbeams that fall on the land on some days when the clouds suddenly open out, as if skimming it with laser beams.

The French doors open out onto a small terrace bordered by a marble balustrade. Three wide steps lead down from here to the rear part of the garden. The steps are cracked and over the years and decades weeds and tender creepers have lodged in the gaps and worked their way patiently toward the glass doors, where in summertime they sway like a green carpet. In winter wind-driven drifts of snow pile up against the doors.

Inside the library innumerable shelves cover each wall up to the high ceiling. When Glass arrived in Visible the bookshelves were practically empty, covered by nothing but dust and twenty to thirty well-thumbed novels. Stella had been no great bookworm. But at some time there must have been real books here, for the smell of leather-bound volumes and moldering, yellowed paper hangs in the air.

When Dianne and I discovered the library we instantly seized on it as our playroom. We chalked hopscotch squares on the parquet floor, which groaned and creaked at each jump. Later, when the game had lost its charm and the chalk marks were smudged beyond recognition, I would often make my way to the library on my own. I would stand in the middle of the high-ceilinged room, bathing in the light of God's fingers, and picture to myself the shelves magically filling up. I had only to close my eyes; as soon as I opened them again, there would be thousands of books, squeezed in together cover to cover, each one a treasure awaiting discovery.

For a long time the shelves remained as empty as when I had first seen them. The few picture books that Glass brought with her when she returned home exhausted after work didn't seem worthy of a place in the library. I didn't have any other books of my own, and Stella's novels were uninteresting to a child. Seated in the burgundy armchair, Tereza used to read us stories and fairy tales every night by candlelight; observing my rapt attention, she advised me to quench my thirst for more by visiting the town's library.

I soon began to bring whole armfuls of books to Visible, and I placed the old armchair in the middle of the library. I made this shabby armchair my throne; seated on it, I would be the creator of worlds, king in the eye of a storm of stories that produced a whirlwind of life around me as I read the books. The backs of the bookshelves splintered apart under the sword thrusts of King Arthur and his knights of the Round Table; thundering black waves high as houses crashed around Moby Dick, the white whale, as he rose out of the parquet floor; the tiny dwarfs of Lilliput threw pin-sized grappling hooks toward me; and on board the *Nautilus,* side by side with Captain Nemo, I explored the depths of a cold, terrifying world twenty thousand leagues under the sea.

Sometimes it was easy to escape from reality. I could totally cut it out for days, sometimes for weeks on end. The books I borrowed transported me into adventures that were as vivid and different from one another as the tales of the Thousand and One Nights, and always had the same effect: they enveloped me like a protective cloak and hid me from the Little People, from the world out there. This was the reason I loved the library. For me it was the center of the world.

Ironically it was to be the books owned by Dianne that eventually filled some of the shelves—not books in the true sense, but about three dozen massive hand-bound volumes with soft leather covers whose pages concealed one of Dianne's secretively hoarded treasures: the herbaries of Tereza's father. Countless plants from all over the world were assembled in them, minute details from the colorful cosmos of botanical life, meticulously pressed and cataloged more than twenty years earlier by the professor in a work of painstaking research.

The herbaries were among the few things of value that Tereza had kept from her late father's possessions. A lot of furniture and all sorts of bits and pieces either had been sold or ended up dumped. Tereza hated reminders. In her opinion they kept people nailed down in the past and prevented them from moving on. As she declared ever more frequently on our summer walks together that Dianne showed an unflagging interest in plants that went far beyond the mere knowledge of their names, she forthwith handed over the herbaries to her.

Dianne couldn't be separated from these volumes. Not a week went by when she didn't make her way to the library, where she would carefully dust the old tomes before stretching out on her stomach to leaf through them for hours on end. As she did so, she would usually have a world atlas at her side—the only present she had ever accepted from Gable—to track down the exact places where the native and exotic plants had been found. The names of the continents and countries, besides a wealth of other information, were entered on each of the pages next to the pressed plants—the exact place of origin, the growth period, the composition and particular features of the soil, the components of the flower head, foliage, and roots, and their pharmaceutical uses. Eventually Dianne began collecting plants herself, and soon her own herbaries were taking their place on the high shelves alongside those already there. A small room diagonally opposite the library gradually filled up with utensils needed for collecting, classifying, and pressing: a specimen container, a plant press, a variety of magnifying glasses, and even a small microscope, a birthday present from Glass that Dianne had asked for. Several compartments on a wobbly old set of shelves housed brightly colored small pots and screw-top glass jars filled with crushed leaves, dried pieces of root, and plant seeds. Every one of them was labeled in Dianne's childish scrawl. I would often sneak into this room to admire the treasures respectfully and study the Latin names on the labels, but I never touched anything. Even more often I would stand in front of the bookshelves in the library and aimlessly look through the many herbaries, not from any scientific interest but simply attracted by their beauty and color. I still do so today, and when I feel like reading I prefer the library by far to any of the other rooms in Visible.

Three years ago Glass also began to go to the library, in which she had previously shown not the slightest interest. On my wanderings in the garden, I can observe her through the double glass doors. She sits on my story throne, her hands loosely resting on its arms. She always turns to the herbaries, with her eyes sometimes open, but mostly closed; at such times I'm never quite sure whether she's asleep or just daydreaming. Since I never see her turning the pages of a book or one of the herbaries, I assume that she's just after some peace and quiet—although there any number of other rooms in Visible where she could find both. Glass is the rarest visitor to this room, where stories begin and end.

If there is any one cliché about Americans that applies 100 percent to Glass, it's her marked preference for junk food. She brings home doughy white bread with the same enthusiasm as skim milk. She regards highly sugary cornflakes or fat-free ham pumped full of preservatives as staple foods, and Glass is possibly the only woman in the world ever to have seriously considered the question whether potatoes are harvested ready-powdered.

As a child I used to hate going shopping with Glass and invariably suffered stomach cramps when I did so. I was bothered by the naked curiosity we were shown in public by the Little People—as if we were some kind of exotic creatures escaped from the zoo. Although the looks thrown at Glass glanced off her as though she were an armored vehicle, I had the impression that I needed to protect her. Not knowing how to do so as a child filled me with frustrating helplessness. Despite this dilemma, the decision taken years ago never to let my mother go shopping on her own if at all possible arose from sheer self-preservation. At some stage I suddenly felt the longing for unadulterated fruit and fresh vegetables, but both of these were items that Glass would buy only if I was there to nag her. In the end it amounted to a straight exchange—I put up with the undisguised piercing curiosity of the Little People for the pleasure of pure yogurt that didn't exude a gale of artificial strawberry aroma when you opened it.

The one thing Glass never brings back from the supermarket is alcohol, which—apart from a glass of sparkling wine on birthdays or at New Year's—she rejects with near religious fervor. The fact that on this particular afternoon she immediately dumps four bottles of Italian white wine in the shopping cart can therefore mean only one thing.

"Soave?" I say when I've taken a look at the labels. "Who's coming to visit?"

"Michael."

It takes a moment for me to catch on. "The fraud case?"

"The very same."

"I didn't know you were still seeing him."

"You're not my secretary, darling. I can manage my calendar without your help."

It occurs to me that in the last four weeks she's been staying out rather longer than usual on some evenings. I hadn't given it much thought, just as I hadn't been thinking about whether Dianne had been out on any more nocturnal expeditions and with whom and what for. My thoughts have been too preoccupied with Nicholas.

"I'm going to the meat counter," says Glass. "Go and get some rice, will you? You know which kind."

I push the shopping cart ahead, put in a packet of rice that has been liberated with industrial precision of all vitamin and mineral content, and sneak in a pound of whole-meal pasta alongside. Glass returns from the meat counter bringing arrestingly pale filet strips packed in Saran Wrap.

"That's not fish, is it?"

"No. They've slaughtered a herd of swine with pigmentation deficit." Absently she flings the filets into the cart. "It's fish, stupid."

"But we've never eaten fish. Since when—"

"Since today."

Four bottles of wine are one thing. But an entire meal is something else. "You're going to cook for him?"

Glass raises both hands as if to ward off a blow. "Take it easy, OK? Why shouldn't I cook for him?"

"Because you've never done that for any man before."

"There's a first time for everything."

Her nervousness is almost palpable. She scoops a can of sweet corn at random from the nearest shelf. I would never have dreamed that my mother would inform me, in a supermarket of all places, that she was at all serious about a man. At any rate, more serious than usual. To avoid looking at me, Glass studies the label on the can as intently as if her survival depended on it. In different circumstances I would have guessed that she was just wondering how it was possible to pack whole corncobs into such small cans.

"Glass?"

"Hm?"

"Don't get me wrong, but . . ."

At this she looks up. "Yes?"

"You haven't the faintest idea how to cook! If you want to impress this Michael, you'd do better to get something ready-frozen and spend money on a new lipstick instead."

"What d'you need a new lipstick for?"

"Very funny, Mom!"

"Don't 'Mom' me, you know how I hate that." She grins and, visibly relieved, puts the corn back on the shelf. "God, you're right. I'll take something from the chiller cabinet. Do me a favor, take that ridiculous fish back, OK?"

I run back to the fish counter, where I hand the fish back to an assistant who is not best pleased. I'm beginning to get edgy. Glass promised to drive me to the town library after shopping, to return a pile of novels I read during the summer holidays. They are just overdue, and I'm going to have to pay a fine.

In the freezer section Glass is thrashing around in one of the cabinets. After a minute or so I'm beginning to get seriously worried about her hands.

"You're going to end up with frostbite if you don't make up your mind soon."

"How about cannelloni—what d'you reckon?"

"Not bad—that'll go with the wine. You need to make a salad to go with that—you can get ready-made dressing in a bottle, and . . ."

Glass shoots upright like a jack-in-the-box. A cloud of

frozen, steaming air surges up after her. "Phil, I really appreciate your concern. But whether or not I'm a good cook is hardly likely to alter the fact that Michael likes me, OK?"

"Why are you telling me this? You're the one who was set on cooking. It's only because you're nervous—"

"I am not nervous! It's going to be cannelloni without any other nonsense, and that'll be it, *basta*!"

"Doesn't exactly sound like a banquet."

"Michael is supposed to appreciate me, not the food! If he's that keen on pasta, he should either invite me out to eat or go to the devil."

Which is where all her previous lovers have gone till now.

That's how I prefer Glass—not because I have anything against her meeting Michael or any other man, but because I can't bear seeing her insecure on account of a man, even if it's just a matter of whether she should cook for him or not. It doesn't suit her—or to be more precise, it doesn't suit my image of her.

"Would you mind," she says a little more gently, "sticking around tonight? Take a look at Michael, you know?"

"You want to know what I think of him?"

"Exactly."

I shrug. "If you want."

"I do." Glass bends down over the chiller cabinet again and almost falls in. "What's in real cannelloni, vegetables or meat? They've got both here."

"Meat, chopped meat." I look at her back, chewing my

lower lip. "Can't wait to see what Dianne will say about your inviting Michael."

"Frankly, I don't give a shit."

Her voice rises out of the freezer cabinet. The coldness enveloping that last sentence strikes me as entirely appropriate.

"You haven't forgotten that you're taking me to the library?"

"I'm thinking of nothing else, darling" comes booming out of the freezer. "These little white things, are they broccoli or what?"

Glass drops me in front of the town hall. The library is in a wing to one side of the building. In actual fact it consists of just one large room that for some reason is never aired and really doesn't merit being called a library. The contents consist exclusively of well-worn novels, nonfiction volumes, and coffee-table art books, with pages that must have been yellowed with age even before I was born. The sovereign ruler of the library ever since I can remember is Mrs. Hebeler. A curiously transparent creature with high cheekbones, Mrs. Hebeler is almost as faded as the spines of the books that crowd the wobbly shelves. She wears her raven-black hair (dyed, I assume) scraped back and knotted at the neck in an ancient style. She's responsible for my not believing in the existence of hormones that release happiness and contentment; if ever her pinched mouth has managed to produce a smile, it's escaped me. Mostly her thin lips open just to inform the rare new reader who has wandered in by mistake that his visit is tolerated only on condition that he places returned books back on the shelves himself and that in the event of books being overdue he will be met with instant and excruciating execution. Hebeler is the self-appointed patron saint of prose and verse; this alone is her essence.

I don't know anyone as convinced of his own unimportance as she is.

As I enter the library there is someone moving among the shelves. This alone is unusual enough. Hebeler's work consists to a large extent of waiting patiently for customers—as a child I often used to watch her carefully to see if she was already gathering dust. Even more unusual is her failure—despite my books being overdue—to bawl me out. I begin to trot out an excuse as she casts a sharp look at my index card, but she waves me away before I can complete my sentence.

"It's not as if anyone's really going to miss the books, is it?" she says kindly.

And she smiles. Hebeler smiles! Expertly, but with verve, she brings the return stamp down on my card and unconcernedly shoves the pile of books to the edge of the counter. Then she glances furtively past me.

Curiosity makes me turn round, and I see Nicholas stepping out from between the shelves. Every drop of blood that I possess seems to rush directly into my heart. Whatever's happening to my face besides turning deathly pale makes the Runner laugh.

"Hi, Phil."

"Hello," I reply.

Purgatory of about ten seconds' duration while I debate all I'd like to say. I don't know whether to look straight past him, shake his hand by way of greeting, or simply run off screaming. He, on the other hand, looks perfectly serene—why shouldn't he?—a picture of composure with disturbingly lively dark eyes.

"Hey," he says at last, "do I come here often?"

In retrospect I regard this as the greatest offensive since General Custer and the Battle of Little Big Horn. All the same I have to laugh. For a moment I feel better and decide to play his game.

"Well, do you?"

"Do I?" Now Nicholas turns his smile on Mrs. Hebeler. "At least for the next three weeks, when I stand in for this beautiful young lady while she's off on vacation—where was it again, Mrs. Hebeler?"

Fiery pink flushes shoot across the librarian's cheeks like shifting sands fleeing from a surging storm tide. She mumbles something that sounds like Ananarea.

"Lovely," replies Nicholas. "Very nice, I've been there once. You'll love it."

Hebeler nods. Nods, swallows, and probably unconsciously pulls back her shoulders, as if to provide Nicholas with an improved view of her breasts, which, although I've known Hebeler for years, I notice for the first time, and furthermore

I become aware that for a woman of such slight build they are disproportionately ample. Her helpless embarrassment makes me feel almost sorry for her. But now, with the Runner's next words, I suddenly have to switch all my empathy toward myself.

"Where were you last week?"

"Last week?"

"And the week before. Thursdays. At the sports field." Nicholas eagerly reaches for one of the books I've returned, opens it, and leafs through it at random. "Missed you."

Now all the blood that had previously drained from my face shoots back into my head as if a flamethrower is being shoved under my heart. Nicholas must notice how I'm blushing. Missed?

"I was . . . just sitting there," I say in a pathetic attempt at an answer.

"Oh. Okey-dokey."

He smiles and looks me straight in the eye. I manage to return his gaze, but of course the whole thing takes no more than a second. If it hadn't struck Nicholas before that it was because of him I stayed behind on the sports field, it must do so now. It's with difficulty that I suppress the urge to back away and rush out of the library screaming—I find the whole thing so embarrassing. And it's not over yet.

"The day after tomorrow, wait for me, OK?"

"What?"

"Wait. The day after tomorrow. You for me." The grin

hadn't left his face. He must be taking me for a complete idiot.

"Why?"

He shrugs. "Why not?"

Bingo! My brain simply switches off—both halves. I feel numb. It's not much comfort to realize at this moment that I'm not the only one that Nicholas has such an effect on. While we've been talking Hebeler has been hanging on his words, absorbing them like parched earth soaking up long-awaited rain.

The reason is not just curiosity. For the first time it strikes me that Nicholas possibly doesn't owe his popularity just to the fact that he's good at sports, but also to the fact that he exerts a magnetic attraction over everyone. It must be his general darkness—dark hair, dark eyes, dark laughter. More than anything it's the smile that gets you.

"Well, I'll just go and put the books back, then," I say, turning to Hebeler. She reminds me of a wretched bird flapping helplessly, stuck to a birdlime-covered branch. Her reply is an incomprehensible chirrup. She's totally under his spell.

I make a grab for the pile of books. Briefly, as if unintentionally, the Runner places his hand on mine. "I'll do that," I hear him say. "Got to get in some practice."

I just can't take any more. I nod and somehow reclaim my hand and in the same instant angrily ask myself how long he would have let his hand rest on mine if I hadn't snatched it away.

The last thing I see before I turn round to leave the library at top speed is Mrs. Hebeler. She has stopped squirming and now sits enthroned on her swivel chair like a sunken Buddha, a delicate smile playing around the corners of her normally pursed mouth. Her prominent cheekbones glow, and for the first time she appears to me to have a physical presence instead of being transparent. Maybe Hebeler is wondering whether to loosen the knot at her neck and, with a toss of her head, let her raven-black hair fall forward with a laugh.

I leave the town hall, run down the high street, and storm into the nearest telephone booth.

"Tereza?"

"No, Pascal."

"Oh, it's Phil. Is Tereza there?"

"Phil, what's the matter with you?" Pascal's Dutch accent comes down the line at me. "It's the middle of the afternoon, and Tereza's at work."

Of course she is. But as Glass is free today, I'd mistakenly assumed that Tereza wasn't working either. Whereas Pascal is practically always at home. Before she moved in with Tereza, she lived somewhere on the Dutch coast, working as a shipbuilder. Nowadays she makes quite a successful living selling hand-carved wooden necklaces and bracelets dotted with amber chips at weekend flea markets.

I hear her breathing on the other end of the line. She's waiting for me to go on and say something else; it's my turn.

Tereza once claimed that her hefty friend was a woman who regarded life as just one enormous trade-off. *My heart for yours,* Pascal had written her on an otherwise blank snow-white postcard at the beginning of their relationship; it hangs to this day on the pin board in Tereza's kitchen. *A life for a life.*

"Would you tell Tereza that I rang? That I need to speak to her?"

"Why don't you jump on the next bus, come here, and wait for her?"

"I can't. Glass is expecting visitors. She's cooking supper, and I promised her I'd be there. Not for the meal, I mean, but . . ."

I bite my lip. Glass will tar and feather me if she finds out that I've been giving away details of her private life. The two women are in a state of uneasy cease-fire, all the more delicate because it was never preceded by open warfare. Pascal knows that for a long time Tereza was in love with my mother. It is a matter of secondary importance to her that many years have passed since then. From what I've gathered from Tereza about her partner, Pascal's jealousy does not acknowledge the passing of time.

"I know about the meal," she replies to my surprise. "Glass asked me for a recipe for a fish dish."

"She asked you . . . ? Hey, was that supposed to take my breath away, or what?"

"Better watch out that it doesn't take your appetite away. Glass can't cook. Just as she can't go in for a firm commitment," Pascal continues earnestly. "If I were you, I wouldn't expect too much of the whole business."

"I believe that Glass has never been as serious as this."

"False comparison, Phil—your mother could only be more serious about this affair if she'd ever been serious about anything."

Tereza once explained that honesty and openness were qualities she rarely encountered in her profession as a lawyer. For four years Pascal has been giving her both. It is one of the thousand reasons why Tereza loves her so much. Unlike Glass, who once supposedly said that Tereza's friend wouldn't open her mouth until she'd considered how much harm her words could do, I like Pascal's directness. For the most part, at least.

"Take care, Phil," she now says.

"About what?"

"The dinner."

"Glass has switched to frozen food. So there's no danger of choking on a fish bone."

"That's not what I mean."

"What, then?"

"What I'm trying to say is you shouldn't let your longing for a father substitute cloud your judgment."

"Thanks for the tip."

I feel like throttling her—her, or better still Tereza, who at some time must have told Pascal the heartrending story of two fatherless children born in the dead of night in the snow and ice.

"If you still want to speak to Tereza, call her half an hour from now. She's leaving early this evening for some conference and is passing by for a moment to collect her bags. She'll be back Friday."

"It's not that important." Actually I'd just wanted to talk to somebody to share my elation. "If she wants to, she could—"

"And disturb the dinner with a phone call? Glass will think she's being spied on."

"It's not Glass she should call, it's me."

"As you like. I'll pass her the message. I don't promise anything."

I step out of the phone booth into the high street, where the evening traffic is moving at a crawl. People are hurrying along the pavement, doing last-minute shopping, carrying plastic shopping bags, pushing baby carriages. Every single one of them ought to be stopping to look at me inquisitively, as my heart is spraying sparks in all directions. It's crazy that I should feel overcome with embarrassment now of all times. I am so used to regarding the residents of the town with disdain, so utterly convinced that Visible turns Glass, Dianne, and me into something special, that up to now I have simply denied emotions such as love or affection to those out there, the Little People, those on the other side. I should have known better long ago, from the stories Glass has been told by so many women.

Then I catch sight of Dianne across the road. She's standing at the central bus terminal, which has existed only since the small town train station (where Glass arrived seventeen years ago) closed down a few years back for lack of customers wanting to take the train. A girl I don't know with short blond hair stands next to Dianne. It must be the girlfriend Kat saw her with at school. For the briefest of seconds I am numbed by the thought that Dianne has a lover—her own Pascal—and I wonder whether it's this blond girl who Dianne goes to meet when she leaves Visible at night.

"Maybe it's in our genes," I mutter to myself.

The two are talking. It doesn't look as if the conversation is at all relaxed; the blond girl is going on and on at Dianne, waving her hands angrily, her head darting back and forth like a bird of prey, while my sister is biting her lip and shaking her head stoically from time to time.

The bus comes. I see Dianne get on, and the blond girl slowly ambles off in my direction. Hurriedly I slip round the next corner. I wonder whether Dianne is on her way to Tereza, and whether I should call Pascal again to ask whether my sister has said she's coming. Then I abandon the thought. If that had been the case, Pascal would surely have told me while we were speaking. I shrug. There are more important things to think about. My right hand is on fire where the Runner touched it. I can't think how I'm going to survive till the day after tomorrow.

I take to Michael right from the start. The first thing that strikes me, to my surprise, is his age. I imagine he's in his early fifties, making him almost twenty years older than Glass. Well, maybe fifteen. His hair is already beginning to thin and is graying at the temples. Faded jeans are topped by a brilliant white shirt, and he wears an old-fashioned watch on his left wrist. He seems cool, elegant, and—despite his somewhat sloppy outward appearance—as serious as an expensive leather briefcase. When I ask him about his profession, he grins, slightly embarrassed.

"Didn't Glass tell you?"

"No."

"No one asked me," Glass breaks in.

The slightly reproachful remark is aimed both at me and Dianne, who has joined us.

The fact that Glass has asked her to be here as well surprises me almost as much as that Dianne has agreed.

"I'm a lawyer," Michael explains. His voice is so deep and resonant that I imagine I can feel my wineglass singing between my hands. He has a slender, striking face, like one of those guys on TV commercials pointing their chins at the camera to advertise twin-blade razors.

I have to grin. "A lawyer in need of a lawyer?"

"What?" Dianne asks puzzled.

"That's how we met," Michael explains. "I was taken for a ride by a client last spring, and suddenly I found myself in deep . . . well, in a very unpleasant mess. The details are boring. Anyway, that's how I came across Tereza. And your mother."

With a smile directed at everyone and no one in particular, he pushes his wristwatch up and down on his wrist. He looks at Glass. He may not know it yet, but he is helplessly lost.

I'm amused to observe that Glass isn't doing much better. She darts around the kitchen like a headless chicken, moving plates and cutlery into place, pouring wine into brilliantly polished glasses, blabbering on without a stop, and smoking like a chimney. It's quite touching to see how hard she's trying to please Michael, but this is making me hellishly nervous—if I'm as panicky as this when I turn up to meet Nicholas, he may regret he ever spoke to me. Finally Michael calms Glass down by suddenly grabbing her after she's put the deep-frozen cannelloni in the oven, sitting her down on his lap, and starting to massage her neck.

"Tense?" he asks.

"Yes, but lower down."

It's the only point when I'm startled. Michael's laughter, together with a genuinely puzzled glance from Glass, saves the situation. Dianne, who's already put down her wineglass, her face showing every sign of imminent flight, relaxes again and decides on a grin. As Michael dutifully slides his hands down from Glass's neck to her shoulder blades, I wonder whether he's aware of the existence of his predecessors, and if so, how he copes with this knowledge.

"Did you want salad?" asks Glass, her eyes closed. "What I mean is, there isn't any, because I wouldn't have known how to make dressing or that stuff."

"You start with one tablespoon of vinegar to three of oil," says Michael.

"Really? Just a bit further left, where you were just—right there, wonderful . . . So, vinegar, what? I don't know, but don't you think it always smells a bit of public toilets?"

Michael is every bit as nervous as Glass, but he's better at concealing it. Unlike her, he just cuts the speed. He speaks more thoughtfully and slowly and makes fewer gestures than she does. But even so, this can't hide the rays beaming out from him like a reliable small heater. If not before, by the time Glass brings the fairly bland cannelloni to the table, she must surely notice that Michael worships her. She could serve him horse manure and he would eat it with the same devotion and admiration. Perhaps it's down to the very fact that she doesn't notice this—or doesn't want to notice it—that she hasn't sent Michael packing long ago. A sentence of Pascal's springs to mind, when she once disrespectfully stated that even the Virgin Mary might have had some objections to devotion if she had screwed half as many men as my mother.

"What d'you think of him?" asks Glass after Michael has excused himself to go to the bathroom.

I look over at Dianne for help. "He's nice, isn't he?"

"Nice?" snorts Glass across the table. "Let me tell you what nice is, darling. Panpipe music is nice. Pink flowered loo paper is nice."

"All I meant was—"

"You could have come up with a slightly less qualified appraisal."

"You're acting as if you want to marry him."

"And if I did?"

Dianne raises an eyebrow—perhaps she's wondering why for the first time in her life our mother is setting store by our opinion. I sense how in the sudden silence that follows, Glass is squirming like an eel between the two of us. She might be blushing, except the unaccustomed alcohol has long since sent the blood rushing to her face.

"And do you?"

"Oh . . . what do I know." Glass gets up quickly and takes another bottle of wine from the fridge. "Well?"

"Well"—I raise both my hands—"I think he's great."

"Dianne?"

"He's all right."

"Good." Glass struggles awkwardly with the corkscrew. "Does anyone know how this thing works?"

One or two more hours go by. We chat, candles burn, and the cheap wine gives the glasses a golden shimmer. Michael is quick and humorous. He behaves as obligingly as if he were the host, and he doesn't bore Dianne and me with questions about school or our future, just chats away happily about God and the world. Apart from Kyle, none of the men Glass has brought to Visible over the years has impressed me so much in such a short space of time. I look over at Dianne. She's thawed out, laughs at Michael's jokes, and is really relaxed—I haven't seen her like this for ages. Even Rosella, who had to give up her allotted place on the kitchen table and has landed precariously on her side out of the way on a shelf, seems to be smiling more happily than usual. It's like a family. Or at least, like I've always imagined a family to be. But for that very reason it appears unconvincing to me, a poor copy of an even poorer TV commercial. No doubt Handel would be deeply affected at the sight of this cozy scene, even sufficiently overcome to make him cover his face. I'm preoccupied by my meeting with Nicholas and also by the fact that Tereza hasn't called.

I'm surprised when Michael looks at his watch and announces that he's going. I was fully expecting him to spend the night with Glass.

"Will you see Michael out?" she asks me. "I'll clear up and make a start on the dishes. Dianne, give me a hand, will you?"

Dianne throws me a searching look, then without a word begins stacking some plates.

The wine has made me so tipsy that I can barely prevent myself from bursting out laughing. Does Glass really think it's time for a man-to-man talk? Michael kisses her on the cheek, which she accepts as if he was no longer present. Then the lawyer who needs a lawyer lets me see him out.

"Imposing stonework," he says as we stand on the porch. He points up at the façade of the building, disappearing up into the night sky. Somewhere a cricket chirps at the autumnal chill. "When you were small this must have seemed like a dream." I let this remark pass. How could he know how frightened Dianne and I once used to be at Visible?

"It was all right," I reply.

"Have you got a boyfriend?"

"Excuse me?"

"A boyfriend. Glass told me that you're gay. I hope you don't mind."

"That I'm gay or that Glass can't keep her trap shut?"

"Both, I think."

"No, I don't mind." It's probably only on account of his velvety, dark voice that I manage to produce an answer at all. It instantly inspires confidence—the perfect tool for a lawyer. "And no, I don't have a boyfriend. Didn't Glass tell you that as well?"

"She didn't know."

I nod and fumble about for something to say to break the sudden silence.

"Hey, I'm sorry, Phil." Michael stretches out a hand, which I automatically grasp and shake. He gives an embarrassed smile, like a small boy. He wears a spicy aftershave, some expensive brand that suits him perfectly, like everything he wears.

"I didn't mean to be indiscreet."

"It's OK."

In fact I actually feel somehow relieved. When Kat predicted that I would encounter problems about being gay once

I turned up with a boyfriend, if not before, I disagreed. That Michael casually accepts it encourages me. I watch him as he goes to his car, his white shirt gleaming, a splash of brightness in the dark. He's left his jacket behind in the hall.

After he's driven off, someone glides out of the door and comes to stand beside me by the veranda rail. I was expecting Glass, but it's Dianne, who emerges from the shadows in her typically noiseless way.

"D'you think," she asks, looking straight ahead, "this time it's going to last?"

"Perhaps. At any rate, it'd be the first time that Glass sent a man home of her own accord. . . . He was all right, don't you think?"

"Well, yes." Dianne gives a quick laugh. "He was nice."

"You know, for one moment as we were all sitting there together . . ."

"I felt the same." Her voice grows soft. "But it's much too late for any of that, isn't it?"

"Could be," I reply in the same quiet tone. "All the same, it'd be great to give it a go. Although I felt damned uncomfortable imagining that we were a family at dinner."

Whispering like this takes us back to when we were small children lying in bed in the same room, talking softly to each other in the darkness.

"Sometimes I think I didn't really want a father," says Dianne, "or I did, but only when I was small."

"You liked Kyle, didn't you?"

"I thought he would stay with us. But he left, and after that . . ." Her face gives nothing away. Only her hands flit and dart along the porch railing, as if possessed with an independent life.

"And after that?"

"I stopped believing in a father. I just wanted a different mother."

I breathe in sharply.

"You think I hate Glass, but I don't," says Dianne with a rush. "It's just our life that I hate, Phil. I've had it up to here with our mother being treated like a leper. For that alone, I hope it'll work out with Michael so that at last we'll be treated like normal people in the town."

"You don't really believe that, do you? I mean, take Stella. She wasn't like Glass. All the same, she complained that no one wanted to have anything to do with her."

Dianne shrugs. "She could have left. Who would have stopped her?"

"She loved Visible too much. Perhaps in spite of everything she felt at home here."

"I do too," Dianne replies. "I like Visible and I like the town."

"But the town doesn't like us," I insist.

"They don't like Glass," Dianne retorts just as stubbornly. "There's a difference."

The conversation has taken an awkward turn. The mood during supper was so relaxed that I've already been wondering whether to ask Dianne about the blond girl I saw her with at the bus stop or about where she was this afternoon. I can forget that so long as we're talking about Glass.

"D'you think," I say, "that she'd have so many clients if everybody hated her?"

Dianne makes a scornful noise. "Those stupid women! They'll still be coming a hundred years from now, because they won't accept that they'd be better off if they walked out on their husbands."

"That's what Glass did."

"Yes, about ten or twenty times a year." Dianne turns toward me. "All she ever wanted was sex, and that's why everyone considers her a slag."

"And you?"

"No. But that doesn't mean that I have to approve of her behavior by a long chalk, does it?"

"Why d'you have to approve of it?" Our voices are getting louder. "You act as if that makes Glass a bad mother."

"My God, I never said that. I'm not completely stupid!" Dianne's voice is slowly taking on a sharp edge. "I know she busts her gut for us and always meant well. But she didn't give a shit the way people gawped at us on account of her escapades. She's made her own rules, and we have to pay for that. Glass was and is totally selfish."

"And? Who says a mother always has to sacrifice herself one hundred percent for her children?"

"Oh, shit, Phil! Maybe someone should have."

Without waiting for an answer, Dianne turns on her heel and marches back into the house. I watch her helplessly. The crazy thing is that I probably wouldn't have been able to answer her, because deep down I agree with her. That Glass doesn't give a damn how she herself, Dianne, or I are perceived by the outside world may indeed be the product of egoistic motives. But it isn't Glass who tells Those Out There how to classify and judge such motives. As for desiring acceptance by the townspeople, Dianne is fighting a solitary battle. She can't count on me. I hardly even need to stop and think about myself as a boy having fallen in love with another boy to arrive at the conclusion that the opinion of the Little People means at least as little to me as it does to my egotistical mother.

chapter 8

how the moon got its spots

Some changes happen overnight. You go to bed one night, sink into a deep, refreshing sleep, wake up next morning, and realize that everything is different.

You can't make out what it is that's happened, because the sun has risen just like every other morning, and that same old picture you've been meaning to take down for ages is still hanging on the wall. The world still looks the same. It's only when you take a closer look that you get the impression that things seem a bit lighter or darker than before—but that's an illusion. It's your own perception that's changed, because from one day to the next you've turned into a different person. And that's what makes you take that wretched picture down.

You notice other changes. You sense them creeping up on

you, slowly but surely, like the changing of the seasons. These changes are preceded by major and minor events that don't seem in any way connected. But something in the deepest recesses of your psyche patiently fits these events and their consequences together like the pieces of a jigsaw puzzle, and in the same way a puzzle takes shape, a change occurs inside you, piece by piece, step by step—a kind of imperceptible rebirth.

There was one year when a whole lot of such major and minor events came together for me.

It was the year that began with my seeing Nicholas on the snow-covered steps of the town church, and then immediately afterward realizing I'd lost my snow globe. Just a few weeks later Glass lost the baby she had set her mind on keeping. Dianne—who, much to my surprise, hadn't displayed either anger or rejection at the announcement of a new addition, but reacted with indifference, almost boredom—became completely disturbed by the outcome. She withdrew totally and wasn't approachable again until Glass was discharged from the hospital, where she'd had to stay for a few days because she'd lost so much blood.

I was helpless. The miscarriage drove Glass into the welcoming arms of a numbing depression that seemed to rob everything and everyone in her immediate vicinity of all color, reducing them to nothing but gray. Glass seemed inaccessible. It took several months before she managed to shake off the depression, hesitantly, as if taking leave of a beloved friend. I lost a friend as well—Paleiko stopped talking to me. It was if the doll had been struck dumb by the fear that had entered Visible along with the miscarriage. Dianne's and my fourteenth birthday also came during this colorless period and passed unnoticed, a lonely business, for no one was in the mood for celebrating. Tereza, who usually marked the occasion every year by recounting the story of our birth with pristine freshness and enthusiasm while Dianne and I wolfed down pastries plastered with colored icing, remained at home for the first time ever.

It was the year when Kat and I got noticeably closer, and the spring of her first as yet ineffectual quarrels with her parents. To see us together at school, laughing or whispering along with Dianne, with whom I shared my newly acquired friend as a matter of course, was a common sight. But at some stage this companionship, restricted up to now to recess times, no longer satisfied Kat.

One day she appeared at the high front entrance to Visible, a little face with bright red cheeks. "You never told me you lived in a castle" was all she said in surprise as she took in the masonry, her head raised majestically. Kat managed to evade all her parents' prohibitions by ruses that would have taken even the most practiced criminals by surprise. Whenever the opportunity to run off presented itself, she would set off for Visible from the far side of the town in any weather. Usually she would arrive tired out and then allow Glass to revive her with some warm beer.

Her presence made Visible a brighter place. Kat cured me

and Dianne of our fear of the dank winding corridors of the house. She challenged us to play hide-and-seek there and would take us by surprise by shrieking loudly as she leapt out of dark corners when we least expected it. She taught us to transform our terror into terrified delight. As only children can do, Kat taught us the thrill of fear. I loved her for that, and in gratitude gave her sand from a small glass bottle that Gable had brought me as a present from some distant shore. The sand was very fine and yellow. I poured it over Kat's outstretched palms, saying, "That's how long you're going to live, one year for every grain. So you'll never die."

Kat usually stayed until her father would drive up in a fury in the afternoon or early evening to fetch his daughter. To start with, he used to treat Glass like a child kidnapper—on such occasions, there would be heated exchanges, with furious accusations leveled from both sides. For Glass these clashes were entertaining rather than annoying, for the two of them were well matched. She thought highly of Kat's father for making a marked effort—unlike his wife—to set aside the prejudices that were hurled against Visible's walls from across the river, like the waves of an ocean that never retreated. Though increasingly exasperated by the escapades of his daughter, at a certain point the man's resistance crumbled, perhaps because he realized that even child kidnapping can become an everyday affair. A friendly undertone gradually crept into the exchanges between him and Glass. Without being aware of it, Kat's father fell under the spell of my mother's siren song like so many others. Since the Battle of the Big Eye, the number of women clients calling on my mother at dead of night had steadily been on the increase.

And so Kat became a regular visitor at Visible, to the delight of not just myself but also of Dianne. Dianne had taken an instant liking to Kat, one of the rare instances when she replaced her customary lively distrust with unreserved friendliness. But it didn't take Kat long to see things as they were. For months she observed the way that Dianne and I interacted, and sensed an imbalance in the scales against her, invisible to us, arousing her jealousy. Finally she dropped Dianne. Her visits became less frequent, and then she stopped coming altogether. At school she told me that Dianne was weird and scared her; she said she'd once observed my sister in the garden, talking to—talking to!—a lizard. She maintained that Dianne was simply mad.

That was the last time I saw Dianne cry. For weeks on end I tried in vain to comfort her. Glass and I were at a loss. For reasons she never explained to us, Dianne regarded the end of her friendship with Kat as a punishment; at that time neither she nor I could understand that Kat's abrupt rejection actually had nothing to do with her. Instead she convinced herself that whatever she touched was destined to fall apart, leaving nothing but shattered fragments. When Kat began visiting Visible again, she would regularly phone beforehand to say she was coming. Then Dianne would disappear for the rest of the day, leaving me alone with my friend and a painfully guilty conscience.

It was the year when on a boiling hot August day I spoke to Wolf. He couldn't understand why I'd left him on his own in the forest the previous summer, and for what reason I avoided him after that. It didn't seem to occur to him that he'd done anything wrong by shooting the fledgling birds. And I didn't dare explain that every time I saw him or thought of him the sight of his strangely horribly vivid forehead appeared in front of me. "What do you get up to without me, Phil?" he asked, without a hint of regret or reproach in his expressionless voice. I couldn't think of an answer. I felt like dead wood.

It was the year when Dianne and I hid under the kitchen table together for the last time, listening to the conversations between my mother and her clients. This occasional eavesdropping had become a tradition for us over many years, and I'm sure Glass knew about it. The soft scraping at her feet when Dianne or I shifted our weight, growing restless or tired from sitting still too long, can't have escaped her, but she never said anything about it. Dianne and I learned some ugly words there under the table, words that weren't in any dictionary. We soon got to tell various visitors apart from the sound of their subdued voices, revealing their secrets to Glass—secrets that were sometimes so trite that Dianne would fall asleep on me and I had to shake her roughly to wake her after the two women had left the kitchen. Then again, some secrets were so awful that even the autumn wind howling round Visible would drop, as if to listen in awe.

It was the year at the end of which Tereza backed out of the customary New Year's Eve bash and drove to friends who had a little house on the Dutch coast, where she wanted to spend a few quiet days. When she returned, she wasn't alone. She introduced Pascal to us, and Dianne and I both agreed she was too broad-shouldered and altogether ugly, her only redeeming interest for us being that she was a boatbuilder, which sounded highly exotic to us. Our dislike of Tereza's lover was sheer jealousy, because Tereza now visited us less and less. We missed the popcorn.

It was the year I received an account of Gable's travels, a crumpled letter from somewhere in one of the four corners of the earth. Gable wrote he'd been able to watch whales, their barnacle-encrusted backs rearing out of the ice-blue water, and he'd heard them singing. The world was colossal, he said, we humans and our problems tiny and unimportant, no more than dust in the hands of time.

It was the year my body changed. My voice became deeper and broke. One morning I woke, my head still full of blurred images, to find a sticky warm puddle on my stomach. The fluid tasted salty, like the skin of the little dry sea horse given me years before by Gable, but at the same time it had a distant, strangely heavy, almost suffocating sweetness.

It was the year I discovered the list on which the number three appeared instead of a man's name.

That year I kept having disturbing dreams, which I remembered in crystal clear detail after waking, probably because so many boundaries began shifting, because I so often experienced reality as dreams and dreams as reality. Familiar smells took on a new intensity. Colors suddenly became much deeper, with hitherto unknown brilliance. Even sounds took on another dimension; it was as if I'd only heard them through a filter before. I went for long walks as if I was sleepwalking, always without Dianne. I discovered the world and my place in it anew. People I'd previously regarded merely as individuals were now suddenly linked in secret groupings, as if an all-embracing, interlocking network had enveloped them. Seemingly insignificant occurrences had far-reaching consequences—to our astonishment, Handel, the new math teacher, told us that the tiniest air current released by the beating of a butterfly's wings in distant Asia could result in a violent hurricane over Europe.

I watched, I listened, I tried to understand, and I wrote down my dreams. I noted them religiously in every detail in dark blue ink in a little exercise book, as if they were the most precious material, which might be woven into fairy tales of the kind that Tereza so recently used to read to two open-mouthed children.

"Have I ever actually told you how much I hate this shitty violin?"

"I've been keeping count."

"Really?"

I grin. "Really. Once I filled up the first notebook, I chucked it." The upper half of Kat's body is hidden behind the open music book propped up on the wobbly music stand. I watch her bowed head dipping forward and then whipping back slightly in a flowing movement, her face a mask of concentration, the eyebrows arched skyward, as fingers and bow dance across the strings of the violin. The air is awash with rippling, vibrating musical phrases.

"Will you be long?"

"Five minutes." She breathes through pursed lips. "You can hear my scraping all over the house, and my mother times me, you know."

I do know. As usual, her mother welcomed me with about as much enthusiasm as you show a stubborn zit that keeps reappearing in the same place for weeks on end. As soon as I enter her house, she behaves as if the thermometer has dropped to freezing; even in summer she makes a point of turning up the thermostats on all the radiators—sheer helplessness in the face of Kat's stubbornness in insisting on my visits.

"Why don't you record that crap on tape and leave it playing so we can clear off?" I say over the sounds of the violin.

"I'm nearly done."

I'm no expert in music, but to me Kat's violin playing sounds wonderful. The final bars sound totally relaxed, body, mind, and instrument forming a harmonious whole.

I can see Kat's determination give way to a satisfied, almost triumphant smile.

I'd originally set out with the firm intention of telling her about my date with the Runner. But now her fleeting smile is enough to make me abandon the idea. That fleeting smile marks the victory over the piece she's practicing. Notes, modulation, rhythm—Kat has internalized them all, has mastered the score, dominates it. It's her piece now. And Kat doesn't like sharing. Once she's monopolized something, conquered it, made something belong to her, she won't let go—particularly if she's had to put a lot of effort into it. She can be honest, generous, or downright magnanimous, but as a rule she only gives in order to end up possessing more. "It's different for you," she never tires of declaring. "D'you still remember when I gave you my nightie, Phil? Not for anyone else in the world . . ." Maybe it's true. That night in the Earnoseandthroat, when Kat was searching for a fellow sufferer, maybe she'd found a soul mate instead and had handed over her nightie out of a kind of intuitive gratitude. But my affection only means something to her because she had to fight for it for so long, not with me but with her parents—of this I'm quite certain. Sooner or later Kat always gets what she wants. If it means launching a holy war, that just makes it all the more attractive. Once she's attained one of her targeted objectives, she frequently gets bored; she can lose interest as suddenly as a child given a new toy will play with it for a short while and then throw it into a corner, where it will stay but not be forgotten—whatever Kat may have acquired as an outcome of clashes remains her inalienable property until she decides to revoke it.

Even her affair last year with Thomas fits this pattern. It was sheer curiosity that made Kat share her body, and maybe her dreams as well, with Thomas. But I'm absolutely sure that at the time she was always standing on the outside observing herself and the short-lived relationship with the clinical eye of a scientist monitoring an experiment. Later on she informed me, with her own special brand of arrogance, that at least she'd had the grace never to let Thomas know that his significance in her life had been little more than that of an experimental laboratory rat. In that instant I saw her before me, hidden behind the curtains in her darkened room, looking out of the window and watching Thomas with satisfaction as he prowled around her parents' house at night, weeks after she'd dumped him, with his unrequited passion burning holes in the snow—a lost sleepwalker in search of his heart, which the blond girl up there behind the curtains held in her hands.

Kat maintains that Thomas doesn't mean anything to her anymore, but I am utterly convinced that her reaction to any girl daring to approach him any closer than ten feet would be one of undisguised jealousy and an aggressive bloody fistfight. Thomas was once hers and therefore belongs to her forever. Or at least until his feelings for her cool off. Or until Kat decides to set him free. This has nothing to do with vanity. The fact that Thomas is still absolutely eating his heart out on her account simply fills her with the calm, barely perceptible satisfaction extended to things taken for granted, and it is this characteristic of Kat's that now makes me unsure. I don't come into the category of a boring toy. I am the exception that for years has confirmed the rule, and this is the very reason I fear Kat's jealousy, because she might believe that she would lose me to Nicholas or slip into second place as a girlfriend. This is why I hold my tongue as the last notes fade away and she puts down the violin.

"You play well," I say appreciatively. "I guess if you wanted to, you could become an exceptional musician."

"Exceptional, eh?" Kat repeats slowly. Her hair falls over her face as she bends down to put the violin and bow in their case. She snaps the lid shut and looks up. "D'you believe in exceptional people?"

I shrug. "I believe in talent."

"Talent isn't enough to make a special person of yourself. Someone really different from others."

"Like who, for example?"

"Glass," she says.

I shake my head. "Glass may be different from a whole lot of other people, but there are plenty like her bouncing around on this planet. Anyone who doesn't know her would probably call her eccentric or a bit mad. But that's all."

"Exactly, mad," Kat agrees. "But not talented, right? Being exceptional has nothing to do with talent."

No, I think, *it has something to do with wounds.* There are only two kinds of people who won't compromise—those endowed with a strong will, mostly combined with a lack of insight, and those who've been so badly damaged that they enclose their hearts with steel plating. In that respect my best friend and my mother are two sides of the same coin. Hardly surprising that Kat has elevated my mother to idol status.

"D'you think," Kat continues the train of thought, "that it's only possible to be truly exceptional if you're mad or something?"

I grin. "D'you take Glass for mad?"

"No. Your sister, more like."

" 'How lightly condemnation trips off thy careless tongue.' "

"Says who?"

I shrug again. "When in doubt, Shakespeare."

"Or Goethe."

"Schiller?"

Kat lifts a finger: "Brad Welby."

"Who the hell is Brad Welby?"

She bursts into giggles. "He writes medical romances that my mother reads on the quiet. And he really is exceptional."

"Madly exceptional?"

"Exceptionally mad, and madly awful."

Kat moves to the window. I stand beside her and look down

on the town rooftops with a haze of September mist wafting above them.

"Perhaps," says Kat thoughtfully, "that's what's missing in this town. There's not enough madness here."

I shake my head. I think of women like Irene, whose profound loneliness made her see UFOs in the sky, and I see Annie Glosser waddling through the streets in red shoes. I think of boys like the Hulk and his pathetic mother. I think of Wolf, of a mist of spraying blood, so much unhappiness.

"Surely it's the opposite, isn't it?" I say. "Perhaps there's too much of it."

"Maybe, yes." Kat shrugs and looks at me. She's beginning to get bored with our conversation. "Fancy an ice cream?"

"Then hit the swimming pool?"

"Right. Let's go."

So we go. And I feel like a traitor.

I can't get to sleep. The more I try to relax, the tenser I get. There are enormous ship's propellers going round and round in my head; no matter whether I keep my eyes open or closed, there are rainbow-colored spots dancing in front of them. One more night—it's the feeling of anticipation like before Christmas or holidays, only I don't know exactly how the meeting with Nicholas will go. What I do know for sure is that there's no point in thinking about it. Picture ninety-nine variations and the hundredth will catch you out.

I haven't spoken to Nicholas at school, partly because I'm afraid Kat might ask awkward questions, and partly because although I've caught his eye during recess in the schoolyard and he's given me a faint smile, he's never made a move to step across to me.

By this time my alarm clock shows two in the morning, and I still feel I'm changing from a person into a coiled spring, so I get out of bed. I patter barefoot across the corridor, and a minute later I'm standing outside Glass's bedroom on the second floor.

"Glass?"

I'm answered by a reluctant growl.

"May I come in?"

"What's the matter? Is the house on fire?"

"No." I stand hesitantly in the doorway. "I . . . well, I've got a date with a boy tomorrow."

"Good for you, darling."

"Mom!" Considering that I gave up the entire evening yesterday so that I'd be able to give her my opinion of Michael, I find her lack of interest seriously unfair.

I hear her clearing her throat. "You want me to tell you what you should do, is that it?"

"Well, yes, sort of."

A short pause. Judging by the sounds that follow, Glass uses it to rearrange her bedclothes. "Right. Well, I'll give you a mother's tip—in fact, I'll give you three if you promise to leave me alone after that."

"Cross my heart," I say hurriedly. My eyes gradually get used to the dark. I see Glass gesticulating. Her hands are two vague, faintly shimmering blobs, huge moths fluttering about wearily.

"First, on no account let him know he's the first date you've ever had. That'll make him just as nervous as you, and if a sexually aroused man is too nervous—"

"Glass, no one's talking about sexual arousal here!"

"Second, never ask him if he loves you."

"Why not?"

"If he says no, you'll wish you'd never asked. If he says yes, you can't be certain whether he's just doing so to avoid an ugly scene. In both cases, you'll be devastated."

"But he might say yes and mean it."

"How old is he?"

"Not as old as Michael." It's too dark to see if or how Glass reacts to this little sideswipe. "About eighteen."

"Then he may still tell the truth."

The floorboards creak as I shift my weight from one foot to the other. "And number three?"

"Wash under your armpits."

"Very funny, Mom!"

"Good night, and see you at breakfast."

"Stupid witch."

"I love you too, darling."

So much for motherly love, I think as I go back downstairs. If anything, the whole interlude has made me even more uneasy.

Following a sudden impulse, I run down the corridor straight up to Dianne's room and knock on the door.

No answer.

I knock again, then carefully open the door. Dianne isn't there. Moonlight seeps in through the curtainless windows, mirrored on the dull parquet flooring—it's like stepping on fog. Dianne's room is furnished even more sparsely than a doctor's waiting room—an ancient armoire of Stella's, a mattress on the floor covered with a plain bedspread, and beside it a small simple standard lamp. One single shelf holds a handful of books and all kinds of odds and ends. No posters or pictures on the whitewashed walls; the herbaries and books attesting to her love for plants are all in the library. In front of the window stands a rickety desk, its surface displaying an almost obsessive neatness—papers stacked edge to edge, pencils arranged in a row according to length, their sharpened points in a straight line.

It's an unwritten law that none of us enters anyone else's room, at least not in the person's absence. My restlessness is the excuse I give myself for having done so. But in truth it's sheer curiosity, prompted by Dianne's nightly disappearance. The same curiosity makes me open the unlocked drawers of her desk.

Well, does it make yer feel good?

Yes, Annie . . . oh, yes!

Ever pinched money from yer mum's purse?

Peeped under yer sister's skirt?

Thought of naked boys and jerked yerself off?

The letters are in the middle drawer. Judging by the thickness of the envelopes that hold them, they must be fairly long. And there aren't just two or three envelopes; there's dozens of them, written, sealed, and never posted, for whatever reason. I eye every one of them, as if I might be able to see through them and read the contents, if only I stared long enough. Each envelope bears just one word.

ZEPHYR

The name of a boy or a girl, a man or a woman? At any rate, it's not someone I know or have ever heard of. Someone—maybe the girl at the bus stop—who induces Dianne to leave Visible in the middle of the night. Glass would have a fit if she ever found out. Since when has Dianne been going on these expeditions? How often has she been going out at night?

It suddenly strikes me as never before how Dianne and I have grown apart. Now, alone in her room, alone among her secrets, the letters in my hand, I have to think back to the Battle of the Big Eye. The day my sister placed herself protectively in front of me and paid for it with a stab wound seems an eternity ago. Love and loyalty are mutually dependent—at the time I took this for granted. Today there is little of either left between Dianne and me. In recent years I haven't succeeded in any of my attempts to get close to her. But perhaps, I'm thinking now, I simply didn't make enough of an effort, didn't try hard enough. Last night when we were talking out on the veranda, even though it was more of an argument, at least it was something like a beginning.

I place the bundle of letters back in the drawer, move across to one of the windows, and look out at the cloudless night sky. The half-moon shimmers, unreal and pale white like in overexposed photos. Mountains and valleys appear like dark ink spots on its surface. It looks so vivid that when I was a child I used to think I could reach out and grasp it.

Then I wrote: *Once upon a time in the summer, there were three children, a dreamy boy with straw-colored hair and two girls, one prettier than the other, who were climbing down into the town sewer. They lost their way among the filth and sewage, and the indignant squeaking of startled rats rose out of the darkness.*

The first girl began to scream loudly. She hoped that the echoes bouncing off the damp walls would show a way out of the labyrinth, but no voice was loud enough to penetrate the maze of vaulted tunnels.

The other girl spoke softly to the rats.

"Give us the silver pendant, the half-moon you wear around your neck," demanded the Queen of the Rats. "Then one of my subjects will guide you back into the daylight."

"Agreed," replied the girl, "but let's make a fair exchange."

Bowing respectfully, she handed the Queen of the Rats the pledge she had demanded and then seized one of the creatures and blinded it, for only the blind, said the girl, find the light. That is how the three children got back to daylight.

Later the boy went back down into the sewer on his own. He had noted the route that the blind guide had taken, and so he had no difficulty in finding his way back to the spot where all hope had been lost yesterday or many weeks ago.

He had brought a knife with him. He used it to kill the rats and cut off the head of the Queen of the Rats. The pendant that he had come to fetch was undamaged. Just a few drops of black blood were left on it; they stuck to the gleaming silver and would not rub off. As the boy left the sewer, clutching the trophy in his hands, a gold light hung over the leaves on the trees.

That is how the summer came to an end.

That is how the moon got its spots.

That is how the straw-blond boy exchanged the pendant for a snow globe.

And woke up, rubbing the sleep from his eyes.

part two

knives and scars

chapter 9

gable's lonely footsteps

Fog hangs over the hills, dense and heavy as the blue-gray smoke soon to rise from the fires in the fields marking the end of the potato harvest. The air is cold and tastes of withered leaves. Rain falls from the sky in broad transparent sheets. Not long now and sports will take place in the gym for the rest of the school year.

Nicholas takes his time. He runs several extra laps along the track, his gaze fixed straight ahead, his pace steady, as if in harmony with the world. With the rain the track has lost its rust-red color; the sandy coating has turned a lumpy dark brown. Nicholas keeps running until the loud, raucous voices of the other pupils in the nearby changing cubicles have gone and the hot steamy air in the showers has cleared, until there's no one left on the sports ground except him and me.

At some point he stops running, stands still, and plants his hands on his hips. He bends forward slightly from the waist. I can see his thorax going up and down, see small, swirling damp clouds of breath. The Runner spits on the ground; his feet scrape the damp sand. Only then does he raise his head, look across to the stand in my direction, and start moving.

"Glad you waited, Phil."

I shrug. "It's fun watching you."

He's standing right in front of me. He wipes the back of his hand across his forehead, where sweat and rain are indistinguishable, and looks at me searchingly, almost as if he's spotted a lie. Then he drops his hand. "Are you coming?"

Without waiting for an answer, he turns and goes ahead. Dark stains on his shirt mark the damp outlines of his spine. One behind the other, we enter the changing room, where the floor is covered with wet footprints. A forgotten clothes bag dangles from one of the clothes hooks. A cocktail of smells hangs in the air: sweat, deodorant, soap. I want to say something, anything, but it's as if my mouth is clamped shut. Instead I watch Nicholas in silence as he gets undressed. His movements flow smoothly, like a dancer's. He slips out of his underpants, turns toward me, and stands in front of me naked. His body glows. I have a problem sustaining his gaze, even more of a problem not looking all the way down him. He takes a step toward me, uninhibited in his nakedness, and it's as if light and air thicken.

"Have you showered yet?"

I nod.

He makes a strange, small movement with his hand; for a second I think he wants to put an arm round my shoulders, to draw me toward him. I begin to shiver.

"Phil?"

"Yes?"

It's like bleeding. The rain has got heavier, and thousands of needle tips are pounding on the roof.

"Come on. Get undressed."

I was fourteen when I was finally allowed to accompany Gable. Glass agreed to my going as a birthday present and made far more of a fuss about the whole thing than I thought appropriate. I actually thought her permission a strange present. I'd asked for new trousers and, most important, for books, books of my own that I didn't have to borrow under the eagle eyes of Mrs. Hebeler.

It was neither the South Seas nor the Atlantic or Indian Ocean that Gable took me to. It was none of the great oceans that I'd been dreaming of forever, but the eastern Mediterranean. After just one day on the not very open sea, my initial disappointment at the somewhat unexotic destination gave way to huge enthusiasm. For two sunny weeks we cruised along the European coastline, and then we reached the Aegean. Gable had borrowed a medium-sized cabin cruiser from a friend who lived near Marseilles. I went on board at Marseilles after a train journey that had seemed endless, with me wishing it would never end. I'd spent most of the time staring out of the window and observing how the world seemed to grow ever larger and the sky ever higher. It was as if the entire universe was taking a deep breath in front of my eyes. I'd hardly eaten or drunk a thing, I was so excited.

Gable met me with a smile and a warm embrace. With a gesture like a king inviting me into his court, he waved me aboard. I was surprised how many people he knew, not just in France but also along the Italian coast, who were his friends. Gable had been cabin boy, ordinary seaman, and mate, and ended up as petty officer. This was how he'd made his way around the globe, and when he spoke about it, it was as if he was talking about centuries long ago.

"I used to let myself be hired by anyone who would take me. I wanted to see something of the world. But most of all I wanted freedom, and the only place to find freedom, Phil, is at sea! Four walls are no good for me, they stifle me. There's only one thing worse—a coffin. I need wide-open spaces, an open view over the ocean. Nothing in the world can give you the illusion of vastness like the blank horizon."

I was surprised to hear Gable using almost the same words that Stella had used to describe the vast view over the world seen from Visible. Glass had told me that Gable and Stella had never known each other, but sometimes when I looked at the photos of my aunt that were hung up in Visible, I imagined how well the two of them would have got on together, and thought that Stella would have made a far better wife for him than Alexa. She would have left Visible to go to sea with him. I pictured them as a couple—Stella with her proud, steely face and Gable with his sad eyes. Even when I was a child those eyes had puzzled me: to me they had seemed far too big for the face of a seafarer. I thought they should have been smaller, from squinting into the glistening brightness of the sunlight on the water, or from being screwed up against the wind rushing at them when the weather was rough.

Gable showed me all over the little ship. He explained the ropes and sails, which at first seemed a complete muddle, almost impossible to disentangle, until I learned to distinguish them from each other by means of their function. That was during my first days on board, which I spent half awake, half asleep. I was away from Visible, away from the town and the Little People, amid a suddenly expanded universe; the world I was familiar with had shrunk to a minute spot on a map, hardly bigger than a pinprick, and was now dominated by water. Everything seemed changed. There was even a different quality to the light, as if the distance between molecules was greater in these latitudes; it simply shone straight through everything, through hemp, timber, and steel, so that nothing seemed to have a tangible substance. The wind tasted of salt and appeared to have unpredictable strength—sometimes I got the feeling that it would take no more than a sudden breeze to sweep me away and make me drift along on it forever. Gable steered the boat over the sea on an arbitrary zigzag course. I was on a constant high. Time had forgotten us; we had no fixed destination. We often put in at tiny harbors, and time and again I was surprised how many people knew my uncle—fishermen and innkeepers and craft owners and the crews of other small boats. Some of them had a sly look. In earlier times, I decided, such men would have been pirates, lawless freebooters, answerable to no one but themselves and their desire for unconditional freedom. Incidents I'd known about up to now only from Gable's stories suddenly took on reality—here was the port where he'd received minor contraband; in another he'd got drunk and subsequently come to in some alley minus his wallet; on this stretch of coast he'd watched dolphins landing a shark; farther on along the coast he'd seen a drowned sponge diver brought ashore, clutching in his blue-white-marble-colored balled fist not a sponge but an unbelievably enormous pearl, brought up from the deathly deep.

"These men can stay underwater for up to four minutes," Gable explained.

"How do they do it?"

"Oh, practice, I expect." He laughed. "The whole of life is a miracle, Phil."

As Handel explained to me weeks later, when back home I questioned him about this phenomenon, deep-sea divers can use meditation to lower their body temperature and consequently their entire metabolism to such an extent that they use less oxygen than under normal circumstances. All a matter of physics, maintained Handel in his own arbitrary way, thereby making the world one miracle the poorer for me.

Gable could spend hours motionlessly observing the changing colors and the movement of the waves on the water. He loved the Mediterranean, and it loved him. When I watched him swimming—as his broad, deeply tanned back rose out of the water following a powerful stroke of his arm and then dropped back in again, and particularly when Gable pulled himself back up aboard the cruiser—I always got the impression that the water didn't rush at him with the same speed as it did at me or other people. It flowed and rippled off him in incredible slow motion, as if it wanted to stay attached to him as long as possible.

"I don't know why it always keeps drawing me back," said Gable. "Maybe because I feel best surrounded by these wide open spaces but know there's firm land directly beyond the horizon."

In the larger ports he introduced me to women who were recognizable as whores at a hundred paces, since they took such pains to sustain the clichés familiar from a thousand books and films that it was almost laughable. Mostly they were garishly made up, and their hair glowed in colors unknown to nature. They strutted through the docks on long legs, like storks crossed with birds of paradise, always swaying a little, as if either tired or drunk or disappointed by love, or maybe simply because their heels were too high, clattering along like joyful castanets. Silver and gold bracelets tinkled and jangled as the women flung their arms around Gable's neck as if he was some long-lost lover—and maybe that's just what he was—and their voices were so rough that you could have grated nutmegs on them.

Some of the women touched me. On such occasions I would blush to the roots of my hair and couldn't help thinking back to Annie Glosser's little orange television containing the forbidden world of thighs spread wide and fleshy pink—sporno. The whores, all of whom looked as if they'd modeled for the tiny nude transparencies in Annie's television, squeezed my shoulders and my thin arms, as if to see whether I had enough flesh on my bones. They laughed as they did so, speaking Greek, in which Gable was able to answer almost fluently, and clutched themselves between their legs, and after an exchange of four or five sentences they would throw back their heads and laugh even more loudly and raucously. Often they would whisper something to Gable, and he would nod, looking at me, a slight smile crossing his face, his broad chin lowered almost to his chest; then he would nod a second time, and my uncertainty would grow boundless. If the whores then turned back to me, talking to me loudly, I would either nod helplessly or shake my head just as helplessly. I thought I could catch a cooing and tempting tone in their voices that pursued me even in my dreams. It even excited me—not the thought of the women themselves but the disreputable air they exuded and the promise they radiated to follow it up, transform it into actions, words, and pleasure.

The reason I found being touched by the whores unpleasant was purely and simply because I believed Gable expected me to react in some way—with enthusiasm or even arousal. Every time we put into a port, I would be afraid he might ask if I'd like to spend the night with one of these women—a gift, a kind of initiation rite he considered appropriate, because I was a man or on the way to becoming one. I could hardly have been more mistaken about Gable, and yet I was proved right. To some extent.

One night we headed for an isolated bay, as it seemed, forsaken by God and man. The entire evening he had been grinning broadly without explaining what was amusing him so much. My skin had meanwhile turned as brown as dark chocolate.

"You've got two hours," said Gable when he'd dropped anchor and the boat had come to a complete standstill.

"What for?"

He pointed in the direction of the beach. It was a moonless night, and the white sand formed a faintly luminous strip. A shadow emerged. It moved and came toward the ship, took a step into the water, and waited. Fear rushed down into my stomach like a plumb line; I felt dizzy as I suddenly heard the cooing and luring whispers of the harbor whores.

"Who's that?"

"Surprise," said Gable. I felt his hand on my shoulder pushing me forward gently, as if afraid to hurt me. The next moment water was surging round my hips, my thighs, my ankles. Five paces, ten—the shadow remained a shadow. Then I stood before him. It was a boy my age, maybe a bit older.

My body no longer seemed to belong to me. It was drained, weightless.

"Hello," whispered the boy in Greek. "Come."

I took hold of the hand held out to me; it was dry and warm. He moved through the night with such certain steps that after hesitating briefly I let him lead me forward. With each step I felt the sand running between my bare toes; it was still warm. Maybe it never cooled down completely but remained warm until the summer was over, though I couldn't imagine that the summer would ever come to an end here. There was an insistent sweet smell wafting through the air like boiling honey, and we left the sea behind us until the beating of the waves on the beach was no more than a distant murmur, a dreamlike echo, a promise repeated to infinity.

When the boy suddenly came to a standstill and let go of me, panic swept over me, fear of the dark. Then I felt his hands on my shoulders, his lips on my neck. I quivered as if struck by an electric shock. He kissed me and whispered, whispered and kissed. I tilted my neck against my shoulder. He moved it back, as if he wanted to look into my eyes, and we stood like that for a while, close together, mouth to mouth. His tongue was firm and rough, like a cat's; he tasted faintly of aniseed. Then he slid his hands down along the back of my legs and came to rest in the hollows of my knees. My hands dropped to his shoulders. His skin was as cool as if the sun had never reached it. I slid my hands through his hair. I melted, turning into fire and water, sand and ash.

Later he disappeared into the night without a sound. A moment before he'd been there, and now he was gone without a word of goodbye, like one of the many men Glass had brought to Visible.

I turned onto my back and stared up into the night sky. As a rule, it was clear and strewn with stars I couldn't see at home; here the Milky Way seemed to touch the earth. But now all above me was black, and it was as if the missing light of the stars was making the resinous smell of the air even more intense. I felt like a vessel, only I couldn't tell whether this vessel had been emptied or filled. In the far distance there came a muffled roll of thunder.

I found the way back to the ship, following the noise of the surf and then the waterline. At first I went slowly, then faster and faster; eventually each of my footprints pounded furiously into the sand. The little ship lay motionless in the sea like a dark nutshell, with a single lamp glowing on board. Gable was already waiting for me. I clambered over a few stones, seized the hand he stretched out to me across the railing, and let him pull me on deck.

"Why didn't you give me longer?" I barked at him as soon as I stood in front of him. "Why just two hours?"

"Two hours, two days, two years . . . it's never long enough," replied Gable, and reduced me to silence by pointing up at the ship's rigging. "Look."

Above the tips of the masts an unearthly weak flickering was flashing and dancing—not a deep blue, as might have been expected, but a pinkish color.

"What is it?" I whispered.

"St. Elmo's fire. A thunderstorm's brewing."

Isolated flames died out amid the crackle of static, immediately replaced by others. The air was filled with a threatening rustling sound, suddenly followed by a barely perceptible smell of ozone.

Something deep inside me rushed up like a wave. I began sobbing uncontrollably, and Gable took me in his arms. He held me for a long while, and as I burrowed my face into his chest, he rocked me and mumbled words I didn't understand.

"Gable," I said at last, "where's Alexa?"

"I don't know."

"D'you miss her?"

"Every day, Phil. Every day and every night."

I moved away from him, wiped the back of my hand across my nose, and sniffed. "Why did you separate?"

Gable shrugged. "I expect it was my fault. She was so calm and settled, and I couldn't bear that. Still, I did buy a house, but I never felt right there."

"Was that in America?"

"California." He nodded. "Not far from the coast, not far from the Pacific, and yet still too far away from it. I'm not made for dry land. I felt like a prisoner in that house, like a tiger in its cage, you know? Had a job in a shipyard, but that wasn't for me. We kept getting at each other more and more, Alexa and I." He shook his head. "God, we were such kids! You had to provoke her to the limit before she'd react, but then when she did . . ."

His right hand sprang to life. It slid slowly up his left elbow, feeling and searching for a place on his upper arm.

"One day . . . Alexa was standing at the counter in the kitchen, cutting up vegetables. I can't remember what we were arguing about, every word we threw at each other—it had turned into a war zone. We were screaming at each other, and one word led to another. Alexa became furious, and well, yes, she had this knife . . ."

His hand finally reached the disfiguring scar that had scared me, even as a child.

"I think she was more terrified than I was," Gable continued. "It hardly hurt; it was just a small wound, barely worth mentioning."

But it left a big scar.

And a deep one.

"When Alexa left, I sold the house along with everything in it. I burned every letter I'd ever had from her, every photo I'd taken of her. I destroyed everything." Gable gave a short laugh. "I even played with the idea of torching the house. I didn't want to keep anything that reminded me of her. Not at first. I knew she wouldn't come back."

He leaned on the railing with both hands. I saw his fingers tense. "Then everything changed, and the only thing I had left of her was this little scar. I was afraid that one day that would disappear as well. That's why once a year I regularly take a knife . . ."

I couldn't bear it. I went below deck. The breaking dawn let enough light in through the portholes for me to study my face in the cloudy mirror. I touched my mouth, cheeks, and ears. I wondered whether the color of a person's eyes changes after the first time he's had sex with another person, or whether the milky gleaming light I thought I'd discovered in them had always been there. Outside, little waves slapped against the keel; I heard Gable's lonely footsteps ceaselessly taking him up and down along the deck.

I can still see myself in this dull mirror. I can still taste the sea. I sense the approaching thunderstorm and the sultriness it drives ahead of it, the pinkish light of St. Elmo's fire dancing across the ropes and sails. I listen to the soft beating of the waves, and above me the creaking of the worn planks under the footfalls of a man who repeatedly wounds himself because he's in love.

"In love? Don't you think that's a bit heavy?"

"Why?"

"Because you hardly know each other," Tereza says.

"I've known him for weeks."

"By sight, if I got you right."

"But we've . . ."

"Screwed. So what?"

Pascal's words. She's balancing a tray with a steaming teapot, delicate cups, and a dish of biscuits on it. Tereza sits on an enormous sofa covered with an Alcantara rug that dominates the otherwise almost empty living room—spacious, light, with few but very select pieces of furniture. Tereza has a flair for transforming the little money she earns in her practice into impressively good taste. Pascal places the tray on a low table that looks as if it's the product of a Japanese designer high on drugs—which it may well be—and sits down beside Tereza. I'm sitting opposite them, sunk in a deep leather armchair.

Whenever I see Tereza and Pascal together, I can hardly believe they're a couple. Tereza's soft peaches-and-cream beauty is in stark contrast to the coarseness of Pascal, whose hands are too large and legs too thickset for such a small body; her dull, tangled hair always looks as if a family of rats has nested in it overnight.

"You can have instant sex with almost anyone." Pascal pursues the subject.

"Rubbish!"

"But love is something that only grows with time. Believe an old woman. Biscuit?" She holds out the tray to me with a smile, and I don't give a damn whether the smile is genuine or affected—in either case I feel like wiping it off her face.

"No, thanks."

She pours the tea. All her movements are jerky. In profile her forehead and the bridge of her nose form one continuous downward line. Pascal maintains that as a small girl she stood looking out at sea, day in, day out, with the wind blowing across her as if she was a part of the sand dunes. It's this little girl that I feel I can sometimes make out under the unattractive outer shell, a kind of flickering and shimmering that sometimes flashes out, as Pascal moves or—a reflex she's never abandoned—with an almost defiant gesture she attempts to push back her formerly long but now razor-cut stubbly hair behind her ears. At such times I get the feeling that this friend of Tereza's is a kind of frog princess, still waiting for the magic kiss to transform her.

Tereza has never made much fuss about her affairs. The little I know about her relationships with women stems from Glass. For a long time she was a victim of her own attractiveness, which other women chose to find inhibiting or even, as Tereza put it on the rare occasions when she used a swear word, too bloody feminine. Since she didn't consider herself either strikingly strong or particularly weak in the early days, Tereza didn't want either to dominate others or be the submissive one; what she was looking for was nothing more than a suitable counterpart to her own character, which enjoyed an equilibrium of self-assurance as enviable as it is rare. As far as that was concerned, Pascal wanted to give the lie to Tereza's assumptions by her sheer physical presence and her gruff manner, but Tereza never tired of asserting that under the rough exterior a gentle loving core lay hidden.

Up to now I've managed to detect precious little of it.

"So what sort of things did he say, your Nicholas?" Tereza asked calmly.

"Or do, after you . . . you know, were finished."

"He got dressed." I can feel the blood rushing to my head under Pascal's grinning gaze. "I mean, we got dressed, and then I was in a complete, well, muddle. The whole time I was terrified that someone might come into the changing room and catch us."

"Horny feeling, eh?" Pascal takes a sip of tea from the fine porcelain cup, which appears too flimsy between her huge hands. She bites into a biscuit, leans back, and carries on talking with her mouth full. "I know about that. Sex in the open, in the fields, in the woods, in a meadow. Turns me on just to think of it."

When Tereza blushes, like now, it reminds me how reticent she must appear to people who don't know her; it's only among close friends or in court trials, as I know from Glass, that she opens up. Then she sends out energy like a firework; then every word that leaves her mouth is like a deadly missile.

"And he didn't say anything else?" she asks me.

I shake my head and mutter, " 'See you tomorrow, at school' . . . something like that, and . . ." I take a deep breath.

Now it's my turn to blush. "And that he wants to see me again, but we don't know where."

"OK," says Tereza simply. She knows I'd like the key to her late father's house, which she's been letting out for the last thirteen years, since her father died, over the summer to holidaymakers who might otherwise end up in the town among the Little People; in the autumn and winter the house is empty.

"Why don't you meet at Visible, you and your boyfriend?" asks Pascal.

"Because I don't want Glass or Dianne to find out."

"About your affair?"

"About the sex part, if you must know."

"Oh ho . . . d'you make that much noise, the two of you?"

"Not as loud as a cow in heat out in the fields."

Pascal's laugh sounds like a trumpet fanfare.

I ought to feel pleased that Tereza gives me the key to the house, enabling the Runner and me to meet whenever we feel like it, unseen, alone. Yet it's all so . . . unsatisfying. After a brief initial hesitation our bodies reacted to each other like well-tuned machines. I didn't take my eyes off Nicholas for a second, searching his almost immobile face and looking into his eyes, which narrowed only for an instant as he came into my hand. I don't exactly know what I expected. No declaration of love, that's for sure, or the heavens opening to shower me with rose-red petals. But nor did I expect Nicholas to turn away from me so abruptly as he then did, as if the sex had just been an incidental interlude, somehow slotted in between his running, showering, and getting dressed—like a chemical experiment where an acid and a base are poured into water to precipitate some kind of salt. Although he assured me he wanted to carry on seeing me, I had rushed—overwhelmed by sudden panic—to catch the next bus for Tereza's place, with a cold feeling in my limbs that I hadn't been able to shake off since I'd been with Nicholas.

Now I do reach for a biscuit, nibble at it listlessly, and drink half a cup of tea that does nothing to warm me up. Tereza and Pascal say nothing. I can feel them staring at me, watching me, so I get up and go to the window and look out. Tereza's apartment is on the fourth floor of a lavishly refurbished old building with a stucco façade, in a street full of lavishly renovated old buildings with stucco façades. Down on the sidewalk, in between expensive automobiles and carefully staked trees lining the edge of the road, a few children are tearing about playing ball, regardless of the shining puddles of rainwater everywhere.

"What's up? Have you just come here to mope?" comes Pascal's voice behind me.

"Oh, shut it."

"You know, there's no point in sulking just because the first guy you have it off with doesn't turn out to be Prince Charming on a white steed."

"You do have such a romantic way of putting things!"

Tereza has stepped up behind me. She places a hand on my shoulder. "Well, now," she says, "where's the problem?"

"Don't know."

I feel her warm breath between my shoulders and wish I could remain standing there forever, taking in the almond scent of her hair and watching the children playing in the street.

"Why don't you just give him more time, Phil?"

"He's had enough, hasn't he?" I mumble.

I hear Pascal give a quiet laugh. "Seems to me our little one has the same problem as Glass. He's afraid the thing might be over before it's even started."

Fury rushes up inside me faster than the mercury in a thermometer suddenly exposed to heat. I release myself from Tereza's embrace and swing round.

"When I'm in need of an analyst, I'll come to you, Pascal. Meanwhile just do me a favor and leave me alone!"

Unmoved, Pascal reaches for another biscuit. Even an earthquake probably wouldn't shake her stoic indifference. "You're just as much of a sissy as Glass. She's done a good job on you."

Suddenly I hate her, her and her dragging Dutch accent that gives every one of her words a special emphasis and makes her—how, I don't know—unassailable. "D'you mind telling me what actually gives you the right to talk like that?"

Pascal shrugs and points to the table. "I'm entitled to criticize anyone who eats my biscuits."

"Your biscuits taste of shit! And you can keep your jealousy to yourself. Glass has had a lot to put up with."

She raises a finger. "Oh, yes? What? I thought she doesn't talk about it." With a sideways glance at Tereza she adds sarcastically, "Except of course with her best friend."

"Glass isn't obliged to talk to anyone about anything!" I shout at her.

"Sure thing. And have you ever thought about what a wonderful scenario she's created as a result? The poor mother who experienced such a trauma that it's prevented her from having a normal relationship with anyone for all eternity?"

I've no idea why she's provoking me like this. I'd really love to smash the grin off her fat face.

"That's enough now, Pascal," says Tereza quietly.

"Why? He asked my opinion, didn't he?"

"That's a matter of interpretation."

"A matter of interpretation? What's that supposed to mean? Am I on trial here all of a sudden, or what?"

"I'll give you the key, Phil." Tereza turns away and leaves the room, which suddenly seems far too big without her.

Pascal jumps up and storms after her in a rage. "You haven't answered my question, Your Honor!"

"Pascal, please . . ."

By the time I leave the house with the key to the professor's house in my trouser pocket, the two are in the middle of a blazing row. In the street the kids are still racing around. I feel like snatching their ball away from them and tearing it into a thousand little pieces.

When I want to be on my own, I go down to a pool in the center of a clearing at the far end of Visible's garden, bordering on the woods. The clearing is hidden and inaccessible, with tall trees, dog rose, and thick hedges of blackthorn growing all around, as well as elder bushes, whose white spring blossoms look like airborne foam. The pool is almost circular. It's obviously fed by an underground source such as an artesian well, as the water level drops only a few inches even during very hot summers. The water is black. It's only toward midday, when the sun is so high that light falls vertically through the treetops, that the water lightens up—a dull glimmer, like the polished surface of an opal lying hidden in moss. To this day the very faint traces of a narrow beaten path are still just visible leading through the grass and moss around the water, evidence that someone must have known and loved this place long before me.

I discovered the pool as a small boy in short pants, armed with a stick, when I set out to explore the terrain. At the time a statue seemed to be pointing the way, the stone figure of an angel with a sword. There were many such statues on the estate; occasionally some disheveled hikers, mostly summer holidaymakers, came knocking in the hope of buying them from Glass, who would invariably refuse. Like the angel with the sword, most had suffered the effects of time; often one or another of their extremities was missing—an arm, a foot, or a leg, sometimes the head—to be found lying in the tall grass some distance away if you took the trouble to look for it.

The angel stood at a precarious angle in front of a tall hedge of flowering blackthorn. The places where it wasn't overgrown with lichen were covered with a network of fine grayish lines produced by weathering and the hundred changes of the seasons. It was leaning to one side so much that it looked to me as if it was about to fall over at any moment, plunging its sword into the soil. Although it was only a head taller than I was, it looked enormous to me because of the breadth of the outstretched wings spreading from its shoulders.

I grasped my stick firmly in my sweaty hands, feeling the summer air weighing heavily on my shoulders. I gazed up in awe into the angel's blind eyes, imagining that they were inspecting me closely, and let my eyes follow the downward droop of the wings and the sharp folds of the drapery, carved from light-colored stone, and marveled at the sword. Then I noticed a gap in the hedge behind the angel, just big enough for a rabbit to pass through. On a sudden impulse I circled the angel at a respectful distance, dropped to my knees, and crawled through the hedge.

My initial delight after I fought my way into the open on the other side of the hedge and saw the pool changed to uneasy fear at the sight of the dark water. It was a fear that changed to horror when I attempted to find out how deep the water was. To do so I used the piece of string, over fifty feet in length, wound round the stick that had once been attached to a dragon kite given to me by Tereza, which had got blown away by the wind the previous autumn. I attached a stone to the end of the string and allowed it to sink into the water. Slowly and continuously the string unwound. At last it was all used up. The stick jerked for a moment as it tautened and the stone came to a halt on its slow free fall.

"Fifty feet," I whispered to myself, and gave a start as a rustling went through the leaves of the surrounding trees, as if in agreement. "And it still hasn't reached the—"

A second jerk shot along the stick, so sudden and unexpected that it all but pulled me into the water. Someone—something—was pulling and straining at the string. The stick slid out of my hands, sharply tearing the skin off my palms, splashed onto the black surface of the pond, and was swallowed up by it. Concentric circles spread out—too fast, it seemed to me—from the place where it had disappeared. The ripples shot across the water, bouncing against the edge of the pond in a flash, as if someone in that moment had fast-forwarded time. I gasped for breath, flung myself backward, and with pounding heart scrambled as far as I could away from the edge of the pool. I thought I heard a groaning in the leaves of the surrounding trees. My hands hurt. Blackthorn twigs scratched and pierced my back as I stared out at the pool, waiting for the water to bubble up and reveal something rising out of the water—something dark, dark and ancient, ancient and very evil. When nothing happened, I felt my way back to the edge of the water slowly, inch by inch.

Nothing.

Black water.

I waited a long time, half an hour, maybe even a whole hour, without a sign of even the slightest ripple breaking the surface. The stick had disappeared. I decided never to go back to the pool but did so all the same, time after time. What's more, I now called it my pool, maybe because fear and terror were the price I had paid for its discovery. When I asked him what was hidden in the pool, Paleiko once again proved distinctly unhelpful with his vague answers. He gave me the obvious but also unacceptable advice not to dive any deeper than was necessary to uncover its secret.

To this day I've never dared to get into the water and swim in it. To this day I'm the only person who knows about the pool—neither Dianne nor Glass knows about the clearing, and I never told Kat about it, not even when I was a kid, as if I was already aware at that time that everyone needs secrets.

Now I get undressed. My body seems to have changed; everything is changed. Shoes, socks, trousers, and T-shirt land in a random heap. I go down on my knees and dip a hand into the dark water. It closes over my wrist like mercury.

The pool remains still.

I sit down, stretch out my legs, and let my feet dangle in the water just below the surface, still warm from the rain that's just fallen. After a moment I push myself forward slowly and glide into the blackness.

I swim a few strokes, then, turning over onto my back, let myself drift across the pool. I look up into the leaves of the overarching treetops. A wind comes up, rushing through the boughs and branches, chasing raindrops down from the leaves. Their soft staccato drumming echoes all around me as they fall. Small rippling waves shoot across the surface. I shiver. Turning onto my stomach, I take a deep breath, shut my eyes, and let myself sink. Cold water closes over my head. I sink down, deeper and deeper, but even as my lungs are beginning to hurt, pleading with me to surface again, I still cannot touch bottom with my feet.

Glass couldn't miss the gleam in my eyes when I returned from Greece, deeply tanned and with straw-blond hair, but she didn't question me outright. The only things she asked about were how I had got on with Gable, how the sea lit up before the sun went down, whether I had seen sharks, whether I'd eaten olives. But a knowing smile played around her mouth, the way I remembered from the times when after Tereza's visits she would innocently ask us whether Dianne and I had been eating popcorn against her wishes (not too seriously meant). I smiled back. I should have worked out for myself beforehand that she'd had a hand in this and had asked Gable for his help. She had a real flair for choosing birthday presents.

Dianne was more taciturn than ever; I got the impression that she had withdrawn even further into herself during my absence. The atmosphere between her and Glass was tense, their interaction almost frosty, restricted to formalities. When they came across each other, the air seemed to fill with static; for days on end I waited in vain for a storm to clear the air. Something must have happened between the two of them during the four weeks I was gone; whatever it was, no one told me. To ask Glass about it was pointless, for unless she decided to talk to me about it of her own accord I wasn't going to find out. I assumed Dianne would be more accessible, but I was wrong.

"Nothing's happened," she said as I caught her outside her room and asked. "Nothing. We had a row, that's all."

"What about?"

"It's between Glass and me. Nothing to do with you, Phil."

"Yes, it is so! After all, I have to live with the two of you. The atmosphere between you two makes me want to throw up."

"So what?" She tried to slip past me through the door into her room. "It'll get better again."

"Oh, yeah?" Her arrogance made me see red. "You know what, Dianne? You're getting to be just like Glass. That's exactly what she would have—"

I only just managed to avoid her hand as it shot out at me without warning. "Don't you ever say that again!" Dianne hissed into my face. "Never, Phil."

Nothing was the same as before. Even the lichen-covered angel guarding the entrance to the pool had finally toppled over in my absence. The arm with the sword stuck up out of the tall grass at an unfortunate angle, hurled there by a storm that had raged for two whole days and nights. The same storm had torn innumerable tiles from Visible's roof, which now lay strewn around the ground like splintered shells. Glass had placed tin pails in the attic as a short-term solution. To have a new roof installed, as she originally intended, was out of the question for financial reasons. She decided to have the damage repaired piecemeal; as a result, Visible's roof looked like a patchwork quilt.

Another victim of this storm, as Kat related to me at our first meeting after my return, was one of the Little People. A boy in the year above us, whom I didn't know but vaguely remembered from Kat's description, had been riding his bike along the country road and had been swept up by a violent gust of wind and hurled against an oncoming car. He was in the intensive care unit of the same clinic where Kat and I had been operated on as children; there was no knowing whether he was ever likely to regain consciousness.

None of these events could really touch me. At first I kept my experience to myself; I didn't tell Kat about it until two winters later, when she had taken up with Thomas and insisted that I'd better get a move on if I wanted to lose my virginity before she did. She was furious because I'd waited so long before telling her, and didn't calm down until she'd dragged the very last detail out of me.

"If you don't even know his name," she ended up by saying, "then it doesn't really count, does it?"

She was reassured. Some unknown boy in Greece, the most fleeting of encounters—that was no challenge to her.

I spent endless days alone at the edge of the pool. After seeing the enormous expanse of the sea in all its bright blue depth in some places off the coast, the black water of the pool seemed foul and brackish to me, and even more unfathomable and terrifying than ever. I kept on and on trying to conjure up before my eyes my encounter with the boy, yet the more I tried, the more blurred and hazy the memory became, and I saw nothing more than my own reflection on the surface of the pool. Gable had been right—no amount of time in the world would have been long enough.

I regretted not possessing anything that would have made the days and—far more important—that one night tangible for me. When Gable appeared at our door a few weeks after my return, the same knowing smile in his eyes that he'd had as he pulled me back on board the ship, the only present he brought me was a little cypress, dug up complete with its root ball. I hardly knew how to thank him. My heart overflowed. I planted the cypress in the garden below the window of my bedroom. Sometimes the tangy smell it gave out at night would wake me, and at the moment of waking, in that short instant of shaking off sleep and adjusting to wakefulness, I would think that the memory had returned.

It didn't take long for me to realize that Dianne, who hadn't asked me anything about my trip and my experiences, was clearly jealous. Whenever I went to water the cypress during the sweltering heat of those last summer weeks, I noticed that my sister had got there before me.

chapter 10

solanum

"Your friend, the headmaster's daughter, Kat . . . ?"

"Yes?"

"You haven't said anything to her about us, have you?"

"Not yet."

"She's jealous."

"You can tell?"

"I think she doesn't like me."

Nicholas tilts his head to one side and shuts his eyes. We're sitting side by side on a wooden bench by the river. The sky is cloudy, a sad, uniform expanse of gray that doesn't match my boisterous mood. One good thing about the inhospitable weather, though—at least it's keeping the Little People indoors. Far and wide there's not a single person to be seen out walking, no children playing, no pensioners out with their dogs. We're alone. Coots paddle busily through the water, little black boats with pointed red beaks crowding through the dried reeds, making lightning dives and seconds later bobbing up again like huge corks to the surface of the water.

"Why are you working at the library?"

"I need a job," says Nicholas, his eyes still closed. "My parents have money, but they keep me short."

At school it's been hard for me, harder than expected, to ignore him and just devote myself to Kat as usual. I kept on wanting to stare at Nicholas. Like I'm doing now. Wanted to touch him, kiss him, tear his clothes off him; there at school, in the classroom, in the toilets, in the schoolyard. In front of everyone, so what. In front of Kat, so what. She's presumably totally unaware of what's going on between the Runner and me and can be left in ignorance for a while longer. I'd better let her know, sooner rather than later, though, and to hell with the consequences.

"Why did you run away from boarding school?"

Now Nicholas opens his eyes, turns to me, and smiles. As if he knows that by turning this dark, magnetic smile on me he can calm me, lull me into silence. As if he knows that his gaze has the same effect on me as my mother's siren song has on her clients. I suddenly realize all the things I'm lacking that prevent me from getting a more satisfying answer out of him than just this smile: lacking any fear of rejection, like Glass; Kat's insistent, adventurous courage, which she uses to expose any blanks in the souls of her fellow creatures; Tereza's sober expertise and calm. I possess none or far too little of any of these qualities. All the same, I continue to pester Nicholas with my questioning.

"Were you there for long?"

"Too long. Like forever."

"What made your parents—"

He interrupts me, raising a hand. "The same reason that makes most parents dump their kids. They want peace and quiet. To follow their careers. It's all too much for them because you haven't turned out to be the cute toy you were intended to be."

"I thought people end up in boarding school because they're too difficult."

"There's always some excuse."

"What was it in your case?"

"As I said, something or other." Nicholas runs a hand through his hair. Every one of his movements electrifies me. His lips have this wonderful swooping curve with edges so sharply defined they seem they might cut if kissed. "In any case, I was hardly ever at home. Or in town. Man, this dead hole . . ." He shakes his head and gives me a questioning look. "How on earth can you stand it?"

"They do great vanilla ice cream."

"And how much of that d'you need to stop you going out of your head?"

Time and again Kat and I have thought about what it

would be like to turn our backs on the town someday. Nicholas did so long ago. The fact that external circumstances forced him into it doesn't make his arrogance any less valid. To be written off once again here must be another sore point, a further backward step.

"What do your parents do?"

"My daddy's rich and my ma is good-looking," he sings softly. "'Summertime,' Gershwin." Then he grins at me. "You're American, aren't you? You've got a crazy twin sister who once hunted down small boys with a bow and arrow. The big boys are your mother's department, although she does render services for the spiritual welfare of her women fellow citizens." Nicholas points straight across the river in the direction of Visible. "And you live in that enormous old house over there by the forest."

"Says who?"

"My esteemed colleague with the scraped-back hair, Mrs. Hebeler. And presumably anyone else in town you care to ask."

He doesn't have any brothers or sisters himself. His father is director of a large metal processing factory somewhere in the region. His mother sits at home all day long, either drinking or knocking back pills to avoid thinking why fate has washed her up on the shores of this godforsaken backwater.

"Platitudes," Nicholas says with a shrug, rounding off the short list, and adds disparagingly, "and pretty painful, at that."

"Platitudes have to come from somewhere." Over the years, Glass has had dozens of clients like his mother. Maybe his mother is one of her clients. But there'd be no point in asking Glass whether she was; she'd never tell me.

"Well, at any rate it doesn't sound as if you're on the best of terms, you and your mother."

"Maybe not."

And maybe the same goes for his father. If all Nicholas wanted was any old job, he could surely go and work afternoons in the factory, at the machines, or in the office in management.

After a long pause, with neither of us saying anything, just staring out at the river, I say, "I saw you once, here in the town. Quite a while back."

"Really?"

"Four years ago. In winter. You were standing on the steps in front of the church."

"Must have been in the Christmas holidays. I don't remember."

He doesn't sound in the least interested. I had hoped he'd remember our first encounter; now I feel a stab of disappointment. And gradually the uncomfortable feeling creeps over me that it's just me asking the questions and keeping the conversation going. *He's a fake,* I hear Kat saying. *Plays the Lone Ranger—hard on the outside, sensitive on the inside. He's actually weak on the outside and boring inside.*

Perhaps I ought to ask fewer questions and go on the

offensive instead, deeds instead of words. I reflect whether to place an arm around the Runner and must have started to make a move, which he perceives out of the corner of his eye, because he immediately shifts away from me a little.

"No . . . please."

"All right."

"Sorry, I—"

"It's OK."

Another moment's silence would be more than I could bear. Nicholas laughs as I present him with the key given me by Tereza. Laughs out loud as if relieved, and then suddenly stops, and his eyes widen as if seeing me for the first time or as if he's about to kiss me with those sharp-edged lips. Which in fact he doesn't do, although there's nobody nearby who could see us.

"You're going to turn into a very good-looking guy one of these days, Phil, d'you know that?"

"Er, thanks . . . much appreciated."

"Shall we go?"

He gets up from the bench and starts walking. It's as if he knows which direction we have to follow. I walk along beside him, concentrating on the sound of our footsteps on the narrow asphalt path in order to suppress the impulse to grasp Nicholas by the hand or lay my arm around his hip or shoulder.

"Just a moment."

At first I think he's going to tie a shoelace as he stops suddenly and bends down. Then I see him picking something up from the path. It's a barrette made of dull brown tortoiseshell with a twisted grip.

"Why d'you do that?"

"What?"

He's already straightened up and spirits the barrette away in his trouser pocket.

"Collect old stuff. I've often seen you do it."

Nicholas shrugs. "Just because. Might come in handy. To give away as a present."

"If you keep everything you find lying around, you must have a whole store full."

"Yup, maybe I do."

Barely half an hour later, as we arrive at the professor's house, the first raindrops come hurtling down violently from the sky like suicide bombers ready for anything. All the same, I first lead Nicholas around the house.

There I stand still next to him. He looks around almost reverently.

It's not the house—which is unremarkable, a two-story gabled building, hardly distinguishable from those around it, standing in extensive grounds—but the garden that immediately attracts attention. Its upkeep by two gardeners from out of town costs Tereza a tidy sum year after year. From early spring to the end of summer it's a riot of blossom, color, and fragrance; in autumn the garden glows, as if gold and bronze have been raining down from heaven. It is breathtaking. The professor made it his life's ambition to surround himself with a microcosm of the flora of this world, insofar as they can flourish in our climate, and over the years and decades he created this minor miracle. This garden is a living, breathing creature, growing lush and rampant, climbing and twining; everything flourishes, is fertile and fruitful. Trees and shrubs stand alone or in clumps, with smaller plants grouped together in beds, making splashes of color in the landscape or in the shade of giant ferns. Dianne often comes here; thanks to the professor's herbaries given her by Tereza, she knows the names of all these plants by heart. There are miniature plants among them whose filigree beauty is visible only when viewed at ground level right up close, for it's possible to inspect their miniature leaves and blooms only from that vantage point. They are sheltered by giant redwood trees, whose spreading branches look like poles stuck horizontally into their trunks; in our latitudes such trees never reach the height of over three hundred feet that they attain in America.

By now we're both soaked to the skin, but, undeterred by the rain, Nicholas continues to inspect the house, the grounds, the garden. He points to a spot, not far from a drooping maple with bloodred foliage, where the ground is slightly uneven. I hear Dianne's childhood voice saying, *This looks like the earth has had hiccups*. The little hillock is covered with plant stems snapped off halfway with leaves withering to musty brown.

"What grows there in the summer?"

“Delphiniums,” I answer, “and campanula.”

Nicholas looks at me inquiringly.

“I just know,” I say, taking the door key from my trouser pocket and jiggling it in front of his nose. “Well, are you coming inside?”

He nods. As we walk round the house, he looks up at the façade and asks: “Who does all this belong to?”

Tereza found her father’s will in one of the drawers of his fine, old-fashioned, ornate russet-colored cherrywood desk. The previous day the professor’s mortal remains had been removed from the house by H. Hendriks, the town’s one and only undertaker, in a zinc container—a battered container, as Tereza told us later; a container, moreover, with one of the four carrying handles missing, making the removal of the dead professor a wobbly affair. The stout H. Hendriks and his assistant, a pale young man with a constantly bobbing Adam’s apple, had sighed and sworn like Trojans—most irreverently, to Tereza’s way of thinking—but she hadn’t had the energy to complain about it.

The aged professor had gone to bed two nights before, fallen asleep, and simply not woken up again. At least, that was what his housekeeper had concluded, having discovered the corpse in the morning, by now turned quite cold. Telephoning Tereza immediately to inform her, she kept on saying over and over again what a merciful death this was, not, God knows, granted to everyone, a truly merciful death. The housekeeper's name was Elsie. She had been a loyal servant to the professor since time immemorial. Elsie was one of the Little People and was quite literally small—barely four foot one in height, she was only just tall enough to be able to reach the mantelpiece without having to stand on a stool to dust it. On the telephone she had sounded like an old hand at composing "sudden and unexpected" press announcements. At the other end of the line Tereza was bawling her eyes out.

Now Tereza was sitting on the floor in front of the open desk drawers, surrounded by mounds of papers, some recent and some yellowed with age, her eyes following the urgent swoop of her father's handwriting with its curlicues of old-fashioned script, which he had refused to modify during his life. She was overwhelmed by feelings of guilt and self-pity—she had visited her father only seldom, and now that he was dead the time for visiting was finally over. Many times she had resolved to inform her loving but morally strict begetter that she loved only women, and then had lacked the courage. Now she could never put right her failure to do so, and thus the absolution she had craved would remain eternally denied her.

In his will the professor had given explicit instructions for his funeral: no cremation and no Christian burial. He wished to be buried on his own land—more precisely, among his beloved plants.

As a nature lover, he did not want a coffin.

It was a wish that Tereza accepted without raising an eyebrow, and proposed to carry out regardless of the circumstances. Of course, she realized that in so doing she would have problems with the relevant authorities. Burying a corpse without a coffin in some old garden went not only against established Christian traditions but in this instance more crucially against state health regulations. No one would appreciate brewing up their morning coffee with drinking water containing dissolved particles of a botany professor emeritus reduced to fluid that had entered the water table, or to be sprinkled with them under the shower. Tereza had to think of something.

"Bizarre," Glass and Tereza agreed years later as they recalled the story for Dianne and me to refresh our memories, for after all we had been there when it came to fulfilling the sacred last wishes of the professor. It was summer now, and we were sitting on the veranda at Visible drinking fruit punch. "The body had already been taken away," recalled Glass, "in this rickety old tin bath. Otherwise we could have just buried him and then reported the old gentleman missing. That way we would have spared ourselves a load of trouble."

In that case it would also have been necessary to keep the old housekeeper quiet. Elsie had worshiped the professor—Tereza assumed she had actually secretly been in love with him, as if it was a law of nature that sooner or later every housekeeper must lose her heart to her employer. But regardless of what Elsie's true feelings were, no one could have persuaded the little woman to agree to a hush-hush burial, that was for sure.

When a pale-looking Tereza turned up at Visible in the evening after the removal of the corpse to ask Glass for advice, Dianne and I were promptly fed with cereal and put to bed. We were too young—four years old—to understand what was going on. But we were old enough to sense that Tereza was beside herself with grief, although she made every effort to put on a brave face. She seemed to ooze grief from every pore; her red hair had lost its usual luster, and the black bags under her eyes looked as if she'd applied them with coal dust.

Tereza and Glass talked far into the night, drinking red wine, and the smell of their innumerable cigarettes penetrated into the farthest corners of Visible. They came up with plans, thought up scenarios, abandoned one idea after another; finally they agreed on a suggestion of Glass's and went to bed. When I went into the bedroom next morning, I found the two women with their arms and legs wound around each other, even their fingers interlaced, locked together like Siamese twins. Sunlight filtered through the window, setting Tereza's long hair, which lay fanned out over my mother's pale skin, ablaze like orange-red flames. Tereza must have heard me come into the room, for she opened her eyes and looked at me for a long time. Her gaze was filled with the unique pain that can be transmitted to a four-year-old—a childhood pain that had neither beginning nor end and cut deep into my heart, so that I turned on my heel and ran down to the kitchen, where I tried to set the table with trembling hands.

After breakfast—fruit juice, masses of coffee, and even more mineral water to deal with their hangovers—Tereza went off to consult her doctor, who had no problem with making her out a prescription for an effective, fast-acting sleeping powder. Two hours later she was back in Visible, and we all piled into the car and drove to the supermarket, where first of all Dianne and I were handed a jumbo-sized bag of jelly bears to keep us quiet. While we stuffed our pockets full, piling up reserves before wolfing more down, Tereza and Glass were buying a pickax, two spades, and three fifty-pound sacks of potatoes. Then we were frog-marched to the ladies' underwear department. Here Tereza kept discreetly out of the way. The Little People knew her father had died, and she didn't want to attract any inquisitive glances. Dianne and I held hands, sticky from the sweets, and looked on as Glass rummaged through a range of white lace-edged underwear.

"I owed Tereza," said Glass, justifying her decision, as we sat on the veranda that evening. "Of course it was by far the biggest sacrifice I was ever prepared to make for anyone, but after all, where would we all be without Tereza?"

The white lacy underwear was all she had on under the shabby knee-length overcoat she'd worn on the journey from America when late that evening she stood in front of the mortician's and rang at the door to rouse the stout—and, more significant, unmarried—H. Hendriks. Tereza had parked the car at the street corner, and we could see Glass bracing herself against the wind that was whistling down the street, and

H. Hendriks opening the door to her. The coat flapped like the torn sail of a stranded little boat. It promised to be a stormy night—in more ways than one.

"What's Glass doing there?" asked Dianne.

"She's visiting that fat man," said Tereza. "The fat man's been looking after my dead papa, and now we're going to collect him."

"What for?"

"Because we want to bury him, sweetie. Dead people get buried."

It had turned cold, so cold that Tereza had to wipe the windshield clear with the sleeve of her jacket from time to time, and the stormy sky threatened rain. From where we were sitting in the backseat Dianne and I could see the mortician's small window display. To this day I cannot think of a more depressing sight than the few items available for a funeral director to put on show as the insignia of his trade—velvet-lined coffins made of wood or synthetic materials that always look somehow too short, urns enthroned on pedestals like lonely little kings, and somewhere in among these a poster announcing that burials at sea can also be undertaken, peace be to you, and are you insured for such a worst-case scenario?

It obviously wasn't a worst-case scenario, as Glass explained to H. Hendriks inside the house, that had driven her to call on him in such weather; rather, it was the professor, one of her family's few old friends.

"What I said to Hendriks," she told us that summer evening on the veranda, "was something to the effect that I wanted to take leave of the old man, but in private, not at the cemetery in front of all those people. Surely he would understand."

It was a classic example of how even a bad reputation can have its uses.

As the stout H. Hendriks listened to Glass, his eyes kept wandering from her face to the spot above her bosom, where the coat was gaping open slightly to offer a clear view of the white lace. Glass let him lead her through the house, where he lived all alone; the assistant with the bobbing Adam's apple was there only in the daytime. H. Hendriks hesitated when Glass insisted on seeing the rooms where he washed the corpses, dressed them, and made them up.

"This isn't at all usual," he blathered.

"But then you're not the usual kind of man either—are you?" trilled Glass, and H. Hendriks swallowed and nodded and set himself in motion like a heavyweight version of a windup doll.

The tiled room that he led Glass into contained two massive closed dark oak coffins supported on simple wooden trestles. They were alike as two peas in a pod. Glass was confused—as if death followed a precisely calculated timetable of one dead body per day or per week, she had naturally assumed that she would encounter only Tereza's father in Hendrik's funeral parlor. Now she pointed timidly at the coffin on the left.

"Is that . . . ?"

H. Hendricks nodded solemnly.

"And is he all ready and correct . . . prepared, is that how you put it, for burial? Or will the coffin be opened again?"

"It stays closed," replied Hendricks firmly. "The daughter's instructions."

Glass nodded. Any other reply would have been a signal for her to take her leave immediately. She took a deep breath in and then let it out, and as if by accident her coat slipped open, further revealing her bosom. An uncertain gleam crept into Hendrik's eyes, while Glass folded her hands, observing a moment's silence as if in prayer—she was indeed praying, but not, as H. Hendriks must have thought, for the dead professor—and then she asked the stout man, who was teetering agitatedly on tiptoe, if he could let her have something to drink.

"Water?" he offered innocently.

"Vodka," said Glass drily.

H. Hendriks led her through the house to his living room, where he hurriedly and awkwardly produced a full bottle of vodka and two glasses, immediately filling them to the brim. Glass sat down on a sofa incredibly overloaded with plush cushions, pulled up the hem of her coat, and crossed her legs. She announced that she was already feeling much better and asked Hendriks to bring her a teeny sip of water.

"Embarrassing!" Glass shook herself in recollection of her

appearance in the role of seductress. "More embarrassing than anything, my acting the dumb airhead, I can tell you!"

As the mortician was on his way to the kitchen, she tipped the sleeping powder prescribed by Tereza's family doctor into his drink. She didn't know whether the powder would alter the taste of the vodka, and H. Hendriks didn't give himself a chance to find out. Scarcely had he returned from the kitchen and sat down in cozy familiarity next to Glass when, excited as he was, he downed his vodka in one single gulp. To Glass's huge relief the powder began to take effect before H. Hendriks had a chance to fling himself at her on the couch or elsewhere, and worked with such force that it positively felled the stout man backward into the sofa cushions.

Glass heaved a sigh of relief, raising her glass in the direction of the tiled room, where the professor lay at rest in the coffin either on the left or the right, and knocked back her first glass of vodka that evening.

Meanwhile Tereza had been waiting patiently out in the car for boredom to send Dianne and me to sleep at some stage. Which didn't happen—there was impending excitement in the air, big things about to happen, at least as great as the second half-empty jumbo bag of jelly bears that lay on the backseat between us. Rain was falling on the roof of the car, and from time to time the soft hum of the windshield wipers would mingle with the monotonous drumming of the rain.

"We're off," whispered Tereza as the front door finally

opened and Glass beckoned to us. As we slid past her through the entrance to the funeral parlor, I noticed goose pimples on my mother's bare legs. Glass was holding her second tumbler of vodka in one hand.

No sooner had the door clicked shut than Tereza grabbed her by the shoulders and gave her a searching look.

"And did you . . . ?"

"No."

With a tender caress she pushed a strand of hair away from Glass's face and kissed her softly on the cheek. "All the same, thanks."

"Anytime." Glass grinned.

Later on I imagined having heard a whispering and mumbling greeting us in the funeral parlor, distant echoes of wailing and lamenting that over years and years had seeped into the respectable display in the shop front. Silence reigned in the presence of the dead. Only by listening closely could we hear a disturbing, repeated whistling sound.

"What's that?" asked Dianne.

"That's the fat man," said Tereza. "He's sleeping."

"If he's asleep, he can't watch over your papa."

"That's why we're here now, sweetie. Glass, show us the way, will you?"

We moved through the half-light. There didn't seem to be any visible sources of light in this house. Light was simply there, coming from everywhere and nowhere, and it was neither bright nor dim—it was simply the most lightless light that I'd ever seen. Soon we were all four standing in the tiled room, and here there was light, horribly cold light, fluorescent light that beamed down from the ceiling as we looked respectfully at the two highly polished oak coffins.

"There aren't any real nails in them, only a kind of screw," Glass explained to Tereza, who had suddenly grown very quiet. "They'll just pop out of the wood. Smooth as butter."

"Which one is it?" asked Tereza soberly.

"The one on the left. I think."

"Glass!"

"OK, OK, I'm sure! It's on the left."

The pins did not pop out smooth as butter. The noise they made as they were being removed put an abrupt end to the deathly silence. It rang in our ears like the rattling of machine-gun fire. The nerve-racking echo rolled around the tiled room like thunder. At last the lid came away from the coffin.

"Full pay for a job half done," said Tereza when she'd inspected the inside of the coffin. "I ought to sue the pig." Her face didn't show the slightest emotion. Only her voice expressed outrage. Curious to see what was upsetting Tereza so much, Dianne and I stretched our necks, but we were too small to be able to look over the edge of the coffin.

"Forget it," said Glass. "Let's get a move on."

When the two women had left the room—Tereza to drive the car into the secluded rear yard and Glass to find the rear exit from the house into this yard—Dianne and I pushed a stool in front of the coffin. We climbed up, stepping on each other's feet, as we satisfied our curiosity, inspecting the corpse that lay between the velvet-lined walls of the coffin like an outsized present packed in white wrapping paper. Apart from the distant, whistling breaths of the fat man from the room nearby, all was quiet.

"He seems to be laughing," said Dianne after a while. "And he smells funny too."

The professor looked thoroughly peaceful, but he hadn't been fully prepared by H. Hendriks, or even made up. At least, his face hadn't been powdered over, and the tiny knots at the end of the wires tying the jawbone to the upper jaw were plainly visible, shimmering faintly in the cold neon light. There had only been one occasion when Dianne and I had seen the professor alive. Since the professor had about as much understanding of children as of exotic birds, he probably wouldn't have left much of an impression on us except that when Tereza introduced us to him, he began flapping his arms around wildly as if we were bothersome insects that needed to be shooed away. He looked so funny with his arms flailing that Dianne and I burst into loud giggles, which only served to increase the professor's irritation and made him wave his arms even more, leading to shrieks of laughter on our part. Now the flailing arms lay motionless alongside the dead body. I looked at the hands and was astounded that they were hardly bigger than mine. A grown man with small, graceful hands as delicate as the tiniest flower.

Another flower came into my field of vision—Dianne's outstretched hand. I thought she was going to stroke the dead old man. But my sister, who a year later was to have a small snail removed from her left ear, simply wanted take leave of the old professor in her own particular way. She had fished something out of her trouser pocket. Without further ado, but with due respect, she stuffed a red jelly bear right up the left nostril of the dead man with the small hands. Back in the car, our second and last jumbo bag had gradually emptied out, and there were only a few left to see us through the long night ahead, which in my view raised Dianne's farewell gift to the level of an almost princely sacrifice. We hurriedly jumped down from the stool as we heard Glass and Tereza come back into the room, panting as between them they dragged the first of the three sacks of potatoes bought at the supermarket.

"The expensive variety," Glass remembered. She looked out from the veranda at the fading evening sky and refilled our punch glasses. "Small, lumpy things. I'll never forget their name—*clementia,* fast-boiling! To this day I wonder why anyone should bother cooking potatoes that are slow-boiling." She put the jug down. Tereza rolled her eyes.

Exchanging the professor for the sacks of potatoes proved to be an exhausting business. Dianne and I were standing on the stool again, having moved it to one side, and watched in silence as Tereza grabbed one of the corpse's arms, which to her relief she could move up and down easily; she had been expecting rigor mortis, but this had already passed by now. The way she moved the lifeless arm eerily resembled the irritated waggling of the professor's arms that now came back into my mind. I had to bite my lip to stop myself from laughing.

Tereza and Glass each seized the professor by the hand and jerked him into a sitting position. The professor's head toppled to one side. There was a gentle hiss as air escaped from his nose. Glass shrieked in terror, let go of the corpse, and leapt backward. The professor toppled to one side, and his head struck the edge of the coffin with a dull thud.

"Please!" hissed Tereza.

"Sorry, darling. I just—"

"All right. Now, once more."

Dianne and I jigged about in excitement as the professor was dragged, pulled, hauled, and heaved through the building. "This is never a hundred and fifty pounds," groaned Glass when they were halfway along. "We should have stuffed some carrots or something into the coffin as well."

"Wheelbarrow," I heard Tereza panting, and this one word, sounding like the vain wish for assistance from an absent fairy godmother, was the last she spoke until the professor had finally been stowed in the trunk of the car and we arrived at his house after a short drive through the rainy, windswept night. Fearing discovery by neighbors or passersby, Tereza hadn't dared to dig a hole in the garden by daylight. She had chosen a spot under a maple tree for the grave, and her father now lay there bedded in the wet grass as Tereza and Glass brandished the spanking new spades. Before she started digging, Glass fumbled in her coat pocket for a cigarette, lit it, and, inhaling deeply, looked down at the lifeless body at her feet.

"Should we undress him?" she asked.

Tereza shook her head. "There was never any question of him wanting to be buried naked."

"Did you ever see him naked?"

"No. And I've no intention of doing so now."

It didn't stop raining as the two women kept thrusting their spades into the soft dark earth and dug a pit, and it took half an hour before they declared themselves satisfied that it was deep enough. From time to time they took a swig from H. Hendriks's bottle of vodka, which Glass had taken away with her. At some point my mother began giggling helplessly.

Dianne and I weren't in the least bit tired. Tereza had sat us down cozily and comfortably on a tall broad stack of wooden logs, under the shelter of a corrugated iron roof. We squatted there like night owls, our eyes having long since adapted to the dark, and when we began to get bored with watching the silhouettes of the two women working away, listening to the sound of their spades breaking up the earth and the stillness of the night, we tried to see if jelly bears melt if held out long enough in the rain.

At last the professor was heaved quite unceremoniously into the pit, a lifeless weight, slumped like a marionette with its strings cut off. Tereza and Glass shoveled earth over the body and then crawled on hands and knees over the grass to weight the earth down with stones. Their long tangled hair hung down over their faces, their clothes stuck to their bodies, and what could be seen of my mother's new underwear, the lacy white edging I had so admired, had meanwhile turned the same color brown as her coat.

Dianne pointed a finger at the freshly dug grave. "It looks as if the earth has had hiccups," she said.

"And now?" Glass had straightened up and, leaning on her spade, looked at Tereza inquiringly. "D'you want me to sing something? 'What I Did for Love' was a high school song we used to—"

"Shut it, Glass," muttered Tereza.

Glass grumbled, "But shouldn't we at least say a prayer?"

"Let's pray for it to stop raining," sniffed Tereza, looking up at the hillside. "I feel quite ill at the thought of the earth being washed away."

"I feel ill as well," Dianne piped up next to me. That was the only warning. She had barely finished speaking when she bent over the edge of the log pile and brought up a flood of half-digested colored gelatin, and—inexplicably to me—that proved the signal for Tereza finally to give way to tears. Her whole body jerked and shook; she sank to her knees and pounded the grass and sticky wet earth with clenched fists, dropping her head to her chin, and bawled. Her mouth opened so wide, I was afraid she would drown in the rain.

"And then, a mere ten hours later, the funeral," Glass continued conversationally. "Not a hint of rain anymore, quite the contrary. Glorious sunshine!"

Everyone ought to be buried in a slight wind and under a sky full of cotton-wool clouds. The cemetery lay at the eastern outskirts of the town. A leaning, weather-beaten chapel stood on the crest of a hill; cascading down the hillside were seven or eight sheer semicircular terraces, interspersed with tall trees dense with foliage, the Little People's God's Acre. Years before the professor had reserved a space beside his wife, who had died young; the plot was five levels down, overlooking the valley and the river. I was delighted to find that even the pewter-tipped roof of Visible could be seen from here. The air was pleasantly warm, and a light breeze wafted the smell of decaying flowers from a nearby compost heap across the cemetery. Here and there fine veils of steam drifted over the ground, where the warmth of the sun met the previous night's rain in the soil, and there were small angels of pale marble patiently standing on some of the gravestones, like dolls waiting to be played with.

I don't remember anything about the funeral service in the chapel—exhausted from the previous night, I fell asleep. But now I was wide awake and was filled with admiration for Tereza. She looked beautiful, in spite of the dark rings under her eyes. She was wearing a deep blue dress and gloves to hide her sore hands, covered in blisters from the night's digging. There were even colleagues from abroad who had insisted on attending, and as an unending line of people in black filed past the grave to pay the professor their last respects and throw some earth on his coffin, Tereza was bravely listening to expressions of sympathy, shaking countless hands, all the while standing dry-eyed and as motionless as a statue.

Glass had red eyes too, though these owed their presence not so much to grief as to excessive vodka consumption and a full-blown cold caught during the night. H. Hendriks was throwing her cross-eyed leers that he must have intended to be enticing but were totally ignored by her. Had he wondered whether Glass might have considered not attending the funeral on account of her immoral reputation, and why she had reconsidered and turned up after all, this was a mystery that remained forever unanswered. Regardless, Hendriks repeatedly phoned Visible in the days that followed and didn't leave Glass alone until she had finally had enough and threatened to spread a story about him and her putting oak coffins to inappropriate erotic use. She had no sympathy for the man. She never felt sorry for any man.

Dianne and I paid careful attention to the way each of those present tipped some damp earth into the grave. Faithful Elsie stayed at the sunlit graveside a long time, longer than anyone else, sniffing, the trowel firmly grasped in her trembling right hand. And for one awful moment it seemed as if Glass had been right in suspecting that Elsie had been in love with the professor, for suddenly the little housekeeper's knees gave way for a second, and it looked as if she was preparing to make a courageous leap. Could have been love or a circulation problem, Glass reflected later, and actually it made no difference; after all, it came to the same thing.

When it came our turn and we stepped up to the graveside, Dianne tapped the vicar on the shoulder, a gaunt, chinless, creepy-looking man who was keeping an eagle eye on the seamless observance of the ritual procedures. "That box down there," said Dianne, "it's only got potatoes in it."

"Yes, of course, dear," replied the vicar sympathetically. He placed a skeletal hand on her shoulder and, looking across at Glass, who must have told her daughter this un-Christian stuff, shot her a glance of boundless, barely disguised fury. Which, however, my mother didn't even notice, as despite her sniffling and sneezing, she was flirting shamelessly across the grave with a handsome, bronzed, dark-haired man with honey-colored eyes, eyes more beautiful than any I have ever seen since. I watched as this man slowly cleared a way for himself through the crowd. Determinedly I grabbed Dianne's hand away from the bony grip of the vicar and instinctively began to march off.

"Trowel!" hissed the vicar.

I let the trowel fall and with Dianne at my side fought my way through a dense forest of black legs. Then we were standing in front of Glass and next to the man, who was by now introducing himself to our mother, stammering in broken English that he was Argentinian—a lecturer in botany, specializing in subpolar mosses and lichens. Glass said something unintelligible in reply. I tugged at his trouser leg. He looked down at me and laughed, a dazzling white laugh, and the next moment I was dangling in the air, swung up by two long, strong arms. I felt as if I was in a swing boat or on a whirling merry-go-round, the blue sky flashing past, the clouds white, the people black; then I found myself sitting on the Argentinian's shoulders.

America, I thought, *America, America . . .*

I was surprised how different the world looked from this height. There was the terraced cemetery, stretching apparently endlessly in its ivy-covered splendor and watched over by all these toy angels. There was Dianne laughing up at me and stretching out her hands to the handsome man from South America—she wanted a go as well, and was going to have one, but not before I was allowed to look around a little longer, and saw Elsie shaking her head in outrage and the gaunt vicar about to lose it altogether; saw Glass with her reddened eyes and Tereza smiling behind her veil; saw the people gathered round the hole in the ground like black grapes clinging to a vine, looking at the Argentinian and at me with disapproval; saw the horizon, a flickering, stripy illusion under the midday sun, and I was the proudest horseman in the world and threw my arms up in silent jubilation. Life was wonderful, death a fabrication.

Then I was lifted off the shoulders and it was Dianne's turn, and all I could do was to gaze in adoration at this beautiful man, touch the fabric of his trousers, cling to his leg, still beside myself with happiness. I wouldn't have had any objections to a lichen specialist as head of the family, but after spending one night at Visible the Argentinian left again, and

I thought sadly of poor, poor Tereza, now with no father either.

"When I was a child," said Tereza as the fruit punch was coming to an end, the sun had set, and the first mosquitoes had arrived, "like every daughter, I guess, I was in love with my father. For a thousand reasons, but above all on account of his eyes. You know, he had these beautiful deep blue eyes. When I walk through his garden today, I look at the delphiniums or the campanula, and I imagine to myself that the pigments that colored his eyes blue for seventy years are somehow floating around in the blooms of these plants."

I looked at Dianne, who nodded and grinned and at that moment was probably thinking the same as me—that somewhere in the red plants, in the rose petals or the dahlias, the pigments of a long-forgotten little jelly bear stuffed into a dry nostril might still continue to shimmer.

That first spring after the funeral Glass visited the cemetery every day, not out of respect for the professor but driven by fear—unfounded, as Tereza continually reassured her—lest the potatoes might have started sprouting, the shoots working their way through the wood of the coffin and the soil around it, and producing the first green shoots on the grave.

"Solanaceae," said Tereza, flapping at a mosquito. "*Solanum.* Just like deadly nightshade—*Atropa belladonna.* To this day some women still use its poison in small doses to enlarge their pupils and make themselves look more attractive."

Dianne tilted her head to one side.

"And taken in bigger doses," continued Tereza drily, "with a bit of luck they can put an end to what their enhanced attractiveness has landed them with."

Dianne, who had been listening attentively, gave a quiet laugh, and I emptied my punch cup and flapped away the mosquitoes with my hands.

Outside broad bands of rain are running down the windows. The streaks they leave behind turn the world beyond into a gray blur. The heating ticks. We're lying naked side by side on sweat-stained sheets on the bed. Nicholas's back and head are dark against the dim light; his right arm forms a straight line against the white background. On the floor beside the bed are two large mugs, both half full of rose hip tea gone cold. All we could find in the kitchen, left behind by summer visitors.

"Full moon," murmurs Nicholas beside me.

"What?"

"Today's full moon. People do crazy things when it's full moon. They steal dead bodies from their graves and bury them in the garden."

"They do crazy things when the sun's shining as well."

He answers so softly, a tired whisper, that I can't make out the words. I watch the condensation forming on the inside of the windows. I'm feeling dizzy and blame it on exhaustion, lack of oxygen, the sticky air wafting down from the ceiling. I assume Nicholas has fallen asleep, but then I feel his hand on my back, warm and light as a feather, feeling its way down one by one over my vertebrae, burning holes in my skin, before it comes to a halt; only then does he fall asleep.

We made love three times. Except that *love* isn't the right word. I turn on my back, stare at the ceiling, and reluctantly admit that Pascal had been right on when she said we'd just screwed; she didn't need to explain that the two can be worlds apart. But I want more, I want more, more than that. At this moment nothing seems more fleeting to me, nothing could fill me with more fear here and now than the body next to me withdrawn into sleep. I want to be the air that Nicholas breathes, to be his blood, his heartbeat, everything without which he can't exist, and I hear Pascal mocking me—I might as well wish for wings of gold.

At some stage I fall asleep. When I wake up the room is in darkness. The rain has stopped, the house is silent. I don't know how long I've been sleeping, but it must be hours. I feel for Nicholas, but there's no one beside me; the sheet is cold.

The day should be over, but it isn't. When I arrive at Visible just before midnight, Glass is waiting for me. She's standing in front of the house. She looks very pale in the moonlight, quite shattered. To my surprise for the first time I notice tiny wrinkles on her face, fine lines that must have found their way there in secret; for the first time I think, *My mother's getting old.* It's as if I've been away traveling for ages.

Glass has no jacket on in spite of the chill in the air after the rain; she's just standing there, far too small compared with the large house, as if she's waiting for a bus. But it's Michael she's waiting for to take her to the hospital. That too is strange; after all, she could drive herself there, and it's quite ridiculous that it doesn't occur to me to ask myself what on earth Glass is doing going to the hospital at this hour, because at this moment all I can think of is that I smell of Nicholas, and I'm still thinking of this as Glass explains to me that we're going to the hospital to fetch Dianne, that I shouldn't worry, she's all right, but there's been trouble.

chapter 11

dianne on the roof

"**Passions, ladies** and gentlemen, passions! Never allow them to take you over! They skew your common sense, so you are no longer in control. And don't talk to me about hormones and the subconscious. Restraint! Control!"

Handel was strutting up and down in front of his desk. With every three or four steps he would come to a halt, bobbing up on tiptoe, and do an about-face like a marionette, casting a glance at his more or less attentive audience as he did so and firing off a fresh salvo of wisdom at us.

"There was once a golden age of reason. The Greek school of Stoics was a small, upright band of courageous souls that saw God's existence in the manifold manifestations in nature and not attached to some cross. The Stoics recognized the passions as the greatest enemy of reason—some of them must already have discovered this within themselves: passion fires a smoke bomb that obscures a clear view of what lies behind things. Burgeoning Christianity recognized the Stoics as supreme rivals and sought to rid themselves of them. They dreamed up the philosophy of driving out pleasure—repression through assimilation—and attempted to rid mankind of passions. Where necessary Christianity achieved this by fire and the sword, but always with passionate zeal—do you see the absurdity of it?

"In the end both value systems remained side by side for a lengthy period. Thus the Stoics succeeded in holding on right up to the late Middle Ages, finally emerging in the Enlightenment. Their principles ultimately collided headlong with the Romantics in one of the greatest and most momentous full frontal confrontations in the history of ideas, didn't they, and so here we are."

Looking around at the dozen or so dropped jaws, I could hardly imagine that there was anyone who still knew exactly where we were or how we had got there, but now Handel was going from the general to the particular.

"An example of the manifold nature of the passions. You are all familiar with our little town hospital, a redbrick structure whose ugliness leaps out at you like some crazed mongrel dog, and whose façade should long since have been refurbished, frightful as it is. . . ."

Handel was absolutely right—the hospital was indeed a

monstrosity. It had nothing in common with the splendid clinic where the alignment of my jug ears had been streamlined by Dr. Eisbert some ten years or more previous.

"Very few of you, however," Handel went on, "will know that this hospital was erected on the foundations of a brewery that formerly stood on the site and fell victim to a great nocturnal fire in the late twenties. Such things do happen and in the usual scheme of things can be subjected to sober scrutiny. But, ladies and gentlemen, was the fire considered to have been due to natural causes at the time? No, it had to have been arson! And arson for the sake of a contemptible insurance claim? Of course not, that would have been too unromantic, and here we have the passionate mix, if you will! Leave aside the characters in the story for the moment—a brewery owner on the verge of bankruptcy and his family, including a pretty, highly sought-after daughter, underpaid workforce, insistent creditors, whatever else—and suddenly the wildest rumors began to go the rounds. There was talk of allegedly unrequited love, jealousy, even of a blood feud! And as if that wasn't enough—"

"The cross," came a voice from somewhere.

Handel gave a small, ironic bow. "Correct, the cross! Whereas the brewery and the adjoining apartment building went up in flames in no time, the brewery owner and his family managed to escape the inferno. And the legend persists that the following day, in the course of clearing up, in among the glowing embers, steaming ashes, and pungent soot a golden crucifix was found that should by rights have melted, indeed vaporized, in the tremendous heat! A cross, moreover, such as the godless home of the brewery owner had never possessed. So: a miracle!"

"What happened to the cross?" someone asked.

"Disappeared! If it ever existed. Naturally it remained in people's minds—call it faith or superstition, as far as I'm concerned it comes to the same. Cross or no cross, the brewery owner and his family leave town, cannot stand the gossip. They disappear without trace in the turmoil of the war—another inglorious, senseless lunacy, that war. Be that as it may: the decision is taken to build a hospital on the charred foundations of the brewery! With the result that today on that spot we have our ugly hospital, where scientists pledged to do battle with cirrhosis of the liver, dilations of the esophagus, jaundice, softening of the brain—in a word, with the consequences of the pleasures of excessive drinking or, depending on one's outlook, of alcoholism as the true outcome of unfulfilled passions."

Presumably I wasn't the only one wondering whether Handel's exposition was solely intended to warn us of the dangers of alcoholism. But he hadn't finished yet.

"I admit," Handel added, stroking his ample stomach in feigned distress, "that it is hard to deny oneself the pleasure principle. After all, everyone wants their little share of fun, don't they? . . . But do not overdo it, ladies and gentlemen, and hone your faculty of reason. Be wary! Otherwise at some stage in your lives you'll find you no longer know where you are."

The idea that anything might happen to Dianne has never disturbed me. At the age when we were still climbing trees, she would never suffer a scratch or a mark. When she used to run along forest trails or on asphalt streets and fall over, she would never cut her knees open or tear her skin or hands. I was actually convinced she could run barefoot over broken glass without getting hurt. Mortality, as opposed to injuries, is unimaginable for children; neither had any meaning for Dianne. The appalling wound she sustained at the Battle of the Big Eye was something that couldn't be measured against a normal yardstick. The resulting peace of mind both she and I had acquired had cost her dear. The blood she had lost in the river had been a sacrifice to both the gods and the Little People in equal measure.

She didn't tell Glass on the phone what had brought her to the hospital at this time of night. The man on night duty at the empty reception area doesn't know much more. Perched in his little glass booth in the corner, lit from below by some light as invisible to me as his hands, he looks as if he is sitting in a trench. His head has retained a few thin strands of hair and looks like a skull with deep dark eye sockets. Glass sweeps toward him like a sailing vessel at full throttle, with Michael and me in her wake.

"Boy attacked by dog," the man informs her tersely. His

voice is incredibly high-pitched and strained, as if he's been inhaling helium. I can't help thinking of brightly colored balloons unleashed into the sky with children shrieking after them.

"What boy?" asks Glass.

"Night sister can tell you more."

Almost imperceptibly the man extends his neck upward, and the eyes in their enormous skull-like sockets climb upward to look at Glass; then he retracts his head once more. At some stage he must have decided to allow his high-pitched voice to be heard as little as possible. I can't think of any other explanation for why he constructs his sentences in such a staccato form, like newspaper headlines, suppressing half the words. I see his arm move. He presses a button, invisible to us, and a soft buzzing can be heard in the corridor. Then his curious gaze moves to me and Michael. I turn away.

Everything looks run-down. There's a battered drinks dispenser, a few hard orange-colored stacking chairs, a low table with a few tattered magazines that have passed through hundreds of hands. The entrance lobby and the corridors leading off it have long since seen better days; plaster is peeling off the pale green painted walls in a number of places, making them look as if they're suffering from cancer or leprosy. The linoleum is polished to a shine but covered in dents and scratches. Ivory-colored lacquer hangs in strips from an unfortunate wheelchair parked half folded in a corner, and the smell of disinfectant and pale, watery tea pervades the atmosphere.

The feeble night lighting achieves one more thing—its bluish light alone would be enough to make everything and everyone throughout the vicinity look ill. Glass was here after her miscarriage.

"I hate hospitals, darling," she whispers in my ear. Michael has gone over to the drinks machine and is waiting for it to spew out coffee.

"I know."

"There are more bacteria floating around here than anywhere else in the whole world!"

Glass has been saying this ever since I can remember. Her nervous, almost intimidated gaze darts here and there. Perhaps I should explain to her that bacteria are not visible to the naked eye.

"Whatever you do, don't let me die in a dump like this, d'you hear me?"

I understand her unease; to some extent I even share it. When I leave Visible, I get the feeling, often for no more than an instant, that I and my immediate surroundings form the opposing poles of the magnetic field. The world repels me. Mostly this feeling is eclipsed by other, stronger impressions. But it is always present, like a static hum that has diminished over the years but is immediately perceptible once you focus on it.

The whisper of crepe soles on linoleum rouses me from my thoughts, and then the night nurse is standing in front of us—not just standing there but rising like a bulwark against the intruders that have come to disturb the sacred, unhealthy calm of the hospital. Below an absurdly small cap is a round, pinkish red face, almost indecently healthy-looking, that the sickly blue light can do nothing to diminish. Her eyes light up briefly enough to reveal that she has recognized Glass. There doesn't seem to be Anyone Out There whom Glass doesn't know. Who doesn't know us.

"You're too late," says the night nurse. "The girls have already left."

I almost expect her voice to be helium-enriched, but it sounds quite normal and pleasantly soft. It strikes me that the woman isn't wearing a badge with her name on it.

"The girls?" asks Glass.

"Your daughter and the other one, who brought the boy here. Kora?"

"Is that Dianne's friend?"

I shrug helplessly. I think back to the blond girl I've seen on two occasions, once at school and then at the bus stop, a blond girl called Kora, who could be Zephyr, the person to whom the letters lying hidden in Dianne's desk were addressed and never posted, or then again maybe not. I know nothing about Dianne. Glass knows even less. Suddenly I feel ashamed on behalf of both of us.

"Where did they go?" Glass points a hand toward the entrance. "Have they gone back home? We came especially by car. . . ."

"They're both at the police station."

"Why the police?" Michael joins in. He's juggling the steaming hot plastic cups of coffee from hand to hand.

"They were reported. By the boy's parents." The night nurse delivers her information in such a matter-of-fact tone, she could be reading the weather report. "The dog attacked him."

She shifts her weight forward and then back again and loudly clears her throat in my direction, possibly because I've been staring at her bosom, still searching in vain for the ID badge that ought to be pinned to her starched blouse informing visitors and patients whom they're dealing with. I don't say a word to this reddish pink woman, have no intention of doing so—let Glass and Michael do the talking—and yet I'm bothered by not knowing her name. I'm so tired, I could fall asleep on the spot.

"Reported?" Glass repeats. "I thought the two of them had brought the boy here. Is coming to someone's assistance the latest form of criminal activity?"

The night nurse shrugs. "I can only tell you what the boy said. He was taking a walk somewhere by the river and saw the girls. They were swimming. At night."

The last words carry a somewhat disapproving implication, pregnant with meaning, an implication that does not escape Glass. "It is now a quarter past twelve," she snaps, "so that this must have happened almost an hour ago! At what time do you consider night begins?"

"When it gets dark," replies the night nurse. "Or at the latest when law-abiding citizens are in bed."

"Oh, yes?" Glass flashes at her. "If every law-abiding citizen is like you, they must all lie there bored to death."

"Well, one way or another, it comes to the same. Not everyone leads such an exciting life as you do."

"Would you kindly explain what you mean by that?"

"No. Perhaps you would be so good as to allow me to do my job. I fully understand your standing up for your daughter, but that's no reason for you to insult me."

Michael has been observing the rapid-fire verbal exchange between the two women, looking from one to the other as if watching a Ping-Pong match. Now he turns to the night sister. "We're sorry, but we are rather shocked, that's all. I hope you can—"

"Never say 'we,' Michael." Glass cuts him short in such a cold and icy tone that I full expect to see the steaming coffee in the plastic cups Michael's holding turn to ice. "I'm not sorry about anything."

Michael simply ignores her and her objection, doesn't even turn to her. If I know my mother, this conduct will be sentenced with the maximum penalty—creeping emotional death by withdrawal of affection—and yet she says nothing more. She looks down at the floor by her feet, as if she's just detected an interesting pattern in the shabby linoleum. Maybe Michael's just been lucky. Glass has been targeting the night sister and is simply too tired for a two-pronged attack.

"What's the boy's name?" Michael asks the night sister.

The woman gives a name I've never heard before. "His parents are still here, in case you want to speak to them."

"Not before I've been to the police and spoken to the girls." Michael reaches into the inside pocket of his jacket. "Be so kind as to give the parents my card."

He is so controlled, so masterful. Glass uses her voice as an instrument in order to bewitch people with her siren songs. Michael reduces people themselves to instruments; he plays them like a keyboard. The smile he grants the night sister is barely perceptible, requesting lenience for Glass, hinting at her confusion, promising a speedy end to the unpleasant, stressful situation. He transforms the night nurse into his accomplice.

"How is the boy?"

The nameless woman smiles back, happy to have found an unexpected ally.

"As well as might be expected in the circumstances." She accepts the business card. "He'll be left with a few scars."

"The face?"

"Not there."

"Good. And the dog belongs to this girl . . . Kora?"

Without so much as a glance at it, she sticks the business card in her breast pocket, the breast pocket from which the wretched ID badge is missing. I've no idea why, ever since my return to Visible followed by the drive to the hospital, I've been standing outside myself in this way, and why of all things this missing name badge is driving me crazy. "No," she says. "The dog belongs to the boy."

Even now Michael still remains calm. His voice doesn't waver, there is no hint of a muscle moving round his mouth, his eyes don't narrow by so much as one iota. "He was attacked by his own dog? In that case, I really can't see any grounds for telling the police."

"Well, you'll have to settle that with the parents. At any rate, the boy claims that one of the girls set the dog on him. He says she talked to the dog." The night nurse has pursed her lips. She now stares straight at Glass. "More than that I don't know."

But I do.

And Glass does too.

She looks at me and whispers, "Damn!"

A perceptible rustling noise comes from down in the glass trench. The Skull has heard every word. He'll construct a brief little story from what he knows, and in his thin high-pitched voice he'll go around telling it, so that everyone hearing it will understand, even if half the words are missing. It never ends, and never will, even if our family has lost the exotic status that stuck to us in the early years, even if by now we are tolerated by the Little People, even accepted by some of them. In such a small town it's impossible to hide. Secrets are all that spread faster here than news. Thanks to the Skull, by tomorrow everyone will know that one of the witch's children has been at work again.

In the summer of the year before the Battle of the Big Eye Dianne familiarized herself with Visible's garden in her own particular way. Some days I would see her lying there motionless on her stomach in the sun, her face in the tall grass as it moved in the wind, her arms stretched out to either side. She lay there as if dead, or as if she was trying to embrace the world. Sometimes shimmering beetles would cling like pearls woven into her black hair, which at that time was long enough to tumble far down her back. Then again, butterflies would land on her sunburnt hands, where they would gently beat their wings open and shut, as if to fan the sleeping girl with cool air.

Dianne's connection with everything that crawled and fluttered around her seemed quite uncanny to me. I happened to be watching once as a bird with ruffled feathers landed on her outstretched hand, and saw his dark eyes return my sister's nonchalant gaze. When Dianne picked flowers, it was as if their blooms stretched out to her and the garden would start whispering; in town scrawny stray cats that gave everyone else a wide berth would rub up to her legs purring, and dogs would beg and whine for her attention. Dianne herself didn't seem surprised by this phenomenon and didn't pay it much attention. She treated animals with indifference, sometimes quite cruelly, sending cats and dogs packing with a hefty kick and a shouted warning that she would tie a tin can to their tails if they didn't leave her alone.

When I told Glass what I had observed, I could see her pupils narrow. She clearly didn't like what I told her, but initially her displeasure fell on me, not Dianne. I thought she considered me a sneak or a liar and was afraid I would spread the story around at school, which wouldn't exactly enhance our dubious popularity. Then it occurred to me she might be afraid that Dianne would turn up one day with a pet, which Glass categorically forbade, being afraid of vermin. But in the days that followed I saw her watching Dianne closely, and if my sister was lying in the garden half awake or half asleep, surrounded by buzzing insects or noisy birds, Glass would immediately wake her roughly and call her in for some time-consuming household chore.

"If you don't want any old mutts jumping up at you," she once blurted out at Dianne roughly, "then give yourself a proper wash. It's your stink that attracts those creatures."

Dianne was unmoved by such remarks. She did whatever Glass asked her to do—cleaned the windows, scrubbed the floors, or washed mountains of dishes—so I soon instinctively began to imagine her in glass slippers, because she seemed like Cinderella to me. But she simply switched off; time went by without there being any change in her relationship with nature.

"What do you do to make animals come to you?" I asked her.

"I don't do anything."

"Well, why do they come, then?"

"To beg. And sometimes they tell stories."

"What kind of stories?"

"About summer and about nighttime."

One evening Dianne disappeared. Glass and I didn't miss her right away; it was only when she didn't turn up for supper and it had long since turned dark outside that we rushed out in alarm into the garden and into the neighboring wood, calling her name. Glass had brought a torch with her. The strong beam of light shook, even when she came to a halt and flashed it around; that was how I realized she was trembling.

Dianne didn't make a point of drawing attention to herself. After we'd already been charging about unsuccessfully for half an hour, a whirring sound coming from above the house made Glass and me look up. My sister was sitting on the roof of Visible, roughly halfway along the ridge, near an enormous chimney, where she stood out plainly, because she was wearing her white summer dress—the same dress she would have to throw away the following year when it got soaked in blood after the Battle of the Big Eye. Like a swarm of lively sparrows, dozens of bats were flocking all around her in a cloud that kept dissolving and reforming. It wasn't till much later that I realized it wasn't Dianne who had attracted the bats, but the mosquitoes and moths buzzing around her.

Glass had already shone the torch upward. The beam of light fanned out so wide across the distance that it scarcely reached Dianne. All the same I imagined I could see my sister's eyes shining.

"How did you get up there?" called Glass.

"Climbed."

It couldn't have been too difficult. On all sides the branches of surrounding trees, solid and as thick as telegraph poles, reached out close to the roof of Visible, and even right over it in parts.

"And what in the devil's name are you doing up there?"

"Nothing."

"Come down this instant. The roof isn't safe."

"No."

Glass gave a short nod, as if she had expected that answer. She switched off the torch and without a word marched back into the house. I presumed she would try to get to Dianne by way of the attic, and wondered whether to run after her or wait out here to see what would happen. I decided to wait. The attic was spooky. There were ghosts up there.

But nothing did happen. I counted the seconds. Five long minutes went by, but Glass didn't reappear, either on the roof or in front of the house. The situation was creepy. I called out Dianne's name but didn't get an answer; she remained silent, a motionless white blob on the ridge of the roof, flickering like an illusion as soon as the black silhouettes of the bats reeled in front of her. I found Glass in the kitchen. She was standing at the stove, where she had put water on to boil for tea, as she did every evening at this time.

"If she thinks she can wear me down, she's got another think coming."

As she spat these words in the air she poured boiling water into the teapot. Then she sat down at the table, lit a cigarette, and disappeared behind a cloud of smoke. She drank the tea trying to appear calm, but her sips were too small and too hurried. I sensed that it was costing her an enormous effort of will to make me believe she was feeling a calm that she wasn't. Quite the contrary—her anger filled the entire kitchen, spreading out from her in concentric circles like rings in water that's had a stone thrown into it. My mouth felt dry, locked tight. I stood in the doorway, a ton weight on my shoulders—the whole of Visible, topped off by Dianne.

"I know what I'm doing" was all Glass said.

Her words may well have been intended as much to reassure herself as me; either way, they filled me with utter dread. Obviously I was the only person who hadn't the faintest idea what was going on here. I just sensed that a battle was being played out—Glass and Dianne were the unequal combatants, our little family and Visible the field of battle. But why were they fighting, and what was the prize? I couldn't really imagine that Glass cared whether Dianne got sniffed at by dogs, or cats rubbed themselves against her, or insects settled on her as if she were a honey pot. There had to be more to it than that.

Glass went to bed without going to look for Dianne or even saying good night to me. I felt I was being unjustly punished and ran outside. Dianne hadn't stirred from the spot; she was still sitting enthroned on the roof ridge, as if she were queen of the bats holding nocturnal court up there. I wondered whether I should climb up to her but didn't know where to start from. The dreaded attic was taboo, so all that was left to me was the route across the tree that Dianne had taken. But it was dark, and I was afraid of falling. An accident would be sure to prompt Glass into some kind of reaction; at the least it would unleash profound remorse, and if I was dead and Dianne as well, then it would serve her right. On the other hand, should I really ally myself to Dianne, who was not only every bit as stubborn as Glass and insisted on some right I knew nothing about, but was also just as self-centered as Glass and simply ignored me and my confusion?

Maybe it was best just to wait. I sat down under one of the trees, closed my eyes, and pressed my hands down on the grass. I pushed my back into the bark of the tree trunk, a silent, watchful, black emptiness inside me. I listened. I wanted to hear what Dianne was hearing, to feel what she felt, but all I heard was the soft whirring of bats' wings beating, the whispering of the wind passing through the branches of the trees, and all I felt was the pounding of my heart. At some point I fell asleep.

I was woken by something tugging at my hand. I opened my eyes. It was still dark, and for an annoying moment I thought I was dreaming because I wasn't in my bed but still in the garden.

"You're covered in spiderwebs," I heard Dianne saying. "You look all silver."

She pulled me to my feet, which were damp and stiff and

seemed barely able to support me, and led me into the house, into our bedroom, where she immediately got undressed and slipped into bed.

"Will you come and sleep in my bed, Phil?"

"Yes."

I got undressed as well and crawled into her bed. She snuggled up to me. Her body was icy. I wrapped myself around her, rubbing her arms and legs with my hands to warm them, then her back, then her bum, chest, stomach. I planted little kisses all over her, as Glass sometimes did after she bathed us because she found the fresh smell of our skin irresistible. My lips burned against Dianne's icy cold skin, which tasted of salty milk.

"Dianne," I whispered. "Why did you do it?"

She snuggled up even closer. I waited. A few seconds later I heard the sound of her regular breathing. A little later, as the gray fingers of dawn crept across the windows and the sound of Dianne's breathing yielded to the first muted twitterings of the dawn chorus, I finally fell asleep.

Glass let us sleep late. When we got up toward midday and pattered into the kitchen, she was on the spot immediately. She made us hot chocolate, which she never normally did, and sandwiches cut into bite-sized pieces—equally unusual—and amused us with lighthearted meaningless chatter. Dianne drank her chocolate and grinned at me triumphantly over the rim of her mug.

And that was that. After this incident I never saw Dianne

surrounded by animals again, neither by insects nor by dogs or cats. Whatever it was that went on that night between her and Glass, it seemed to have destroyed my sister's power over living nature, and Dianne didn't give the impression that it particularly mattered to her or that she missed anything.

Yet a few years later when Kat informed me in a whisper that she had seen Dianne talking to a lizard, and made this her excuse for wanting to keep away from my sister, it gave me a start. Dianne hadn't forgotten. She was only pretending.

"You didn't understand then, did you?" says Glass. She's lit a cigarette, drawing on it far too quickly and too often.

"How could I?" I ask in reply. "I was a child. We were both children! To be honest, I don't understand to this day."

The car glides through the night, the engine a soft spooky sound. It isn't far from the hospital to the police station, but we're stopped twice by red lights, and I wonder why they keep on working at night, as apart from us there's no one about. I see Michael cast a brief glance at Glass before looking at me in the rearview mirror. I shrug.

"There isn't much to understand," Glass explains. "I wasn't bothered by any old animals, creepy-crawly creatures, and all that. It was . . . I don't know—this exaggerated empathy that Dianne had at the time."

"In what way?"

"For heaven's sake, Phil, are you blind?" Glass winds down

the window, flicks the glowing cigarette end out into the night; the wind sweeps through her hair. Then she winds the window up again. "Don't you see what happens to such people? You listen closely to your inner self, or worse still, you listen to everything around you. And this is how you stagger through the world at large, head in the clouds, trusting everything and everyone, and then . . ." She stops for a moment. "And then things start to happen."

"What sort of things?"

Even as I ask the question, I know I'm not going to get an answer. Glass turns her head and looks out of the window.

We drive past a small bunch of rowdy drunks propping each other up. They wave at us. One of them is standing by the wall of a house, supported by one hand, his body bent into an absurd question mark, his trousers hanging round his knees. Urine runs across the pavement. A streetlamp casts a sharp circle of light over part of the man, positively cutting him in half. I shiver.

"Where were you, Phil?" asks Glass.

For days she didn't ask how my date with the boy went, on account of which I had drummed her out of her sleep. I answer her reluctantly.

"With my friend."

"What's his name?"

"Nicholas."

"You haven't told Kat about him yet, have you?"

It's the second time today that I've heard this question. Only when it came from Nicholas as we sat on the bench by the river, I was less tense than now. And also less tired.

"What makes you say that?"

"She called. Wanted to come by and watch some TV movie with you."

"Did you tell her where I was?"

Glass casts a thoughtful glance at me over her shoulder. "I didn't know where you were, darling. I said you were spending the night at Tereza's."

I listen to the comforting purr of the engine. My body is quivering. I want to be with Nicholas.

"What you're doing isn't fair to Kat," says Glass after a while.

"You know what she's like. She gets jealous so easily." To tell her now that I had made up my mind to speak to Kat tomorrow about Nicholas would sound like a cheap excuse, if not an outright lie.

"She's your friend, Phil."

I bend forward a little. "So what? Tereza's your friend, and does that mean you've ever told her about my father?"

From the backseat I can see Glass only in profile, but that's more than I need to sense her total resistance. "Phil, I thought we'd discussed this subject more than enough."

"Discussed? We've never discussed anything! All you've ever said a hundred times over is that there's nothing to discuss."

"And that's the way it is. I consider this discussion terminated."

"Fine, and I consider it postponed! You can't avoid the issue forever."

Naturally she doesn't answer. I sink back in my seat. It's not just Glass but myself that I've driven into a corner. I feel hot, I feel dazed. I wish I could get out of the wretched car. Michael has listened to our short dispute without saying anything. I'm grateful to him that he doesn't try to ease the tension with stupid jokes, but grateful too that he doesn't take sides, for he could easily now touch Glass, take her hand, put an arm round her, and make me feel excluded as a result. But he doesn't do any of this. Goodness knows what he must think of us. Maybe he thinks I'm selfish. It's supposed to be about Dianne, not about me and Number Three. But that has to do with Dianne as well. It's all connected: somewhere in America there's a man I don't know, who has no idea that his daughter gets up to wild midnight antics—who doesn't even know he has a daughter, and who, even if he did know, probably wouldn't give a damn, and if he *had* ever set eyes on her would care equally little whether his daughter was acting up the way she does.

Asshole.

"Your Nicholas," Glass pipes up from the front. "Why don't you bring him along to Visible one day?"

I sit up in surprise. This is something new. Giving in isn't usually her style. I wonder whether it's thanks to Michael that she's turned placatory so quickly, whether he has some magic touch that can tame her temperament and deflect her defensive rages. And I'm too tired to reject her peace overture.

"OK. If he wants to."

I breathe a sigh of relief as we finally arrive and Michael parks the car in front of the police station.

If there's one thing I won't forget about this night, I already know that it's the quality of the light. In the hospital it filled the air like a cold blue fog; here in the office we now enter it torments you and wraps itself around you like a slow-moving stream of yellow water. It's enough to suffocate you.

Wearing one of her dun-colored dresses, Dianne is standing in front of a painfully neat desk. Perched behind it, hunching his back, is a gangling young police officer, in the process of trying to fit a sheet of paper into a manual typewriter. I recognize him instantly. It's Acer, the policeman who turned up at Visible two years ago on account of the graffiti on the office walls of the UFO's gynecologist. He must surely remember us just as well as we do him. Wonderful.

The other girl, Kora, is sitting on a wooden chair. She looks gaunt and tired. I don't know whether it's Dianne's choice or whether Acer has elected to make my sister the spokesman for the two. Neither do I know where on earth Kora's parents have got to, and whether they are likely to turn up here at all. Dianne smiles when she sees us. Acer himself only looks up briefly, signals us to wait, then finishes putting the paper into the typewriter and turns to Dianne.

"What were you doing by the river?"

"But I've already explained."

"I need it again for the report." Acer's gaze is firmly glued to the typewriter. He doesn't notice how beautiful Dianne is, that as she speaks she gently moves her arms up and down and how as she does so her hands slowly flutter as if around a flame.

"We were swimming. Is that against the law?"

"Wasn't it a bit dark for swimming?"

"There's a full moon."

"Were you wearing swimsuits?"

"What for?"

Clack, clickety-clack, clack. One of the typewriter keys sticks each time it's struck. Acer has to pry it up awkwardly with his fingers.

"Do you often meet to do this? Swim at night?"

"Yes."

"When did you notice that you were being watched?"

"We didn't. The guy was crouching in the bushes somewhere jerking off."

"According to you."

"No, I know. His pants were still down when we found him."

"Where was the dog at this time?"

"How should I know? It's his bloody dog." Dianne is still moving her hands about; now it's as if she's winding thread, her fingers fluttering. "The creature was probably just crouching in the reeds, watching his little master wanking."

The blond girl, Kora, sniggers. Acer raises his head; a single glance from him, not angry, not warning, just a glance, is enough to silence the girl. He is no longer the novice I encountered two years ago. At least there is no more of the nervous hiccuping that nearly made him choke in the kitchen at Visible, or maybe it's just a territorial issue, as he's on home ground in his police station.

And Dianne isn't Dianne. I've never seen her like this—so self-assured and potentially aggressive, and certainly not so gross as this in her choice of vocabulary. In her own use of language Glass has never been particularly restrained, but it's the first time I've heard Dianne using coarse language.

"What happened then?" asks Acer.

"We heard growling. Well, a kind of growling . . . At first I thought there was another storm coming—after all, it had been raining during the day. Then there was a cracking sound somewhere in the bushes. We climbed out of the water—"

"At that point you were in the water?"

"Yes."

"Whatever prompted you to go swimming in the river at midnight of all times?"

"Are you going to ask the boy what prompted him to take his dog for a walk at midnight of all times as well?"

"Did you ask him that?"

"Is that relevant?"

Out of the corner of my eye I see that Michael is about to move forward, but Glass holds him back by the sleeve of his jacket. Could be that Acer is trying to confuse Dianne with his strange and repetitive questioning, or it may well be that he's proceeding according to a form of logic known only to him. At any rate, so far Dianne is managing to defend herself perfectly well on her own.

"You get out of the river. Then what happened?"

"The boy began screaming, which was all to the good, otherwise we wouldn't have found him so quickly. By the time we reached him he'd managed to calm the dog down. At any rate, the creature had let go of him by then."

"And he didn't have trousers on?"

"Yes, but they were round his ankles. And there was blood everywhere. It looks quite black in the moonlight." Her hands stop moving, and Dianne looks up. "Did you know that?"

"Yes." Acer looks fixedly at his document. "And then?"

"We dragged him to the hospital. After all, it wasn't far. The stupid mutt cleared off. You ought to find him. Maybe he's acquired a taste for it."

Clickety-clack . . . clickety-clack . . .

"Did the boy say anything to you, speak to you?"

"Would you talk to someone who's just caught you masturbating?"

"No."

"There's your answer, then."

Click.

I wonder whether Dianne is consciously copying Glass, and if so, whether she's doing so only in order to snub her in front of Michael and the policeman, or in order to demonstrate that over the years she's learned to put up a fight in her own defense.

"That's all." Acer pulls the paper out of the machine and pushes it across the desk to Dianne. "Once you've signed here, you can both go."

Kora gets up uncertainly from her chair. Dianne signs her name and without so much as another glance at Acer marches straight toward the door.

"You ought to read it first before signing," Michael advises her as she goes past him.

"Why? To correct the typing mistakes?"

She pushes past us and goes outside, followed by Kora. Glass rubs her forehead, then reaches for the report and skims through it.

"You ought to look after your daughter better," says Acer.

"Really?" I can almost feel Glass beginning to seethe. "Nothing happened to her, did it?"

"But something might well have done. You have neglected your parental responsibility."

"Are you going to report me for that?"

"Why should I?"

With the exception of Michael, we all know why he should. It would be a golden opportunity for him to get his own back for the day when Glass brought him to the point of nearly choking on his own hiccups. There's no better way of expressing his superciliousness than the superbly indifferent way in which he dismisses Glass and the two girls with a wave of his hand. I have to admit reluctantly that his conduct could possibly be a sign not so much of condescension as of fairness. Earlier on she hadn't got anywhere with the night nurse at the hospital, for all her aggressiveness. I'm tired. Perhaps we're all tilting at windmills.

Michael offers Kora a lift home from the police station, but she turns him down. I see her close up for the first time. She's neither pretty nor ugly. She's one of the residents of this vast no-man's-land inhabited by unremarkable-looking people who never get a second look, but what does that amount to? For Dianne she doesn't belong to the Little People, in the same way that I don't consider Kat does. I suddenly feel jealous of this girl. I can't remember the last time I touched Dianne.

In the car I attempt a feeble grin, but Dianne looks straight past me into space. She says nothing all the way home. None of us says anything. I get the feeling my stomach is being filled with lead. The journey home lasts less than five minutes and in that time Glass manages to smoke two cigarettes. Not until we arrive at Visible and get out of the car does she turn to Dianne.

Within seconds the situation escalates.

"OK . . ." Glass takes a deep breath. "Did you or didn't you?"

"Did I what?"

"Set the dog on that boy?"

"What's that supposed to mean, Glass?" Dianne places a hand on her hip, a gesture I never would have associated with her. "What makes you believe a total stranger rather than me?"

"Because I know you."

"If you knew me, you wouldn't ask me those kind of questions."

"How can I possibly know someone who's as spaced out as you are?"

"Spaced out?" Dianne's shoulders stiffen. "What's so spaced out about having girlfriends whose interests aren't in guys or fucking?"

The word catches even me like a hammer blow. Glass was going to have to cave in at the unbridled anger of this accusation. I ask myself how much energy she has left, how long this trial of strength with Dianne can go on.

"This is nothing to do with me," says Michael tersely.

He goes inside the house. Glass watches him go and waits for the light in the entrance hall to go on. Then she turns back to Dianne. "Did I do something wrong?"

"D'you really want an answer?"

"Yes, I bloody well do."

"How long have you got?"

Without waiting for an answer, Dianne flounces off, not into the house but in the direction of the trees rising into the night sky behind the wooden shed.

Glass looks down in resignation, poking around in the gravel with the tip of her shoe. She shakes her head.

"I give up."

"Mum, you weren't really trying." I'm convinced that Dianne hasn't gone far. She may still be nearby, listening, as she does to Glass and her clients. "Why don't you go after—"

"Now listen, Phil!" Her head shoots up. An index finger flashes out at me as if about to drill a hole. "You have absolutely no idea, d'you understand? Just no idea."

"Well, there's a way to change that. I'm here. I'm not running away. What is it? What's gone wrong between you and Dianne?"

"Nothing you can help me with."

"Who says I want to help anyone?" It's doing my head in. "I just want to know once and for all what's up with you two. I've a right to!"

"No, you don't! So do me a favor and keep out of this!"

"Out of what?"

"For God's sake, Phil. If you're so interested, why don't you ask your sister?"

"Because, damn it, she's just as pigheaded as you are!"

"I'm going to bed."

Glass turns away and strides into the house. I feel like running after her, grabbing her, and giving her a good shake. I can't believe we've just been having exactly the same exchange almost down to the last word as I did with Dianne when I came home from Greece three years ago.

"Shit," I whisper.

Clouds race across the night sky, and as they pass near the

moon they change into small bronze-colored ships. I hear a rustling sound. Dianne is standing next to the shed, barely visible between the trees, whose low-hanging boughs and branches embrace her so that she merges with wood and bark and leaves.

"Dianne?"

"Leave me alone, Phil."

"Won't you come inside?"

"In a moment."

"Listen, I—"

"Another time. I feel lousy. I'm tired. Let's talk another time."

I stand and wait, one minute, two, without Dianne making a single move or saying anything. The longer she stays back there among the trees, the more her outline starts to blur before my eyes until at last she's completely dissolved into the darkness. Maybe she doesn't see me anymore either. Maybe she's closed her eyes and is listening to the night, waiting for the clouds to open up again, for the moon to bathe her in its light and wrap her in protective silver.

People do crazy things at the full moon.

Two girls meeting at night by the river, to be alone together and bathe nude, isn't crazy. Nor is a boy slinking after them and secretly watching them, and if he plays with himself a bit as he does so, that isn't crazy either. Crazy is for a night nurse's missing ID badge to throw me into a panic, a bunch of rowdy drunks, or the clattering of a faulty typewriter at one in the morning. Crazy is that Glass, Dianne, and I don't live according to the rules of the Little People, that each of us has reasons to feel like an outsider, that we have more in common with each other than just the blood that flows through our veins, and that even so, we find it impossible to speak to each other.

chapter 12

to

love

Next morning I wait for Kat outside the school. To the east the sun hangs like a golden soap bubble over the hills. It shines as confidently as if its summer strength would last forever, as if autumn hadn't long since spread its burning red hands across the land. The air is as crisp and clear as cold water. It's a good morning to make my confession to Kat.

I see her on the other side of the road. As she catches sight of me, she waves and begins running, regardless of the cars honking furiously, forced to slam on their brakes. I often think the way that other pupils keep her at a respectful distance—the headmaster barrier, as Kat calls it—is a bit much for her, despite assertions to the contrary. It's understandable that she doesn't want to attract any additional penalty points by being seen getting out of the headmaster's car every morning like some diva of humanistic educational ideals.

"One of these days you're going to make the national headlines," she greets me. "This business with Dianne is all over the place!"

I shrug. I've no intention of talking about Dianne, even though I've already guessed it can't be avoided. She wasn't the first to leave her room this morning. When I knocked on the door, I got a snub by way of reply, not too harsh, but unmistakable. As usual after any quarrel, Glass behaved as if nothing had happened. Which may also have been due to the fact that as I came into the kitchen, Michael was patiently initiating her into the mysteries of preparing scrambled eggs without oversalting them.

"Well?" says Kat eagerly.

"Well what?"

"What happened last night?"

"How many versions have you heard?"

"Ranging from three to eleven." She blows her hair away from her forehead. "Well, let's just say two. At any rate, my mother had two phone calls during breakfast alone."

The phone lines must have been buzzing all over the wretched town this morning. Dianne had good reason to decide to stay home at Visible. Gradually the schoolyard fills up, and I hear whispering from all sides. The Skull with the helium-filled voice has done a good job, as expected. My heartfelt wishes are for him to contract some disgusting infectious disease at the hospital. Not just because by spreading a doubtless distorted and sensational version of yesterday's events, he's opened up old wounds again, but because with every second that ticks by with Kat and me discussing this subject, deep holes are being torn in my resolution to tell her about myself and Nicholas. Suddenly the morning seems far less bright than a moment ago.

"Now, come on," Kat insists. "What's behind this story?"

"D'you know, you're really just as much of a sensation seeker as the rest of the pack."

She waves her hands dismissively. "To be honest, Phil, I don't think it so strange that she's supposed to have set the dog on the guy. I still remember that business with the lizard. . . ."

"Kat, I'm sleeping with the Runner."

It certainly isn't the most elegant way to make her shut up. But it's very effective. Kat's mouth snaps shut as if she's just been dealt a left hook. A tiny upright crease appears on her forehead. Two or three heartbeats pass as she stares at me in sheer disbelief.

"You're joking?" she says at last.

"It's not a joke."

"Since when?"

"About a week."

"With Nicholas? With the famous Nicholas?" Kat looks left and right as if expecting help from one of the other pupils or searching for a means of escape. Her eyes flash. "Shit, Phil. You really might have told me before!"

"I didn't want to frighten the horses unnecessarily. I wasn't even sure myself."

That's only half the truth—even less than half, and judging by the expression on Kat's face, she doesn't believe even that much. I let a second go by and take a deep breath. "Apart from that, I was afraid you might think Nicholas would want to take me away from you or something."

"Idiot."

"I'm sorry."

"I hope you get covered in zits, you asshole!" She shoves her hands into the pockets of her jeans, looks down and then up again, and shakes her head. "Man, I need time to take that in!"

At any rate, so far there haven't been any reproaches of betrayal and breaking friendship, tears or outbreaks of jealousy. All the same, I don't feel good. I watch Kat's face working, and jump at the noise of a chestnut landing on the ground like gunfire.

Kat sniffs. "What's he like?"

"D'you expect me to give you an objective opinion?"

"For goodness' sake, stop answering questions with questions!" She jabs a finger into my ribs. "Getting anything out of you is like pulling teeth—after all, you owe me! So go on, tell me. Did he come on to you, or you to him?"

Kat grins at me full on. Perhaps I ought to go down on my knees and beg for forgiveness. I'm sorry that I misjudged her so badly and, worse still, that I painted such a false picture of her to Nicholas. All the same, I start out slowly in order to be on the safe side. I begin with the day when Nicholas spoke to me in the library, but Kat barely lets me finish.

"And you're really in love with each other? Is it wonderful, is it cosmic?" She turns around on the spot, like a windup ballerina on a toy clock. "Will you marry and have children? And which of you will be the mother?"

At that moment I love her for making it so easy for me and accepting my laughter for an answer. And because I don't have to tell her that there's never been any mention of love between Nicholas and me, that up to now he hasn't even kissed me, and how ridiculous that is, since my lips have covered every inch of his body except his lips. Or that I lose certainty under his gaze and his touch rather than gain it, and for that reason I am feeling more and more as if I've got to cross a rope bridge slung across a ravine a mile deep.

As Kat has a keen instinct for sensing when I'm preoccupied with such thoughts, I steer her attention toward something closer at hand. "Nicholas thinks you don't like him."

"Rubbish," she snorts. "After all, I hardly know him."

"That can change. He should be here any minute."

She grins and gives me a punch on the shoulder. "Man, Phil! And you really thought I'd make a scene? What's he like in bed?"

Only Kat can ask two such totally different questions in one breath.

"In bed?"

"Well, on the floor or a stool, for all I care. What's he like?

I mean, you do it together, don't you?" Suddenly she's looking at me with wide-open eyes. "Or maybe not?"

"Of course we do it."

"Well, then," she mumbles, reassured. "And what's it like?"

"Listen, Kat—"

"My God, don't be so coy. After all, I told you everything about me and Thomas!"

"No, you did not. You said that you'd been to bed together exactly once, that it wasn't so bad, and that you'd had a fantastic orgasm."

"So I did," she said soberly. "But not till later. Once I was back on my own again."

Her laughter shoots up into the sky like New Year's Eve fireworks. We walk across the schoolyard slowly, side by side.

"Whatever," I say. "At any rate, there weren't any details, and I didn't want any either, otherwise I would have asked."

"And I would have told you."

"A blow-by-blow account, no doubt. But I don't want to talk about it, OK? Nicholas and I sleep together, it's great, and a lot more besides."

" 'Sleeping together' sounds so technical."

"Everything else sounds vulgar."

"Well, yes, but vulgar is so much more fun." Kat stops abruptly and shakes her head. "I still can't believe it. You and the Runner. What a scandal that could make!"

"Do me a favor, try to like him, OK?" I say quickly. "I'd be really stuck if my best friend rejects my boyfriend."

"Oh, never fear. I'll put on my best smile for him. A bit like . . ."

Kat pulls her face into a grimace baring all thirty-two teeth. When I realize that her leer is directed not at me but over my shoulder, I turn around. My heart misses a beat as I see Nicholas coming toward us.

No sooner is he standing in front of us than Kat lets fly. "I know all about the two of you, all the gory details."

Someone heaves a quiet sigh. It's me.

"And?" asks Nicholas, unfazed.

"Hush money!"

The seconds that follow between the two of them are like a flurry of sparks, groping closer, weighing up, sizing up sympathies, a first assessment of each other's boundaries.

"How much d'you want?" asks Nicholas.

"Fifty thousand."

"In low-denomination used notes?"

"In large, unused scoops. Cherry flavor."

"Could be arranged."

The skirmish is over. Nicholas and Kat are smiling at each other. A lead weight drops from my shoulders.

"Have you been admitted into the circle of Phil's seriously psychopathic family yet?" asks Kat.

Nicholas shakes his head.

"My mother certainly wouldn't object," I break in. "She told me she'd like to get to know you."

Nicholas looks at me skeptically. "Does she know that we . . ."

"Yes."

"And it doesn't matter to her?"

"Nothing's ever mattered to her. She's, well, different from other mothers, I guess."

"Yes, so I've heard." He chews on his lower lip. "Being seen with her apparently doesn't exactly enhance one's reputation."

"Sleeping with Glass doesn't enhance one's reputation, but in your case there's hardly likely to be any danger of that," says Kat drily.

"Are you quite sure?"

"QED."

"What?"

"Quod erat demonstrandum."

"*Erit,* in this case." Nicholas grins and points across the schoolyard without letting Kat out of his sight. "But not here, in front of all these people, surely?"

"Guess you'll have to sort that out with Glass, not me," counters Kat.

"Well, then." For a second he is hesitant. Maybe he's thrown by the gawping from all sides, which he cannot know is aimed not at him but at me, the witch's son with the weird sister. "What d'you say we all go out sometime together? I could ask my father to let me borrow his car."

I'm taken by surprise. "You have a driver's license?"

He nods. I don't like having my nose rubbed in the fact that Nicholas is a year older than me and that he's repeating this school year. His having a license only serves to emphasize that he has the edge in experience over me. At least, that's how I see it.

"Today?"

"No, sometime soon. I'll have to put in some groundwork first. My father doesn't like lending his car."

"Super idea," says Kat. "The knight on the white steed whisks us away from the dreary gray of the little dying town."

"He'll do just that, but first he will wend his way into the dreary gray of this little old school." Nicholas looks at his watch. "I have to go. See you later in Handel's class."

He moves off and mingles with the pupils streaming in through the main entrance. I really wish for once he'd turn back to me, wave, anything.

It's good to know Kat is beside me. She puts an arm around my waist and pulls me close to her. We form a small island in the surging waves of pupils thronging into the building from all sides.

"Does he always just leave you standing like that?"

"Yes."

"No kiss?"

"No."

"Well, in your place, I'd insist. . . ."

Then something strange happens.

Every voice and sound suddenly stops. The air dissolves

into liquid glass that casts waves. Standing beside the bicycle shelter, his face as red as a beetroot, is Thomas, looking straight at Kat and me. He is quivering with pent-up energy, a lighthouse radiating jealousy. And through the open door I catch sight of Wolf inside the building, deathly pale, a thin hand on the banister staircase leading up to the first floor. The crowd of pupils parts around him like the surf around a rock. I stand there paralyzed, as if frozen to the ground.

"Kat?" I whisper.

Someone's walking over my grave. That's how Glass would describe a flash of premonition. I get a different feeling. It's a bit like how my scars itch before a change in the weather. I can't put a finger on it; it's just a presentiment, some age-old instinct. But at that very moment something is set in motion. It's irrevocable and final. I think of a herd of galloping wild animals with trampled grass and dark earth flying up from under their sharp hooves.

"Phil." A voice penetrates the silence. "Phil?"

"Hm?"

"What's the matter?"

"Nothing."

"Well, come on, then. Let's go inside."

Kat releases me from her hug and pulls me after her. Thomas and Wolf have disappeared like ghosts.

A week later, by which time I am no longer counting on Nicholas even remembering, he asks whether Glass would still like to meet him. He says he'll come in the late afternoon, as soon as he's finished training at the running track. I call Glass at her law firm and ask her to be home on time.

Nicholas arrives at Visible shortly before her. We're still both standing in the entrance hall when Glass storms through the door on stiletto heels wearing one of these sober serious secretary suits with a snowy white blouse that she absolutely loathes but that Tereza positively insists on. Right away I see she's brought home a mound of paperwork. I can tell not so much from the briefcase full to bursting point under her arm as from the undecided way she's dithering about—rather like a squirrel faced with a tree full of available holes, trying to make up its mind in which to store its supplies.

"Give me an hour, darlings," she calls over to us, "then I'll make us some tea, OK?"

Darlings. She probably now sees me in this impossible plural of two halves blended into one blissful unit that she herself detests so much. She rushes past us, frantically fumbling in her briefcase as she goes.

"Mum!"

"Hm?"

"I want you to meet Nicholas."

"Oh." Glass comes to an abrupt halt, spins round, and stretches out her free hand to Nicholas. "Good to meet you, Nick. Sorry, my head's in a fog today."

"Please take your time, ma'am."

"How formal you are in this country!" she calls back over her shoulder as she clatters on her way. "Just call me Glass, OK?"

I fill in the time by showing Nicholas round Visible. I would never have believed that anything could impress or surprise him. But now he follows me like a little boy on his first visit to a fairground. Unlike Kat, who swept along with the natural arrogance of a conqueror without looking to left or right on her first visit, Nicholas views Visible with near reverence. He insists on my showing him every single detail. I take him everywhere, allowing him to go into every room from the cellar to the attic, with the exception of my own room and those of Dianne and Glass. While I tell him stuff about the house and its history, Nicholas touches the walls, the wooden beams, the worn banisters, attentively studies the photos of Stella stuck all over the walls, and listens to the creaking of the well-worn floorboards beneath our feet. I'm pleased that he moves so carefully, as if Visible was a sleeping creature, not to be woken. He remains standing for a long time in the library, taking in the tall shelves and their contents, Dianne's herbaries, the few books left behind by Stella and the many by Tereza's father. He spends longest looking at the threadbare red armchair, my story throne.

We go down the rickety staircase behind the library into the garden, where waist-high dry yellow grass bends and waves like seaweed in the cool autumn wind and the sandstone statues stand in imperturbable silence. We look up at the house, at the wide cracks and slits and the noticeably stained plasterwork, which the evergreen ivy scarcely hides.

"Well, what do you think?" I say. "When will the walls cave in on us?"

"Never," replies Nicholas softly. "Houses like this are built to last forever. It's beautiful, Phil!"

Five minutes later we're sitting at the kitchen table, under the imperturbable gaze of Rosella, as Glass battles like a prizefighter trying to pry a couple of tea bags out of the packet. She has changed clothes and is wearing jogging pants and a top that look as if they've been dug up from the props basket of some cheap TV soap. I'm excited and don't know why. I ought not to care what impression Nicholas makes on Glass. Nor for that matter should it make any difference to me what her opinion of Nicholas will be—after all, apart from Michael, she's never asked me my opinion about any of her men.

"How d'you like Visible, Nick?" Glass has at last succeeded in dropping the tea bags into the teapot, and sits down at the table with us.

"Wonderful," says Nicholas. "I'd like to buy it from you on the spot. The garden must be fantastic in summer."

"I gave up the garden long ago. Weeds everywhere, and all kinds of creatures crawling about in it." Glass wrinkles her nose. "Did Phil ever tell you the business with the snake?"

"Mom, please, I—"

"Don't 'Mom' or 'please' me."

The kettle whistles. Glass goes over to the stove. Nicholas grins at me across the kitchen table. I smirk and make a helpless gesture. The prospect of Glass dishing up that old childhood story is horribly embarrassing. Before she even starts, I know she'll exaggerate hugely. She can't help herself.

"I was busy in the garden, pulling up weeds and that sort of stuff. Phil and Dianne were there," she begins as she pours hot water into the teapot. "They were still very small and were getting under my feet with their little plastic spades and rakes and buckets. It was really hard to know where to begin in that jungle, with fallen boughs and broken branches and undergrowth all over the place."

I don't like thinking back to that day. It was at the time when Glass had tried to wrest Visible's garden back from the wilderness, the futile attempt that had ended up with Glass employing Martin—Martin of the towels, Martin with his unending laughter, Martin and his smell of summer and garden soil.

"So there was this tree trunk," Glass continues, sitting down at the table again. "Actually, it was only part of a tree trunk. Maybe it had been cut down for firewood ages ago and then left there—no idea. And I'm thinking, *You can do it, it can't be that heavy,* so I roll it over, intending to move it off the grass."

Nicholas nods.

"And then there was a snake lying under it, coiled up tight.

It was black with these light vertical markings, a—what's it called again, darling?"

"A viper."

"Exactly. Viper. And suddenly"—I shrink as Glass shoots both hands into the air—"it wasn't coiled anymore, it was a rope jerking up in the grass! And it hissed and I screamed. . . ."

"It only darted its tongue, Mom."

Her arms drop, and my objection is swept aside with a single flick of the wrist. Glass begins pouring the tea. "And then it comes shooting toward me, hiss, hiss, and I tell you, Nick, this creature was enormous!"

"Glass!"

"E-normous!"

Even then I had sensed that the snake—more of a feeble relative of the truly venomous American vipers, and whose bite, as I later discovered, was never lethal unless you happen to have a weak heart or poor circulation—must have been far more afraid of us than Glass, Dianne, or I was of it. It was only reacting instinctively as it signaled its readiness to defend itself by opening its jaws wide, and it would probably have cleared off if only we had left it in peace. Apart from that, Glass was wearing rubber boots. Nothing could have happened to her, even if the snake had bitten, but that didn't stop our mother from screaming. It was this terrible scream that made Dianne and me go for it.

"Phil and Dianne hacked it into little pieces," continues

Glass chattily. She blows into her cup. "With their rakes and their spades. They fell on the creature like lunatics. Quite quick about it too. Lots of teeny-weeny pieces. Sugar, Nick?"

Nicholas laughs and passes her his cup. I'm hoping he thinks Glass has a tendency to ironic exaggeration. It would be embarrassing for me if he knew that she meant every single word quite seriously, has set the scene like a second-rate actress from one of her beloved soap operas. She carries on babbling and prattling for half an hour more, smoking cigarette after cigarette, and Nicholas must realize that she's flirting with him outrageously. That at least can be explained later on—it's instinctive with her. Glass flirts with all men and is nearly always successful at it. It is the inexhaustible source of her self-confidence.

It's hardly any surprise that Nicholas tells me, as we go upstairs soon after, how much he likes my mother.

"She's quite young, isn't she?"

"She's thirty-four."

"Then she was a teenager when you were born."

"Yes."

"Where was your father?"

"No idea. I don't know him. He walked out on Glass."

"What a fool."

And no further questions relating to Number Three. Another hurdle overcome. Relieved, I guide Nicholas into my bedroom. He looks round very intently.

Looking at the familiar through someone else's eyes

sharpens your own perception. All of a sudden I feel like a stranger in my own room. It's large and as high-ceilinged as all the other rooms in Visible: two bay windows, no curtains, very light. In one corner is the tiled stove, with a few logs from the last cold spell. On the worn parquet floor is my mattress, covered in gleaming bedlinen (one day Glass discovered a chest in the cellar containing dozens of white sheets). On the floor beside the mattress is a small cheap lamp, the only one to light the room, and next to it my telephone. Books are piled up against the wall. There's a wide rickety bookcase with two whole shelves reserved for the treasured oceanic pieces I've received from Gable over the years. The others are an assembly of dust-covered remnants from my childhood. In among threadbare furry animals and a few toy cars Paleiko peers out like a tired black comma. At some point I brought a worm-eaten old desk up here from Visible's simply inexhaustible cellar and placed it under one of the two bay windows. A sole chair stands in front of it. For someone with few friends, there's no call for providing seating for visitors.

"Where's your gear?"

"In a closet outside in the corridor. I can't bear armoires."

"Really?" Whenever Nicholas smiles, like now, it makes my heart give a leap. "Nor can I."

The white-painted walls are hung with pictures that Gable has brought me and dozens of postcards he's sent me from all over the world. Most of the space is taken up by the two enormous old torn display panels I stole from the cellar at school in the company of Wolf—the pinpricked world map, covered in creases and frayed at the edges, and the map of North America, spattered with spots of brown mold.

Nicholas goes toward the bookshelf, stretches out a determined hand, and takes down one of the two potbellied glass jars with a screw-top lid from the upper shelf. I can't help grinning. "A sweet jar," I explain. "I've got two of them, and Dianne has one."

"Do I get to see her as well?"

"Probably not."

I can't possibly tell him about what went on last week without going into details. Everything is so intractably intertwined. It would take too many explanations, in turn requiring further clarifications, and in spite of every effort to keep the ten or twenty threads of a very long story separate, it might just end up with a highly confusing Gordian knot. In any case I can't just go over Dianne's head.

"She's asleep, I expect. Something stupid happened last week. She's still staying home and doesn't want to see anyone, because—"

Nicholas cuts me short. "I heard about it. Where do these jars come from?"

What I find surprising is not that he's aware of the far-reaching bush telegraph of the Little People but how nonchalantly he dismisses the whole affair, thereby freeing me from the wretchedness of having to unravel it for him.

"From an old man," I reply in relief.

"Grandfather?"

"No. Someone in the town I knew as a child and was very fond of."

Nicholas looks at the glass for a long time, tracing a wavy line over its dusty surface with his index finger. A faraway look of deep concentration appears on his face. It's almost as if he's listening to the inside of the glass, as if his eyes, like his finger, are trying to find the countless images reflected on its surfaces that have long since turned cloudy.

"Tell me about the old man and his glass jars."

"You'd just be bored."

"Oh, QED." Nicholas smiles. "Or maybe not?"

I believe I was terrified by most of the Little People because they just seemed so unreal to me, as intangible as the two-dimensional figures in a black-and-white movie. They all had the same transparency I was later to discover in the figure of Mrs. Hebeler, for example: skin that had life flickering through it without apparently having any hold on them. When I was a child the residents of the town seemed strangely bloodless to me, and with the same unhealthy pallor as the face of Tereza's father bare of makeup and with a badly stitched-up jaw. There were exceptions, of course. Annie Glosser was one of them, but long before Annie—two years, to be precise—there was Mr. Troht.

Mr. Troht ran a gloomy, unsuccessful grocery store that only really brightened up when the door opened with a creaking sound because it had such tiny perpetually filthy windows. An old-fashioned bell would then promptly tinkle. Everything in Mr. Troht's shop seemed utterly old-fashioned, both the contents and the owner. There was a giant cash register, covered with all kinds of embellishments, that looked as if it was made of cast iron, and its drawer would spring open with the terrifying sound of a snapping crocodile jaw. On the wall behind the sales counter was a round clock with a cracked porcelain face and wonderfully ornate metal hour and minute hands that never appeared to move.

Mr. Troht himself had such a tiny head that I could hardly believe it could contain a full-grown brain. I decided that at some point this head must have been bigger, probably in Mr. Troht's incredibly distant youth; with age it then shrank and became as wrinkled as a discarded potato. However, Mr. Troht's eyes were enormous, admittedly only when he decided to open them wide. But that happened only rarely; most of the time they were screwed up into two small slits, for Mr. Troht was extremely shortsighted and wore glasses with lenses as thick as a finger, which he appeared to clean as seldom as the windowpanes of his shop—in effect never. Presumably because he was virtually blind, there was only one single, dim lightbulb, which gave just enough light to reveal itself. In a word, Mr. Troht lived in a world of profound darkness. Yet when the door of the shop opened, the darkness was illuminated. Then light would fall, like a magic beam from a conjurer's wand, onto the object of my longing: a row of potbellied jars, each tapering upward to a narrowing neck with a screw top. They stood right next to the cash register and displayed small, round sweets for sale in all colors of the rainbow. Glass sometimes took Dianne and me to this shop, just to show us the brightly colored sweets or to smell them—it seemed to me they even smelled like a rainbow—but she very rarely bought anything there, because to her regret Mr. Troht didn't stock any ready-prepared foods.

This didn't seem to bother Mr. Troht. He was an institution among the Little People, many of whom still remained loyal to him after the supermarket opened in competition, even if it meant buying just a bit of butter, some cigarettes, or the daily newspaper. Possibly it might have been better for Mr. Troht's takings if he'd sold information instead of groceries, for he knew everyone, just as one and all knew him, and he always had time for a little chat. In view of this it would have been surprising if he'd never heard anything about the American whore and the witch children. But regardless of what he may have heard, it never stopped him from chatting with Glass like an old friend. At the time I could have sworn blind that it was Mr. Troht's sweets that won me over. Today I believe it was his way of treating people without any prejudice.

"Been in several wars," he explained to Glass on more than one occasion in words as dry as if his ancient vocal cords had been wrapped in blotting paper. "You want to have fun? Then have fun! Life's too short to waste it on wars. You give love?

Good for you, I say! Too little of it about, too little love in the world. Everyone should make love, that's my opinion, old Troht's opinion. All these wars, and not enough love." With that the enormous slit eyes rolled in Dianne's and my direction. "And you two little birds, have you done a good deed?"

From time to time the two little birds received one of the alluring sweets. These brightly colored gobstoppers were incredibly hard. Dianne and I were in the first year at school, and in the whole class Mr. Troht's sweets were legendary. Some children maintained he had them made specially in some exotic Asian country—no doubt Mr. Troht's slit eyes behind the lenses were the source of this assumption—and it was said that the sweets didn't break or even get the slightest scratch if hurled with full force against a stone wall or on an asphalt pavement. Which neither Dianne nor I ever did, the sweets being far too precious. What mattered to us was that by reason of their absolutely magical hardness, they lasted for many hours. But we didn't get the sweets for nothing in return—the question whether the little birds had performed a good deed was asked so regularly by Mr. Troht that I soon arrived at the conclusion that for some reason best known to himself he thought we were Scouts or our mother a representative of the Salvation Army. Whereas initially I would reply that I'd caught a grasshopper and then let it go again, I'd picked a bunch of flowers for my mum while out on a walk, I'd stuck some chewing gum under a desk at school but taken it off again immediately—I used to rack my brains before each visit to the shop in order to come up with as attractive a good deed as possible and pocket an accordingly generous reward as a result—Dianne would always give the same answer: "I sat on the toilet to do a wee." And she would thereupon unfairly receive exactly the same number of sweets as me.

And so I realized that Mr. Troht didn't really care what our good deeds were. Shortsighted to the point of blindness as he was, he seemed to ask the questions just in order to hear our voices, for regardless of the answers we would be showered with sweets as he called out, "To love, to love in the world!" I would have loved to sit on his lap, just to listen to him, to hear his voice, as he heard ours. But I never saw Mr. Troht sitting down; he always stood behind the counter. It was as if he had no lower abdomen, or as if it had long since melded into the counter. Mr. Troht must already have been old before Glass came into the world; perhaps he was already old when he himself was born. "In any case, he's by far the dearest old heart this town has ever seen," Glass once said. Dianne and I both agreed that was the greatest compliment we'd ever heard our mother utter about one of Those Out There, even though it didn't seem quite proper, as we thought she'd said *fart* instead of *heart*.

When Mr. Troht wasn't deploring the lack of love in the world, he would talk about the war. "Bee-dven-dyets," he would keep saying, and it wasn't till years later that I realized he meant B-28 bombers. "Those were the worst! Came from

America, like you! Hatch open and all hell let loose, and d'you know, my little birds, we deserved it! We did terrible things in the war and long before, for which no God can ever forgive us! I've had it with all those wars." He shook his wrinkled head slowly. "You're Yanks as well, you little birds, but so what, there's too little love in the world."

As I did with all men, I also stared at Mr. Troht's hands. They were repulsive, ugly—as big as shovels, with thick blue veins that branched out on the back like a river delta. These fingers fished about in the sweet jars like tweezers, because that was the only way Mr. Troht could get through their narrow necks to the contents that Dianne and I were excitedly waiting for. "And what does a polite child say?" he would ask after he had stuffed our greedy little mouths full, after which, prompted by a light tap on the back of our heads from Glass, Dianne and I would thank him politely. My gratitude went so far as to make me consider at length whether to give him a kiss on the cheek sometime, in spite of his ugly hands. The impulse was there every time, but respect for a man who had been in several wars—who might not be able to see me if I came up to him with pursed lips and might even take me for an approaching Bee-dven-dyet, which might be too much for his heart—canceled out the impulse, and so Mr. Troht remained unkissed by me. Which I truly regretted when one day he simply wasn't there any longer. "Where is he?" I asked Glass. I'd wanted to pop into Mr. Troht's shop on the way home from school in the hope of a sweet. But the door was locked.

"He was too old to carry on with his shop. His daughter came to collect him. Mr. Troht lives in an old people's home now."

"Is it far away?"

"Much too far," answered Glass.

"Further than the moon?"

"Nothing's further than the moon, darling."

I was surprised that Mr. Troht had children of his own; he'd never mentioned them. His shop remained closed for a long time. For months on my way home from school I squashed my nose flat against the dirty small windowpanes, behind which there was nothing to be seen apart from a few capped electric cables dangling sadly from the ceiling, the broken clock on the wall, and the emptied shelves slowly disappearing under a layer of dust. The cash register had vanished. In the end the shop was refurbished, the old windows removed and replaced by new, bigger ones. A fashion boutique opened there, and for me the world was the poorer by one form of magic. I wondered what had happened to the glass sweet jars and angrily came to the conclusion that Mr. Troht must have taken them with him to the old people's home, where the colored balls were disappearing in exchange for good deeds between shriveled lips and toothless mouths.

One long, sweetless year later a well-groomed older woman was standing in front of Visible. She introduced herself to

Glass as Miss Troht and told her in a matter-of-fact way that a week before, Mr. Troht had died peacefully in his sleep. Then she handed Glass the three huge glass jars, filled to the top with gobstoppers in all colors of the rainbow.

"Expressly for the children," said Miss Troht, "and I was to tell you that you should continue as before. Do you know what he meant by that?"

Glass nodded.

"'Died peacefully in his sleep' means," she explained when Dianne and I arrived home from school to be surprised by the treasures, "that you shouldn't mourn for Mr. Troht. He came to the end of his road peacefully and with a smile on his lips."

I never heard her speak the same way again after that.

"Is he dead?" asked Dianne.

"Of course he's dead." Glass sniffed.

"And will he be buried?"

"Naturally, sweetheart. Everyone gets buried when they die, you know that. Like Tereza's father." Glass sniffed again and then pointed to the enticing shining glass jars. "But Mr. Troht left you these sweets. They ought to last until you're at least as old as he was." She smacked each of us lightly on the backside. "Well, and now both of you go and write a thank-you letter to his daughter."

Dianne and I nodded obediently, crept into our room with a day's ration of sweets, and wrote old Miss Troht in our best rounded children's handwriting telling her not to be upset, because although her father was gone, he hadn't gone nearly as far as the moon. Apart from which, he was the nicest old fart the town had ever known, with best wishes. Dianne and I thought this incomparably long for a letter—it took us half an hour to cobble the sentences together—and so Miss Troht was spared a postscript saying it would have been all right to send us the sweets by post. We thought it really great that she had taken the time to come all the way to Visible after all the trouble she must have had after her father died, what with the three sacks of potatoes and the burial in her garden.

"I knew him too. And it's true those sweets of his were awesome." Nicholas taps the empty jar. "Have you got any more of them hidden away somewhere?"

"Eaten up, the lot of them. Years ago."

"All those good deeds?" Nicholas turns the sweet jar slowly, very carefully, in his hands, as if it's made of the thinnest crystal. "Troht. I'd forgotten the name. No, actually, my mother wasn't too keen on the shop either. Too dark and stuffy for her."

"So why did she go there then?"

"Just for small things." He places the jar back on the shelf. "Amazing that you remember all these old stories so clearly . . ."

"Everyone has stories like that in their past."

"I don't."

He goes over to one of the windows and opens it wide. Cool

air flows into the room. Leaning on the window seat, Nicholas looks out. I look at his upper body, dark against the dull light, like a painting bordered by the light window frame, black on gray surrounded by white. His back leaning forward slightly, the narrow hips, the two handfuls of tight bottom, the long legs, all of it so perfect, his black hair curling into his neck. I don't know why my heart has chosen to rest on him of all people, has opted for his silence and his irritating reticence. I feel like stretching out my arms to reduce the distance between us. Nicholas could at this moment turn round and leave the room without another word, without even looking at me. He could fall victim to a lightning flash of amnesia, could forget me before his hands even leave the window seat. He could, like Stella in her time, fall out of the window—maybe it's this very window beneath which she lay on the drive with a broken neck and blood dripping from her nose; I've never asked Glass about it. He could—

"Would you like to come and visit me? At my place?" Nicholas turns round to me and crosses the room with long strides. "There's something I want to show you."

"When?"

"Whenever you want."

"Do your parents know about us?"

"No."

He sits down on my mattress, pats the space beside him, and as I sit down next to him he clasps my face with both his hands. He touches me as gently as he touched the glass jar before. I look into his eyes, trying to fathom their blackness, but there is nothing, only the mirror of my blindness, and for the moment that's enough for me.

He kisses me.

chapter 13

a room of his own

The stinging nettles at the foot of the castle tower are so heavy they can hardly stay upright. They prop each other up like the lances of exhausted battle-worn soldiers. Kat and I are wearing coats, as it's turned distinctly cold. The wind tears through our hair and turns our foreheads and cheeks a raw red. October is almost over; it's one of the last chances to go up the castle tower again with a visitor before winter sets in. The past few days have been stormy. The treetops are almost completely bare; as we look down on them, they're like a dark rustling sea of thousands of opened but hole-filled umbrellas. A broad bank of mist rolls over the town from the hills. It makes me think of a huge roll of gray, grainy gift wrap unfurled by some mighty hand to wrap up the toy houses of the town.

"Well, are you going to take it back?"

"What?"

"Saying he's superficial."

Kat gives a sniff. "If he ever decides to talk a bit more about himself, then maybe."

"Blank spots?"

"By the acre, I guess."

I look down on the river, disappearing into misty nothingness in the hollow of the valley below, opaque and sluggish.

"He doesn't let it all hang out like I do."

"Adds to the attraction." Kat reaches into her coat pocket and pulls something out. It's a small red plane made of folded paper. "Have you been to his house yet?"

"No. But he asked whether I'd like to come sometime."

"And?"

"His parents have no idea. I don't feel like putting on an act in front of them."

"Maybe you'll want to put on an act once you've met them."

"They live on Fox Pass." I point to the right, where a large hill rises out of the mist with a single extended row of houses nestling up against it. "I always thought the rich were so decadent that a gay person in the family wouldn't make any waves."

"Money doesn't necessarily breed tolerance."

"Does make it easier to put up with all sorts of pain, though."

"Says who?"

"Says me."

"Oh, yeah?" Kat gives a quiet laugh. "Well, then, I hope I won't ever have to suffer pain. My credit's next to nowhere."

The paper plane whizzes past with an elegant swoop over the tower, sails straight ahead a little way, and then spirals downward, getting ever smaller till its outline is lost among the treetops and the red shape is swallowed up in the mist.

The plots along Fox Pass are much bigger, the houses more imposing, the gardens more luxuriant, and the fences higher than in any other part of town. The unrestricted view they offer across the valley is magnificent. The town is a sea of red roofs, Visible a splodge crowned with tiny pewter ridges at the far end of the world. I've only ever been here once, on a brilliant summer day when I was a little kid exploring his world and its close borders on my bike. If God should ever decide to take up residence among the Little People, I thought at the time, He would choose Fox Pass. In the eyes of the kid I was then, the sky had stretched itself across the land like a canopy of deep blue silk. Today it's gray and sad. I find the house number Nicholas told me on a shuttered garage. To the right a winding stairway of black basalt slabs flanked by nodding shrubs leads upward. There is a mailbox and another box for newspapers.

The house itself, a complex structure of snow-white bricks that drops away at the rear, appears to grow directly out of the hillside. Above it, all the way up to the broad crest of the mountain, there is nothing but wild vegetation and dense thickets of trees. I ask myself how a three-person household can fill this enormous house. Visible is bigger, but we use only a fraction of the rooms. Fearful of discovering possible damage to ceilings, walls, or any of the wiring, Glass hasn't looked into some of the rooms for years.

I ring at the door, and Nicholas answers. Immediately I notice he's wearing a dark blue shirt. He never usually wears shirts, only T-shirts or sweaters. Maybe there's a different dress code up here among the rich. He smiles, steps outside the door, and lets it close behind him. Without stopping to greet me, he grabs me by the arm and pulls me along behind him.

"Come along. This way."

I stumble along after him. Dull grass fans out damply under my footsteps from yesterday's rain. In between islands of shrubs and flower beds, most of which are already covered with mulch and fir branches to protect them from early frost, we go across a carefully tended enormous lawn around the house.

"Where are we going?" I ask.

"To meet my mother."

"And where's your father?"

"Abroad, on business."

"Is he away often?"

"As often as possible. He's away more than he's here."

His mother is very slim. She has black hair, like Nicholas. She wears a figure-hugging lime green dress and a necklace of tiny silver-white beads. She has a preoccupied introverted look. Her mouth opens and closes soundlessly. She's talking to herself and walks up and down as she does so, six steps one way, six steps back, to and fro, forward and back again. Nicholas and I are standing behind a box hedge. I'm staring through an enormous floor-length window at this unhappy automaton behind glass. I don't like to look, because the spectacle upsets me so much. But I can't turn my eyes away.

"This isn't at all what I expected," I whisper.

Nicholas shrugs indifferently. "This is as near as you can approach her safely." He doesn't even bother to lower his voice. "That applies to me as well."

"That sounds really awful."

He doesn't look at me. His gaze is fixed spellbound on the spectacle behind the window. He nods gently in time to his mother's pacings.

"Doesn't your father ever take her along with him when he travels abroad?"

"The two of them hate each other. One of these days they'll kill each other."

"Would that make you feel better?"

Now he throws me a sidelong glance, his forehead furrowed. "You do ask the strangest questions, Phil. Come along, let's move on."

Again I stumble along behind him. Something inside me is gasping for air. I'll never be able to ask him why he detests his parents so much. I'll never get anything other than evasive answers from him. His mother and I may stay on different sides of this window, but Nicholas remains behind glass as far as the two of us are concerned.

We cross the stone slabs set into the grass to go round the house and pass several windows fitted with wrought-iron grilles. Several items of garden furniture made of heavy, weatherproof timber stand on a spacious terrace. A pale marble birdbath filled with water from yesterday's rain waits for visitors. Behind the terrace is a single-story annex—two windows and a door—that may once have housed garden implements. Now it's where Nicholas lives. He takes a key from his trouser pocket, unlocks the door, and steps aside.

"Go ahead."

I don't exactly know what I expected. Posters and photos on the walls, some sort of pennants. Or medals, cups, and badges brought home from innumerable contests, hung up or displayed on shelves for all to see.

Nothing of the sort.

I'm confused, because the room immediately conjures up a feeling of familiarity in me. The walls are white, and yet they don't seem to reflect the light entering both windows. It looks as if the room itself radiates light, fed from some invisible source, projecting it outward. There is one single shelf halfway up the wall. Below the window is a small desk with a flat electric typewriter on it. Heaped up on all sides are notes and papers, jotters, pads, and different colored pencils. In the center of the room, accessible from all sides like the supporting columns of a temple roof, are four showcases divided into open compartments.

And suddenly I know what this room reminds me of—the old school cellar that I explored with Wolf. Suddenly I feel myself catapulted back in time and see the dusty conglomeration of outworn useless and forgotten items—the tattered books and atlases, the glass containers with dissected rats and frogs, the stuffed animals with their gleaming dead button eyes that haunted me in my dreams. Here, despite all the light filling the room and despite the absence of dust and decay, a similar atmosphere prevails. The same aura of oblivion pervades everything. It emanates from the strange objects on the shelf and from the contents of the four glass cabinets.

"This isn't your real room, is it?" I ask Nicholas.

"No, but this is where I stay almost all the time."

"What is it?"

"My museum." He laughs softly, almost embarrassed. "At least, that's what I called it when I started collecting all these things."

"When was that?"

"When I was nine or ten. I sent a lot of stuff back home from boarding school."

Nicholas hasn't shifted from his spot since he ushered me into the room. He has closed the door behind him and follows each of my movements. I crouch in front of one of the cabinets and look at the contents of the compartments, stand up again and inspect the shelf.

"Have your parents ever been in here?"

"They're not interested. My father considers it kids' nonsense, my mother thinks it's strange. I guess she's worried about my mental health." Nicholas pulls a face. "Probably since she's discovered how quickly you can lose it."

"And what do you do with the stuff? D'you look at the things every day, or what? Like someone who collects stamps?"

"I invent stories about them."

"Stories? About things like this?"

An entire shelf is awash with countless buttons, all colors and sizes, that look like seashells washed up on the beach. There's a whole army of keys in all shapes and sizes and metals, dozens of combs made of tortoiseshell, metal, or plastic, their teeth cleaned, partly broken, and an enormous collection of writing instruments—wax crayons, lead pencils, colored pencils, ballpoint pens. I discover at least five fountain pens among them—no cheap varieties such as schoolkids use, but items that were obviously expensive. Two of them are gilded.

Nicholas reaches for one of the gilded pens. "To start with, you ask yourself what sort of person uses a pen like this. Did he buy it himself? Is it a present or maybe an heirloom? Was it stolen? Why is it gold, not silver, and when and where"—he points to a tiny cracked place on the cap—"did the lacquer come away?"

His enthusiasm is muted, perceptible rather than visible. He'd be shattered if I was to laugh now or show I was amused.

Nicholas points to the four cabinets. Each of them has nine compartments. Each compartment contains a single object. Thirty-six compartments, linked to three dozen stories. "But it's only the individual pieces that are really interesting," he explains. "I know that a button possibly has a more exciting story to tell than something like this"—his fingers glide over a faded little blue and red boat, a mini-steamer made of plastic—"but everyday objects are just less attractive."

"Some people would disagree with you about that."

"And you?"

"You don't need to take things so seriously, do you?"

I look at the little plastic boat and ask myself whether Nicholas replaces old objects with new, more interesting ones, and what he then does with the older pieces. Maybe nothing. Maybe he just gets a new showcase. There's an old vinyl record with three small crosses scratched on it. A single ice skate, scratched and covered in rust, with torn red laces. A small simply framed picture of a butterfly with colored iridescent wings. A beautiful pocket watch on a gold chain, without its cover. The face is made of white enamel with the numbers painted in delicate thin brush strokes, and it has just one strangely curling hand pointing to half past twelve. Honey-colored horn-rimmed glasses with one arm secured at some time with a Band-Aid. A small pocketknife fanned out with three different-sized blades and a mother-of-pearl handle. A red scarf of fine, soft wool that looks freshly washed. A heavy silver cigarette lighter with a monogram engraved on the case, half worn away with frequent use and now no longer legible.

I crouch down again. In the bottom compartment of the second cabinet stands a small box made of thick nut-brown wood, about half the size of a shoe box. The hinged lid is covered with tiny mother-of-pearl inlay work.

"Who could lose a box like this?" I say to Nicholas. "It's quite big."

"Don't know."

"Was it empty when you found it, or is there still something inside? Does it have a story?"

"Of course."

My gaze wanders across to the typewriter. "Are the stories in your head, or d'you write them down?"

"I write most of them down."

It's the second time he reveals his uncertainty to me. This consists of nothing more than a barely perceptible narrowing of the eyes and a rapid movement wiping his lightly perspiring hand on his jeans. "You don't think it . . . crazy, do you?"

"Well, there certainly are less exotic hobbies." There are also less weird hobbies. The objects in the showcases make me uneasy, and I don't know why. It's almost as if they're asking—commanding—to be touched. "But how did you hit on the idea?"

"Pity."

"Pity for a few things?"

Nicholas shrugs.

"D'you remember Handel saying the other day than if you want to appreciate the beauty of what man has created, you must look up? That all beauty strives upward, because that way it comes nearest to God?" He grins. "Even if that doesn't apply to Handel in person."

"Sure. Cathedrals, pyramids, and the tops of skyscrapers, the crowns of kings and popes, and all that."

"Well, I thought about it," says Nicholas. "Handel's right. What I find is lost or thrown away. All very far removed from God, if you like. There are psychologists who maintain that you don't lose things unintentionally, or at least not subconsciously. In one way or another everything you see here is a symbol of neglect. Things that are no longer wanted, for whatever reason."

"But you didn't know or think that when you started collecting."

Nicholas shakes his head.

"And what you think up about these things . . ."

"They're just any old stories."

I look at him intently. He can't possibly think I believe him. "Would you show me one?"

"Which one?"

I reach into one of the compartments at random and take out the lovely pocket watch with the missing cover.

"What about this?"

The watch is heavier in my hand than I expected. But it doesn't send out any sparks and doesn't come to life magically between my fingers. It wouldn't have surprised me. Meanwhile I feel like Hansel and Gretel must have felt deep in the dark forest when they realized their trail of bread crumbs had disappeared.

"Does it still work?" I ask Nicholas. "Can you wind it up?"

"That's part of the story. Wait."

He rummages among the papers on the desk, pulls out three sheets of paper, and hands them to me. I sense his eyes on me as I start to read.

SHOWCASE 2
4TH COMPARTMENT FROM TOP
THE WATCHMAKER WHO GOT LOST IN TIME

A watchmaker once lived in a small kingdom. The king had ruled over the land as long as people could remember, and would continue to do so when the world didn't need people anymore. So the regent ordered the watchmaker to make him a watch—a pocket watch, to measure eternity.

So the watchmaker sat at his workbench, where escape wheel, barrel bridge, sweep hand, jewel bearing, and set-hands arbor formed a glittering assembly, and his nimble fingers fitted one piece to another. He worked for days and nights on end without a break, and then the work was complete. The watch shone and ticked, to the satisfaction of the watchmaker. All he had left to do was to fasten a glass cover to the body of the watch, but by now the watchmaker was tired; his eyes closed with exhaustion, and so he fell asleep.

When he woke up, he found himself on a white expanse, flat as a mirror, stretching in all directions as far as the eye could see. And in the way when you're dreaming you know that the place you're in can't possibly exist but you still accept it without question, it didn't bother the watchmaker that it was the enamel face of the watch where he'd ended up. See, there was a watch hand turning toward him already, ticking to its own time and quickly moving on.

And just as every dream conveys its own necessity to the person sleeping, so the watchmaker too knew what his task was—to follow the hand of the watch.

Immediately the watchmaker started out. But hardly had he taken his first steps when he had a terrible fright. For he was finding it absolutely impossible to make out where he was in relation to the watch hand! No matter whether he placed himself in front or behind the watch hand, it was less a matter of physical distance than of chronological definition. When the watch hand was immediately behind the watchmaker, then the watchmaker might be one or more circuits behind it in time, and the watch hand that he was trying to catch up with was actually in front of him. However, if the watchmaker was ahead, then the watch hand would straighten out, knowing it had to catch up, and consequently would place itself behind him.

All this was highly confusing. Also, since the watch

hand was constantly on the move, making it necessary for the watchmaker to either pursue it or run ahead of it, the watchmaker never got a chance to think about the problem, as he was in a constant hurry. And as if to mock him, the watch would even swing round and come toward him, so that the position of the watch hand made no more sense.

So there was nothing that the watchmaker could do but to keep up by rushing around the watch face, sometimes in this direction and then in a circle, just like a terrified rabbit running away from a fox. The spot where the least movement took place, the watchmaker reflected at some point, when he could hardly bear the exhaustion and dizziness any longer, was probably at the center of the watch face, at the axis of the relentlessly rotating hand. Yes, that was where he would set out for right away; there he would be able to rest.

Imagine the watchmaker's surprise when, having reached his target at the axis of the watch hand, he found a small piece of paper, and what was more, with writing on it! There were six words on it, six words in writing so tiny it was hard to imagine where in the world such a thin pen existed that could write that way. Well, could it be that the author of the words had used not a pen but a hair to write with? But then again, did a creature with such fine, thin hair exist?

The watchmaker screwed up his eyes and read.

THAT'S NOT PART OF THE DEAL

But scarcely had he deciphered the last letter and read the six words when the mechanism of the watch stopped working. The hand came to a halt, and the watchmaker felt himself swept away by a fierce wind as the last fraction of the last passing second swallowed him up. No one knows what became of him, for he disappeared forever in time and was never seen again.

And the king waited in vain for his wish to be fulfilled.

Nicholas smiles as I hand him back the sheets of paper, maybe because I still don't manage to get rid of the furrows that have crept over my forehead as I was reading. "It's good," I say hesitantly. "I mean, it's well written, but . . . well, to be honest, I don't understand a word of it."

"There's nothing to understand."

He places the sheets back on the heap of papers stacked high on the desk.

"Are the other stories also so . . ." I'm about to say "complicated" but stop myself, although by now it doesn't really matter. I must have long since seemed like an idiot.

"You hit on the most abstract one of the lot. Most of them are more like fairy tales."

"Sorry if—"

Nicholas stops me with a wave of his hand. With that brief movement the light in the room seems to dim, as if a cloud had passed across the sun. He doesn't take his eyes off me as he slowly unbuttons his shirt. I follow his movements as his hands move downward.

And so the autumn passes. Nicholas keeps his job at the library long after Mrs. Hebeler's holiday is over, having offered to sort out and catalog the library stock two afternoons a week. That's only a part of the time lost to us. Nicholas spends even more time running on the deserted sports field or doing cross-country. I'd love to have more time with him.

One day he drives up to Visible in a red sports car, on loan from his father.

He waves and opens the passenger door for me. I jump in laughing and pull back the top, and Nicholas grins and lights a cigarette, the one and only time I ever see him smoking. We go and pick Kat up from her house, leave the town behind, and race along remote country roads through the late autumn landscape, dissolving in flaming orange and heavenly blue. It's one of those days when the world seems to be taking a last deep warm breath before handing itself over to winter. We cover mile after mile; the air is filled with the rich hum of the engine, the blaring of the radio, and the whirring of the tires on the asphalt. Kat's wearing a brightly colored head scarf that flaps in the wind, and outsized sunglasses. She puts her arms round me and Nicholas in turn from behind, and she's constantly laughing and squealing, especially when Nicholas takes one hand off the steering wheel along a straight stretch of road. In the rearview mirror, or when we turn round to her, we see her crooked incisors, and when we get home, music from a single roaring in our ears, we name the brilliant, drunken, exhausting day the Gap-Tooth Day.

At school, Nicholas takes care not to spend more time with Kat and me than with his many admirers. When the three of us are together, he pays as much attention to Kat as to me. It's as if every time he talks to us, when we laugh or talk about everything under the sun, he makes a hole in an internal punch card that he is constantly checking in order to be fair to each of us. Nicholas and Kat get on famously. It's only when we are alone together that he touches me. Meanwhile it's become a trademark of hers to put her arms around him and kiss him in front of everybody.

Tereza and Pascal are going off to Holland together for a few weeks. Tereza didn't take time for a summer vacation, and now she's making up for it. She sends us a postcard from the coast, where she and Pascal are hiding out in a comfortable little guesthouse. Between autumn and winter they go for long walks along deserted beaches, defying ice-cold rain, storms, and coastal fog. *The food is good and Pascal is getting fat,* writes Tereza. *I'm going to frame her and sell her as a three-dimensional multimedia artwork à la Rubens.*

Michael stays at Visible so often now that I hardly notice, whereas I get almost nervous when he's not there. The lawsuit he was involved in has been settled in his favor. Michael's always saying how impressed he is with Visible's architecture—if it was his house, he wouldn't change it by one iota. He goes on long exploratory walks and discovers nooks and crannies that even I didn't know about, and gets as excited as a little boy when Glass surprises him one day with the design plans for the house, which she's found in the cellar in one of the millions of cardboard boxes stacked away down there. I find it barely comprehensible how much Michael loves Visible, and wait with curiosity for the winter, when Glass will make him chop wood by the ton in order to heat the drafty rooms. I like his calm, reflective manner. He is passionately fond of chess and tries to get me interested. I like the look of the hand-carved, stern chess figures, the symmetrical contrast of black and white, but the game itself is beyond me. I'm incapable of planning more than two moves ahead, and we soon give up the effort, more to Michael's regret than mine.

Glass blooms visibly under the strange magic that I still believe Michael works on her. It is a calm bloom that glows, perceptible just by looking at her out of the corner of your eye or without focusing sharply. Sometimes she moves through the house humming softly and unexpectedly breaks into the occasional little dance step. Then again, on one of the rare evenings she now passes without Michael she'll sit wrapped in a blanket on the far too cold veranda and smile for no apparent reason at the world at large. The nervous energy given off in restlessness or frenetic babbling that has been part of her for as long as I can remember is now dropping away day by day. Glass has less and less time for her clients, whom I can never think of without seeing Gable's horrific scar before me. Poor Rosella with her missing ear and crooked grin is getting covered in an ever thicker layer of dust. The rainy day for which Glass was saving for years seems to have retreated into the remote distance.

As for Dianne, I keep on indicating I'm prepared to talk to her if she feels like it. She doesn't make a move. I console myself with the thought that she doesn't show any interest in my concerns either. On one occasion I catch sight of her when the door of her room happens to be open. She's sitting bolt upright on her bed and waving her hands around, just as she was doing that night at the police station, when there was a full moon. Then it made me think of flames dancing around each other. Now it looks as if the hands and fingers are spinning an invisible cocoon around Dianne's body, terribly slowly, like an animal that has already lowered its metabolic rate in preparation for hibernation.

Dianne still sets out in all weather on her endless walks to God knows where, and also goes on meeting Kora. At school I see her outside during break laughing with other girls; maybe that's down to Kora's influence. Maybe Dianne still takes the bus somewhere from time to time, and maybe she carries on writing letters to Zephyr, a name that fades in my mind, as it does on the letters addressed to him, and maybe that's all she needs to be happy.

There is still no communication between her and Glass. When the two of them happen to meet, they restrict themselves to exchanging polite trivial noncommittal remarks. Neither of them seems prepared to give way by a fraction of an inch. It's a situation I've been aware of for years. Now I'm beginning to get used to it.

And then there's Nicholas, Nicholas over and over . . . When we're alone together in Tereza's father's house or at Visible—never again in his museum—I tell him about Stella and Glass and Dianne, about Tereza and Pascal, prompting him to observe at some stage that my life was defined by women to such an extent, things could end badly; a masculine counterweight was missing. What am I supposed to answer? That essentially he's right and I've always missed having a father, that I still do, because I feel that Michael may have appeared in time for Glass but too late for Dianne and me? That on the other hand I can understand what Tereza once maintained, namely, that men are useless because they never grow out of being children, that out of fear of being hurt and a deep-seated fear of life they prematurely enchain their hearts, and that as a result of this self-imposed imprisonment they pass on their insecurity from generation to generation? Insecurity that makes them so restless that at decisive moments in the lives of their wives or children they are anyway never at home but somewhere out there, convinced they are obliged to conquer worlds.

A vague feeling that I may hurt Nicholas makes me keep all

this to myself. Instead I unload further, talk about Kat and Gable, mendacious doctors, and knife-wielding children with no eyelashes, about divinely inspired nurses and transparent women librarians. I tell him about UFOs making their ghostly appearance on silver bromide nights, women mincing along in red patent leather shoes being swallowed up by holes in the road, and boys who revere their dead mothers' curls as icons.

"I used to believe that fate had it in for me because it regularly took away all the people I came across who meant something to me. Annie, Wolf, Mr. Troht . . ."

"Surely there were plenty of others?"

"Yes, but they might as well have been dead."

"No, I mean Glass and Dianne, Tereza, Kat . . ."

"They don't count. They're part of the family. More or less."

"Your family can also abandon you."

"No. No, family is forever."

The more I reveal myself to him, the more I put myself at his mercy. The less he divulges about himself, the more closely he binds me to him. For the first time I believe I understand the simple yet complex dynamic behind Kat's explorations of her famous blank spots chart. For the first time I understand that it's fear that sends people on voyages of discovery. If I don't wish to lose Nicholas, I have to discover him. The only secret he's entrusted me with is his museum of lost things. I ponder over what he was trying to show me, I rack my brains over the wretched clockmaker and eternity, but I don't get it. Nicholas has handed me a key that I don't know how to use. And to ask him for more stories would only add to my confusion.

When we meet we sleep together.

His kisses are still rare, gifts offered hesitantly.

I never ask him if he loves me.

"There's post for you," Dianne greets me when I get home. She's sitting at the kitchen table peeling an apple, intently absorbed on removing the peel in one piece. "A small packet."

It's late afternoon. Heavy dark gray presses against the windows from outside. I accompanied Nicholas to the library, stayed for a while browsing among a few shelves under Mrs. Hebeler's gaze—ever watchful but now turned soft as butter—and then left. When Nicholas works he does so oblivious to his surroundings and with the same total concentration that I've observed when he runs.

"A small packet? Where is it?"

"On the stairs in the hall."

"Is it from Gable?"

"There's no sender. But the stamps are just ordinary."

Gable signed on in the summer with a freighter carrying spices through the Indian Ocean. In his last letter he wrote that he would try to spend the end of the year with us. Christmas is only a few weeks off; he'll have to hurry if he's actually going to come.

"You've got a boyfriend, haven't you?" says Dianne without looking up from the increasingly long apple skin.

I've just been taking some milk from the fridge and shut the door more heftily than necessary. "Who says?"

"Kora heard. There were some guys talking about it during recess."

I don't know why this piece of news immediately makes me think of Wolf—maybe because I'm convinced that he sees more than other people do. But whom would Wolf talk to? At any rate, Nicholas will be less than pleased if he hears about it.

I gulp some milk straight from the carton. "Did they mention any names apart from mine?"

"No. Would that be so terrible?"

"It's nobody's business."

"Not even mine?"

Dianne sounds quite composed. All the same, I get nervous. I wish she'd at least look up once and pay less attention to that stupid piece of fruit and more to me. Perhaps I ought to tell her that it's idiotic to peel the apple. Most of the vitamins are in the skin or directly under it.

"You know, you've been avoiding me for weeks and months, Dianne. To be honest, I didn't get the feeling my life particularly interested you."

No reply.

"And why should I have told you at all? After all, you didn't tell me anything about Kora, even though you've been meeting at night down by the river all through the summer."

She doesn't even ask me how I know. She just shakes her head. The apple peel falls onto the table. Now she begins to divide the apple into eight equal segments on the plate. It looks almost as if it falls apart by itself without Dianne having to exert pressure on the knife.

"I've been thinking about a lot of things, Phil."

"Oh?" I take another sip of milk then put the carton back in the fridge. "About you and Glass too?"

"Naturally."

"And?"

"And I've come to the conclusion that you simply have to accept things that can't be changed."

"You've chosen a pretty easy option."

"You think so? It strikes me as bloody hard." She holds out a piece of apple toward me. "Want some?"

"Thanks."

"Thank you yes or thank you no?"

I sit down on the edge of the table, accept the piece of apple, and take a bite. Dianne hasn't bothered to remove the core. "Can't we talk together properly sometime?"

"That's what we're doing."

"Longer. And without ending up by arguing or you quitting halfway through."

"OK. But not yet."

"Then when?"

"Soon. When I've finished thinking."

Dianne arranges the seven remaining apple sections into a star shape on the plate. "Are you happy with your boyfriend?"

"Well . . ." I chew on what's left of the piece of apple. "I ought to be. But it isn't that simple. He shuts me out. I'm not certain what he wants from me." More as a way of diverting her from Nicholas than out of curiosity, I try a shot in the dark. "And you, are you happy with Kora?"

"I'm not in love with her, if that's what you're asking," Dianne replies quietly. "I'm not like Tereza. Kora is just a friend, that's all. But yes, I'm pleased we're friends. What's your boyfriend's name?"

"Nicholas. And I'd be grateful if you keep that to yourself, even as far as Kora's concerned."

"Don't worry." Dianne gets up, takes the plate with the apple pieces and moves to the door. "Maybe the packet is from him." And with that she disappears into the hall—glides away, with her own special, strangely floating, completely silent walk.

I remove the apple skin from the table, throw it away, and go into the entrance hall to fetch my packet. At most Dianne has had a ten-second start, but she's already out of sight.

She was right, the packet does come from Nicholas. I recognize the handwriting instantly. I have to grin. He didn't say a word about it, didn't give the slightest indication there was a surprise waiting for me at Visible. I shake the packet; something rattles. I take it to the library, sit down on the story throne, and hold it in my hands for a while before opening it. On top, a sheet of paper typewritten on both sides. Underneath, a smaller sealed envelope firm to the touch, probably a card. Finally the heaviest and biggest part in the packet is something packed in wrapping paper, about the size of a lunch box. When I give it a slight shake it rattles. It makes me think of a nest of Russian dolls. I stick to the order in which the contents were packed, and first of all I read the typewritten text.

SHOWCASE 1
BOTTOM COMPARTMENT
THE THREE SISTERS

There were three sisters, all very different, who lived together in a very old house. The house was surrounded by a dark garden, and the garden was surrounded by a very high fence. Beyond the fence there was a war going on, and no one knew when it had begun or whether it would ever come to an end.

Although the sisters were so different, they all agreed with each other, and none of the three could leave the others on their own. If the youngest sighed, then the middle and oldest did the same; if the oldest closed her eyes, then the middle and youngest would also fall asleep.

Now, there came a time when the middle sister wanted to see the world. Every day she would go up to the attic and look longingly out of one of the windows in the roof, on to the world beyond the fence and on to the life on the far side.

"That's where I want to go," she said to her sisters.

"Then go," said the youngest.

"No, stay," said the oldest.

There was a loom in the attic. The middle sister sat down at it, clamped her mouth shut, and, because she couldn't make up her mind whether to go or to stay, started work on a carpet. Thread by thread and color by color she wove and worked; tirelessly the shuttle shot through her hands, and the carpet grew bigger and bigger and more and more impressive, for all the wishes and desires of the middle sister worked their way into the carpet, without a word crossing her lips.

The youngest sister whispered and tempted her: "Go out, take what you're longing for! What are you weaving this carpet for when everything you long for is waiting for you outside the door and behind the fence?"

But the oldest sister said the opposite and commanded her: "Stay here, for here you are safe and sure, but out there death awaits you. Can't you see the quagmire overrunning the garden, the deadly spears and lances waiting for you beyond the garden?"

Thus they sat in the attic, disagreeing about what to do, and the air was filled with encouraging whispers and threatening mumbles and the silence of the weaving sister.

Time passed. Days turned to nights and nights to days, and summer came to the land and gave way to autumn. And still the oldest and youngest sisters talked at the weaving sister, and as they did so they lost vitality and became weaker and weaker, and were not aware of it.

But as every kind of weaving and working eventually comes to an end, so the carpet was finally finished and glowed so brightly and beautifully, brighter than the sun, more glowing than the moon and more sparkling than the stars. Then the middle sister looked at her raw hands and what she had achieved with them, and finally she opened her mouth and said: "Now it's good."

One single tear escaped her eye and fell to the ground. And where it landed it covered the border of the carpet, and as it did so the three sisters saw the carpet go up in flames, set alight by this one single tear.

Soon there was a blazing fire. It spread rapidly, for it was a magical fire: it swallowed up the house from top to bottom, and its flames were not hot but cold. It seized the three dying sisters and transformed them into blazing silent torches. Nothing remained of them but three little heaps of icy ashes. A wind came up, tearing and sweeping into the ashes until they merged into one and were swept away. But the flames of the fire continued to flicker—they burned and blazed, they darted and searched and devoured. For three whole days they were visible from near and far; orange and red, they burst through the roof and out of the windows.

And outside it snowed, for winter had taken hold of the land.

I look at the box covered in gift wrap without touching it. Then I reach out for the envelope. It contains a plain white postcard.

Phil
This belongs to you. I did see you that day in winter.
Nicholas

Perhaps I'll never really understand him. I tear the wrapping paper and find I'm holding the little box of nut-brown wood in my hands. I open the ivory-inlaid lid and tip it upside down.

It's gleaming white, flaming red; it snows, it burns.

It's my snow globe.

chapter 14

his little friend

Handel is adept at shamelessly exploiting his popularity. He's the only teacher who categorically refuses to wipe his chalk scribbles off the board at the end of the lesson. He prefers to make one of his eternally grateful students responsible for this task—today it's my turn.

The damp sponge swishes across the board, erasing formulae and symbols that look more like Egyptian hieroglyphs to me than mathematical statements. I'm alone in the classroom. I don't turn round at the sound of footsteps behind me. I just stop cleaning the board and smile, thinking that Kat or Nicholas, waiting for me in the schoolyard, has got impatient and come back.

The profile entering my field of vision from the side wipes

the smile off my face, as it belongs to neither of them. It belongs to Thomas. He stares at me for some time without saying a word. The devil knows what actor in some second-rate B movie he's impersonating. I wait a while, then take a deep breath.

"What d'you want?"

His index finger moves across the board and leaves a straight line on the dark green surface, which hasn't yet dried. The shining trace is like an enlarged version of the razor-sharp line of his compressed lips.

"Keep your hands off Katja."

I could pretend to be surprised, but I'm no good at acting. I'd be bound to give a pathetic performance, which Thomas would just take as confirmation of his jealousy. The little I know about him comes from Kat. He's not stupid, but he's no genius either. He's one of those people who once they've got their teeth into an idea don't like to drop it, even if they've long since realized they're actually on the wrong track.

"I've never touched Kat," I say over my shoulder, and start cleaning the board again. "But you could try hacking off all my fingers and you still wouldn't believe it."

"Too right."

"We're friends. Ever heard that word? We've known each other since we were five. That's it. Now leave me alone, OK?"

"Forget that."

"You bet I will." I put the sponge down. "That's why I'm off now."

"You'll stay here and hear me out."

"The hell I will." I take a step toward him. He doesn't retreat an inch. "You've got the wrong address, can't you understand? If you want something from Kat, then do me a favor and go to her."

"She treats me like dirt."

"Maybe, but that's not my problem and has nothing to do with me either."

"It's got everything to do with you."

I look into his glassy eyes. I know that look, and I imagine I know the pain that lies behind it. There were men who'd lost their souls at Visible and for weeks on end never missed an opportunity to try to get them back. They wrote letters pages long. They telephoned day and night. They begged and threatened. They lay in wait for Glass when she left the house in the morning and when she came back from work in the evening. Some of them screamed and raged, others wept; most of them just looked like wounded animals. They pursued my mother like hunters without realizing that it was they who were the prey, long since bagged and forgotten; maybe they couldn't understand because their mortally wounded hearts were still beating and felt like raw flesh. I saw a few of these men. They all had this look.

"I don't know what she sees in a wimp like you," says Thomas roughly. "But I don't want to see the two of you together again."

"You don't have a choice."

He doesn't move. He's rehearsed this speech a dozen, a hundred times, and he won't stop until he's got through the last sentence and the last word.

"If you ever dare to go near her again . . ."

The pathetic threat remains unspoken. He's not going to kill me, but he will fight me. I can take it, in terms of both height and strength, but that isn't important now. Two things become clear. Regardless of who wins if we do fight, Thomas will never believe me. And the Battle of the Big Eye is finally consigned to history. There's no heroic aura left to protect me, because it's never again going to be children who will threaten me. Those children have meanwhile grown up and now belong to the Little People. Bow and arrow are no longer an adequate weapon to face them with.

"There's nothing I want from Kat." I take another step toward Thomas. "Or any woman."

I place my hands on his shoulders and sense pounding, trembling heat. We're practically the same height; I only need to raise my head very slightly. Thomas doesn't resist. His lips are firm and warm. I can hear how unevenly time races; it has taken on the drumming pace of my heartbeat. Thomas doesn't move. I persist, push myself closer against him, open his lips with my tongue, thrust against his teeth, and taste them. Hunger shoots through my body like a torrent. I could drown in Thomas, I could wound him. For the flash of a second he thrusts his lower body toward me; maybe it's just an instinctive movement, although I can feel . . .

Then the moment passes.

"D'you understand?" I whisper.

Thomas pushes me away violently. I fall backward and bang my left hip against the teacher's desk. Pain flashes through me.

"You'll pay for this, you filthy swine!"

He stomps off furiously, knocking his shoulder against the door frame as he leaves the room. It's as if all the colors from the pictures and posters hanging on the walls drain away, flow together in pursuit of him. All that remains is black and white. Pain from my left hip travels in all directions in breaking waves. I wipe the back of my hand across my mouth and close my eyes. It should have been an end, but it feels like a beginning.

As I open my eyes Wolf is standing in front of me. My heart takes a painful leap. It feels as if it's beating backward, just this once. Just to remind me how vulnerable I am, that it can beat differently, that it can stop beating if it decides to do so. I can handle Thomas. But I'm afraid of Wolf.

His face has become more striking in the passing years, the mouth more defined and the lips fuller than I remember. But otherwise nothing has changed. The wild straw-blond hair that I would so like to have stroked back then still doesn't seem to be familiar with a brush to tame its beauty. The gray-blue eyes still lack any life or expression—they gleam neither cold nor warm; they hide everything yet don't hold anything back. Those eyes that I saw weeping only once are nothing more than a combination of eyeball and pupil, iris and retina. That's what makes them so sinister. Wolf has seen everything with these eyes.

"I saw it all."

Oh, yes, that he did. He saw everything, everything. The sentence echoes in my ears. Wolf uttered it as a child would, uncertain, defiant, threateningly. Any minute now he'll add, *And I'm going to tell everything.* And suddenly I feel laughter surging up inside, because I'm suddenly struck by the thought that I'm later going to have to repeat this performance over and over again. That all the boys in the school will line up in front of me to be kissed and be convinced, that the worst imaginable horror is no fantasy, no illusion, wafting up before them during wakeful overheated sorrowful nights, that they'll use me as litmus paper in order to establish which way they're inclined when their saliva has mingled with mine and discover whether they too are misfits.

"Did he hurt you, Phil?"

"Yes."

Wolf raises one hand and strokes my chin. His breath smells of peppermint. There's nothing to release me from his vacant gaze. No amount of violence from Thomas could have been worse than this cool, gentle touch.

"Good," says Wolf, smiling. "That's good."

Kat has always been an enthusiastic advocate of the view that you don't need any excuse for a celebration. Saturday evening finds her and Nicholas standing arm in arm on the doorstep of Visible. Kat has allowed three bulbous bottles of champagne to accompany her from her parents' well-appointed cellar, one for each of us.

"Cold in here," Nicholas remarks in the entrance hall. His fingers slice through the small cloud of condensation his breath has left behind.

"I know. You'd have to cut down half the forest to heat this place properly."

We've got Visible to ourselves. Glass has permitted Michael to talk her into spending the whole weekend at his place. For her, who's never been away from Visible longer than one night at a time, preferring to have her men come to her, this is very much a first. For Michael, I can only hope that he knows what he's let himself in for. Dianne bade me a very friendly goodbye before going off to spend the night with Kora. She was in such a good mood and so relaxed when she went that I toyed with the idea of calling out after her that it had turned too cold to swim in the river.

Nicholas hands me a plastic bag. "Here."

"What's that?"

"Tea lights." He laughs, brushing the hair back from his forehead with one hand. "A hundred."

"Wow!"

"Where are the champagne flutes?" asks Kat.

"Very funny."

We take former mustard jars from the kitchen and bring

them upstairs to my room. There we put the tea lights inside them and place them along the window ledges, distribute them along the walls, and group them in small islands on the parquet floor. They have the pleasant bonus effect of heating the room and so relieving me of the task of having to bother with the erratic old-fashioned tiled stove. November is hurrying toward its melancholy misty end; at night the temperature drops to below freezing. In the morning my first glance on waking is directed to the ice flowers blooming on the inside of my windows.

In the news an early freezing winter is predicted.

Kat claps her hands in delight like a little child once all the tea lights are lit. The flickering of the candles is reflected in the windows, and the room resembles a shimmering, waving sea of light. Nicholas looks about him inquiringly.

"Don't you ever listen to music here?"

"Only the radio, in the kitchen during breakfast."

"I could have brought my violin." Kat giggles.

"You play the violin?" asks Nicholas respectfully. "I'm impressed. You must know the Brahms second violin concerto. It's . . ."

I run downstairs to the kitchen and fetch the radio–cassette recorder. I don't waste time switching on the stair light; on the way back I simply follow the sound of Kat's laughter. So I only just miss tripping on the stairs. If I stopped for a moment, I'd probably start to think why I'm rushing. And needlessly rushing at that, because my thoughts catch up with me.

I'm jealous of Kat.

There's no point in denying it. I don't like the intimacy that's grown up between her and Nicholas, plainly evident in the way the two of them were standing arm in arm in front of the door. I don't like the way Kat's laughing either, for the simple reason that Nicholas responds so uninhibitedly. It crosses my mind how often she's been laughing recently when the three of us have been together. I dismiss the thought as stupid, only to have it wash over me even more strongly as I enter my room and see the two of them sitting side by side on the mattress. Kat is saying something about one of our classmates—no doubt she's been prying again in her father's confidential files—and Nicholas is listening. Not just listening, but watching her with this fine, barely perceptible mixture of reserve, amusement, and the tiniest element of arrogance. I ask myself whether Kat has also told him about his own file.

"The radio," I say feebly. "D'you want me to find a classical station or maybe—"

"Plug it in and turn it on!" commands Kat, and I can't for the life of me see what's so funny, making them roll over the mattress with laughter.

Then the first cork pops and thunders against the ceiling, foam and bubbles rush out of the bottle, our glasses clink. All my suspicions vanish under the influence of the champagne. We empty the first bottle in praise of Kat's father, the noble unwitting donor, the second in praise of us all, life, and the inventor of the minute tingling bubbles in the champagne.

With the third bottle I'm filled with happiness, and a strange numb feeling sinks into my lips and gradually spreads over the whole of my face, then travels downward from my neck, spreading through my arms into my hands, which suddenly don't know what they're doing anymore.

"Winter holidays," says Kat at one point. "This time you'll never guess—the shitty old Aps!"

"The Alps!"

The radio plays, we sing along at the top of our voices with the latest summer hits, and sadly with the ones each of us has known forever and ever without knowing where or when we first heard them. At some point it switches over to commercials.

"You know, I've been thinking," murmurs Kat, clutching the last champagne bottle, long since emptied, in her hand. "Anyway, I'm going to dye my hair. I'm fed up with being blond!"

She grins. Her mouth seems bigger than usual, but maybe I'm mistaken and it's her eyes that may be too small—but her hair color seems quite OK to me.

"But blond suits you."

"I want to go black."

"You'll look like Paleiko."

"My hair, you idiot, it's only my hair I want to color, not my whole, you know, body or something. . . . Where is the old doll, anyway?"

Nicholas points to the shelf. He's wearing a white sweater,

and as he moves his arms through the air, a light streak remains behind. I'm wondering whether I ever told him about Paleiko, which makes me feel very tired and takes up a lot of time, because in my next wakeful moment I already see Kat singing and whirling through the room with Paleiko in her arm.

"Dance, little doll, dance . . . !"

"Don't drop him, Kat."

"Why are you—"

"Careful, right?"

"Why are you actually named—"

"Kat!"

"—Paleiko?"

One minute Paleiko is still clutched to Kat's breast as she dances, pressed to her like a defenseless sleeping child, and the next he's sailing through the air, does a single somersault, and smashes into a thousand pieces on the floor.

"Too late," says Nicholas beside me.

For her ninth birthday Tereza gave Dianne a doll that could pee and had long blond hair that you could comb. I got a football. I didn't even try to hide my disappointment. A football was by far the stupidest, most useless present that I could imagine. For a time I hoped that Tereza had reversed the presents by mistake, for I would have loved a doll. But the allocation remained as it was. I was quivering with suppressed anger and indignation. Even the sight of the birthday cake, a miraculous confection that Tereza covered with hundreds and thousands of sprinkles like a spray of meteors, couldn't soothe me. I refused to blow out my nine candles.

For weeks if not months before the birthday I felt I was under Glass's increasingly watchful eye. Sometimes I felt her gaze weighing on me like a delicate but noticeable weight. I became aware that Glass watched me only in certain situations—when I set the table in the kitchen, when I tidied Dianne's and my room, as it always seemed untidy to me, or when I would tie the same shoe twenty times, until both bows were exactly the same size. All these situations must have had something in common that escaped me. The fact that there were other things I could do without attracting the telltale gleam from my mother's eyes made it all the more confusing for me.

And now, thanks to Tereza and her useless present, I had a new problem.

In the days following my birthday Glass appeared to be concerned with only one thing—that I should at least try out my new toy.

"Don't you want to play with your new ball, darling?"

I shook my head.

"But why not? Tereza spent an awful lot of money on it. And it's such a beautiful ball, Phil!"

"No!"

I had no intention of struggling with this ball, either kicking it around on the grass or fooling around with it somewhere the way I saw other boys doing in games lessons or during recess at school. And with the best will in the world I really couldn't see anything beautiful in this thing consisting of a honeycomb of black and white leather pieces sewn together, apart from the shape, which I liked because it reminded me of soap bubbles and Christmas tree baubles. As soon as Glass stopped nagging me to use the football, it ended up in some forgotten corner of Visible. For the first time I was grateful that the house possessed so many hidden nooks and crannies. On hot summer days thin flies would eat their way into the rotten timbers of Visible with lightning speed in order to lay their eggs there. I hoped there was some insect species whose larvae were programmed to feed on leather.

One fine summer's day when Dianne and I came home from school, there was the leather horror in all its ugliness suddenly lying on my bed, as if it had fallen out of the clear sky. Three months had passed since my birthday, and all the rather ungrateful wishes for its destruction had long since been forgotten. But now there it was again, fat and round and conspicuous. Glass had found it. At first I believed she had just placed it on my bed the way you put a lost toy back in its place as a joyful surprise for the owner. Without a moment's hesitation I stuffed it out of sight under my bed. I had no way of knowing that returning the football was the prelude to a comedy stage-managed by Glass and Tereza, which, contrary to their expectations, I really didn't find at all funny.

The following Saturday Tereza came to visit us. The

weather had been glorious for the past week, and although it was only halfway through July, the heat had already begun to build up at Visible. A picnic basket was packed, Dianne stuffed her doll and all sorts of bits and pieces in a bag of her own, and we all set off for the meadow by the river, which held an uncomfortable, fateful memory for me. I instinctively put my hands over my ears as we got there, to make sure they hadn't reverted to their original shape.

"We're going to play a game, Phil," announced Tereza as soon as she'd emptied out the picnic basket.

"What kind of game?"

"A funny one. It's a kind of test," she declared. "Well, actually, they're three tests. But if you pass them, you get a present."

At the word *present* Dianne looked up hopefully. Her blond, eternally peeing doll was obviously not enough for her.

"This is a game we can play only with Phil, OK?" said Tereza in her direction.

Dianne nodded, and that was all. Loud protests were not her way. But I had suddenly grown suspicious. Another present didn't interest me in the slightest, no matter how beautiful it might be. Glass had also referred to the football as beautiful, so clearly there were concepts of beauty that lay miles apart. On the other hand, my curiosity was aroused—but only until, to my horror, Glass extracted the football from the basket. She handed it to Tereza, who smiled at me.

"Don't be afraid, Phil. It's really just a game."

She clamped the football under her arm. I began to see my chance.

"Ready?"

I nodded.

"First test," said Tereza quietly. "Whistle with your fingers."

"What?"

"Whistle between two fingers. It's not very difficult. Look, I'll show you how."

She let the ball fall on the grass and showed me. It was impressive. Her whistle was so deafening and piercing that I thought I could see tiny, frightened waves leaping over the river, glittering in the sun.

"Wow!" said Glass. She was sitting cross-legged on the blanket spread out on the grass, fiddling about with a thick, cone-shaped cigarette.

"Now you," ordered Tereza.

I hesitated briefly. Then I stuck both index fingers and thumbs in my mouth and puffed, but all that came out was a slightly loud breath. I repeated the performance following Tereza's instructions. Patiently she showed me how to place the fingertips against the teeth and press the tongue against the fingertips. This time spit sprayed out of my mouth and ran down my chin over my T-shirt. I ended up by shoving nearly my whole hand down my throat, but apart from making me feel like throwing up, this attempt too did not produce the desired result.

"Don't look so embarrassed. You did very well!" Tereza

lifted my chin up, smiled, and ruffled my hair with one hand. Then she sat down on the blanket next to Glass. "Time for a short break."

Did very well? I'd failed!

Glass lit the cone-shaped cigarette, took two puffs, and handed it on to Tereza. Gray-blue clouds of smoke wafted like little misty animals through the still air across the meadow. The smell was pleasantly sweet in my nostrils—damp hay with sugar frosting. It must have been this nice smell and not, as I'd secretly feared, my poor performance that caused the two women to keep on giggling stupidly. It was something of a consolation, if only a weak one. So long as they were giggling, they weren't thinking about my failure.

"Second test," announced Tereza merrily when the cigarette had gone out. She got up from the blanket, swayed a little, and pointed to the football, whose black and white leather gleamed evilly. "Throw the ball!"

"I've had enough."

"Do it for me, darling," wheedled Glass. "Please!"

I looked at Dianne for help, a little envious. She was happily sitting in the grass, combing her doll's hair and making her pee for the hundredth time. The pee was refilled from a bottle dragged along for the purpose, and filled up every few minutes with fresh water from the river. The weird tests I was being subjected to didn't seem to interest her in the slightest. Then I turned back to Glass, who was still looking at me pleadingly.

So throw the ball it had to be.

Couldn't be that hard.

Twice the ball simply slid out of my hands and plopped onto the grass. Once I threw it straight up, so that it almost fell on my head. The last attempt twirled it right in the middle of the picnic china, where it made a cup handle bite the dust with a protesting crack.

"Oh, well. Who was it said breaking crockery brings good luck, Phil?" said Tereza with a broad grin.

I laughed back bravely and hoped that she didn't notice how my lower lip was beginning to tremble. An almost intolerable burning crept up behind my eyes.

This time there was no cigarette interval.

"And now shoot!" announced Glass and Tereza both at the same time, prompting another outburst of inappropriate merriment.

Shoot!

That was it, the last and most treacherous of the tests demanded of me. Didn't the two women notice this was the summit of all summits, the mother of all tortures? How could they possibly believe I was able to shoot a ball that I'd already been too stupid even to throw? By now I was totally discouraged, but it seemed best to get the altogether undignified business over and done with.

I placed the hateful leather object in front of my feet and stood there uncertainly. Should I take a run up to it? Shoot standing? With my left foot or my right?

Tereza nodded at me encouragingly.

"Now come on, have a go, darling," Glass egged me on.

"But, Mom—"

"Just do it!"

The scars behind my ears began to tingle. I stared into my mother's large, enthusiastic eyes with their strangely contracted glistening pupils. Then I stared into the other, deeper gleam I thought I could detect behind the pupils, and this was the moment when I knew what Dumbo must have felt before he jumped down from his sixty-foot tower into the porridge. In some terrible way Glass had changed into one of Those Out There.

Dianne had at last put her doll aside and was now watching me as well—lusting for sensation, it seemed to me. Tereza was standing next to me looking slightly vacant. There was no dribble oozing from her half-open mouth, but all the same she looked like a drooling idiot.

I smiled and hated every one of them.

I bundled up my hatred, took a run, and shot.

I hit the leather precisely with the tip of my foot; the kick could not have been better aimed. The ball detached itself from the ground and in a magical dreamlike way described a perfect parabolic arc. I stretched my neck and gazed after it. No wobbling, no swerving, just this shining noiseless black-and-white rotation around its own axis. Passing the vertex. Then the gently described downward arc.

And landed in the river.

There was a gentle splash, and I wasn't clear who or what had caused it, the bouncing of the ball or my heart, which had just lurched down into my stomach, turning it to liquid. I held my breath.

"Passed!" shrieked Tereza beside me, and clapped her hands. "That was brilliant, my little one!"

"And that's it?" asked Glass doubtfully. She was watching the ball sailing happily down the river, swept along by glittering waves. "You can tell someone's gay if they're no good at games?"

"Rather if they don't want to be good at games."

"Well, I don't know. . . ."

"But I do!" Tereza insisted. "I have it from a reliable source. Every gay person knows about these tests, and they laugh themselves silly over them. Believe me, your son's a fairy!" Tereza bent down and planted a kiss on my forehead. "I'll never forget how he wanted to be Sleeping Beauty, and that's years ago."

I couldn't understand why I was a fairy, let alone what a fairy had to do with Sleeping Beauty. All I knew was that I'd just kicked this expensive football, my birthday present, into the river, which therefore made it sacred, even though I'd detested it, and all the fundamental laws of reason were turned topsy-turvy because no one, absolutely no one, was cross about it.

Glass now tipped up my chin with one hand, stroking my head with the other.

"If that's the way it is . . . well, that's the way it is, then." She looked at me thoughtfully. Something flitted across her face, a dark shadow that came and went as quickly as the blink of an eye. "Well, it's all right by me."

At last she smiled. I breathed a sigh of relief. I'd searched her face for telltale signs, for the slightest indication that having a fairy for a son wasn't all right by her, and which she might relentlessly attempt to correct, surgically if necessary, like the position of my jug ears. Had this thought been behind the fleeting shadow over her face, it was now forgotten. Evidently being a fairy was nowhere near as reprehensible as having protruding ears.

"I was on the point of giving up when he kicked the thing. Nonetheless"—Tereza burst into another fit of giggling—"Nonetheless, he's a hero. You're a hero, Phil! And now there's cake for everyone. Boy, I really feel like something sweet!"

So I was a hero. Which was incomprehensible to me, because in my eyes I'd failed miserably, whereas in the view of my mother and Tereza I'd given a brilliant performance, making me a hero nonetheless. It was a good feeling that kept getting better the more I thought about it, and in the days that followed I wished there was someone I could tell about my glorious deed, like Annie Glosser or Mr. Troht. But for the past year Annie had been in that dreadful sanatorium, where they wrapped her in diapers and maltreated her with electric shocks, and as for that kindly old crock, Mr. Troht, an eternal smile playing on his lips, it was already two years since he'd ended his days, going straight up to heaven. There was no one I could trust. All I could do was wait for Gable's next visit.

While Tereza, Glass, and Dianne pounced on the cake Tereza had brought along, with much clattering of plates and cups, I made my way through the whispering grass to the river and tried to catch a last glimpse of the football. But the current had long since swept it away; by now it must already have passed the Big Eye, and it was no longer to be seen. That was exactly what I wanted to be sure of. The prickling behind my ears hadn't gone, and that worried me. It had something to do with my newly acquired status as a fairy, the implications of which weren't clear to me, and above all, for all the giggling and laughing, with the way Glass had said, *Well, that's the way it is, then.* A brief hesitation had preceded the words, and she hadn't laughed as she hesitated. And not afterward either. Afterward this shadow had flitted across her face in a flash.

Well, it's all right by me.

Suddenly I knew what this shadow had meant: anxiety. Not any old anxiety, but very specific anxiety regarding my future. Never mind the hero bit; all of a sudden I was no longer sure whether it would be easy to lead a life as a fairy.

What I was absolutely sure about was that the life that lay ahead of me was closely connected, however mysteriously, with the football I'd kicked away. After all, it had all begun with the football. So I continued to stare into the water. I was nine years old and I knew there were no evil spirits and no slimy river god covered in algae that could reverse the flow of the water to bring back the football. I knew it, but I wasn't absolutely sure.

So I kept my eye on the water.

Just in case.

I felt a hand on my shoulder. "There's someone I want you to meet, my little one."

I turned round to Tereza and found myself gazing into the face of a black doll.

"This is Paleiko," said Tereza. "He's something very special, Phil."

The doll was smaller than Dianne's, smaller and a lot older. Big white eyes shone out of the dark porcelain face, and the naked sexless body was covered in scratches. Paleiko was no match for his blond counterpart, but it was precisely this that made him irresistible and beautiful in my eyes. A tiny pink stone was embedded in his forehead, a fragment of coral or gemstone that seemed to me to glow softly.

"Paleiko was a present from my mama when I was a little girl," said Tereza. "And she got him from her mama when she was little. He's very old and has seen a great deal. Sometimes he'll speak to you and answer your questions. You're his little friend now."

"Why does he have such a funny name?"

"That's a secret," said Tereza, "and the only question you must never ask Paleiko."

"Why not?"

"Because that will make him shatter."

I took the black doll and flopped down on the spot into the grass by the riverbank and pressed his mouth to my ear. I couldn't think of anything to ask him there and then, and so all that I heard was the gurgling and murmuring of the nearby water, the rustling of the grass between Tereza's calves as she went back to Glass, and the sound of the two of them talking quietly.

"He's too old for a bloody doll," said Glass.

"You're never too old for a doll. Just look at how he's treating Paleiko. He's in love with it already."

"I don't know. . . . Is that just a cliché or another of your weird bits of evidence?"

"Both and neither, my beloved. Your boy is a little fairy, mark my words!"

"Is there a difference between a fairy and a gay person?"

"Is that important?"

There was a moment of total silence.

"At any rate, he's a dishy-looking fruit," said Glass at last. "With very handsome, tailor-made ears."

"Oh, he certainly is, no question. Sooner or later the men will be at his feet." I heard Tereza stifling a snort of laughter. "In any case, that's the only place they'll be safe."

"I want to be a fairy too!"

I lowered the doll and turned round. Dianne, who'd been listening and watching the whole scene without a word, alternately chewing on a piece of cake and her long hair, now turned to Glass. Doll and pee were forgotten. Her dark eyes blazed with envy, and I didn't begrudge her it. I was a hero, I was a fairy, and I had Paleiko. There was now no way Dianne could be a heroine, because the football had disappeared. In order to achieve the esteemed status of being a fairy, her only hope was if she exchanged her vapid blond doll for a dark wonder like Paleiko. And she knew that she wouldn't get Paleiko from me. She hadn't lifted a finger to protect me from those tests.

"You can't be a fairy, sweetheart," said Glass, trying to distract her.

"Why?"

"Because you have to be a man to be one."

"Then I want to be a man."

"Dianne, don't be silly, of course you can't."

"Why not?"

"Too expensive," said Tereza drily. Then, shrieking with laughter, she rolled onto her back.

You see, my little friend, Paleiko whispered in my ear, *it's not that easy. You're the only hero.*

Kat lurches. She holds out her palms to me; they gleam white. "Oh, shit. I . . . I'm so sorry, Phil."

I don't know what to make of Paleiko's being dead. It's years since he spoke to me. Damn it, he never spoke to me, he was just a toy! But he was Tereza's toy too, and it's this that makes the sight of the shattered pieces strewn across the floor so painful. After she'd given him to me—*entrusted,* a voice inside me whispered, *she only entrusted him to me*—she never asked about Paleiko again. I don't have to tell her what happened; it might unnecessarily hurt her. And I'll never have children of my own to pass Paleiko on to.

She only gave me to you for safekeeping, and you didn't look after me.

Time is completely out of joint. Smoochy music comes from the radio. I crawl along the floor, avoiding the tea lights glowing with heat, and search for the pink stone that had been sunk into Paleiko's forehead, hunt for it and hunt and hunt. It's nowhere to be found; maybe it's slipped down in between the floorboards. I sit down with my back to the wall, next to Nicholas, who's been watching me hunt without making a move, and scratch tiny splinters from the palms of my hands. Kat hasn't budged.

"Hey." Nicholas puts his arms round me and pulls my head onto his chest. "Don't cry, eh? Don't cry. We'll just stick him together again."

"OK."

"I'll get a dustpan and brush."

"OK."

"We'll pick up all the pieces, every little scrap."

"All right."

"And then we'll glue him together again."

"Mm."

"Don't cry."

"Come," says Kat. "Get up."

She pulls Nicholas and me up from the floor by the hands, puts her head on my shoulder and an arm round Nicholas's waist. Slowly, carefully at first and swaying together in time to the music, we move closer and closer toward each other. I close my eyes, swing round and round. When our bodies touch, it's as if I'm stumbling through an open window. Under my feet broken pieces crunch and splinter, we're going to knock the tea lights over, soon the hot wax will spread across the floor, we're going to set Visible alight. I feel lips on my lips, on my neck, very gentle, and don't know whom they belong to, Kat or Nicholas or both.

It's one in the afternoon when I wake up on Sunday, with my head feeling as if my brain's been transformed into the air bubble inside a spirit level, being tilted to and fro. I stumble out of bed, tear open the windows, and soak up the cold air that hits me. The world on both sides of the river is hidden under a finely woven glittering cloth of hoarfrost.

Kat and Nicholas left around three in the morning. They turned down my offer to stay overnight, and I was too tired to persuade them. I look at the aluminum-gray containers of one hundred burnt-out tea lights and the shattered pieces and splinters that are all that's left of Paleiko. Then I put on woolen socks and go downstairs to the uncomfortably cold kitchen and make myself some strong coffee. It's so hot that I burn my lips and tongue, but it does succeed in bringing the air bubble in the spirit level to a tolerable equilibrium. I don't even attempt to light the fire or the decrepit water heater in the bathroom. Instead I call Tereza, who is pleased to hear from me, as she's free all afternoon because Pascal is still busy producing amber jewelry for the opening of the Christmas market. As I'd secretly been hoping, she invites me for coffee. I don't make the slightest allusion to Paleiko's passing and intend to leave it at that. But the sound of Tereza's voice is enough to unleash the guilty conscience that until now has remained hidden in my aching head, like a rabid dog running away without its chain and dragging me with it. At the end of the call, I sweep up the broken pieces and throw them into the garbage can in the kitchen. It's pointless trying to piece them together; there are just too many of them. I still can't find the pink stone from Paleiko's forehead anywhere. Sometime I'll hunt more thoroughly.

On Sundays the buses run only every two hours. I'm standing in the deserted marketplace almost half an hour early, in the icy cold. Only now and again a car roars past; there are hardly any people about. Colored Christmas lights and candles flicker inside two or three windows of the surrounding houses, and it occurs to me it's the first day of Advent. I stamp my feet and rub my hands to keep my circulation going. I'll ask Tereza if I can use her shower, or better still her bathtub. Even the two soldiers on duty by the fountain duck down against the cold and look as if their frozen hands can barely hold on to their rifles fitted with bayonets. On more than one occasion Handel has attempted—in letters to the editor of the local paper, and at meetings of the town council—to draw attention to the fact that an enlightened society really cannot afford the anachronism of armed soldiers looking heroic and warning against war, but as usual he got no response. He must feel terribly misunderstood, a lone voice in the wilderness. I ask myself what could have brought a man like him to this sad little provincial town at the back of beyond. Maybe he suffers from excessive missionary zeal.

In the bus I close my eyes, lulled by the dry warmth, my thoughts on the past night. I'm being unjust to Kat with my jealousy, which probably isn't jealousy but envy—envy of the uninhibited direct way she has with people, that I'm accustomed to from her, for which I admire and like her, and which I myself utterly lack.

Shit.

It's five minutes' walk from the bus stop to Tereza's. The street with its fine old buildings lies still and quiet. Inside the windows there are considerably more candles, electric and wax, than I saw earlier on in the marketplace. Christmas music filters into the stairwell through one of the doors. Pascal opens when I ring. She looks the way she always does, sullen, bedraggled, and half asleep.

"Hail to thee, Maria," she growls. She stands aside. "Come in."

I hang my coat up in the closet and peer down the hallway. "Where's Tereza?"

"Gone."

My heart sinks. "But she—"

"She asked me to tell you she was sorry, but some important client called and she was off. She did try to call you, but there was no one at home."

No, I'd been at the damned marketplace, standing till I was fit to drop in the lousy cold.

"If you can put up with me, you're welcome to stay. Except that I've got work to do and"—Pascal looks at her watch—"I have to disappear in an hour at the latest."

"I know."

"Won't you stay all the same and have a coffee? You look as if you could do with one." She's already turned round and started off in the direction of the kitchen. "Have you been having a good time?"

"Yes. Actually, I'd rather have a hot shower."

"You can have both."

"Even better."

"Anything to please a guest," Pascal calls over her shoulder. It sounds more as if she means guests ought to be shot immediately on entering the apartment.

"Come into my workroom when you're done."

I could stay under the shower forever. I let the hot water rain down on me for ages before I turn the control to cold and a short icy burst drives the last gray cobwebs from my brain. When I leave the bathroom I feel newly born. Barefoot, with wet hair, and wrapped in nothing but an enormous Turkish towel, I pad across the soft carpet through the apartment. The door to the kitchen is open, and the aroma of coffee wafts into the hall. As I pass the pin board on the wall the white postcard that Tereza received from Pascal five years ago catches my eyes.

My heart for yours.

A life for a life.

I'm familiar with Pascal's workroom, her little jewelry factory, as she calls it. To me it looks like major chaos. Tools strewn about on a large work surface make me think of miniature medieval instruments of torture. Design drawings are pinned to the wall with tacks. Silver wire and nylon cord spill out of open drawers. Boxes and small baskets are filled with amber in varying stages of completion, from rough unpolished lumps to the finished milky translucent pieces with typical reddish brown inclusions. But Pascal's speciality is actually the tiny, carefully polished chips that she arranges in openwork patterns mounted on pieces of wood she has polished herself.

The muddle has its own particular quality. This isn't particularly evident in the individual pieces of jewelry—intended not as an unkind criticism but as an observation that Pascal might be the first to agree with. It's plain to see that every one of the amber pendants mounted in silver or wood on long chains and each ring set with a large stone has been produced with a certain lack of enthusiasm. Maybe the impression is different when you look at just one piece on its own—Pascal displays them on draped velvet and brocade for sale—but in here the items of jewelry lying about look as if they've been turned out on a production line, interchangeable products made without loving dedication or creative impulse.

"And," Pascal greets me, "how are you and the fairy-tale prince? Has your range spread beyond the bed by now?"

"It has."

"But all the same there's a problem." She turns back to the piece of wood she'd been working on with sandpaper when I entered the room. "Or you wouldn't be here, would you?"

Too kind of her, coming straight to the point like that. I'd much rather be talking to Tereza. But I get the feeling that just now I can't be choosy. Apart from which, although Pascal may well be challenged on a number of issues—such as tact as well as sensitivity in dealing with other people's feelings—she certainly isn't lacking in practical life experience. So I take a deep breath, and then I tell her about my being jealous of Kat, and that she's far better at getting Nicholas to open up than I am.

"Are you so sure about that?" Pascal looks up for an instant from her work. "He may just react differently to her than to you. But that doesn't mean to say that he lets her get any closer to him. Why don't you ask Kat about it?"

"She might take it for distrust."

"Well, that's what it is, isn't it?"

"Well, yes, but—"

She shakes her head. "What do you want of Nicholas, Phil? What is it you really want from him?"

"I don't know. More certainty, I suppose."

"That doesn't exist in any relationship."

"Right. Well, then, that he doesn't act so reserved all the time. He knows everything about me, I reveal myself totally to him, and I get nothing back from him." I draw the bath sheet more tightly around me and reflect. "The funny thing is, I love him all the same."

"How romantic. Try substituting 'all the same' with 'because of it,' and you might be nearer to an answer." Pascal puts wood and sandpaper aside and tips out a few amber chips in front of her on the table. "And what if his silence just means that he doesn't have anything to say?"

"I don't believe that."

"Yeah, yeah, that's because you love him." Now she reaches for a magnifying glass in order to inspect a couple of amber chips more closely. "If you ask me, love hardly comes into it if there's one doing all the giving and the other does nothing but take."

"You know what I can't stand about you, Pascal?" I say after a brief pause. "That you love telling people what they don't want to hear."

"Well, someone's got to. . . ." Without putting down the magnifying glass, she waves one hand at me. "Give me the tweezers over there."

I watch her as she carefully dabs one of the tiny chips with adhesive and inserts it into the piece of wood she's prepared. Then she attaches a pin to the back of the brooch. Hard to believe that her thick fingers can do such delicate work.

"That wasn't particularly helpful," I say at last.

"Phil, now listen to me." Pascal puts the finished piece aside and looks up at me. "It's your life, not mine, and you're responsible for your own problems. I'd advise you if I could, but I don't know about men, nor do I want to know about them. OK?"

"OK."

"Would you still like some coffee anyway?"

"Sure."

"Then go and get dressed, for heaven's sake." Pascal gets up, pushes past me, and points at the bath towel. "Or are you waiting for me to tear it off and throw myself at you?"

"Would you do that?"

"Oh, who knows," she says drily. "What would life be without exotic adventures on the edge of perversion?"

She's waiting for me in the living room, with coffee and yellow butter biscuits on the table.

"Hey." I point at them. "Are those leftovers from the summer?"

"They're fresh, you idiot! D'you think I'd have cut out bells and Christmas tree shapes in the summer?"

Under her distrustful gaze I eat a few biscuits and nod at

her enthusiastically—they really do taste fantastic—and I notice how at some point her expression changes and becomes thoughtful.

"What's the matter?"

Pascal clears her throat awkwardly. "Well . . . actually, Tereza intended to tell you this today, but as she isn't here . . . Wait a minute, will you?" She leaves the room and is back in a second. A folded piece of blue paper lands in front of me on the table.

"Read this. We've got a whole collection of them."

It's a letter, just a few lines, hurriedly scrawled in thick black felt pen. I don't know what's worse, the gross ugliness of the words, which strike me like a punch in the face and make me blush, or the brutality they express.

"Who writes stuff like that?"

Pascal shrugs. "Some guy for whom the notion of two lesbos screwing doesn't make him jerk off for once, but puts his nose out of joint." She pulls a face, presumably to show her indifference to this letter, but it ends up as a grotesque, lopsided grin.

"And why . . . why are you showing me this?"

"Huh." She moves her hands, trying to smooth her short hair behind her ears. "Shit, I'd rather Tereza had told you, but she's been trying for weeks and simply can't bring herself to do it. Well . . . we're leaving, Phil."

"What?"

"We've thought it over hundreds of times, and there are as many reasons." She points to the letter. "That's only one of them."

I get the crazy feeling that if only I can manage to leave this room quickly enough, I can reverse what she said. If I act as if I hadn't been here at all. "And the others?"

"For example, that I'm feeling homesick for my country," says Pascal. "Or for my previous career. Or that Tereza's sick of clients whose only problem is the neighbor's dog shitting in their garden."

I stare at the letter. "So when?"

"Next year, sometime in the spring."

"In the spring!" That soon. My thoughts rush in all directions. "And what about Glass? She'll lose her job. She'll go crazy when she finds out you're going to move!"

"She already knows."

"She already knows! Why didn't she tell me?"

"Because she thinks it's up to Tereza. And because she seemed quite relaxed about it herself."

"Relaxed about it . . ." I must stop repeating each sentence like a scratched record. "But what about her job?"

"There are dozens of lawyers in the area," says Pascal calmly. "Glass is good; she expects she'll find a new job anytime. She could even work in Michael's firm."

"And Tereza?"

"She's tracked something down in Holland. She was looking round while we were there on vacation. International law.

She'll have to do some more studying for a few months, but she's definitely got a job."

Of course she's right. Holland isn't the other end of the world. We'll be able to visit each other, we'll telephone. All the same, my stomach turns at the thought of not having Tereza nearby any longer.

"Well, that's about it." Pascal empties the rest of her coffee, looks at her watch, and gets up. "I've got to go."

"It's all right."

"You could come along and help me set up if you like."

"Don't feel like it."

"Well, stay here, then. Make yourself at home. I expect there's something in the fridge you can heat up. Oh, and clear these dishes, will you?"

She's already taken three steps toward the hall when she stops and turns back to me once more. "And as far as your Nicholas is concerned . . ."

"Yes?"

"Maybe it would help if you took the initiative more and acted less like a detached bystander drifting around the world." She grins. "That's precisely what I can't stand about you."

chapter 15

secale cornutum

A postcard turns up, this time from Cape Town—Gable announces he will definitely be coming for Christmas. This is the signal for Glass to apply herself to planning the Christmas festivities with military precision. Tereza and Pascal are invited; Michael's presence is taken for granted.

I find Glass in the kitchen sitting at the table with a pile of cookbooks and a heap of scribbled notes on scraps of paper in front of her and, as is customary at this time of year, deep in concentration over the composition of a multicourse Christmas menu. I've long since ceased wondering why she spends so much time on something that will never get beyond the planning stage. Glass has never so far sorted out one of her strange menus. She didn't buy the cookbooks herself—they belonged to Stella. Like all the festive meals planned by Glass, Christmas dinner will end up consisting of just one course: chicken in a ready-made marinade with roast potatoes. When I tackle her about Tereza's plans to move, she doesn't even look up from her jumble of papers.

"Of course I shall miss her, darling," she mumbles.

"And what are you going to do?"

"Not think about it."

"I mean, what will you do when you lose your job?"

"Well, what d'you suppose? I'll find another one."

Glass snaps one of the cookbooks shut, opens another, and makes some cryptic notes. The tiled stove roars into action, filling the kitchen with pleasant warmth. I've had to pay for it with blisters on my hands—and there'll be no end to the wood chopping before April next year.

"And don't think I haven't often thought about it before now," Glass continues. "I've been in that law firm longer than the longest-serving houseplant. Actually, I should be grateful to Tereza. If she wasn't going, I'd never shift my ass."

"Will you start working for Michael?"

"Of course not! I can work for Michael or I can sleep with him. Doing both is out of the question." She pushes the scraps of paper aside and reaches for the next book. "Tell me, darling, what d'you say to chicken with potatoes for Christmas?"

"Terrific idea."

"Isn't it?" Glass looks up, beams at me, and begins crumpling the hundred scraps of paper. "Why don't you and Dianne each invite your friends as well?"

Dianne stays with Kora nearly all the time now or with her in their girlfriends' homes. When I ask her whether she'd like to invite her friend to Visible for Christmas, she just shakes her head dismissively.

"Kora's only seen Visible from afar, and that was enough for her. She says there's something magnetic about it. She maintains there are probably dozens of water veins crossing energy lines below the foundations."

"Water veins and energy lines?"

"Well, she believes in that sort of thing."

"And you?"

"Well, maybe." Dianne cocks her head to one side. "At any rate, Kora says that houses like Visible would devour anyone entering them."

"I don't want to upset you, but that sounds a bit nuts."

"If you like. But believe me, Phil, there's no one more clearheaded than Kora."

Asking Kat whether she feels like eating chicken and roast potatoes elicits the information that she's off with her parents over Christmas and New Year's to endanger the Alps on skis.

"Definitely the last time," she declares over a pre-Christmas session of violin scraping while I'm visiting her at home. "And this time I'm going to have a wild time, after that Malta disaster in the summer!"

"Are you still on the lookout?"

Kat pulls a face. "What are you giving Glass and Dianne for Christmas?"

"We're not doing presents—we're broke."

"What about Nicholas?"

"No idea."

Apart from running, he doesn't have any hobbies. Of course he has his strange museum, but he might consider it a betrayal of confidence if I told Kat about it. And to be honest, I relish the idea that this confidence gives me the edge over Kat.

"We've arranged to do a bit of Christmas shopping together," she says without putting down the violin. "He's really great fun to be with, don't you think?"

"Depends."

"By the way, he thinks it's a great idea."

"What idea?"

Kat lowers her violin. I can almost hear her mother pressing the stopwatch somewhere in the house. "Oh, that I'm going to have my hair dyed black."

"Kat!"

I decide to make a display case out of wood for Nicholas. It's a project that is totally beyond my capacity until I quickly decide to ask Michael to help me. It seems there's nothing he can't do. One of Visible's empty rooms is selected as a workroom. We plunder the cellar, where we find well-seasoned timber, and in the days that follow we're busy together hammering and sanding and nailing and sawing directly after

Michael is back from work in the early or, more frequently, late evening.

"What d'you intend to do after high school?" he asks me at one point.

"No idea. Maybe study, but don't ask me what. But I can just as well see myself sailing round the world for a bit with Gable."

"I can't wait to get to know him." Michael brushes some wood shavings off his sweater. "You're very fond of him, aren't you?"

"As a child I always wished he was my father."

At which Michael looks at me thoughtfully in a way that could mean everything or nothing, more likely everything. I smile at him and turn back to my work. Should he and Glass decide to move in together, they'll announce it soon enough.

The row with Nicholas happens as quickly as a sudden summer storm. And it's over just as quickly. But in the same way that one of these brief summer thunderstorms rarely clears the humidity from the air, our argument also leaves a hint of more to come, a background rumbling that I seem to be hearing even days later. Nicholas arrives at the house of Tereza's father, where I'm waiting for him. As I open the door to him, he stomps into the hall in a state that I've never seen him in before.

"It's all over the place—they're all talking, saying you're gay."

"Who's saying?"

"Kat's ex-boyfriend! He claims you groped him, and that's putting it mildly!"

"Didn't. I only kissed him."

"You did what?"

The room temperature seems to plummet by several degrees. A hole forms somewhere in my insides through which all my strength and energy drain out.

"Kissed him, so that he'd leave me alone."

"Are you completely out of your mind?" Nicholas raises his arms, and for a moment I really think he's going to hit me. "How can you possibly provide these people with ammunition?"

"Let the idiot say what he likes! I could say the same thing about him. I could let people know how much he enjoyed it."

"Don't be so damned naïve. Haven't you given a moment's thought to Kat?"

"She ought to be pleased I've saved her having to use her powers of persuasion."

"Which she didn't ask you for!"

His face is flushed with fury. The dark eyes glitter angrily. I think of chess. When I was trying to learn how to play, Michael explained to me how to maneuver one's own pieces or those of one's opponent into certain positions. I can't remember whether it's stalemate or a draw when no one can make another move without checkmating the other person's king. But this is just how I feel at this moment—defeated.

I ought to ask Nicholas why he's hiding behind Kat when it's really just that he's afraid to be seen with me. I ought to ask him why I have to defend myself to him when he's obviously the one with the problem. But to do so I'd have to be able to suppress the quiver in my voice and calm my racing heart. I lack the courage to go over to the offensive, the way Pascal advised me to do. Since he turned up here in a razor-sharp fury, I'm consumed with fear he might go off and leave me on my own. He must see this fear, for suddenly his face softens.

"Phil . . ."

I turn away so that he can't see I'm fighting back tears. He places his arms round me from behind. His breath brushes my neck.

"Phil, I'm sorry."

"It's OK."

"I don't want to fight with you."

"I don't want to quarrel either."

"Come along, come."

Later, after we've slept together, we're lying on the bed staring up at the ceiling and listening to the now familiar ticking sounds of the heating. Darkness and wind push against the windows from outside. I ask Nicholas if he wouldn't like to come over to Visible one day over Christmas.

"I can't. My parents and I are visiting relatives."

"Why go with them?"

"I can't leave them alone."

"If things are so bad, surely it won't make any difference whether you're there or not. With you there too, that'll make three of you to give each other hell instead of two."

"You don't understand."

I turn on my side to face him, tracing the outline of his eyebrows and stroking his hair. "Is there some dark family secret you haven't revealed to me?"

"No. There's nothing."

"But if you tear each other apart, why d'you go to relatives, then?"

"When there's nothing left to hold on to, you cling to the old rituals." Nicholas grips my hand in his firm grasp and pushes it down onto the mattress. "Roll over onto your stomach."

"Be careful. . . ."

With someone as reticent as Nicholas it's hard to tell when he's withdrawn even further into himself. All the same, in the days that follow I get the impression that his rare kisses are becoming even rarer and the touching less. It's only the sex that remains the same—a hunger that can't be satisfied.

The weathermen didn't get it wrong—it turns into a freezing cold winter. By the middle of December there's already a thin bluish white covering of ice over the pool at the bottom of the garden, which I haven't been down to since the summer. Now and again some powdery snow falls, but it's never more than a ragged veil blown against tree trunks and the walls of houses by a Siberian wind, where it clings like a dusting of icing sugar. Everything freezes solid. Frost bites deep into the soil and seals the earth with an armor plating of invisible ice. Perhaps it's the unbearable cold that makes Dianne decide to shed her own armor.

One Saturday afternoon she tracks me down in the room that Michael and I have transformed into a carpenter's workshop.

"Phil, have you got a moment?"

"Does it have to be now?"

My hands and clothes are spattered with green paint. The display cabinet, Nicholas's Christmas present, is finished at last and thanks to Michael's help looks really professional. I deliberated for a long time whether to leave the beautifully grained wood as it is or to give it a coat of paint. In the end I decided to paint it with a coat of matte lacquer.

"I can come back later," says Dianne. She looks at the cabinet. "Nice color."

"I was thinking of yellow at first."

"Green's OK."

"Green like the paint on Hoffmann's consulting room?"

She grins. "Yes. Sort of."

I get back to work. Dianne stays standing in the doorway watching me. I apply one, two strokes with the brush, then I give in and lower it with a sigh.

"OK, then. What's it all about?"

"D'you still want to know what the problem is between Glass and me?"

I almost drop the brush. I'm completely taken by surprise. She could have asked me in just the same innocent way whether I prefer coffee with or without milk. All I can do is nod.

"Then come with me."

One of the pearls of wisdom that Glass sells her clients like chocolates with sweet or plain fillings according to taste is that there's a time and a place for everything. Could be that Dianne has taken this piece of wisdom to heart, but I don't ask her. My curiosity outweighs my interest in her motives. I follow her along the corridor and into the cold entrance hall, surprised to find us making for the library. Dianne goes straight up to one of the shelves, takes out one of the leather-bound herbaries compiled by Tereza's father, and opens it—hardly needs to open it because the pages almost fall open of their own accord at a certain place.

Suddenly the feeling hits me forcibly that it was a mistake to have followed Dianne here. Then comes the longing to turn on my heel and run away, the awareness that I never should have asked my sister questions without being prepared for the most terrible answers. She points at five purple-black tiny nail-shaped seeds attached to the page with a nearly transparent strip of adhesive tape.

"What's that?"

"*Secale cornutum*. Ergot. Not really a plant, but a fungus. I still have almost a whole jarful of it."

"Dianne, I—" But of course there's no stopping her now; the words are as good as uttered.

"Ergot contains an alkaloid. In small doses it causes cramps, especially cramps in the involuntary musculature. Midwives have used it for hundreds of years to induce or increase contractions."

Glass lost the baby at the end of January, almost exactly four weeks to the day after she had revealed to me on the bridge over the frozen river that she was pregnant. It happened at night; Dianne and I were woken by her screams. Outside it was snowing unremittingly for days on end, the world was clothed in white, and a wind was blowing, not very violently, but loud enough to make me think afterward that I might have not heard Glass screaming the first two or three times. Not that it would have made any difference.

"Phil! Phiiiiiilllll . . . !"

I informed the emergency service. I didn't need to hunt for the telephone number—Glass had drummed it into me and Dianne almost as soon as we'd learned to say the word *telephone*. She'd even taught us the secret maneuver that every schoolchild in America can perform, a kind of hold that can prevent someone from choking on a food morsel by removing the foreign body stuck in the esophagus. Glass had warned us about bleach and detergents, tablets, ointments and lotions, about nasty men, nasty women, about knives, forks, scissors, lightbulbs, everything to protect us, and now she was the one too late to be protected.

It was only later that it occurred to me to phone Tereza as

well. By the time she arrived at Visible the walls of the entrance hall were already reflecting the rotating blue light of the ambulance, standing in the drive with the engine running. Snow was blowing in through the open front door, snaking in glittering lines across the cold tiled floor. I sat cowering at the foot of the stairs and cried, because I thought Glass was bound to die.

"What's happened?" asked Tereza, as breathless as if she'd run all the way to Visible. She was wearing old-fashioned red and blue striped pajamas with an open coat thrown over them. She must have driven like the devil.

"She wasn't feeling well already this afternoon."

"Where's Dianne?"

"Upstairs. She's cleaning up."

"She's . . . ?" It took a moment for Tereza to understand. "Oh, my God, Phil . . ."

She embraced me briefly, then ran upstairs. She left a trail of ice-cold air behind her like an invisible train. Outside the ambulance was driving off. I didn't move from the spot. If I just stayed sitting here and didn't move, then Glass would stay alive. I began to cry again.

In the late afternoon, shortly after Glass had complained of feeling nauseous, the contractions had begun. They set in as suddenly as the cold that spreads through the countryside just before a hailstorm. Glass had filled a water bottle with hot water and taken it to bed, and remained lying there stoically, even when the contractions began to get worse and she exchanged the water bottle for a bag filled with ice cubes, which did just as little to help. This time she had to pay for her reluctance to call on help from outside and inform a doctor right away.

It was a few minutes before Tereza came back downstairs again. She glided slowly down the staircase, holding Dianne by one hand, and in the other a crumpled sheet with a red stain soaking through in one place. Dianne's lips were pursed tight. Her eyes were glassy. Something glittered and shone. With every step my sister took down the stairs, the half-moon-shaped pendant I had given her for Christmas fell against her heavy dark sweater.

"What's in there?" I whispered, pointing at the sheet.

"Nothing a child needs to know," said Tereza.

I'd never seen her so pale before. God alone knows what my mother's bedroom looked like, God and Glass and Dianne and Tereza.

"Go and pack a few things, Phil, and you too, Dianne. Clothes, toothbrush."

"What sort of clothes?"

"Anything. Hurry now."

After I packed and joined Dianne in her room, not a word passed between us. I was worried because her arms were rising and falling in exactly the same mechanical way as I imagined the movements of the Tin Man in *The Wizard of Oz,* which Tereza had read to us. I knew Dianne disapproved of the men who used to come and visit Glass. Which was why Glass and

I had feared that she might react strongly when told about a baby. Strangely enough, she had accepted it quite calmly—she hadn't burst into tears of joy, but there'd been no screams of horror either. It must have been wishful thinking on my part, but I had assumed that secretly she was actually looking forward to the baby, maybe like a doll, for soon after she began behaving really affectionately, plumping up cushions for Glass before she sank onto the sofa by the chimney, making her endless cups of tea, and preparing breakfast and supper for her.

The front door was still open when we came out of our rooms and back downstairs into the entrance hall. It was dreadfully cold. All the warmth seemed to have left Visible along with Glass. Tereza was sitting on the staircase, on the same step where I'd been sitting before. The red sheet had disappeared. She bundled Dianne and me into her car, took us with her, and put us up in her apartment. Next day she sent for two men from a cleaning firm to go to Visible.

"How long are we going to stay with you?" I asked her the first evening. The three of us were sitting on the convertible couch that Tereza had opened out for Dianne and me in the living room. The light from a standard lamp threw long shadows against the walls, and Dianne stared at these shadows as if she could bring the pattern of the black outlines to life with her glassy gaze.

"Till Glass is allowed to leave the hospital," said Tereza. "Maybe even a bit longer. As long as you like."

I snuggled up to her. I never wanted to go back home

again. I was fully convinced that Visible would collapse on top of me because the walls and the timbers of the house could not bear the misfortune that had befallen my mother. That first night I dreamed I was back in the old cellar at school. I was standing in front of a row of glass jars filled with formaldehyde. The jars had been carefully dusted, and in one of them, as if weightless in the dirty yellow fluid, floated a delicately veined sleeping baby, its tiny fists pressed into its face, the little legs curled up. Suddenly the fluid turned red and the baby opened its eyes and screamed. It had the same big blue eyes as Glass.

Dianne slept beside me like a stone. But Tereza heard me crying and came to me. Straightaway she took me into her own bed and spoke to me comfortingly.

"Imagine life as a huge house with lots of rooms, Phil. Some of these rooms are empty, and others are full of junk. Some are big and filled with light, and others are dark and hide terror and grief. And from time to time—but only from time to time, mind you—the door to one of these scary rooms opens and you have to look inside, whether you want to or not. That makes you terribly frightened, like now. So you know what you do then?"

I shook my head.

"Then you imagine it's your life—your house, with your rooms. You have the keys, Phil. So you just shut the door of that scary room."

"And I throw the key away!"

"No, you mustn't do that, ever," replied Tereza. "Because one day you may realize that this scary room is the only way you can reach a bigger, more beautiful part of the house. And then you'll need the key. You can lock out your fear for a while, but at some point you have to face up to it."

"When I'm bigger?"

"Bigger and braver, my little one." Tereza stroked my temples with the back of her hand. "And perhaps not on your own anymore."

I couldn't wait to visit my mother in the hospital, because I wanted to see with my own eyes that she was still alive. But because she had lost a lot of blood and something had gone wrong with her abdomen, Glass was ordered total rest, and so only Tereza was allowed to see her for the first few days. And so, for all the reassurance offered me by Tereza that the worst was over, I continued to worry. Up to now I had believed there was nothing worse than life without a father. Now I was consumed by the nightmare prospect of a life without parents—if Glass hadn't survived the miscarriage, Dianne and I would have been orphans. Something akin to gratitude welled up inside me. The baby, a brother or sister, was lost, but Glass was still there. But despite the knowledge that if she had died Tereza would have raised heaven and hell to keep custody of us, the thought of life without my mother filled me with a terror that I was never to shake off completely. Weeks after her return home, I was still inventing scenarios of Glass meeting her death in the wildest ways, and these fantasies would repeatedly surface, recalling the cloth that Tereza had carried down the staircase at Visible, the crumpled sheet with the glaring red bloodstain. I had visions of Glass wrapped up in it like a toga or a sari, covered with it like a shroud; I saw it in the form of a hideous turban wound round her head.

Tereza did her utmost to keep Dianne and me occupied. On the third or fourth day she bundled us into the car early in the morning and set out on a drive, lasting hours, to a big city, only to end up in front of the closed gates of the zoo where she'd wanted to take us.

"Zoos are shut in winter" was Dianne's laconic observation. It was the first sentence she'd uttered since the terrible night at Visible. I gave a sigh of relief. Up to now I'd been uncertain whether she simply couldn't find the words to communicate or whether the shock of witnessing the event had robbed her of the power of speech. It was only Tereza's relaxed reaction to her silence that had reassured me somewhat.

"Of course," said Tereza. "Of course zoos are shut in winter." She sat down on a snow-covered bench and burst into tears.

I would have liked to comfort her, put an arm round her, but instinctively shrank from doing so. Something in Tereza rejected any form of sympathy.

Glass was more than a friend for her, and love never dies; at best it changes. Tereza had to let out her grief on her own. I looked at her red hair hanging limply, the tiny holes in the snow at her feet made by her tears, and thought back to the stormy night when we'd buried her father, how Tereza had dropped to her knees on the dirty wet earth of the burial mound and howled her grief at the sky, and I felt a lump rising in my throat. At this moment I'd have given a kingdom for a bagful of jelly bears.

When at last the day came that Dianne and I were allowed to pay Glass a brief visit, I was so wild with excitement that Tereza threatened to go and buy a dog leash and put it round my neck. But all that was required to calm me down was the sight of my mother. Glass was lying limp and pale in her bed in a room that seemed distinctly too cold to me, with a penetrating smell that brought back unpleasant memories. She could barely raise her head to greet us. She'd also been too weak to prevent Tereza from registering her as a private patient. Dianne and I sat in silence on the edge of the bed next to Glass for a while; I took her hand, which was surprisingly warm, and squeezed it without getting an answering squeeze, and all the same for that moment I was blissfully happy. At some point she fell asleep.

"Will she get completely better?" asked Dianne as we left the hospital with Tereza.

"Yes, but it'll take a while."

It took months, well into the summer. Physically Glass recovered relatively quickly, and after ten days she was back at Visible. But it was as if a black web had unfurled over her spirit and retreated only slowly and hesitantly. When the last remnant had dropped away, she appeared to be the same old

Glass, but by then I knew her well enough to realize that she had only regained sufficient strength to cover her eyes with blinkers.

From the day Glass came out of hospital, Dianne was a changed person. She blossomed and emanated an inner light. For weeks her face had been pale, and now for the first time a flush of color came back. She was lovingly attentive to Glass. Just as she had been before the miscarriage, once again Dianne now turned into care personified, and moreover proved an exemplary nurse. First thing in the morning she would scurry into the freezing cold kitchen, prepare food, make tea all day long, run soothing baths in the bathroom, read aloud to Glass from the newspaper, and do her very best to cheer our mother up, even if it was to no avail.

It didn't take long for me to consider her an angel.

"I put it in her tea, in small doses, so that she wouldn't taste it," said Dianne. "In case it had a taste. I never tried it myself."

She closes the herbary, puts it back on the shelf in its allotted place, and remains standing there. I see the back of her head and her back, bent forward a little, as if expecting blows. Her arms stretch out to either side; her hands cling to the spines of a few books.

"That's all there is to it," I hear her say quietly. "Now you know why Glass hates me."

"She doesn't hate you."

My own voice suddenly sounds like that of a stranger. I

don't know what has hit me harder, Dianne's confession or the almost casual way she has delivered it. I feel as if my entire body has been scooped out with a knife.

"Yes, Phil, she does." Dianne turns round to me. I've never seen her eyes look so dark. "Don't you understand, I could have killed her! I had no idea what sort of doses to give!"

"How did she find out?"

"She didn't. At least not by herself." Dianne moves slowly toward the French doors, where the wind is flinging snow crystals against the glass. They rattle on the panes like hailstones. "At one point we had a row. You were in Greece with Gable. We really let fly at each other—it was because . . . oh, it really doesn't matter what. Anyway, one thing led to another. Glass was screaming and threw a tantrum, and then I couldn't stop myself from telling her. Just flung it at her."

"God, Dianne . . ."

"It's got nothing to do with God." Again she's speaking very coolly, as if talking about two strangers. "That did it. She made me show her the herbary, and then for months she'd be huddled here in the library gawping at the wretched leather tome. I tried a hundred different ways to prove to her I was sorry, but she just withdrew totally."

"Can you blame her?"

"Phil, I'm not proud of what I did, believe me."

"You were jealous."

"Elementary, my dear Watson!" One corner of Dianne's mouth curls scornfully downwards. "Of course I was jealous! I was only thirteen years old, and years before that Glass had pushed me so far that I'd climbed up on the roof, just because I couldn't think of any other way to protest against her and scare her to death at the same time, and there are probably ten more reasons I could think of to excuse myself. But I am sorry."

"You should have told me all this long ago."

I get no answer.

"At least you ought to speak to Glass about it. Dianne, she's waiting for you to do so! Why won't you just get it over with?"

"Because to do so I'd have to take her seriously, and I can't. D'you remember what she was always going on about when we were little—'I love you the way you are'? Shit, Phil! If she'd really meant that, the whole thing wouldn't have happened."

"But she only wanted the best for you."

"Oh, did she? Well, I suppose that's what's known as the curse of a good intention."

Dianne stares out the window, very pale, very calm. Something churns through my insides. It won't stop and shakes me like tiny random electric shocks. My eyes wander and come to rest on the green paint spatters on my hands.

"Dianne . . . ? Did you set the dog on that boy the other night?"

She gives a soft laugh. "So do you take me for some kind of monster now as well, like Glass does? No doubt the boy repeated some kind of crap he heard sometime. We're the witch's children, remember Phil? It takes a long time for these old stories to get forgotten."

"So it wasn't you?"

Then Dianne turns round to me. "Don't be such an asshole! Did it ever cross your mind that I would have called the dog off—provided I'd had any influence on it, confused as it was, because the smell of blood must have made it completely mad?"

"But there was a time—"

"That's all over and done with. It's in the past, Phil! Unlike Glass, I realized that ages ago."

I don't know when she finally left. I stay on in the library. For a long time I sit on the throne, my story throne that's nothing more than an old armchair covered in threadbare red material, and stare at the shelves and walls and the spines of books in a room that has nothing more to tell me.

I don't even call Nicholas but set out an hour later to find him. He's been working in the municipal library, and I don't want to disturb him there or give Mrs. Hebeler the satisfaction of seeing me in such a state. He must be at home by now.

The streets are too icy to go by bicycle, so I go on foot. As I cross the bridge where Glass told me she was pregnant, tears come into my eyes. It takes me a good half hour to reach Fox Pass, running fast and then still faster, my face heading into the biting cold wind. I rush up the black basalt steps, go round the house, across the garden in the dusk, and past the window. Today there's no one moving behind it, and why should there be when they can talk to their reflection anywhere in this house? Past the barred windows that prevent misfortune from entering or escaping through them, past the terrace and the marble birdbath, up to the museum of lost things and invented stories. I step up to one of the windows, join my hands around my eyes, press them against the glass, and peer inside.

Even when you look into the room from outside, there is still the impression that it creates its own light and transmits it to the outside. A warm yellow glow. I was wrong on my first visit when I thought that it was the objects on the shelves and in the showcases that create this glow. It must have emanated from Nicholas, as it does now in pulsating beams that break like waves against my eyes. The light rises from his naked body, lying stretched out on the floor and still bearing the last bronze-colored traces of a summer suntan.

It streams like water over his slightly splayed legs, over his wiry arms, his beautiful hands. It even plays over his lips, a golden torrent, as Nicholas opens his mouth as if to give a silent scream. I pull back from the window, not because I'm afraid of being seen, but because I'm afraid the sounds rising in my throat like black spiderwebs surging out of a burst cocoon might be heard in there. If I could, I'd run with my eyes shut now.

But I've long been back in Visible now, and even after I

fetched the ax from the garden shed, yelling as I smashed it into the showcase made for Nicholas, till all the strength drained from my arms and the floor was strewn with thousands of splinters, I can still see the tensing, arching back and the back of the girl's head as she sat astride Nicholas very gently—as if she didn't want to hurt him—rocking up and down with careful, circular movements of her hips, and I see the head with its black hair thrown back, Kat's black hair, which only yesterday was still blond.

"When and where do things begin, ladies and gentlemen? It is thought that life follows a particular plan, a somehow crafted pattern, an open or a secret sense. Why?"

As usual, Handel simply casts the question into the room, and as usual it is purely rhetorical. I'd prefer it if he would suddenly digress for no particular reason and lecture, and in so doing—unlike when he's teaching math—not care whether anyone answers his questions.

"We believe in sense, because we cannot bear the thought that everything is simply a matter of chance. We believe in signs, but believe me, there are no signs. Beethoven created some of his greatest compositions after he became deaf—important things occur in silence. Catastrophes occur without the heavens darkening beforehand. The birth of children who go on to become historic personalities who leave their mark on the world is not heralded by thunder and lightning. Groundbreaking discoveries are made but are not accompanied by a flower of outstanding beauty blooming somewhere on earth. There are no signs, ladies and gentlemen. At best there are coincidences. All else is superstition."

There were times, like now, when Handel fell silent after an extended performance, bobbed up and down, collected his thoughts, and then continued.

"At some time after man had learned to walk upright and mastered fire, he must have realized, ladies and gentlemen, that despite his fellow creatures who painted the outlines of mammoths and saber-toothed tigers on the walls of caves with wet earth pigments in the light of flickering flames, he was alone and had only himself to rely on. This realization drove him to despair! And it was on this despair that religions were founded, in a desert of meaninglessness and pain, and it is this consolation that is the only thing that they are really good at. For religions dispense consolation but no understanding."

Someone put up a hand in protest, but he simply ignored him. " 'Faith,' " he quoted some philosopher in conclusion, " 'is an insult to common sense.' "

It was a remark that nearly cost him his job. The school board considered transferring him—reluctantly, as I discovered from Kat; Handel had everyone's sympathy, and in the end her father decided simply to sit the whole affair out, but without sticking his neck out too far and publicly defending his best math teacher. Some parents didn't calm down even after weeks had gone by. The Little People were brave and upright Christian souls.

If God was dead, as Handel had maintained in his by now infamous lecture, this piece of news had at any rate not reached them yet.

"Maybe a few of the men," granted Glass as we were sitting together in the kitchen, discussing the scandal. "Otherwise some of them wouldn't incur the awaited divine wrath by beating their wives with predictable regularity to the point of needing hospital treatment." She thought for a moment. "It was probably also the men who bumped him off. After all, they were the ones who invented him as well, weren't they?"

"Why don't you go and talk to Handel about it sometime?"

"Oh, he's a bit too plump for my taste."

"Mom!"

Glass laughed. "You know, he's quite right, your Handel. There's no sense to life. It's completely random. All it wants is to carry on. And as far as that's concerned, I've done my duty and fulfilled my obligations."

I listened to her and saw a shadow rising behind her on the wall, Handel's shadow, nodding in agreement. But even Glass, and maybe Handel too, would have admitted that everyone reaches a crossroad in their life, with paths going off in different directions, and they have to decide which one they will follow. Someone who finds no meaning in his life can at least still try to set himself a goal. With luck, at some point the two can merge.

So when and where did things begin? Maybe they began when nearly two hundred years ago a butterfly flapped its wings in Asia and the air moved, as a result of which the weather in Europe changed and a wind blew in the face of one of my ancestors, who savored change. Or when Glass decided to leave America after my unknown father had left her high and dry. Maybe things began when Tereza realized that I would never in my life learn to whistle with two fingers or play football. When I met a bandaged little girl with a passion for cherry ice cream in Earnoseandthroat, when I saw Nicholas on the snow-covered steps of the church, below which he found my snow globe, or when Dianne took refuge up on Visible's rooftop, swarming with bats.

Maybe things already began millions of years ago as some blind, bored God snapped His fingers and set off the big bang.

Yes, definitely. That must be it.

part three

chasing the winter blues away

chapter 16

phantoms

Monday passes in a timeless, blank vacuum. I've told Glass and Dianne that I've gone down with flu. Retreating to my room into the protective hollow of my bed, I erect towers of thoughts yards high from identical bricks, knocking them down again piece by piece, or watch as they come crashing down of their own accord. Staring numbly at the wall for hours on end, I see Kat and Nicholas before me, Nicholas and Kat, all the while rolling the snow globe like a fetish between my hands, not knowing whether it brings me good or bad luck. The room is overheated. I don't leave my bed except to go and get more firewood from the shed.

I dream about my pool. Its waters close over me, pitch black and cold. I sink deeper and deeper; even in my dream my feet are searching for the bottom. It's a feeling of movement in utter calm and utter darkness—free fall, floating downward, unending.

On Tuesday Kat telephones.

"What's up with you?" comes down the line. "Why aren't you at school?"

"Flu."

"Oh . . . well, you haven't missed anything. So near the holidays—there's nothing much going on. Handel brought in biscuits and read us *A Christmas Carol* by Dickens. Candles on the tables and stuff—it was really cozy. You'd have liked it."

"Can you tell them why I'm away?"

"No problem. I'll pass it straight to my dad."

There's a short pause, interrupted by a soft crackling on the line. I shut my eyes.

"Yuh . . . well," says Kat hesitantly, "I don't know if I'll get to drop by again. Christmas shopping and all that. Packing too. We're off tomorrow. In the afternoon."

"It's OK. See you after New Year's."

"Yup. Well, then . . ." Each of us listens to the other's words trailing off. "Till next year, then. Have a good one and all that. And look after yourself."

"Kat," I add in a rush.

"Yes?"

"Did you do it?"

I think I hear a sharp intake of breath, but maybe I'm just imagining it.

"Do what?"

"Dye your hair?"

"What? Oh, yes, sure! It's black now. I don't expect you'll like it, or will you? But I feel like a completely new person."

I sob into my pillow after she's hung up.

The next hours pass in surreal clarity. I look out onto the bare trees in front of the window. I can clearly make out, like an X-ray image, frozen vascular bundles in the twigs and branches, hidden below the bark. Life is suspended there in the form of minute icy crystals. I count fantastically linked molecules and inaudible, softly pulsating atoms.

Later, at some point between waking and sleeping, Dianne is standing in my room—at least I think I see her standing there. Outside dusk reigns and everything is indivisibly gray, the room, the light, Dianne herself. Only her eyes shine out, as remorselessly white as the porcelain eyes of Paleiko before he was broken into a thousand pieces.

Don't expect me to help you now, Phil.

No . . . It's because I left you on your own, is it?

For years you didn't give a shit about me. Did you want me to change into a shadow?

No.

The water in the river was so cold. And the moon shone so brightly that its light burnt my eyes.

I'm sorry.

That's what people say who don't know anything, or don't want to know anything.

Stay with me.

I can't, Phil.

Nicholas looks more real than Dianne. And more alive. Hard to know exactly why, but he appears more alive to me than ever before. He turns up on Wednesday, the day Kat goes off on holiday. He stands in my room as if surrounded by an aura of fizzing blue oxygen. His black hair gleams, the dark eyes glitter, his face is the color of a healthy apple. He's wearing expensive gloves of very fine light brown leather that he doesn't remove.

"You look terrible. Kat says you've got flu."

"It's on the way out." I could ask him why he hasn't been in touch for days, but he'd only lie.

"I brought you something." Nicholas produces a little parcel. Christmas tree baubles and candles and children's toys are printed on the wrapping paper. "But not to be opened till Christmas, promise?"

"Will we see each other again before you're off with your parents?"

"That's going to be tricky." He goes over to the bookshelf and places the package on it. "We're off on Friday, and before that I've got to—"

"Do Christmas shopping. And pack, of course."

"Exactly." My sarcasm escapes him. He pushes back the sleeve of his overcoat and looks at his watch. "Actually, I'm already a bit pushed for time."

I can't attack him, because I'm busy defending myself.

Nicholas sits down on the edge of the bed and strokes my cheek with his gloved hand. I stop myself from thinking of the hands inside the soft light brown leather or of the warmth of his skin. Then he kisses me on the forehead. His lips are cold. I protect myself from his smile by making myself think of mutilated corpses, the mangled bloodred debris in some war zone.

"I'd like to see you again before you go."

"Can't it wait till after Christmas?"

"No."

He grins. "It's not terminal flu, is it?"

"Would you stay if it were?"

Instead of an answer, he gets up and smoothes down the front of his coat with his gloves. "I've really got to go now. My mother's waiting for me to drive her to go shopping."

Suddenly I'm so furious that I have to clench my fists under the bedspread to stop myself from jumping up and hitting him. "What about tomorrow?"

Nicholas shakes his head.

"Then the day after, Friday?"

"OK. I'll come and fetch you—in the morning." He doesn't say it reluctantly, but he's in a rush and is practically out of the room. "Provided you're better by then."

I remain lying on my back after he's gone and try to make out the pattern on the white ceiling in order to arrange the red and blue glowing sparks of my anger around it.

Later Glass pops her head round the door. "What is it

you're supposed to drink when you've got flu—hot milk and honey or eggnog with wine?"

"It's hot lemon juice." I turn on my side and stare at the wall. "Leave me alone. I'm tired."

"What's the matter, darling? Trouble with Nick? He barely stayed five minutes."

In the past she'd never have done that, asked how I or Dianne was feeling. In the past we were fledglings who had to learn to fly by ourselves. I don't answer.

"Don't you want to talk about it?"

"No, I do not want to talk about it!" Bitterness wells up in me like bile. "You know all about that, don't you?" I don't turn round to face her. She ignores my question anyway.

"I'll run you a hot bath. By the way, Tereza wishes you better. And I've got this for you from Pascal."

An envelope lands on my bed. On the card inside are just two short lines. I scrunch it up angrily, hurl it across the room, and silently curse Pascal and her goddamn intuition.

Half an hour later I lower myself up to my neck into steaming scented foam. Glass comes back with a fresh large towel. She sits down on the edge of the tub, hands on her knees, staring past me at the old brass boiler. I know that she can wait forever—she does exactly the same with her clients, giving the women time, time to breathe, to find the right words to express their emotions. For a time I give myself up to the soothing scent of the foam bath and savor the feeling as the tension in my muscles gradually melts away. Sleepily I watch condensation spreading down the black tiles in small overlapping rivulets, and think of Michael's chess game.

"Mom?"

"Hm?"

"Dianne told me. You know, the business about . . ."

I cannot bring myself to utter the word *miscarriage.* Glass continues looking at the boiler. Her only visible reaction is a tiny head movement, the suggestion of a nod. "Is that why you're feeling so bad?"

"No." The sound of soft popping of thousands of shining tiny foam bubbles bursting before my eyes. "Well, yes, that too."

"You're asking me why I didn't tell you?"

I nod.

"If I had, wouldn't you have thought I was trying to set you against Dianne?"

"Perhaps."

"No, quite definitely." Glass wipes her hand across her forehead, which is covered in tiny beads of perspiration. The boiler is giving out intense heat. "After she told me, I hated her. And when at last I felt ready to give in, then she hated me. To be honest, I simply have no idea how to break out of this vicious circle if she isn't prepared to play along."

She puts her head to one side, takes a deep breath, and then breathes out again. Maybe she's crying. I can't help her, and I don't think she expects me to either. I've tried often enough to mediate between her and Dianne.

"Well, all right . . ." Glass sniffs loudly, an indication as good as any that for her the subject is now closed. "And what happened just now between you and Nick?"

I have to blurt it out quickly. If I hesitate, I won't be able to say it at all. "He and Kat slept together. Neither of them has any idea that I know."

Whether what followed really happened or whether I just imagine it did I can't really tell afterward, just as I couldn't really distinguish between sleeping and waking these past few days. At my words Glass looks at me, and the familiar features in her face seem to rearrange themselves. Her forehead and the corners of her mouth droop, and an expression of such consternation enters her wide-open eyes that I have a crazy impulse to laugh out loud. I feel terrible, for the whole business is terrible, but there are worse catastrophes than betrayal or loss of love, and even both together shouldn't trigger such a reaction.

As if you'd had your skin torn from your flesh and then had salt rubbed in.

The words rush into my mind, voiceless, soundless, speechless, more the scraps left from the memory of speech—a memory of Glass. An old memory—moreover, it's worn like the ragged edges of a much-handled photo, and even the colors are faded, strangely washed out and sepia-colored.

". . . or could you imagine sharing him with Kat?" asks Glass.

I'm certain I missed the first part of the sentence, and equally certain that my imagination or my tiredness has been playing tricks on me, for Glass is still looking at me, and her face shows no sign of consternation or sadness. There is just a lively interest, and behind it a trace of empathy. At her question, I shake my head forcefully.

"No, stupid of me, who could possibly do so?" she murmurs. "I was just thinking . . . Maybe that's what Nick wants. It doesn't have to mean anything, his sleeping with Kat. It may have been a one-off for the two of them."

"I don't believe it."

Glass shrugs her shoulders. "Maybe he isn't gay at all. Or maybe he feels the same for men as he does for women. Has that ever occurred to you?"

"Yes. And even if that was so, I still wouldn't want to share him with Kat. Just as Kat wouldn't be prepared to share him with me. Hell would have to freeze over first."

"Give me your hand, Phil."

Glass strokes the whispering foam and the drops of water from the back of my hand. It's one of those rare physical gestures—I used to think that Dianne and I received so few of them because her lovers demanded so much for themselves.

"It's not fair," I whisper.

"It never is, darling."

"What am I going to do?"

How often must Glass have been asked that question—a hundred, two hundred times? Even more? And how often have I heard her answer this question, sitting with Dianne under the kitchen table in the late evening or at night, eavesdropping on her talks with her clients?

"What are you worth, Phil?"

"I don't know."

"Whom do you love more, yourself or him?"

"I don't know."

Glass lets go of my hand and stands up. "Well, now, once you do know, you won't have a problem anymore."

"Thanks a million for your help."

"Don't mention it." Her gaze softens. "I'm quite serious, Phil. Don't do yourself down just because you don't want to lose Nicholas." In the doorway she turns round again. "And don't stay in the tub too long. You're getting all wrinkled."

I wait till the sound of her footsteps fades away down the corridor; then I shut my eyes. I take a deep breath, hold it, and let myself go under. Water and foam wash together over me. I listen to the intensified booming, creaking, and whispering of Visible, the metallic clanking of the ancient pipes, and hear the pulsating rush of the blood streaming through my veins. At a certain point my lungs threaten to burst. Red spots begin to dance before my eyes.

Pascal's postcard says: *How much longer are you going to play the bystander and keep on feeling sorry for yourself? Wish you better.*

I come up again, very slowly.

Late on Thursday morning when Glass is at the law firm and Dianne at Kora's, there's a ring at the front door. I rush out of my room and tumble down the stairs into the entrance hall driven by the vague hope that it's Nicholas, who's made his way here a day earlier than planned.

The cold rushes at me as I open the door. A boy roughly my age is standing there. He's wearing black jeans and a dark coat. His face is so pale that it merges into the whiteness of the snow behind him. I notice barely perceptible freckles that must have been more pronounced in the summer. His short hair is not quite red, more bronze-colored, yet his eyebrows and eyelashes are blond, almost invisible. The boy is almost girlishly pretty. And slightly embarrassed—it goes through my mind that had he been standing here on the same spot a hundred years ago, he would probably have been twisting a cap uncertainly in his hands.

"Hi."

"Hallo."

"Is this where . . . Dianne lives here, doesn't she?"

"As well."

"Can I . . . Well, you know me, don't you?"

I reflect. Suddenly I'm certain I do know him. I rummage in my memory, but I can't place this pale face right away, so I shake my head.

"I used to live here. Not in your house, of course," he adds hurriedly. He nods his head in the direction of the river. "On the other side, in the town."

He looks at me expectantly, his mouth half open. Then he reaches in his right-hand coat pocket and pulls something out.

A pocketknife.

I gasp, less out of fear than surprise. There's only one boy in the world who would hand me that knife. I might have recognized him sooner, but his hair was even shorter then, stubbly, and his face rounder, like every child's face.

"You're the guy who went for Dianne with the knife, at the Big . . . down at the river!" I say in amazement.

He nods and puts the knife back in his pocket. Back then Dianne had dropped the knife in the river after she'd pulled it out of the wound in her shoulder. The boy must have gone back for it later. He looks at me expectantly. He has very pale green eyes. Sometimes when I dreamed about him, about him and his knife and Dianne's wound, where the flesh split open like overripe fruit when he stabbed her, I studied these eyes. As a child I had thought I detected meanness in them, an evil intent, if such a thing exists. But even in my dreams there had been something more—I remembered how the boy had hesitated before lunging out and how the hesitation had been evident in his whole posture and in his eyes. Then there came a time when I virtually forgot the episode. After the Hulk and the little stabber had left town I scarcely ever thought of them. In my memory they had turned into phantoms that disappeared into the shadows, cast over the world by Dianne's and my own superhuman heroic figures.

"What do you want?" I ask the boy.

"To see your sister."

"What for?"

"To apologize to her."

I can't help grinning. "After all these years?"

He looks down at the ground again. It must have taken a huge amount of courage to turn up here.

"Come in for a minute before you freeze to death." I guide him into the kitchen. Glass lit the fire earlier in the morning, and it's still warm. I poke around in the glowing embers, blow on them, and wait for the first flames to flicker. The boy has sat down at the table and is looking round. He hasn't taken off his coat.

"And?" I say.

"What?"

"Is it like you expected? The witch's house?"

He relaxes. It's as if the warmth from the fire is thawing him out. He has dimples when he laughs. "When we were kids, we really believed it—you and your sister gave us all the frights." He spreads his arms out. "Now all I can see is a kitchen and a guy who seems quite nice."

"Thanks."

"Maybe I'd see things differently if we'd stayed here in this little backwater. The people here are a hundred years behind the times."

"Things have improved a bit over the years," I say. "You left pretty quick after the business at the river, didn't you?"

The boy nods. "About three months later. I hardly remember. It was more like escaping than moving away. My mother packed a few bits and pieces, and we did a disappearing act, and that was it. Off down south, near the border. The old man was sitting watching TV."

"Does your father still live here in the town?"

"He died two years ago. Drank himself to death."

"Oh."

"No need to feel sorry," said the boy coolly. "The guy was a real loser. Boozing, thrashing, more boozing. I didn't feel sorry, none of us did."

"D'you have brothers and sisters?"

"A brother and an older sister."

I sit down at the table facing him. Perhaps I ought to offer him coffee or tea, but getting the fire alight has drained me of all my remaining energy. I've been lying in bed as good as dead for days, and now I'm completely done in.

"Did you ever see your father again after you moved away?" I ask.

"Just once. I was twelve or thirteen at the time. Actually, I did a runner to go and see him. Funny or what, when he made life such hell for us?" He considers his slender hands as if they had something to do with that hell or with his father. "Anyway, when I arrived, he was so drunk, he didn't even recognize me at first. And then at some stage he started bawling and yelling that my mother was a whore and so on. And then I asked myself—who wants an asshole like that for a father?"

Strange that I've never thought of it before—that Number Three, if I ever met him, might turn out to be not the longed-for great savior and wonderful father, but someone who beat, drank, and raped—one of those men, in fact, whom Glass's clients usually spoke about in hushed voices, the way you do about sleeping monsters, for fear of waking them just by whispering their names in the air.

"Actually, I have your mother to thank," the boy continues. "If it hadn't been for her, we'd never have taken the plunge."

"I thought she only spoke to the Hulk's mother at the time."

"The Hulk?" The forehead furrows above the green eyes. "Oh, him, yes. That was what some people called him."

"D'you know what happened to him?"

"No idea. In any case, our mothers, yours and mine, did talk. Otherwise we'd never have got as far as doing a runner and that."

"And now you've come back all that way to . . ."

"No." The boy shakes his head. "My mother's come to visit a friend. I just came along with her."

A silence follows that I'd fill with questions if I could think of any. The fire gives out soft popping and crackling noises and the hissing sound of warmth drawing through the chimney. The disconcerting situation must be even more embarrassing for the boy than for me—at least I have the advantage of being on home ground. All the same I'm relieved when I hear the jingle of a key followed by footsteps approaching the kitchen. Then Dianne is standing in the doorway.

"You've got a visitor, Dianne. This is . . ."

The boy has got to his feet. Suddenly he appears as embarrassed as he was when I opened the front door to him.

"Dennis," he says.

Dianne narrows her eyes and just stands there for a few seconds, tilting her head slightly to the side, her cheeks reddened from running in the cold. Finally she nods, as if she's just found the answer to a question that's been bothering her for ages.

"Dennis," she repeats.

"I just wanted to—"

"You know what, Dennis?" Dianne interrupts him. She goes toward him, throws her bag on a chair, and leans on the table with both arms. Her face is so close to the startled boy that the slightest movement further forward would bring her near enough to kiss him. "I would have stabbed you then if I'd had my own knife with me."

Dianne steps back. I look at Dennis, and he looks at me out of his pale green eyes, and from me he looks at Dianne, and from her back at me. The witch's children. And then all of us, Dianne included, burst out laughing.

On Friday morning Nicholas comes to fetch me from Visible. He suggests going in the direction of the sports field, and, unprotesting, I trot along after him. We cross the bridge to the town, and on the Little People's side we turn off to the left along a footpath. The winding trail follows the river for almost half a mile, alongside community gardens and a few isolated houses. The sky is gray; it's one of those sad winter days that get lost between dawn and dusk, as it never really gets light.

At some point Nicholas branches off the well-trodden track and plods through the snow-covered grass. He talks about his relatives, superficial uninteresting little stories that I hardly pay attention to. I hear him speaking next to me, and from out of nowhere a feeling steals over me as if I'm detached from my own body and floating somewhere above us, taking in all the immediate surroundings with every one of my senses—I sniff the empty classrooms with their smell of chalk, see the Christmas tree with a pathetic string of lights, rise beside the war memorial in the market square, hear the rustling as the UFO turns the pages of a photo album looking at pictures of her husband, feel the ice spreading outward from either side of the river, taste the sugar on roasted almonds being packed into pink bags by a stall holder outside the supermarket.

"In other words," Nicholas concludes, "my entire family consists of boring rich people who feel bound to get together at Christmas and talk, talk, talk incessantly so they don't run the risk of realizing how useless they are during the long stretch of imposed leisure."

"If they're that boring, why do you go and visit them?"

"It's what we do."

The words bear no contradiction. I recall that when we

were having a row some weeks back Nicholas had said something about having to keep an eye on his parents. I don't remind him of it.

We pass Annie Glosser's abandoned house, which has gradually been growing derelict over the years. It looks like a bewitched gingerbread cottage from a fairy tale. Snow weighs down on the roof, and two of the shutters are swinging open. They hang crookedly from their hinges, and the windowpanes behind them are shattered. I stand in front of the fence and look at the white garden, where legions of wild roses grow rampant every summer, as red as Annie's shoes. Suddenly I long for this crazy fat woman like nothing else on earth. And from one minute to the next it seems the easiest thing to spit in a church font or confront Nicholas. Only it's hard to do so while I look at him. I plunge my hands into my coat pockets and stare into the darkness beyond the broken windowpanes.

"I saw you having sex with Kat."

"You did . . . what?"

"I wasn't spying on you," I add hastily. "It just happened."

"I could say the same."

"What?"

"That it just happened," says Nicholas slowly. "With Kat and me."

"Do you love her?"

"No."

"Do you love me?"

I still don't dare to look at him. My words have pursued a singular, sober, and merciless logic, emerging inevitably from what has gone before. Now they've been spoken, and hang in the air vibrating silently, and can't be retracted.

"I need you," replies Nicholas. "But I don't love you."

"That's pathetic."

"No, it's honest."

"And altogether practical, isn't it? Probably soothes your conscience after you've made use of people like stuff on sale in a ten-cent store."

My legs have gone weak. If I don't move, I'll fall or vomit. I turn round and go off following the line of the hedge whose proximity offers protection and safety. Nicholas stumbles after me.

"What's the difference between loving each other and needing each other, Phil? Who's to say that what you feel for me is love? How can you be so sure? And damn it, how can you judge me so self-righteously? After all you've told me, what your mother gets up to is no different from me."

"Glass has her reasons."

"Everyone has reasons for what they do."

I wish I could draw comfort from the thought that he's just hiding behind rhetorical hairsplitting. I wish I could reply by saying that Glass, unlike him, speaks about her reasons, but of course she never has. I feel I've been driven into a corner, and I quicken my pace.

Nicholas grabs me by the arm. "Phil, what difference does

it make whether I love you or not? I like you. We get on well together. We spend time together. We have good sex."

I stop walking and shrug him off. "I want more than that."

"For example?"

"For example, that you take me into your confidence."

"I do."

"No, you don't! You don't tell me about yourself, not really. I don't know what goes on inside you. Actually, I don't really know anything about you."

"There's nothing to know."

"Is that so? Have you ever tried explaining that to Kat? She'll be even less satisfied than I am just to jump into bed with you! And even less inclined to share you with me. Sooner or later you're going to have to decide on one or the other of us."

Nicholas shakes his head. "I like you both. It's not a question of deciding."

"For me it is. And if you're not able to do so, then I'll have to."

I turn away from him and trudge on. To the right of me the hedges part and open onto a small meadow. Around the edges stand closely ranged snow-covered fruit trees. Some of the trees were cut down in the summer; a tall pile of logs is stacked up at the end of the meadow. I don't realize that Nicholas has stopped following me until I no longer hear the sound of his footsteps beside me and I turn round to him. He's standing some feet away from me in this white nothingness, an island all alone. Then he comes slowly toward me, cautiously, almost as if he's afraid the snow might give way under him and the ground might swallow him up.

"What do you mean?"

"Nicholas, I want to feel I'm safe with you! Is that so hard to understand? And I can't be with someone who claims to need me but is ready to drop me at any time. I'm worth more than that."

"So what will you do?"

"Go. Just go."

He remains rooted to the spot. And there it is. For a brief moment the armor plating that Nicholas surrounds himself with opens up. I see it in his gaze that flickers like a startled, frightened bird. Fear grips me so intensely that my knees threaten to give way. The beautiful face, normally so controlled and unmoved, now changes expression several times within seconds, just as if invisible hands were pulling a series of Greek tragedy masks over it in rapid succession—fear gives way to helpless despair, childlike surprise, burning hatred.

"No."

And then the moment passes. Nicholas is once more in complete control. His face relaxes. Whatever it was that rose briefly to the surface has sunk deep down again. But everything has changed, first making my heart miss a beat and then making it beat faster, so that I'm now desperate to take back everything I said.

I go toward Nicholas and stretch out my hand.

"I'm sorry, I didn't mean—"

My hearing and seeing coincide. What I hear is a dry crack, as if a branch has given way somewhere and snapped under the weight of the snow covering it. What I see is Nicholas's right eye opening above the pupil before his head jerks to one side as if hit by some invisible blow, and he collapses into the snow.

He screams. Oh, God, he screams loud enough to make the heavens tear apart and the earth open up. And above his screams I hear words, words I've heard once before, life completing a dreadful full circle. Suddenly I can smell the nearby river, it's summer, the air smells of algae and butterbur, and somewhere there's a flash of pink and silver as a rainbow trout shoots away through the foaming water below the Big Eye.

"He's—"

"Ohhh . . ."

"Get away!"

Nicholas is lying in the snow clasping his right eye with both hands. I fall on my knees in front of him.

"Let me . . . Nicholas! Take your hands away!"

"Noooo . . . !"

"Nicholas, let me see!"

There's hardly any blood, just pale, clear fluid. It sticks to his gloves, it oozes from what a moment ago was still an eye and now looks like a squashed small flower. Nicholas clamps his hands back to his face, doubles up, and writhes in the snow, yelling. Then I hear the crackling sound of rapid steps running away. I spring up and dash off.

Ten yards ahead snow sprinkles down from some of the fruit tree branches that reach right down to the meadow. The branches bang against each other and close, obscuring a shadow disappearing out of sight. There's the stack of cut logs, brown and wet, and tall enough to hide behind quite easily. I chase round the pile.

Wolf is cowering on the ground and stares at me, his eyes a ghastly clear gray. He's wearing neither jacket nor coat, just a painfully thin striped shirt. Blond curly hair falls heavily over his forehead, tangled and wiry with a life of its own. The air gun lies across his arms, and Wolf slowly rocks himself to and fro with it. His hands are frozen, the veins standing out purple from his skin. His mouth moves; his blue lips croon the same three words over and over again across the glittering snow, barely audible above the hideous screams of Nicholas: "The poor Runner, the poor Runner, the poor Runner . . ."

When I whisper his name, I feel ashes in my mouth. When I call up his image, ice settles on my thoughts. When I imagine myself stroking him, scalpels cut my fingers and hands open.

He was taken to the same clinic where Kat and I first met, two hours away from me by car. He refuses to see me or take my phone calls. He doesn't want me to utter his name again. I'm history. I don't know how to reach Kat at her holiday resort. I don't know whether I really want to either.

I learn from his mother that the eye is damaged beyond repair, making it blind, but that the bullet from Wolf's air gun was removed from the back of the right eye socket and did not cause any further harm. His mother is a very unhappy woman. Her loneliness cloaks her like the stink of decay. I introduced myself to her as a school friend of her son's. I don't meet his father.

The bullet was meant for me, and only intended as a warning shot, according to what Thomas told the police. I don't discover how he got to Wolf and how he managed to win him over. Once he had wormed his way into Wolf's heart and mind, it wouldn't have taken much persuasion to turn Wolf into the willing tool of his jealousy. Day after day they had waited for me outside Visible, waiting in the freezing cold, till they saw me leave with Nicholas and followed us. Thomas couldn't have guessed that by the time Wolf fired the shot he would already have turned the gun away from me and aimed at the boy beside me. And maybe he wouldn't have cared.

chapter 17

talking in the dark

It doesn't stop snowing for days. People are getting excited at the prospect of a white Christmas, and Glass keeps putting on Stella's ancient scratchy record of the soulful relevant Bing Crosby song. Streets become impassable for a while, and outlying districts are cut off. The massive weight of the snow brings down whole trees or makes them lean dangerously to one side, and every now and again there is a threatening rumble of protest from Visible's roof.

Gable shows up at Visible two days before Christmas Eve, and on his arrival the weather turns. As he stands at the door in the early afternoon, his sailor's kit bag over his shoulder, it stops snowing. It's almost as if Gable has tumbled out of the sky accompanied by a thousand stars—suddenly the day is unbelievably bright and clear, the air motionless and the sunshine warm. The screams of delight that Glass greets him with travel all the way up to my room, where I'm abandoning myself to dark thoughts about guilt and atonement, love and death. I've been staring at the wall for hours, trying to make my eyes bore a hole into Visible's masonry. The image of a horrific flower swims before my eyes, opening and closing in unending time-lapse frames, and with each completed loop spews this clear, gall-like fluid from its shattered center.

Apart from general expressions of shock and regret, reactions to what took place are somewhat varied. In characteristic fashion Glass's view was a sober one. Nothing and no one, she maintained, was of sufficient importance to bring the world to a standstill. I should count myself lucky that the accident—*And after all, it was an accident, wasn't it, darling?*—with Nicholas occurred at a point when I happened to be morally at a very low ebb. She very politely pointed out that although she had every sympathy for my wish once again to remain shut away in my room wrangling with my destiny, she was in no way inclined to support my gloomy contemplation of my navel with constant deliveries of food and drink.

Both Michael and Tereza had offered to represent Nicholas in court if he or his parents decided, as might be expected, to institute legal proceedings against Thomas. I told both of them that they would have to go straight to Nicholas if they were interested in the case, as I had no wish to concern myself any further with the matter. I was by no means polite, and later regretted my behavior. I apologized to them, and hated them afterward for being understanding.

Pascal earned penalty points from all sides with her observation that the best thing would be for all men to be issued guns—that way the world would soon be rid of one huge problem. Dianne couldn't help grinning when I told her. Apart from that, to my relief my sister kept her opinions to herself.

The loudest reactions came from across the river. It's grotesque, but then I hadn't really expected anything different: not knowing any better, the Little People blame me for what happened. Thomas spread some filthy story about me, and I couldn't help thinking of Irene, the unfortunate UFO, and her tormentor, Dr. Hoffmann, and the role reversal of victim and culprit. I received several anonymous letters all bearing the local postmark. Two of them were written by hand. For the third, someone had gone to the lengths of cutting up the local paper, extracting individual words and several capital letters, and rearranging them into an alphabet of hatred, something new to me but long familiar to Tereza and Pascal.

Now when I hear Glass kicking up a racket, I jump out of bed, rush downstairs to the entrance hall, miss the bottom step, and sprain my left ankle. My yells of pain mingle with Gable's laughter until at last the floodgates open and I lean against Gable's chest and his comforting murmurs, needing no words, for he sounds as if he's brought the ocean with him.

His hands glide across my head, stroke my back, my shoulders and arms. Gable knows exactly what to do. Under his touch the first wounds gradually begin to heal.

Yet Nicholas remains present. It's not concrete memories that persist in my consciousness; the only image that repeatedly appears before me with inescapable clarity is the ghastly sight of his burst eye. Other than that there is just the feeling of irreparable loss and the vague thought of having narrowly escaped a punishment actually intended for me rather than Nicholas, which I believe I deserved. There are times when I manage to suppress these thoughts, but even then Nicholas is still there. He stands in the dark corner of an otherwise brightly lit room and is only waiting to step forward out of the shadows. When it all gets too much for me, I close the door to this room, turn the key, and remove it, just as Tereza told me to do years ago when dreams of bloodstained sheets and worry about Glass robbed me of sleep. But I don't know where to keep the key. Its weight is heavier than all the memories put together.

One of Glass's long-held wishes is for once in her life to see the whole of Visible lit up in the full blaze of Christmas lights. She dreams of strings of Technicolor Christmas lights framing the front door and every single window, stretching across the façade and roof, and encircling the railings and uprights of the veranda. Every little ridge and each of the tiny bull's-eye windowpanes in the miniature towers that Dianne and I never looked out of as children, because of our fear of the attic, is to be decorated.

"Now that I think about it, the trees could be lit up as well," she says to Michael as the three of us are decorating the Christmas tree in the room with the fireplace. "I really don't know what you find so great about these smelly wax candles. And what's more, they're dangerous."

"Leave me out of your tacky American gimmicks," Michael replies from the top of a wobbly wooden ladder. "A real tree has to have real candles!"

"I didn't want a real tree!" says Glass grumpily. "We've managed very well all these years with our plastic one, haven't we, Phil? Now it's stuck down in the cellar and—"

"Pass me the wire," Michael interrupts her with a grin. "I wouldn't put it past you to serve hamburgers under the tree."

"We're having chicken and roast potatoes," Glass declares importantly. She hands Michael the wire. "Provided Gable's in luck down at the supermarket and there's still one left."

I could hardly believe my ears when Dianne announced she was going to accompany Gable to do the shopping. And yet it fits with the change that I've observed coming over her in the last weeks and months. Dianne has become gentler and more approachable.

"Oh, Michael, it's beautiful!" Glass beams. Previously she would never have shown her delight as openly as she does now when the decoration of the Christmas tree, a magnificent specimen over six feet high, is complete.

"Just wait until we've lit the candles," says Michael. "You won't believe your eyes. Electric candles indeed!" He shakes his head in mock horror.

"All right, all right!" says Glass. "Phil, would you put that record on again, the one with—"

"I know."

To the strains of "White Christmas" and Glass's off-key accompaniment, I distribute round the room plates piled with the Christmas biscuits that Pascal has baked for us by the ton. A blazing fire crackles in the chimney. Michael has arranged branches of pine and orange peel in front of it, filling the whole room with the aroma of a spice store. All that's missing is a heap of gifts at the foot of the Christmas tree. We've decided against them. This time even Gable has arrived empty-handed, which suits me fine—I depend on his hands. I don't know what it is or how he does it, but when he puts his arms round me—which he frequently does—it somehow makes me feel better. For the first time I have a sense of what Michael must mean to Glass.

When Gable and Dianne return home from shopping, Glass shuts herself away in the kitchen: Operation Christmas Chicken. The outcome is no culinary revelation but looks and tastes acceptable.

"Good," mutters Michael appreciatively.

"Just good?" asks Glass defensively across the table.

"It's superb. The mother of all roast chickens." It would never occur to Michael to criticize the shortcomings of the Christmas menu. He has this enviable unerring sensitivity to other people's weaknesses. I feel a painful stab thinking of Kat, who's the exact opposite in this respect.

Michael's eyes light up when shortly afterward he lights the candles on the Christmas tree. The room is bathed in a warm glow, though it can't compare with the beams of happiness radiating from Glass. She goes over to Michael and gives him such a long kiss, it's almost painful to watch the two of them. Tootling away in the background are the scratchy sounds of "White Christmas," and I'm considering how many different ways there might be of murdering Bing Crosby.

Then we sit round the flickering fireplace, Glass, Michael, and Gable on the ancient beat-up sofa, Dianne and I on kitchen chairs, and listen to Gable, who untiringly tells us about the hopelessness of the people living in the slums of Calcutta, of the poverty and hunger in the small Pacific island states, the names of which were all new to me, of the horror that infested Southeast Asia like the plague following the civil war there. He talks about the death of countless cultures brought about by ships landing on every distant shore over the centuries, which were then presented to their European princes and monarchs.

It's the first time I've heard Gable speak of such things, the first time he shows that there's more to his life than the filigree beauty of black coral fans or dried sea horses.

Later, when everyone's gone to bed, I go and fetch the parcel Nicholas left for me and take it down back to the fireside. Single flames flicker up from time to time out of the embers.

The wires and Christmas baubles on the tree reflect the dying glow from the fire. The parcel weighs heavy in my hands. For days I've been on the point of opening it, driven by curiosity, but for some reason I've stuck to the promise I made to Nicholas not to open it before Christmas. Now I kneel down in front of the fireplace and undo the gift wrapping with trembling fingers.

It's a book with a blank cover, bound either by Nicholas himself or goodness knows who. It contains thirty-six stories, two of which I already know. I hastily leaf through them, scan a few sentences, and read the titles, and the museum of lost things springs up in front of me.

BUTTERFLY'S WINGS

THE KNIFE THAT CUT ITSELF

THE SHIP WITHOUT . . .

I slam the book shut. Then after a moment's hesitation I open it again, tear out the pages one by one, and feed them into the hissing embers in the grate.

Tongues of flame lick slowly across the black letters and white spaces in between. Then the odd page suddenly flares up and crumples as if in pain before the paper burns away. I start as I hear a rustling sound behind me.

"Still up?"

"Yes."

"I can't sleep either." Dianne has slipped down beside me.

She crouches and points at the fire, where the last pages of the book have just crumbled to ashes.

"What was that?"

"Nicholas."

"A present for you?"

I shake my head. Dianne puts an arm round my shoulder, I weep, then I start talking, and we stay like that in front of the fireplace until the last embers have died away.

On Christmas Day Tereza and Pascal appear. They arrive in the early afternoon and in seconds the whole of Visible resounds with their yells and squabbles and shrieks of laughter in their attempts to prepare a Christmas goose stuffed with apples and raisins. They transform the kitchen into a battlefield and whisk a five-course menu onto the table that Glass graciously pronounces fantastic. All the same she eyes the bird suspiciously.

"My God, the poor thing looks frightful!" She points to the spread-eagled thighs of the goose, covered in crispy brown skin. "So obscene and so dead."

She herself would never cook anything bigger than a chicken, having been compelled as a child to watch a turkey being slaughtered—a gory bloodbath, if she is to be believed.

Pascal winks across at her—since she knows Glass to be in safe hands with Michael the situation between the two of them has eased noticeably—and is already making snapping motions with the poultry shears. "It was only a little mannikin, I believe. No need to get upset."

Michael and Gable look at each other, and both roll their eyes at the same moment. They've only known each other a few days but are already getting on famously in this strange way, unfathomable to me, that most men have—with few words in an unquestioning, silent agreement about God and the world and probably about women as well.

"It's just as much a puzzle to me as to you," Tereza confides to me in the kitchen where we're making tea and coffee after the meal. "Put two men who don't know each other in a room, and they circle around each other quickly and sniff each other, just like dogs."

"And then?"

"Then they'll either go for each other's throats or the two of them will terrorize the neighborhood with their barking."

I watch as Tereza stacks cups and saucers on a tray. As yet I haven't tackled her about her plans to move. This would be the right moment, but I shy away from doing so—the childish belief that nothing will happen as long as you don't talk about it is deeply embedded in me.

"Tereza?"

"Mm?"

"Are you happy with Pascal?"

"Sometimes more and sometimes less. But happy enough to move to Holland with her, in case you— Phil! Don't, don't cry, little one."

I sniff against the crook of her elbow and imagine I can detect the almonds that her red hair used to smell of. But it's Christmas, all the world smells of almonds, and habits change, even if it's only in the choice of shampoo.

After coffee, we all go off for a walk. Almost instinctively we follow the path leading along by the river to the Big Eye. In small groups we trot along behind each other through the dazzling bright winter landscape—Dianne arm in arm with Tereza and Pascal, Glass shuffling through the snow arm in arm with Michael. Gable and I bring up the rear.

"When d'you have to go again?" I ask him.

"New Year's Day. I'm taking the train north, and I'll board ship in the evening. And then I won't be seen on dry land for a week." He already sounds relieved even though only half his time here has gone.

"Where are you going?"

"America." He gives me a sideways look—probably because he knows the effect this word has on me.

"You could come with me, Phil. Provided, of course, that you'd like to." I stand rooted to the spot. I can only stare at Gable.

"It's a big freighter," he goes on. "Cars, electronic instruments, I don't know what else. I've never been interested in the cargo."

"I could . . . You mean I could simply come along too?"

"There's always room for an extra pair of hands." Gable grins. "Apart from which I know the captain."

"What about school?"

He looks at me as if he's concerned for my sanity. "You cannot be serious!"

I can't remember the last time I was so excited. My heart is racing, beating fast like a tireless engine, and already I'm thinking of ships, of mighty turbines and powerful propellers churning up the sea. "Well . . . I'll think about it, OK?"

"Take your time."

"And Glass mustn't know about it yet."

"That's up to you."

On the way back Michael moves off on his own. He leaves Glass with the other women and walks along close to the riverbank. He's smiling and looks down at the ground, lost in thought, taking big strides and sometimes kicking into the snow like a little boy. At some point he laughs out loud for no apparent reason, making me wonder at what stage this man, whom my mother is getting to love more day by day, learned to have no fear of being alone.

Back at Visible I go to my room and look at the old map of the world. I remove all the green pins marking the oceans and the continents, more than twenty of them, and pin them on to the map of North America all the way down the East Coast. I take two steps back and consider the green winding ribbon that glows at me like a promise. I have dreamed about accompanying Gable more times than I can remember. But I was a child at the time, and the thought of going to sea amounted to no more than a desire for crazy adventures, the longing for the broad view into eternity.

If you go now, I hear Paleiko whisper, *it's like running away. Taking flight.*

No, it's not.

You think it would be a fresh start? How can it be when you have nowhere near finished things here?

Give me time.

Even if it would be like taking flight, I've only to think of Gable's scar to know that there are certain things you can't escape from. He's taken his disappointment with him all the way round the world, just as Glass brought Number Three with her to Visible. Gable's scar has always disturbed me because the crazy self-inflicted renewal of this disfigurement has taken hold of his entire body and soul. Only . . . over the past few days I have constantly tried to get a glimpse of it. But Gable always wears long-sleeved sweaters or shirts, and contrary to his habit on previous visits to Visible he no longer runs around with a bare chest on his way to the bathroom. I have a vague feeling that he no longer wishes to see the scar himself.

Things change, Paleiko.

Just like Tereza changing her shampoo? You can't force changes, my friend. Or would you go just the same if it wasn't America but some other country?

Maybe.

You want to look for him, don't you? That was the first thing you thought of when Gable made you the offer. Number Three.

Yes.

D'you think that's a good idea?

For goodness' sake, be quiet, Paleiko. You're dead. Just because I still haven't found the pink stone from your forehead—

Wrong! I'll never die, Phil. That's the blessing and the curse of Tereza's present. I'll always be with you.

Yes, as a guardian. But I can look after myself.

Quod erit demonstrandum. Who was it said that?

Deciding is easy. I'm still putting off talking to Glass about it because I'm afraid she'll raise objections and try talking me out of my travel plans. But I tell Dianne. Her reaction is to screw up her eyes as if a speck of dust had got in. "Does Glass know about it?"

I shake my head.

"It's a good idea," Dianne says drily.

"And that's all?"

"D'you expect me to burst into tears?" She shoots me a glance, expressing distrust or care, I'm not sure which. "You will come back sometime, won't you?"

"Naturally."

"Well. That's it, then."

The next day I go to Gable and tell him I accept his offer. His delight—a round of tiny sparks dancing in his eyes, a glow that sweeps across his face—is balm for my soul. He rushes to the phone, and in the space of half an hour everything's arranged. We're leaving Visible together on January first.

"You can still change your mind," says Gable while the look in his eyes urges me not to.

"No, I'm coming with you." I look at him, slightly uncertain. "But I may stay in America for a while."

"I thought as much." He places a hand on my shoulder. "Once you've done what you set out to do, you can join me again at any time, Phil. I'll show you the world."

"Yes. The world."

Once Handel brought two pictures along to a lesson. One of them showed a green landscape, like a crater, that no one in the class could identify—the best suggestions were an abandoned meadow following the death of three cows, a meteor landing on an alien planet, and a bird's-eye view of a rain forest. The second picture was a maple leaf. The first was a magnified version of the second. I may not always have heeded the advice that Handel associated with these two images, but I've never forgotten it: things look clearer from a distance. And what I need above all at the moment is to see things clearly.

Two days before New Year's I can't stand it any longer. Glass, Michael, and Gable have set out for some unknown destination early in the afternoon. Dianne and I could have joined them, but we both declined. I wanted to be on my own, but by now I'm fed up with my own company. Dianne appears unexpectedly as I'm pulling on my boots in the hall.

"Where are you off to?"

"To the clinic, to Nicholas."

She looks puzzled. "Didn't he say he doesn't want you to visit him?"

"Don't care. I'm going all the same."

Dianne reflects for a moment. Then, with a decisive movement, she reaches for her coat. "All right, I'll come with you."

"To the clinic?"

"Yes, but not to Nicholas," she adds, noting my look of irritation. "There's something I need to show you before you disappear with Gable."

More than that she won't say.

We take the bus. As I ask the driver for two tickets, she slips in beside me. I stare in surprise as she pulls out a season ticket and shows it to the driver. I suddenly remember that summer day when Nicholas spoke to me in the library, shortly after I'd seen Dianne arguing with Kora before getting on the bus.

"OK," I sigh once we've sat down. "Are you going to tell me right away, or d'you want to surprise me?"

"I'd prefer to wait until we get there."

"I don't like surprises."

"Don't worry."

The bus crawls along at a snail's pace through the snow-covered countryside. It stops at each village, but few people get in or out. There are little Christmas trees decorated with Christmas lights in front gardens. People wrapped in heavy overcoats are out and about, with children pulling sleds along behind them. The sky promises more snow. I look away and down at my hands. I've never enjoyed the run-up to New Year's, considering it an unreal time, enforced waiting in a no-man's-land on the border between yesterday and tomorrow.

"I'm going to miss you," says Dianne as we approach the town.

"I should hope so."

"Seriously, I mean it, Phil." She places a hand on my knee. "The past few years have been really shitty between the two of us. And now just as I'm getting the feeling that things could improve, you're disappearing."

"Will you cope here on your own?"

"I'm not alone. I've got Kora, and I've got Visible and Glass." She brushes aside my look of surprise. "You're thinking that there'll be nothing for it once you're gone, that I'll have to talk to her, aren't you? Because we'll be dependent on each other or something of the sort."

I nod.

"Could be that I'll do it." Dianne looks out of the window. "What did you think of that Dennis?"

"Quite nice. Attractive. Very brave."

"Me too." She draws little patterns in the condensation on the window. "Funny, isn't it? He's coming again. In about two weeks."

"To Visible?"

She nods.

We get out at the bus terminal. The clinic lies beyond the town, nestling between hills, roads snaking along them. The nearer we get to our destination, the more anxious I become. Nicholas is lying somewhere in this gigantic complex. At the reception I ask for his room number; then I follow Dianne. The confusing number of corridors and passages leading through the hospital like an anthill that so terrified me when I was there as a jug ears have lost nothing of their labyrinthine character. Dianne threads her way through without looking left or right. With a sleepwalker's assurance she finds the correct turnings, stairways, and locked doors that open automatically with a quiet hiss by means of unseen floor electronic sensors. It's crazy, but at any moment I expect to bump into Senior Nurse Marthe and have to explain to her that her one-time jug ears has long since stopped wearing strange girls' nighties but has taken to other boys' pajamas. That certainly wouldn't please her—Lord God, no way. I shake my head and push the thought aside.

At some point Dianne and I are standing in front of a wide closed door fitted with two glass windows. Dianne presses a bell.

"Are we in the right place?" I look at the sign next to the door. "Intensive care?"

"Yes. Wait a minute."

The door opens with a brief hum. Dianne enters. Through the window I see her talking to a young nurse in a small office, gesticulating with her arms in my direction. The nurse firmly shakes her head. Dianne gets worked up—her voice carries to where I'm standing, but I can't catch what she's saying. An older doctor comes up, and Dianne shakes his hand. Their gestures and the way they're speaking to each other suggest intimacy, as if they've known each other for years. The doctor looks me over briefly through the window, nods, and disappears from view. Seconds later there is another humming noise.

"Here, put this on," Dianne greets me inside the door. "Regulations." She hands me a blue gown, then slips into one of her own and ties it up at the back.

I'm less handy than she is and fumble with the tapes. How often has Dianne been here, I wonder, in this station, put on a sterile gown like this, while I was under the impression that she'd been going off for walks? Twice a week, at least, dozens of times a year, and how many years has it been going on? My God.

"OK," Dianne says. "Come on."

The background noise is muted. The sound of bleeps from various monitors fills the room along with the pneumatic hissing of unfamiliar machines and a distant gurgling glugging, all very faint, as are the mumbled exchanges between doctors and nurses. No object throws a shadow under the cold fluorescent light that falls vertically from numerous tubes. White screens, strategically placed, shield the patients hidden behind them from the curious gaze of visitors.

The bed that Dianne leads me to stands as if forgotten in

the far corner, farthest away from the nurses' office. Lying in it is a boy. His eyes are closed. The bare arms lie on the cover like leafless branches.

"He doesn't always look this bad," says Dianne almost apologetically. "The business with the tubes, I mean. There's a central attachment, but sometimes . . ."

Attached to the lips with tape, a heavy tube leads from the boy's mouth to a machine, with a monitor across which green wavy lines run continuously from left to right as if in a time warp. A thinner tube, transparent and filled with yellow-brown fluid, runs into the boy's nose.

The body is so emaciated that its sharp outlines hardly bulge through the blanket reaching up to his chest.

"This is Zephyr," Dianne says softly, as if afraid to wake the boy. He does actually look as if he's merely asleep; his cheeks are even rosy. His chest rises and falls in the painfully accurate rhythm regulated by the machine, filling his lungs with oxygen and thereby preventing suffocation. He has light brown very close-cropped hair and a face without any sharply defined features, as if the coma had condemned him to eternal childhood.

"Zephyr," I repeat quietly. "That's not his real name, is it?"

"No. There's that 'Ode to the West Wind': 'Oh, lift me as a wave, a leaf, a cloud! / I fall upon the thorns of life! I bleed!' Yuh, well, sounds a bit kitschy, I guess." Dianne looks at me. "His name is Jan."

In some remote recess of my memory a bell sounds a soft

alarm. Jan—that's a name I've heard once, briefly, a long time ago.

"How . . . how did he come to be here?"

"He had an accident."

"Not recently, or what?"

"No." Dianne has moved over to the bed. "More than three years ago, in the summer."

She stretches out a hand and strokes Zephyr's cheek. There is such gentleness in the action that I look away. I ought to be jealous of this boy, lying in a coma on the border between sleep and death. In some way, without knowing it, he's taken my sister away from me.

"He was riding his bike," says Dianne. "And there was a storm. It was so violent it blew bricks off Visible's roof. Afterward Glass had to have it patched up all over the place. And at the back of the garden one of the statues even fell over, the angel with a sword, you know the one?"

"Yes."

I look at the tubes, the cannulas inserted into the back of the boy's hands, looking as if they're growing out of them; artificial veins and drips distributed over the surface, drip-feeding liquid nourishment and anticoagulant.

"He was on his way to see me at Visible," says Dianne. "I'd only got to know him a few weeks before. You were away then with Gable in Greece."

"Yes, I remember."

"You weren't there, Phil. You just weren't there."

I put my arms round her and hold her close. She doesn't cry, but her body shakes, as if her heartbeats had somehow made their way to the outside and were beating on the surface of her skin. I wasn't there for her, neither before Zephyr's accident nor after. I let myself be carried away by the perfume of cypresses, while Dianne was getting entangled in her love for a boy who would never again look at her, touch her, or kiss her. I think of the letters she wrote, all those letters. . . .

"I've been visiting him at least twice a week," Dianne whispers into my shoulder. "I thought, without me . . . I thought he'd die without me. Crazy, isn't it?"

"No."

"It was so easy to love him. He couldn't defend himself. But by the time it was over I'd already forgotten what color his eyes were." She detaches herself from my embrace. "Glass was against it. But that it came to an end was thanks to Kora. She gave me a talking to."

"Down by the river?" I grin, although I'm feeling shabby. Shabby and small. Small and treacherous. "Looks as if your friend stood by you better than your brother."

"Yes."

A painful silence follows. Dianne looks at me unblinkingly. I wish I could read that look, but we've lived in different worlds too long for that. At last I look down at the floor in embarrassment. The fact that she's brought me here is both a reproach and evidence of trust. Nothing has been lost, but we need a lot of time. It will be up to me to write letters to Dianne, letters from all over the world.

"You still want to go to Nicholas," she says at last.

"Yes." I hesitate; then I point to Zephyr. "Is he going to . . . I mean, is there any chance that he'll ever recover?"

"No, he's dead," Dianne answers soberly. "If the life support were turned off, it would be over. But his parents won't allow it."

"You know them?"

"Very well, as it happens."

"Why do they let their son stay hooked up to this machine?"

"Because they love him."

"Seems very selfish."

Dianne shrugs. "Love always is, isn't it?"

She stays with Zephyr. We're to meet again later at the main door. I leave the intensive care section, and as I pass along the complex layout of the hospital passages that don't seem to follow any logic, I think of the color of Nicholas's eyes and begin to wonder whether it's such a good idea to visit him against his express wishes.

As I expected, Glass is not exactly enthralled at the idea of my shooting off to America in the company of Gable. She doesn't question my decision, but I can see her thoughts ticking away behind her forehead. I take her presumed displeasure for normal maternal anxiety, but there is more to it than that. Right up until New Year's Eve Glass holds back. I must be blind, because I don't notice that all this time, just like me, she is constantly thinking about Number Three.

Maybe my blindness is brought on by the sleet that begins to come down just before it gets dark. It turns Visible into a glittering crystal palace, spreading out over the white landscape like a glass tablecloth over a feather quilt, and transforms the Little People's town into a raft sailing on an unreal reflection of a royal blue sky. The sleet also turns the roads into icy toboggan runs; Tereza and Pascal arrive at Visible two hours later than planned for the New Year's Eve party.

"It's only because you're buggering off tomorrow, otherwise we would never have ventured out on this ice rink," snorts Pascal. She throws her rucksack at me—on loan for my trip. "There's a sleeping bag inside. But don't you dare mess it up using it with some guy, got it?"

"Oh, Pascal, do shut it! Come here, Phil." Tereza clasps me to her, then pulls me by one ear.

"Careful, they're only sewn on!"

"They need pulling all the same. You might have let us know earlier what you're planning."

"Just like you told me you're going to Holland?"

"One-nil to you." Tereza smiles. "What do you actually intend to be when you're grown up?"

The entire evening is centred on Gable's and my imminent departure. Tereza and Pascal have cooked and baked ahead like crazy and immediately requisition the kitchen, alternately laughing and arguing as usual. Glass and Dianne have carried the kitchen table into the room with the fireplace and set it with all the odd, mismatched dishes, glasses, and cutlery from Visible's kitchen, making it look as festive as if we're about to celebrate some millennium jubilee. Michael has raided his wine cellar and to Pascal's utter consternation has brought along shiny gold and silver party hats with elastic chin straps.

"You're trying to make me look a complete dolt with that thing on my head!" Pascal fights him off as Michael grabs her near the oven and attempts to fit the little hat on her head.

"It's all a question of habit," replies Michael "Or could it be we're vain, by any chance?"

Pascal grunts, reaches out for a carrot, and demonstratively saws it in two under his eyes. Michael shrinks back in feigned horror. Later, as Pascal serves the first course—fish soup—together with Tereza, she's still wearing the mini-hat.

The feast goes on and on. It's fantastic and worth every moment. The wine—although I'm hardly a judge—could inspire even a hardened connoisseur of the rank of Handel to write an ode to the sun. For the hundredth time everyone wishes Gable and me, but especially me, all the very best. If at all possible, the mood is even more harmonious and more relaxed than it was already at Christmas. And today Gable restricts himself to stories of beauty and wonders, as if he doesn't want to frighten me unnecessarily before we set out. I make up my mind to ask him about his scar once we're away.

I don't know why, but I postpone packing. When I finally leave the table and go up to my room with Pascal's huge rucksack over my arm, it's already eleven o'clock. Barely an hour to go before midnight and the New Year. This time tomorrow Gable and I will already have finished the first leg of our journey and embarked. I pack the bare minimum. Gable warned me that I might have to carry the rucksack for days, mile after mile across country, once I'm in America. One last time I look at the two wall maps: America. The world. I go over to the shelf, stroke Mr. Troht's sweet jars, peace be to his ashes, and place my hand where for years and years Paleiko used to sit and look out at me serenely. With one last look out of the window at the river and the lights of the town, I put out the light and leave the room. I put the rucksack down in the hall. Now there's just one more thing I'm going to pack.

Moonlight reflected by the snow and ice falls into the library through the tall double windows. This is all the light I need. I go over to one of the shelves and let my hand wander across the backs of the books.

"You'd never go without a book, would you?" I hear Glass say behind me.

"No."

I turn slowly to face her. She's sitting on my story throne, barely visible in the moonlight. Her hands blend into the arms of the chair. Her head is leaned back in deepest shadow. I can't make out her face.

"Which one are you going to take?"

Stella didn't leave many books, but there's one that I must have read a dozen times. It's appropriate for a sea voyage, but I'd also take it if I were flying to the moon. I take it down from the shelf. *"Moby Dick,"* I say in the direction of the story throne.

"Is it good?"

"Yes. It's . . ."

I stop. All at once I know why Glass has been waiting for me here. My hands close round the book and begin to sweat.

"I have a suggestion," says Glass. "You ask me whatever you want to know. Either I'll answer or I won't. But I'm not prepared for a discussion."

"Agreed." Inside my head everything is in turmoil. I take a deep breath and try to put my thoughts in order. "Right. What's his name?"

"Next question."

"Oh, thanks! Very encouraging."

"Phil . . ."

"It's all right, OK." My head feels like it's made of wood. I think hard. "What was he like?"

Glass hesitates. For a long time she says nothing. So long that I'm tempted to abandon this stupid game, almost before it's started. Then I hear Glass take a deep breath.

"He was wonderful, Phil. He was the most wonderful man you could ever imagine. The best."

The words strike me like blows below the belt. Gold and bloodred stars flash before my eyes. "If he was so wonderful, what made him walk out on you?"

"He didn't" comes the answer out of the dark. "He loved me too much for that."

My anger fades away almost before it has flared up. And only now it dawns on me that I've roused phantoms better left asleep. I recall the bubbling up of dark air during that dim and distant night following the Battle of the Big Eye. Then, even before Dianne confessed she had been aiming her arrow at the Hulk's heart, I'd already sensed she was going to say something I didn't want to hear. It's the same now. Once again the air is dark, but instead of Dianne's whispering there is just the smell of old books here and the relentless voice of my mother.

"He was so gentle," I hear her say. "When he touched a flower, it would bloom soon after, I swear, Phil. I saw it. Once we went to a circus. We walked past the cages with the big cats, and the creatures that had been pacing up and down and roaring as we approached just lay down quietly. Your father put his hand through the bars and stroked the head of a lion. He was unafraid."

My chest is too tight to contain my pounding heart.

"Dianne was just like him," said the darkness. "Just as sensitive. When she was little she could hear the world breathe, just like her father. That's why I thought her just as vulnerable. That's why I wanted to protect her."

My hands grip the book more tightly, so tight that my fingernails dig deep into the cover. "What happened then?" I whisper.

"I became pregnant. From that moment on your father didn't just love me, he worshiped me. He was as pleased as a little child and planned our future. He wanted to marry me. He wanted to build us a house. And he would have done all that."

"What happened?"

"He had a friend. A best friend. Gordon paid court to me, and I was so mad for him that I felt drunk just to think of him touching me. I couldn't get enough love, never mind who from. I was so damned grateful that the very thought makes me quite ill now. I would have taken any man. Later on that's just what I did, to extremes."

Glass laughs out loud, a short, bitter sound. I lower my head. The parquet floor at my feet shimmers. Dianne and I used to play hopscotch here long ago. Somewhere in the cracks between the individual floorboards there are ancient remnants of chalk dust. I remember how the dry dust lit up and shone when it was caught in the light of God's fingers.

"Phil?"

"Yes?"

"Look at me."

I raise my head. Glass has leaned forward. Her face looks like a ghostly mask. Her lips are thin dark lines.

"I behaved like a whore."

"No, Mom. Please . . ."

"Your father caught us. His pregnant girlfriend in bed with his best friend. After that I couldn't look him in the face any longer." Glass gives a weak smile. Tiny dots of light dance in her pupils. "With you at least I want to do so."

"Mom, you mustn't say things like that." My entire body feels paralyzed. "It simply isn't true."

"I know. But for years I thought it was. And that's why I had to say it at least once." Glass leans back again into the shelter of the shadows. "Whatever, I decided to leave. At first I didn't know where; finally I thought of Stella. Your father . . . he begged me on his knees not to leave him. He beat the floor with his hands till they bled. My God, he humiliated himself before me. And I felt so ashamed, Phil."

"You could have stayed with him."

"No. I couldn't guarantee that the same thing wouldn't happen again. And again, and again. I would have kept on wounding him. He didn't deserve that. No one deserves that."

A hand detaches itself from the arm of the throne. I don't know when Glass started to cry. Perhaps she couldn't help thinking of how my father felt when she left him. He must have said it was as if someone had torn away his skin and rubbed salt in.

"Couldn't you have . . . with the other one?"

"Gordon wasn't interested in a pregnant woman," came the short reply. "Nor I in him for the long term. We were kids, Phil. He wanted his freedom, I wanted mine."

The irony of the story doesn't escape me. For years all my thoughts had centered on Number Three. But the real reason I never got to know my father is Number Four, the man whose name is next on the list. No, I correct myself, that's also wrong. The real reason is Glass herself, who grabbed at love or what she thought was love whenever and wherever she could. And once we go down that road, searching for the explanation for her conduct, then we get to—oh, then we're back with the passions and the question of the when and the where of the beginning of all things. Better, ladies and gentlemen, to get on with the story, if we don't want to do our heads in.

"Why did you never tell Dianne and me?" I ask into the darkness. "Why did you make such a huge secret of it?"

"Because of Tereza, darling."

"I don't understand—"

"I lied to her," Glass interrupts me. "The first time she asked me about your father I told her he'd walked out on me and I'd been so badly hurt that I never wanted to talk about it again. Tereza accepted that and never broached the subject again. Instead she helped me and put me back on my feet. Without Tereza there wouldn't be you or Dianne, there wouldn't be Visible. There'd be nothing."

"You could have explained to her later on. She'd have understood."

"Maybe . . . but I kept putting it off, and every day that passed convinced me that I'd done the right thing. To make myself out as the victim made everything a whole lot easier. What I have and what I am all comes from this one lie. With time it began to weigh more and more heavily on me. But at the beginning it didn't seem such a high price to pay."

Silence returns to the library. It's as if Visible is straining to catch Glass's every word. I can't hate Glass. We've all paid for her lie, Dianne far more than me. But Glass is the one who's punished herself all through her life for this lie, with every entry on her list, to confirm to herself and others that she deserved the label she'd given herself—the label one of Those Out There had also promptly scratched on the paintwork of her car one day.

"You have told Michael, haven't you?"

"Yes, he knows. . . . He may be moving to Visible," she adds after a while.

"That's good."

"Maybe."

My fingers can't keep hold of the book any longer. I put it back on the shelf. My hands slide over one of the herbaries, and I shrink back as if I've had an electric shock.

"Mom?"

"Yes?"

"What did he look like?"

"Dianne takes after him. A bit. She has his hair." In the darkness two flat palms open wide in a gesture of regret. "It's crazy, but I can't really remember much else."

"What's his name?"

The hands drop. "No, Phil."

"Mom, please! I could try."

"That's not a good idea. He may well be married by now, have a wife and children, who knows. Would you want to destroy him?"

"It doesn't have to be that way."

"No, of course not. He might also be holed up in some corner still waiting for a miracle. He would build a shrine to you. He would worship you as he worshiped me. Is that what you want?"

I hang my head. Everything's been said; the audience is at an end. When I look up again, Glass has got off the throne. She goes to the door and opens it. Light from the hall falls into the library.

I look at Glass, and I can't help myself—I have to grin.

She looks down at herself uncomprehendingly, then places a hand on her hip. "What is it?"

"Mom, how . . . how could you tell me all that with both of us wearing these ridiculous party hats?"

Glass reaches under her chin. She pulls off the little gold hat, and even as she is still considering it in amazement like a foreign body, a small alien that chose her head for an emergency landing, we both burst out laughing. Tears follow the laughter, and after the tears we sober up. Nothing seems to have changed, yet everything is different than it was before. My knees are shaking. Nothing is simple.

"Oh, and I mustn't forget this," sniffs Glass. She pulls an

envelope out of her pants pocket and hands it to me. "Happy New Year, darling!"

I open the envelope, look inside, and gasp. "Glass, you're crazy! Where did you . . . ?"

I rush past her into the kitchen. The table is still in the other room with the chimney, where laughter rings out. My eyes run across the shelves and countertop.

"She's dead," says Glass. She stands in the doorway and dangles the little gold paper hat by its elastic from her index finger.

"You slaughtered Rosella?"

"Oh, it was very quick," replies Glass. "I can promise you, she didn't feel a thing."

"I can't take this money. It belongs to you."

"Don't get the wrong idea, darling." Glass puts the little hat back on her head. "I'm not the welfare department. I've divided it into three—a third for me, a third for Dianne, and a third for you."

"Mom . . ."

"I won't take no for an answer, understand?" Her voice has dropped to a whisper. "I had nothing when I arrived here, Phil. Just the two of you and a little suitcase, and I was scared out of my bloody mind."

Only now does the tension that's been keeping me together evaporate. I feel I'm swaying, and I'm afraid I'll collapse any moment. With her revelation about Number Three she's pulled the rug from under my feet. I don't know how to cope with my confusion, with the disappointment that for the moment at least is greater than the hesitant understanding I'm beginning to feel for my mother. All I know is that it's good to go off with Gable, to put some distance between me and Visible and my life, which feels incomplete through and through and which I'm slowly losing sight of.

"Come here," says Glass. She folds her arms around me and holds me close. We stay like that for a while, embracing like a pair of lovers, clinging to each other like little children afraid of the dark. "Promise me you'll take care of yourself, sweetheart."

"Cross my heart and—"

"Shh . . . don't say that."

Glass lets go of me, places her hands on my shoulders, and looks at me intently. "I lied to you. I can remember him very well. Dianne has his hair, but you have his eyes. And his mouth."

"Do I have his ears as well?"

"No, absolutely not." She wrinkles her nose. "Only Dumbo has your ears. And even he's far better-looking than you."

Tiny furrows appear at the corner of her mouth. I wait. Slowly Glass bends forward. She rises on tiptoe. I close my eyes in expectation of her goodbye kiss. Then I feel her lips close to my ears, feel them open and close.

She whispers his name.

It is the final minute of the old year. We all troop outside and gather on the veranda, where we chant the remaining seconds out loud. Then the booming of the church bells crashes through the air, the first rockets shoot up into the clear star-studded sky and explode, rainbow-colored fountains rush toward the ground. Whooping, we all fall into each other's arms. Corks pop, champagne foams from ice-cold bottles, and everyone clinks glasses. Glass strikes up the first bars of "Auld Lang Syne," and we all join in, Gable leading us in his deep bass voice. In the sky above Visible a firework bursts open, growing bigger and bigger and ever more glorious. It turns the winter night to day and is reflected on the icy landscape in a blurred and strangely magnified form. Michael has bought jumping jacks and firecrackers—the noise is meant to drive away the ghosts of the old year—and we greet each explosion by cheering loudly.

Later Pascal and Tereza fool around in the icy snow, which crackles like splinters of the thinnest glass. Dianne has promised she will look after the cypress. She sips her champagne and keeps nodding as Gable talks to her quietly. Now and again the two of them laugh out loud. Arms round each other, Glass and Michael sway in the semidarkness of the veranda to old songs by Billie Holiday. I stand in the driveway looking up at Visible's walls and wish I could embrace the house. I still feel as if the ground is swaying under my feet, but I'm no longer afraid of falling. It's a lovely feeling. It's the feeling of life in motion.

epilogue

phil

I lean over the rails of this incredibly large ship and stare down at its sides covered with broad streaks of rust. Yesterday was stormy and so cold that no one went on deck unless they really had to. Today the air is mild. The sky has no beginning or end; it is turquoise-colored, and the wind riding on the broad back of the ocean carries a sweet smell. Maybe it comes from Nomoneas, from Semisopochnoi or from Tongatapu. For days I've had the tast of salt on my lips. From somewhere I feel a tiny glimmer of luck creep into my heart.

I knew I'd made the right decision when I saw Nicholas in the clinic. His parents had seen to it that he had a room to himself. He was asleep as I opened the door and stepped up to his bedside. He actually had on one of those black eye patches reminiscent of pirates or a carnival—something I really wasn't prepared for. The blanket was thrown loosely over his chest, and his arms were stretched out to either side. I tried hard not to look at his hands. I could have woken him, or waited till he awoke. The problem was that I had no idea what to talk about. Everything had already been said between us, or at least, what could be expressed. The desire to say goodbye to Nicholas and inform him that I was going to America had arisen purely and simply from the foolish hope that he would ask me to stay. Just one single word from him would have been enough to make me abandon all my plans, just as it had been one single word that had caused me to make them.

As he lay there, it wasn't by chance that Nicholas reminded me of Zephyr and how, defying all logic, Dianne had loved the boy for years. Loving Nicholas was equally impossible. I saw him in this bed, a white face on a white pillow, the collector of lost things now lost himself, a teller of stories without a story of his own. And suddenly I no longer saw Nicholas but a blank sheet of paper waiting to be written on. I knew that I would never be the one able to do so, not here and not now.

I shut my eyes and see Nicholas running along the red dirt of the cinder track, his concentrated gaze looking straight ahead not in harmony with the world and himself but on the hunt for it. Perhaps on that very first day at the sports field I should have embraced him, held him close, and prevented him from continuing to run. But what did I know then? And actually, I'm quite sure that Nicholas wouldn't have let himself be stopped by anything or anyone.

If anything more lasting develops between them, Kat is going to have problems with this attitude of his. She doesn't like people retreating from her. The fact that I've gone will be a shock to her. I can't let myself think any more about her. It's too painful. I already miss her. I wish she'd drop dead, and I love her.

That much I've learned: love is a word only to be written in bloodred ink. Love drives you to do the strangest things. It makes you hand out rainbow-colored sweets, it makes you dance through the streets in red shoes, and it lets you hack graves in paradise gardens till your hands bleed. Love causes deep wounds, but in its own particular way it also heals scars, provided you have faith in love and give it time to do so. I won't touch my scars. I'm bound to get fresh wounds, even before the old ones have healed, and I will inflict wounds on other people. Every one of us carries a knife.

Those are the rules, Paleiko.

The sea is troubled. Small greenish blue waves splash about; they break up in foam in the wake cut by the ship as it moves at full speed through the churned-up sea, and cling together one on top of the other, seemingly reluctant, but in reality following some physical law of nature. Nothing is what it appears to be. Truths are as fragile as the people who have formulated them. The water here is hundreds of feet deep. It looks uninhabited. But somewhere in the unfathomable deep there are grotesquely formed phosphorescent fish swimming about. Gable says it's miraculous how these phantoms of the deep resist the unbelievable pressure that the ocean exerts on them, truly a miracle. For better or worse he has never lost the capacity to see the world with the eyes of a child.

If I turn my gaze to the left, I look in the direction of America just half a day's journey away. Finding Number Three on this continent will be as difficult as the hunt for the proverbial needle in the haystack. But I know his name.

What lies ahead of me, what I am enmeshed in, is a search, not an escape.

There is nothing I need fear. And for that reason, regardless of whether I've found my father or not, I shall return home sometime. Once enough time has passed. When I come to chant the word like a prayer: *Visible, Visible, Visible . . .*

I turn up the neck of my windbreaker, stroll along the deck, and turn the heavy metal wheel to open the door of the hold. Behind it work awaits me.

Strange, but I miss Handel.

my thanks

I adore thank-yous. I've always harbored a secret dream of being a film director, just in order to win an Oscar and see Tom Cruise or Sean Connery break down in tears during my thank-you speech. And then to comfort them.

I thank:

The Stiftung Preußische Seehandlung, Berlin, whose generous grant sponsored work on this novel.

Donner and Ackermann, who opened up ears and watches for me, and Almut Gebhard for providing remedial tuition in pharmacology.

Dr. Friedbert Stohner, Ursula Heckel, and Cornelia Beger for their willing and friendly support in editorial and publishing issues.

Klaus Humann and Cordula Duffe, whose great enthusiasm and even greater commitment provided impetus and encouragement.

My family: Hiltrud, Dirk, and Björn—you are the center of my world.

about the author

Andreas Steinhöfel is the author of numerous books for children and young adults. He has a degree in English and media studies from Philipps-Universität Marburg and works in Germany as a translator, scriptwriter, and reviewer. *The Center of the World* is his first book for Delacorte Press. It won the prestigious Buxtehuder Bulle Prize for Best Young Adult Novel in Germany and was short-listed for the German Children's Literature Award.

166926